"In Yael Unterman's stunning debut she presents her readers with a galle., ... compelling characters in headlong pursuit of the spirit and the flesh. That they often find these goals to be mutually exclusive turns out to be a source of both heartbreak and riotous humor. How she manages to embrace such extremes in stories that are also poignant, passionate, and brave is a mystery whose result is a deeply irresistible experience."

— **Steve Stern**, author of *The Frozen Rabbi* and *The Book of Mischief*

"It would be wrong to characterize Yael Unterman simply as a writer—she is a force, a spirit of turbulent and joyful query. Her devotion to ideas, to Jewish thought and literature in particular, to two languages, Hebrew and English, the intersections of Orthodoxy and the contemporary world, can't help but fascinate readers. Her sketches of life in modern Israel and the Diaspora evoke the sweetness and melancholy of Chekhov. Her passion to understand, to find a way to live a life of meaning both in a commitment to tradition and to *derech eretz*, the way of the world, however, give them the spice of something unique and original. One feels throughout *The Hidden of Things* a furious and original energy. These stories are not just witty and insightful. They search the world of modern Jewish life in Jerusalem, the suburb of Katamon, the frustrations and foibles of religious women, for answers. The plight of the woman and man who find themselves single in their early thirties searching references from matchmakers, friends, Internet dating sites for a soul-mate is anatomized often with a breathless laughter."

—**Mark Jay Mirsky**, author of *Blue Hill Avenue* and *Dante, Eros and Kabbalah*, and editor of *Fiction* magazine

"From Zion has come forth an outrageous, wise, and funky voice. I've already started re-reading it, that's how good this book is."

—**Ruchama King Feuerman**, author of *In the Courtyard of the Kabbalist* and *Seven Blessings*

"Each story is a jewel strung upon a glittering chain that joins complexity with deep insight. I found it difficult to stop reading. The insights into singleton Orthodox life for women and for men were cogent and compelling. 'Katamonsta' and 'The Hidden of Things' quite blew me away—the former with its brash humour flecked with poignant awareness and intelligence, and the latter with its agonising representation of a woman in search of her identity and of peace, possibly in all the wrong places."

—**Yvonne Fein**, author of *April Fool* and *The Torn Messiah*

"In this rollicking book—simultaneously empathetic, tragic, and comic—the playful scenes and the ironies, the joy in language, and the cleverness of the dialogue delight. Unterman has an Austen-esque touch where seemingly small moments are experienced as profound; at the same time, a Malamudian darkness permeates some of the stories and sinks into the soul. But the hiddenness of things in this book is in its female friendships. This hiddenness illuminates a quiet undercurrent of support, compassion, humor, comfort, kindness, and connection. You will find both kinds of blessings in this book: hidden and revealed."

—**Eve Grubin**, author of *Morning Prayer*

The Hidden of Things

Twelve Stories of Love & Longing

To the Alberts
Lovely to meet you
Best of luck
Yael ☺

The Hidden of Things

Twelve Stories of Love & Longing

Yael Unterman

Yotzeret Publishing
St. Paul

First edition

The tzaddi logo is a registered trademark of Yotzeret Publishing, Inc.

Cover photo © Vince Clements/Shutterstock

Frumster and Frumster.net are registered trademarks of Frumster Inc. Used with permission.

Glove was first published in 2012 on Jewish Fiction .net

Publisher's Cataloging-in-Publication data

Unterman, Yael.
    The Hidden of things : twelve stories of love & longing / Yael Unterman.
    p. cm.
    ISBN 978-1-59287-102-5 (Pbk)
    ISBN 978-1-59287-302-9 (Kindle)
    ISBN 978-1-59287-303-6 (Epub)

1. Short stories, Jewish. 2. Jews --Fiction. 3. Jews --Anecdotes. 4. Dating (Social customs)--Fiction. 5. Jewish fiction. 6. Man-woman relationships --Fiction. I. The Hidden of things : 12 stories of love and longing. II. Title.

PS3621 .N68 H53 2014
813.6 --dc23   2013955362

For my dear friends Shlomit Ben-Michael and Tania Hershman, who were so generous with their time and support.

Also in memory of Shaindy Rudoff, without whom these stories would not exist.

Acknowledgments

It is truly wonderful to finally be at this point. The first of these stories was written in 2004, when the period described could still be termed current affairs rather than history. There were times when I was uncertain my characters would ever make it into print; but Sheyna Galyan of Yotzeret Publishing rescued them from the dark and dusty drawer and here they are, alive and breathing, talking a mile a minute, pulling ridiculous faces and demanding to be paid.

To introduce my thanks, I would like to share the following story, heard from Rabbi Shlomo Riskin of Efrat:

> Rabbi Israel Baal Shem Tov, founder of the Hasidic movement, was in the habit of praying the Musaf (additional Sabbath) silent prayer at great length, taking a full hour. His disciples, who always finished much more quickly, grew impatient and bored, so one Shabbat they decided to go home and have a l'chaim (alcoholic drink) while he prayed. Finishing their silent prayers, they tiptoed out one by one. As the last disciple was leaving, the Baal Shem Tov unexpectedly took three steps backward and three steps forward, marking the end of his prayer. It was long before the usual time, and the shocked disciple hastily called the others back. All stood looking at their rebbe in astonishment. He explained: "You see, when I pray, I ascend a ladder to the Divine Throne: the ladder built of your presence in prayer. This morning, halfway through the ascent, I suddenly felt my ladder crumbling and had no choice but to finish my prayer."

The point I want to make through this story is that my achievements, I have come to understand with maturity, are not really mine. From my parents, through God's grace, I inherited talents; my teachers shaped me; and the support and feedback I received from friends and colleagues were the ladder upon which I made that prolonged climb to publishing a book.

I want to thank the following people, and hope that I merit being a rung in your ladders too:

First, my thanks go to the good folks whom I encountered while studying in the Shaindy Rudoff Graduate Program in Creative Writing at Bar-Ilan University.

To my professors for their wise insights on the creative process—Steve Stern, Allen Hoffman, Atar Hadari and especially Mark Mirsky, whose instruction, "Write what you fear to write about," opened the floodgates to these stories.

To the members of my class, Sharon Bacher, Judy Labensohn, Gladys Liebner, Jonathan Udren, Sheryl Robbin and Leeora Rabinowitz and especially Gila Green, Nadia Jacobson, Karen Marron, David C. Muller and Yaeer Talkar for all the time they invested reading and critiquing.

I owe a debt of gratitude to the late Shaindy Rudoff, the founder of the program. Without her vision, this book would likely never have been born.

Thank you Nira Azriel, Reena Barnett Tasgal, Michael Berger, Stewart J. Brookes, Lisa Daniels, Naomi Slutzkin Fisher, Catriella Freedman, Kibi Hofmann, Yehudit Malkiel Finfer, Reva Mann, Rachel Reinfeld-Wachtfogel, and Yael Valier for all your amazing feedback. To Shlomit Ben-Michael and Tania Hershman—your generosity, warmth, advice and critique was much appreciated and hence I dedicate this book to you.

From the bottom of my heart I thank my publisher Sheyna Galyan for believing in these stories, and for reminding me that happy endings do come about. My editor Leslie Martin was a delight to work with and made excellent suggestions, though the final product still contains too many references to the digestive system for her liking.

Thank you to my beloved family: Abba and Ima; Yossi, Sandra, Michael and Yoni; and Avi, Pearl and Kinneret.

And finally: I thank the One who created me and made me a writer. I apologize for, in my early years, experiencing my creativity as a burden—in fact it is a gift (though an instruction manual would have been helpful).

In brief—thank You God for everything in my life, especially the hard stuff, without which this book would have read simply: *Acknowledgments. The End.*

Yael Unterman
Jerusalem 2013

Author's Note

This book is peppered with Jewish and Israeli expressions, the language in which its protagonists instinctively think and speak. It is awkward to continually define terms, so where this has not been done, the reader is invited to turn to the glossary at the end.

These stories are intended to be read in order, as they are interlinked and build on each other.

Table of Contents

Bubble (aka "Ode to Odium")

There lies a spot upon a hill in the Middle East where creatures crowd together, competing for shade under an excoriating sun. Where ancient predators catch vulnerable little things that scuttle alone in the dark.

Its inhabitants gather inside an enormous translucent bubble, its walls shot through with fine filaments of silver. Hundreds of individuals, yet each at its precise epicenter, absorbing the faces roundabout. There are many faces, and they shine with a light without heat, in a *fata morgana* of normality and joy. A closer examination reveals: triangles of cheekbones, hollow ovals of eyes, starved faces hidden 'neath fleshy cheeks. Here is a glimpse of the faces of the damned, captured by pirates, forced to walk plank, now but bloaty corpses, their mouths a floating 'O'. The startled onlooker recoils, and wishes they would return the customary mask.

Of the starving what can one can say? They feed on their dreams, they have no choice. Yet dreams choke instead of nourishing. Constant movement conceals lifelessness: the eyes blink, the lips part, the voices mutter, complain, analyze, describe, request. Mouths flap without rhyme or reason, words billow aimlessly, patchy and worn from years of repetition; shot out at random angles in hopes of hitting a target by some happy chance. Splinters of words that together do not make a broadbeam:

height?
body type?
ready for relationship?
meet you at 9 o'clock
passionate
looking for completion, my best friend
trust your gut
at a sweet little café on Ben Yehuda
meet you at 8:30
too modern
take it slow
let's be friends
completion, my other half
just friends
great guy, but not for me
shopping list
slim
educated
at a meat restaurant in the German Colony
spontaneous
sporty
good sense of humor
blue eyes
meet you at 6:15
chemistry
mensch
completion, my best friend
do for a living?
in the tiny park in Nachlaot
not my type, maybe for you
so tell me—what are you looking for in a mate?

All this frantic activity causes the bubble to undulate and fling out pseudopodia, like a frenetic disco amoeba. Words and phrases flutter like snow in a paperweight, like pieces torn off a survivor's shirt, like birds migrating in the wrong direction, like roof tiles in a hurricane. The words speed up, the mouths flap, the eyes flash, the voices grow shriller and higher, the heedless conversation, the dull flirtation, no face fully turned toward the other, fake-smiling then instantly turning aside, faces fleering and jeering, mouths emitting high-pitched noise like myriad bagpipes played concurrently or bats trapped in a belfry or sirens funneled through a needle's eye.

The sounds buffet the faces, sending the bubble into peristaltic paroxysms; at unexplained moments, the faces turn, revolve, so as to get close to another face, any face, turning immediately from that face to find the next face, babbling at a face, gyrating, revolving, smiling at a face, the hundredth face, the thousandth face, their haunted hunted souls, starved behind powdery cheeks, kohled eyes, pink-red lips. The faces fissure and crack apart, untold mouths weeping and pleading, and always the faces, the eyes, flapping, circling, spinning, oscillating, splintering apart, the eyes, the faces, the talk, the sound, the sound, the unbearable sound . . .

Yesterday, today, tomorrow
All eyes hollow

These Old Katamonians,
these Katamoaners, Katamonsters,
these Old Caterwaulers
yearning for

a different night
            a different light
                        an end in sight

And the years go by.

* * *

There lies a hilly spot in Jerusalem
where herds of aging singles live as gracefully as possible
under the weight of waiting.

Here are some of their stories.
Proceed with care.

Cold Dates

February 1999

"Break a leg, love!" says Emma. "Preferably his!" Thus she launches her sweet-smelling flatmate on yet another date, giving Shari a little push out the door as if she truly is that champagne bottle on the end of a rope. Shari hopes that this time she will not end up smashed against the ship's hull—just this once.

Shari steps out into the cold night, heels medium-high, blush puffed on cheeks, perfume dabbed upon neck and wrists. All the seductive bones and joints—collarbone, elbows, knees—are fittingly covered up. Thus, both prettiness and mystique are assured. Shari knows their necessity. Even religious male heads, most properly arched over a book, turn at a slim ankle and delicate cheek. For this reason, before every date, Shari spends twenty minutes blow-drying her hair into a shiny brown waterfall. Always give it your best shot. People reject based on the littlest things. She knows.

Tonight will be the third new man in two weeks—number eighty-eight of the total tally of lawyers, accountants, yeshivah students, teachers, rabbis, academics, and businessmen with whom Shari has sat over the past decade in cafés, restaurants, lobbies, parks and cars. They include Americans, British, Canadians, South Africans, Australians, Israelis, a French Moroccan with a distracting monobrow, and a gregarious convert from Peru. These men are debonair, intellectual, witty, intriguing, sweet, shy, shallow or downright tedious as they fumble their way through the procedure, narrating their stories, evaluating, deciding, listening-not-listening through evening after evening of strained conversation. And all the while under the polite surface whirls a vortex of fears and silences. Two extended selves stretch and yearn, yet always seem to fall short of something tangible.

Shari's list grows like an unchecked weed, covering ever more pages of her journal with vile statistics. Upon her return she will write:

February 1999. Number 88.

Moshe Toledano.

Age 31. Canadian. Rabbinical student.

Set up by: Hannah Kaplan.

Hannah went out with him last week, and now she has passed him on to Shari. This is accepted practice in the 'hood: *He wasn't right for me but I thought of him for you*—a weary game of pass-the-parcel.

There is also a category called *Number of Dates*, which she will record when it ends. All too often the number is a 1, its solitary straight line resembling the lonely word "I." One-dimensional, just like the experience itself with its stale aftertaste. But there is always hope. Perhaps it will be a higher number this time. Three will be excellent; seven will necessitate the blessing upon a miracle.

Shari leans upon a lamppost outside her building. The stone houses of Old Katamon—some with Arabic-style arches and high ceilings; others rectangular apartment blocks, Western and functional—are bright with an indoor warmth. She wishes she did not have to go out, but duty calls. Down the road, the supermarket where the singles do their shopping is closing. A bus passes. Next to Shari stands a blue municipality sign that proclaims: *The name Katamon comes from the Greek kata toi monasterioi ("below the monastery"). A strategic point during the 1948 War of Independence, Katamon was conquered on May 1st by the forces of the Haganah and Palmach. Today, the neighborhood is known as Old Katamon, to contrast it with the Katamonim, the newer housing built for immigrants in the early years of the State.*

Shari has never read this sign all the way through, for when standing on this spot she is always waiting for some man, too anxious to take in enlightening words. She does not much care about the official history of this neighborhood; rather, she cares about her personal history in its streets. The word Katamon, for her, long ago transmogrified in her mind into *Cat o' Moon*, as if the lunar orb houses some gargantuan feline, fathomlessly distant yet naked to the eye, purring contentedly as if all is right with the world. The thought generally comforts her; she has even found herself actually reaching out a hand as if to pet the moon. Tonight however, in her mood of despair thinly laced with hope, *Cat o' Moon* makes her think of the Jerusalem cats stalking streets by moonlight and yowling suddenly from green dumpsters. These lanky, dirty street cats with their angry wails scare her. There's one now: a compact furry creature gliding the walltop on soft pads, icy eyes glinting at her momentarily before moving on.

Shari shivers. She wonders whether to go back for an extra layer. She suffers badly from the Jerusalem winter that numbs her feet and hands. She wishes she could live in Tel Aviv, whose clime is far more pleasant for winter months; but the religious social life there is too limited. In the end she remains where she is, but changes position, curving her hip so that her right foot is splayed out in front of her, and tapping at her thigh with her long painted nail to a Jewish traditional tune playing in her head.

"Shari?" says a voice.

She blinks, and quickly arranges a sweet smile on face. "Oh, hi, hello." She cannot look at him, at first.

"Sorry I'm late. So, uh . . . where to?"

"You decide?" She says this to show him that she is not out to dominate, is flexible. It is also a good way to find out quickly if he is a man-with-a-plan, one of the items on her checklist. She smiles brightly, glancing up at him briefly though she is too nervous to really see him.

"OK, let's go," he says, and they begin walking toward town. He does not offer to call a cab. She says very little, walks quietly beside him, her heels making a muffled clip-clop, her face buried for warmth in her scarf. She risks a sidelong glance at his profile. He is tall, close to six feet. He sports short brown hair, cut close except for two small sidelocks curling out over the pronounced ridge at the sides of his broad skull. Light grey eyes. Skin that seems not flesh-colored but white in the moonlight. Pale blue shirt with a pen in the breast pocket. A thin coat (how can he wear that in this weather? why do men never get cold?). She likes the way he looks—dignified, yet with a certain boyishness.

At the entrance to the restaurant Moshe has chosen, Shari pauses, her eyes sweeping the area, apprehensive of encountering her students. The last thing she needs is their curious eyes, their whispers and giggles behind unsubtle hands, their eighteen-year-old pity for an old maid of twenty-nine, fueled by their certainty (and had she too not once felt that way?) of avoiding the same fate. But the girls adore burger joints and bagel bars, not fancy restaurants, and none of them are here tonight.

Seeing her hesitate, Moshe urges: "Come." The soft pressure in his voice calls up an unexpected image of his hand on her back steering her inside—she can practically feel the bones of his fingers pressing against her vertebrae. Disturbing. This is not helpful! She tries to banish the idea back to the murky inner place from whence it escaped. But she feels thrown off balance, and immediately after sitting down she orders a glass of mulled wine, to warm and calm.

The restaurant boasts elegant palm branches, delicate paintings in reds and browns, and an expensive fish menu. It has good heating, and Shari is delighted to be able to remove her jacket. Moshe orders and Shari allows him to choose for her too. As she drinks, she is finally able to relax enough to take a proper look at him. She notes now that although he is quite handsome, his knuckles are somewhat reddish (eczema? is he healthy?) and his eyelids have a way of drooping, making him seem somewhat reptilian. This unattractive feature is redeemed by the acutely inquisitive light in his eyes, which rove quickly over their surroundings, taking in everything. Everything but her. She waits, upset, for him to look her way, as he talks about the décor, speculates about the family of four who have ordered mounds of chips and about the scruffy middle-aged man at the back, chewing slowly over his plate, complains about the slow service, talks of this and that. When at last his glance falls upon her face and lingers there, his attention feels to Shari like the blast of hot summer air that hits you when you emerge from your air-conditioned plane at Ben Gurion airport. Finally, he asks something about her.

She opens her mouth to answer but just then the food arrives. And now begins the serious task of dating, eating and talking simultaneously. The soups (tomato and spicy bean, with toasted bread and garlic butter) are accompanied by conversation about their Jewish childhoods in Toronto and Boston. Shari still takes pleasure in recounting her biography, even after so many repetitions. It anchors her and reminds her of who she is, even while trapped in the company of this unceasing succession of male strangers.

— *I hated school. What a waste of a childhood.*

— *I loved school. The teachers were great. I am still in touch with some.*

— *My brother and I used to collect goldfish and lizards*

— *I used to make up stories in my head when I was bored.*

— *Like what?*

— *Umm . . . I remember one was about a hot air balloon filled with peanut butter and—no, it's too embarrassing.*

— *Go on!*

— *. . . and piloted by a . . .*

— *by a . . . ?*

— *a donkey . . . named Kitniyos.*

— *Awesome!*

The fish course (grilled salmon with baby greens and rosemary-flecked potatoes, fresh trout with curried rice) brings intellectual discussions. In Shari's mind the association of intellect with fish throws her straight back into family meals past. Little Shmuli and Avi both groaning, "Yucky fish, mommy!" and her mother insisting, "Fish is brain food!" Somehow her mother always manages to intrude into Shari's mind on dates. This is not helpful.

Shari and Moshe discuss:

— *Should yeshivah students be exempted from the Israeli army?*

— *How does Jewish law jibe with scientific truths?*

— *Are Orthodox women's prayer groups legitimate?*
— *Should land be given to the Palestinians if peace could be guaranteed?*

Moshe expresses hope that peace has arrived at last, that the current lull in terror attacks will, God willing, prove permanent. In truth, Shari feels cynical—she does not trust the Palestinians to be satisfied without full right of return. But she does not verbalize this; she just tells Moshe that she hopes he is right. Aware that they are outsiders to Israeli politics, they soon move on to other subjects, such as the expected rise in tourism for the millennium next year, and the short attention span of today's students.

Over the next hour, Shari raises many topics, always asking Moshe what he thinks. She smiles frequently, plays with her hair, and opens her clear brown eyes wide in a way she knows makes her look pretty. She often says, *"That's a good point,"* and *"Oh yes! You are so right."* Always be warm to men, that's the rule. Make them feel good; don't scare them off. But once or twice, against her own better judgment, she finds herself arguing passionately—though she knows, she just knows that it is too early to disagree with him. These processes are so fragile, people can reject for the slightest things. You have to be perfect in all ways, until he is hooked. She knows that you wait until the fourth date before speaking your mind, yet here is her mouth opening of its own accord and declaring, "Fine, but on the other hand . . . ." She is angry with herself.

In any event, Moshe does not let her argue for long. Though he is a gentleman, twice asking, "Shall I order you more wine?" he prefers to hold forth than to listen, and frequently steamrolls over her attempts to speak. In her experience many men seem to have this habit and Shari knows it is not malicious; but being interrupted repeatedly makes her feel increasingly irritated. Also, his rapid-fire jokes are not as funny as he thinks. He is rather arrogant, and she does not like arrogant.

With regret—for he is an attractive man—she imagines herself mentally marking a "1" next to his name on the list. At this point, she stops trying to appear intelligent, and suffices with smiling and letting him talk on. She sneaks glances at her watch and over Moshe's shoulder at the fish-guzzling man in the corner, who has asked for the menu yet again. Does he have four stomachs?

The minutes pass, and Shari looks vacantly into Moshe's face, seeing his wide cheekbones and the round shape of his skull, watching the way his jaw moves when he talks. She idly wonders who will be her number eighty-nine. Or, for that matter, one hundred and eighty-nine, her one thousand and eighty-nine . . . endless, endless men to date! A shiver runs through her, and she suddenly envisions dozens of journals overflowing with names of men long forgotten and long married, while in the latest one she pens some horrendous four-digit number in a shaky old-lady hand. Her smile droops suddenly, as if someone snipped the strings attached to the corners of her mouth.

The meal is winding down. Their fish is now a pile of sharp bones, small scrapings of flesh clinging to them. In the last few minutes, there has been an unexpected turnaround, unprecedented in all of Shari's dating experience. Mellowed by his Chardonnay, and perhaps by Shari's polite attention, Moshe's dead-white cheeks have turned a patchy apricot hue, and here, out of nowhere, comes a stream of shy confessions and sweet compliments for her:

I've wanted to be a rabbi since I was eleven—my uncle is a rabbi, he's my hero. But my folks are threatening to cut off support, and they do have a point, I'm thirty-one already, feeling the pinch . . . . You've already been teaching for five years, look how far ahead you are of me, you're amazing . . . . Tell me about your worst date ever. Was it awful? You shouldn't have to suffer like that . . . . I hate first dates, they're so corny and I'm no good at them. I bet you get lots of shidduch offers, a pretty girl like you. Really? I can't understand why you don't have a long line of suitors banging down your front door . . . .

Shari thrills, her inner cavities glowing. She is used to meeting at the shallowest end of things, the shiny surfaces where man and woman, oil and water, mix; but now she actually feels seen, for once. Moshe's eyes under his half-lowered lids suck her in greedily. She feels herself melting. She loves the trapezoid shape of his facial bone structure. He is a great catch after all, she decides: sensitive yet masculine, Torah-learned yet worldly, articulate, confident, shy. *Check, check, check, check.*

And yet! And yet, caution always. Even with tongue lubricated with wine and heart with sweet words, Shari keeps things airy. Heaviness is never a wise course on the first date. She knows. So she laughs at Moshe's statements about dates, though it is no laughing matter, though her heart aches. Dates, she jokes, are generally about as enjoyable as being stampeded by a posse of drunken yaks, as her flatmate Emma would say. Nonetheless, they are still preferable to "Friday Night Live," aka the scene, those crowds that spill out of various synagogues such as Ohel Nechama and Yakar into Chopin and Kovshei Katamon streets, barely bothering to move aside when honking cars try to pass. The men, hands in suit pockets, eyeing the women, who chit-chat and chirrup, strutting about and stretching their necks like a flock of flamingos.

Moshe snorts and tells her that the Jerusalem scene is nothing compared to the meat market—that's *meat*, not *meet*, he laughs wryly—on New York's Upper West Side, where he lived for three years. She listens in fascinated horror as he describes huge gaggles of gorgeous Jewish twenty- to sixty-somethings milling about and making small talk, always someone new to meet, always the promise of something better 'round the next corner. Her stomach turns. "I prefer to meet naturally, in intimate settings, such as Shabbat meals," she informs him. She enjoys hosting, and in fact hosted a meal this past Shabbat. Oh, yes, it was very pleasant. That is (*pause; laugh; toss of shiny hair*) until some random horse-faced Israeli woman showed up halfway through, claiming that a mutual friend had sent her. Shari would not have minded so much—she always makes plenty of food, just like any good Jewish woman (*laugh; toss of hair*)—but the visitor dominated the conversation for the rest of the evening with the entire story of her dreadful divorce. Shari is careful not to mention any names, as that would be *lashon hara*, gossip, but she entertains Moshe with imitations of her unwanted guest and her own unexpressed thoughts.

"The only thing that eventually shut her up was a humungous piece of chocolate cake—"

"Which you wished she would choke on!" cackles Moshe with not-very-rabbinical glee.

"—but by that time everyone was totally depressed and just wanted to go home!" Shari cannot join in his laughter. After sweating all day in the kitchen to create a delicious and relaxing meal, and taking care to invite balanced numbers of men and women to meet in an unpressured environment, having one self-absorbed individual spoil the whole thing was infuriating. And even worse—though this is not something she would ever tell Moshe—was the Shabbat lunch she attended the next day. A women-only meal, at which one of the guests said at some point, "Well none of us have boyfriends, I assume, otherwise why would we be here at this meal?" Exposing the unspoken shame. Making her (at twenty-nine!) feel pathetic, spinsterish, old.

But there is no point dwelling. Shari orders herself to snap back into the present, where there *is* a man, to whom she should pay attention if she does not want to lose him and go back to the all-girl meals.

". . . Israelis," he is saying. "They like to talk and not listen, as a whole, don't you find? It can get annoying."

"Yes, very true."

"Mm! Good wine!" Moshe downs the dregs of his third glass.

"Yes, very good."

He continues to reflect on Israelis, and, nodding automatically, she drifts away again to imagine a Shabbat meal sometime in the near future, hosted with Moshe, with whom she has developed a wonderful romantic connection. All Friday they will cut and chop and talk and laugh and flirtily fling dishtowels at each other, in lieu of anything more forbidden. Just before Shabbat, the doorbell will ring and there he will be, spruce and handsome in freshly ironed Shabbat shirt, bringing roses or lilies, and she will blush and act surprised, burying her nose shyly in the fronds. After synagogue, they will serve their erudite guests steaming bowls of chicken soup with *kneidlach*, potato *kugel* and rice, chicken wings in honey, spinach salad with strawberries, cabbage salad in soy sauce. For dessert, her delicious home-baked brownies that send the guests into raptures. On the table, a nice Merlot from Tishbi or Carmel. As they rehearse playing house, the other singles at the table will sniff the air like hungry bloodhounds, enviously scenting the Real Thing. *The Real Thing.*

Dessert arrives: pistachio ice cream with chocolate swirls, and fresh dates straight from the freezer. Moshe makes a pleased little-boy face; pistachio is his favorite. He tells her of the New York kosher eatery that featured pistachio ice cream on the menu and yet on a dozen consecutive occasions "happened to be all out." The day before he left New York, Moshe bought a tub of pistachio ice cream and presented it to the bemused owner with an elaborate bow. Ha ha!

Shari smiles at him, enjoying his pleasure. She picks up a date and slits it lengthways with a manicured nail, checking for bugs. Moshe, about to pop the fruit straight into his mouth, notices her action and stops to do the same. Watching the fine movements of his hands, she is judging him. How could he, a rabbinical student, forget the bug laws which, under certain circumstances, are five times worse than eating pork? She is still thinking about how this bothers her when Moshe holds out the pitted date to her and says the words, "Feed me!"

This is very last thing Shari expected. The two words seem to hang in the drowsy air between them like the echoes of the *shofar* blast on Rosh Hashanah. *What did he say?* Shari's muscles seize up, all motion has stopped in her entire body down to the smallest organ, it seems. She runs the words through her brain again and again to see if she can possibly have misunderstood his intention. *Feed me . . . ?* Shari is by nature obedient, and generally does what she is asked to do, especially by men, but . . . .

For an endless instant the fleshy fruit, its black skin glistening with tiny diamonds of water, is suspended between them. His hand does not tremble. Then—

"Feed me!" he repeats, a little more insistently, persuasively, looking at her through his lazy lids.

Her heart slaps in her chest and her clothes feel itchy, prickles of sweat breaking out in all sorts of odd places. As if under a spell, feeling as if her hand belongs to someone else, she reaches forward slowly, and taking the date from him with great care, transfers it to his mouth. She tries to keep her fingers as distant from his lips as possible, but as he sucks in the food quickly, he catches the ends of her fingers with his tongue. Shari pulls her hand sharply back to her side of the table. Frowns. Giggles. Frowns again.

Shaking her head as if she has water in her ears, she tries to paste her sophisticated smile back onto her face as if things like this always happen, but fails, and instead looks fiercely down at her fingers clenched in her lap. *I don't understand. What the . . . ?* This is not the behavior she expects from religious men, from rabbinical students—*frum* guys! Hands are kept to yourself. What happened to modesty? Roses bloom in her cheeks. Her fingers still feel wet, and she wipes her hand repeatedly on her skirt until all vestiges of his saliva are long gone. Only then does she manage to resurrect the dating smile, a wobbly, pale shadow of its former self.

"Coffee?" she says in a faint voice. Moshe looks at his watch. Twelve minutes to midnight. Late. Long day tomorrow. I'm sure you understand.

No, she does not understand. She does not understand! She herself desperately wants a coffee, but her tongue cleaves thickly to her palate, so Moshe obliviously goes off to pay the bill. Her hands seem to have forgotten how to function, and it is with some difficulty that she manages to take out a small plastic sheet from her wallet and say Grace after Meals. *Who nurtures the entire world with His goodness,* she mumbles absently, slurring the words into long run-on sentences, and finishing: *I have neverseen a righteousperson abandonedtheLord shallgiveHis peoplestrength the Lord shallblessHis peoplewithpeace.* As she mouths the last paragraph, her eyes rest unseeing on the plate before her, where three date pits swim in melted pistachio between two long spoons exactly two inches apart.

Moshe returns and they leave in silence. A cab is flagged down, though she cannot afterward recall how. They travel back to her neighborhood. Moshe points out the building where one of his rabbis lives and prattles on about what he has to do tomorrow. She nods and 'mmm's. They arrive in Katamon and she gets out, and so does Moshe, while the taxi waits to transport him to his apartment in Kiryat Moshe.

That unwieldy moment has arrived, as it always does, for saying or not saying, for clues in body language and tone of voice as to how things will play out. Will hurt be given or received? The judgment, the verdict, or a postponement? At this point in the date, Shari often becomes overwhelmed by a sense of futility and despair. Somehow the men she likes inexplicably reject her, while in situations where she would, as Emma once put it, "rather date a three-legged ferret with lethal halitosis," the men are keen to continue. What a cruel joke, this mismatch of desire, this unmet reaching out for connection, a prank played by God on innocent men and women. Like the pustulant, stubborn Job, Shari has a bone to pick with the divine order of things—if anyone would just listen to her. But tonight she feels an odd excitement prickling in her scalp. For a change, something interesting has happened on this first date, though she still cannot grasp exactly what. Something meaningful, for a change! So she waits, concealing her nervousness, for his next words, while a cat watches them silently from a wall.

Moshe is relaxed, leaning against the taxi door. He bows in an affected manner and says, "Well, Ms. Shari, you've been great company."

"Thanks," whispers Shari.

"You have, if I may say so, a compelling personality."

"Oh—th-thanks," Shari stutters, not sure what to make of this.

"So, um, thanks for a great evening. We'll talk." Moshe smiles gently, and with another minuscule bow, gets back in the taxi, roars off. Shari waits until it is out of sight, then walks into her building on numbed feet. Only when she enters her home does Shari realize that Moshe, the rabbinical student, totally forgot to say Grace After Meals.

"Compelling personality?" Emma screeches, bouncing on her heels in her ill-matched pajamas.

"That's what he said."

"Well what the 'eck is that when it's at home? Is that him saying, 'You'd be a great teacher fer my kids—which I will be having with another woman, yer great ugly dollop?'"

Shari blanches. Emma claps her hand over her mouth. "Sorry! Sorry! You're not ugly, don't be silly, that's just—I mean, I'm so knackered, I don't know which way up I go right now. I put a cheese sandwich down somewhere two hours ago, and I've been looking for it ever since, it's driving me 'round the bend. Please forgive me; and just be careful where you sit till I find it."

After obediently making sure it is cheese-sandwichless, Shari sits down on a chair and rolls her long lovely hair into a tight ball behind her head. "Emma," she moans, "this was the bizarrest first date experience I've ever had. I'm so confused!"

"Sandwich, sandwich, where art thou?" Emma mutters, shoving her hand fruitlessly into the depths of the sofa.

"Earth to Emma!" says Shari loudly.

Emma looks up. "Too much drama; it's all too much," she explains, plunking herself down apologetically on the sofa. "OK, so what happened? Tell me all."

"Sure you want to hear? I know it's late."

"Yuh!" says Emma. "I'm all ears! Well, some of me is ears, anywoz. Blab away."

Shari obediently blabs away. But even two heads—or, since this *is* Emma, one and a half heads at least—cannot quite make sense of it.

"Only time will tell," Emma yawns in conclusion, stretching her arms along the back of the sofa, and then yelps in glee as her hand encounters soggy, cheesy bread.

Time tells.

Shari has just come home from a long day at the seminary—teaching and endless paperwork. Her hair hangs in long limp strings, just like the spaghetti she is cooking. She really ought to wash it at some point soon.

Emma enters the kitchen. "Wotcher, Shaz!"

"This apartment is cold, why is it always so cold?" complains Shari.

"So did he call yet?" says Emma, opening the fridge. A salad dressing bottle falls out and smashes on the floor, eliciting a word that Shari has never heard before but imagines should not be employed in her Torah classes. Her flatmate grabs up reams of paper towel and squats down to clean up. Unnerved by yet another of Emma's little accidents, Shari says, "Huh?"

"The fruit-fetish blokey. Has he rung? Written? Yodelled? Sent a pigeon?"

"Er . . . none of the above."

"Spotty git! How long has it been?"

"Ten days."

Emma stops cleaning. "You what? *Ten days?* Insufferable! Auntie Em says forget him and move straight on to the next victim."

"Victim?" says Shari in an insulted tone.

"Feller, chappie, whatever, you know what I mean. Just move on!"

Shari sighs. "I know, I know."

The spaghetti is overcooked and it slips soggily from the spoon at an unexpected angle, landing on the floor near Emma's mess. But Emma just cheerfully cleans it up too with her huge wad of dripping paper towel, and adds firmly, "Next time when I tell you to break his leg, you do it!"

Shari inhales wearily. "Yes, Auntie Em. I've had it with all these . . . these—"

"Selfish prats?"

Shari nods. "These morons, these—" She wishes she had a stock of dirty words, like Emma. "These lying, misleading, self-absorbed . . ." She fumbles for a word that expresses what she is feeling. *"Clowns!"*

Emma stands up and pats her arm with a hand smeared with salad dressing. "Cheer up, duck. There's someone for everyone. Every Bonnie has her Clyde, every Jekyll has his Hyde."

"Yeah, er. Thanks."

"Anytime!"

She takes the unappetizing pasta into her room and, after lackadaisically examining the oily streaks on her sleeve, sits down on her bed and gazes into space, the spaghetti uneaten. Her fingers are feeling once again that unexpected moistness— the cold impress of frozen dates followed by the warm, fleeting feeling of human tongue. She once more makes that wiping motion on her skirt, though she knows it is an irrational act. Looking around in disgust at her untidy room, she spies her journal on the floor, its pages bent, and leans over to pick it up, almost falling off the bed. This is the first time she has written in it since the date with Moshe. She scribbles:

How dare he eat from my hand? What is this, the Song of Songs? Am I some shepherd girl to play around with? Can he just knock at my door and then vanish?

This is all she can write for now. Breathing hurts. She is glad that she feels so bad—this is what happens when red lines are crossed, she scolds herself. Women ought not to be intimate with men who are not their husbands. Even the smallest touch infringes the prohibition of *"To a woman in her impurity thou shalt not come close."* She has always kept the law so carefully till now. She believes that its purpose is to preserve holiness in human relationships, and particularly to protect women from men's strange, primitive urges. This incident just proves the law is true, down to the last detail. A rabbinical student, of all people! Disgusting.

Turning to the list of names, she fills in the number 1 next to Moshe's entry. Then she writes furiously:

Eighty-eight down, how many to go? Soon I'll hit the big one hundred and then I'll have a party and invite all of them to come and tell the story of "my date with Shari." Oh how we'll laugh!

She shivers violently. Her teeth are chattering and she can barely hold the pen straight. *So shall I always be alone, a never-married widow? Buried alive in a single grave, while the rest of the world lives and loves?*

Wet tissues gradually litter her bed in yellows, oranges, and whites. Sad, bloated caricatures of roses.

Four weeks later. Hearing Moshe's voice makes Shari grimace, but she plows on, affecting a vivacious tone. She is a good actress, as teachers often are.

"Oh, hello, hi, yuh it's Shari Eisenhart. Remember me? We went out a few . . . yes, how are you? Yes, yes, fine, thank God . . . . Look, I'll cut to the chase. You seem like a great guy and I, uh, thought that I could set you up with someone. Every pot has its lid, so they say." She laughs artificially. "Are you fr—? Oh, of course. Well her name's Galit Peretz. Very attractive woman. About thirty, quite tall, slim with lovely green eyes. A sports teacher. Born in Israel, but speaks an excellent English . . . . Uh, good question, I don't really know . . . actually, I don't know her very well, she's a friend of a friend, I just met her once . . . . Religious, of course! Oh, and divorced—is that OK? Listen, I know you'll like her, she has a—a compelling personality. Give it a chance, why not? It's just a coffee. Great, I'll give you her . . . here's her number . . . ."

As Shari hangs up, she feels nauseous. There is a twisted smile on her face, and it is not her dating smile. *For you, sir. One talkative Israeli, special delivery.*

Number ninety-four is called Ron. He works in the diamond business. Built like a bison, dark-skinned with a huge smile full of large teeth, his features seem oversized; they fail to fit together properly. He looks like the Mr. Potato Head toy Shari played with as a child. She is without any make-up, and as they stroll through the Katamon streets, they make a suitably hideous pair, she thinks. She doesn't care. Her new ambition is to hit the big one hundred by Pesach, and she has been recklessly accepting all offers coming her way. She has little to lose since it never works out anyway. She even recently went out with a freshly divorced rabbi, father to a small baby, a red line she had never crossed before, frightened of that word "stepmother" with all its nasty fairy-tale associations. A man named Immanuel, charming but clearly still very damaged, not at all ready for a new relationship, and not ready to be passed on to Hannah. Hannah might be too feminist for him anyway—most men couldn't handle that. You couldn't always just pass the parcel.

Shari's comfortable flat shoes make no noise as she walks at Ron's side. He is interested in history and philosophy and everything in between, and has already covered about seventeen topics, from Rabbi Samson Raphael Hirsch to the invention of the motor vehicle, from Communism to the Dead Sea Scrolls. Every moment brings a new trampling of the English language. He has already told her that "consistency is the gobhoblin of the little mind," and that he believes that Judaism is essentially "floralistic" and is not about "pilosophy" but rather action-based. Shari marvels at how eager he is to chew over all these issues, this hulking jeweler. She has noticed before that in Israel, the local tailor may be a learned Talmudist, the butcher an expert in Maimonides. A land with a scholar under every bush. She finds herself wishing that she could fall for this friendly giant, who will make an excellent husband and father, but then he laughs his large silly laugh that echoes off the stone buildings, and Shari knows she could never spend her life with someone so uncontrolled and incautious. She just knows.

The pair walk down Palmach street, then up Lamed-Heh to Hachish street and around back onto Palmach to start again. It looks like they will keep circling the block until Ron runs out of steam or the Messiah arrives, whichever comes first (Shari is betting on the Messiah). Ron's breath clouds in the frosty air as he talks. Shari is wondering how soon she can end the date without seeming rude. Noticing her shivering, Ron suggests they find somewhere indoors to sit. Shari does not want to prolong the date and insists she will be fine. They walk around the block another couple of times, and now she is losing sensation in her lips. She is about to ask him to walk her back to her apartment, when Ron stops and, looking at her quizzically, says:

"So tell me, Sherry—why you so sad?"

A guilty hand flies up to her face, as if to search for her lost smile, and she fumbles for a suitable reply. Ron pulls a crumpled granola bar out of his pocket, offering it to her. She refuses, trying to work out how she can shift the conversation back to him but he looks at her with compassion, which makes her feel like sinking into the earth.

Just then a figure emerges from a nearby building. She tries to turn away, but it is too late.

"Hey, Shari, is that you?"

Moshe.

"Hello, yes, hi, Moshe . . . this is—this is, er—"

"Ron. Shalom." Ron genially clasps Moshe's hands in both of his. Shari is trying to think of a way to escape this situation. She cannot tell whom she hates more at this moment: Ron, Moshe, or herself.

Moshe says, "Pleased to meet you. Hey Shari, I am *so* glad to run into you! Thank you *so* much for introducing us, I really can't thank you enough!" From behind him, Galit exits the same building, wearing a black raincoat with a fake-fur collar. "Shari!" she shrieks. "*Eyzeh keta!* I don't believe it!" She runs over and hugs the stiff Shari. Introduction to Ron is left to Moshe, for Shari is speechless.

Galit tells Ron in rapid Hebrew, "Hey brother, this woman is a saint and a sweetheart! Don't let go of her too quickly. I crashed her Shabbat meal and she was so gracious. I was so depressed and thought if I ate on my own I would die, but she and her friends made me feel so much better, they were all so nice to me. Oh and she makes a wicked chocolate cake!"

Ron smiles.

"And best of all, she found me this wonderful, gorgeous hunk." She grabs onto the flap of Moshe's coat and gives it a tug, and he smiles, his eyes lighting up, his cheekbones rosé. Galit turns to Shari and says in English:

"You are fabulous, Shari!" She pronounces the word *farbulous*. "I'm your number one fan!"

Ron grins proudly.

Moshe agrees. "You're the greatest, Shari!" He and Galit stand close, intimate. Shari's head is spinning. She sees Moshe's eyes glinting in the moonlight and remembers how they stared at her in the restaurant. She remembers the cold feel of the fruit in her hand as she held it out to him. She wonders if the incident even survives in his memory. Or was it so trivial to him as to simply drop out of sight?

Galit smiles, her face alive with joy. Moshe looks at her and says proudly, "Well, it's not quite official, but we can tell you, our matchmaker. We just got engaged."

Shari makes a very small sound in her throat.

"You got a third of paradise now, Shari, you're going to heaven—*yalla*, pack up your bag!" They laugh together, synchronized, intimate.

"But not at this moment I hope, yes?" Ron laughs, his big body shaking. "We still on our first date." Shari stands frozen in horror while the three of them look down at her fondly as at some delightful child.

"She's a good one," says Moshe, wagging a finger at Ron. "Don't let her go."

"I'm sure not let her to go without a smile tonight," promises Ron. He puts a heavy arm around Shari's shoulders. "Right, my cherry?"

Shari's shoulders twitch involuntarily. She wants to wriggle an escape from under his arm but it would be rude, she knows. She wonders what her students and colleagues would think if they saw her, standing here in the street with no make-up, being cuddled by a large Israeli man. She looks up at the faces of Moshe, Galit, Ron.

Lizard face. Horse face. Potato head.

A tremor of hilarity makes its way up her body, and suddenly she bursts out laughing: not even ordinary laughter, but a manic screeching like Emma's. For a short while she is entirely unable to stop, and has to practically gag on her hand to stifle her giggles.

"There!" says Ron, his lumpy face aglow.

"*Sh'koyach!*" says Moshe, smiling.

"*Hee hee,*" titters Galit.

"*Farbulous!*" Shari exclaims, and claps her hand over her mouth again. Shivers of laughter run through her body, feeling like waves of nausea, and she cannot suppress them.

Soon Moshe and Galit will make their goodbyes and walk off together, their bodies inclining toward each other in comfortable intimacy. Then the awkward moment will come with Ron, and it will be time for pass-the-parcel and number ninety-five. She knows.

At this moment, however, three people are laughing fondly, are smiling their sweetest smiles at her. And Ron's arm around her thin shoulders—this knobbly forbidden fruit—feels so warm, so very, very warm.

Species

October 1999

Sukkot, falling in September-October time, is designated a festival of autumn, that sly red-backed fox that slips unnoticed between bulkier seasons. In Britain, Sukkot falls in dead winter (try, if you will, to enjoy the lopsided shack you have built in your garden as rain drenches your decorations and dilutes your chicken soup), while in Israel, late summer hums and scorches, making your Sukka booth a sauna, and soaking your underarms with unfestive sweat.

Hannah had known both extremes, shuttling between climes from year to year. This year she was spending the festival on a religious kibbutz in the North of Israel. This was the nearer North, a lush area that abuts onto the Jordan Valley, where at night Jordan's lights glint as close as your breath. She looked forward to seeing Liron and Zak, a lively couple with feet-on-the-coffee-table hospitality and a plump, rumbly-tumbly baby, at whose home she was not a pitied thirty-year-old single, but rather a friend, beloved for intellect and spirit.

On Sukkot morning, Hannah stumbled out to the balcony of the apartment where she was staying (how generous, how relaxed these kibbutzniks were, letting strangers sleep in their homes while they were away). She squinted through sleep-gritted eyes at the surrounding hills, a patchwork of faded greens thirsty for the rainy season, and at the modest white cubes that were the kibbutz homes. It looked like another hot day.

Suddenly Hannah felt happier than she had for a long time. Perhaps life was manageable after all. Beauty existed that no human could spoil. "Hello there!" she called coquettishly to the sun, a young stallion pawing at the horizon. The golden orb remained indifferent, nestling majestically in thin strands of cloud.

She returned to the kitchen to assemble her *arba minim*, her "four species." The shaking of the species—taking four different types of vegetation and shaking them in all directions—was a bizarre ritual to which she looked forward every year. Recently some of the old practices, to which she had clung for years, had lost their charm and seemed a little threadbare. Protracted single life seemed to wear things down in general, she was finding, important things like family connections, hope and faith; it replaced them with disturbing questions about religion, the role of women, where one fit in and what it all meant. She felt herself teetering on the edge of daunting changes, of which she herself had only a half-formed notion, knowing only that they had to do with the alarming label "feminist" that, once embraced, might change everything.

But for now, at least, she still loved this Sukkot festival with its outlandish plants. Eagerly, Hannah went to redeem the willows from their moist confinement inside a rolled up T-shirt in the fridge. The most vulnerable of the four to climate, they had to be kept wet. If they died, Hannah would be obliged to shake the "three species," which wouldn't do at all. She picked them up gently, the cloth cold and damp in her hands. The long leaves dangling over the top reminded her of smiling lips, which in turn brought to mind the traditional explanation that the *arba minim* represent the human body. This was an idea she had first heard many years ago, sometime in her childhood—certainly before she understood what a body really was (and did she really, even now? She had only lately breached some of the restrictive taboos, like a child wobbling on her first bike, an explorer *sans* map).

The *aravot*, willows, the teacher had told them while pointing to herself in illustration, symbolize the mouth; the *hadassim,* the myrtle leaves, are like eyes; the *lulav,* the palm branch, is the spine; and the *etrog,* the knobbly lemon-like citron fruit, the human heart. The children all drew little people with willow mouths and *lulav* spines, and when Hannah's father brought home his *arba minim,* in her six-year-old naïvete she put the citron to her ear, hoping to hear a heartbeat. Disappointed by the silence, she had refused to touch the *etrog* for the rest of the festival, leaving it to sit idle in its little hair-lined box except when her father needed it.

Carefully she inserted the willows into the green woven holder next to the palm branch and the waxy myrtles. The three of them lay there patiently on the kitchen counter, awaiting the embrace of her hand. Hannah picked up the *etrog* that would soon—very soon—complete their little coterie, and, making the blessing on scents, drew its genteel citrusy flavor deep into her lungs. This must be the fragrance of the world to come, she thought, the scent of paradise. Didn't some scholars believe this was in fact the seductive fruit eaten by Adam and Eve? A druggy bliss spread through all her parts, and she slowly lifted her arms in a yoga-like stretch, on the exhale breathing, "*Chag sameach!*" to the sun and not caring that no response came. It was about time for some joy.

The previous day, Hannah had traveled with the *arba minim* in their plastic transparent carrier on the bus to the Central Bus station in Jerusalem. As she stared out the bus windows, holding the carrier awkwardly between her knees, she saw many signs that Jerusalem was preparing for the millennium and its anticipated huge influx of tourists. Hotels were being renovated and new ones built, and the already thronging streets would soon be even more packed. This should have been a reason for celebration but Hannah was not in the mood. All she saw was the dust and the hordes.

At the Central Bus Station she struggled in frustration to schlep her case, her handbag, and the *arba minim* off the bus without falling over. With her delicate build and fragile wrists, Hannah was always having to go to her neighbors for help with impossible-to-open jars. So when a stranger stopped her, she hoped that he was about to offer help with her bags. She would never be too much of a feminist to refuse such old-fashioned chivalry. The man was of indeterminate age—a wrinkled forty? A youthful sixty?—with pale, forgettable eyes and a small beard. Pointing, he had asked in a French accent:

"Eet's your *lulav*?"

"Yes," she said irritably. It did not sound much like an offer of assistance. Was it some strange Jewish chat-up line? Why was she always a magnet for obnoxious people who wanted things? They would come up to her and ask for things point-blank—not only in Israel where reserved people were a persecuted minority, but even in her travels in England, Spain, and Russia. What was it about her? Did she look exceptionally harmless? Just a few days earlier a woman had stopped Hannah in the street and requested that she phone her cell-phone, lost deep in the recesses of her bag, so that she could locate it. Hannah wondered what she did when she lost her socks.

Around them people raced to catch their buses to Afula and Yerucham and Hod Hasharon for the festival. Passengers streamed to the left and right around Hannah and the Frenchman, a clump of dry land in a Red Sea of people: beanstalky teenage boys with small knitted *kippot*, girls in long denim skirts and identical backpacks, old Iraqi and Moroccan Jews shuffling along in cloth caps, pot-bellied Hasidim and urbane yeshivah students in black Borsalino hats. Many of the men carried their own elongated plastic carriers, bashing other people as they dashed by. It was lucky, Hannah thought, that no one poked out an eye.

But the stranger was not finished. "Your own?" he pressed.

She raised her eyebrows. "Yes!" Did he want to buy it from her? She wasn't selling.

"You weel shake eet?" he persisted.

What did he think she was planning to do with it—make a salad for tomorrow's lunch? She held her tongue and just nodded. Recently she had found herself becoming angry without much provocation. Puffs of rage arrived and departed quickly, leaving her at the mercy of her emotions. She had once been polite, but that seemed to be fading fast. And still the interrogation continued.

"Mademoiselle, tell me please, from what community you come?" Her shrug forced him to explain his meaning: "You are Conservative woman, weeth *lulav?*"

Finally Hannah understood. It should have been obvious to her from the start here in stereotypesville Jerusalem. Imitating his accent she had replied, grinning at her own bravado, "I am Orthodox woman weeth *lulav.*"

"Oh! Orthodox woman? *Mais oui, c'est vrai?*" He looked at her appraisingly for a moment. "Mmm-hmm. Well, I learn something new. Orthodox woman. Mmm-hmm."

Nodding and smiling, he had given her a little wave of parting. Sighing impatiently, Hannah had flattered herself that she had pricked one more balloon of religious chauvinism.

The synagogue was much like other kibbutz synagogues she had seen. They all bought their furniture from the Kibbutz Lavi furniture factory, granting them all a certain sameness, though each had a slightly different architecture. This building was decorated with a light tan-beige wood. Triangular in shape, its apex soared grandly in an inverted V above the ark, the two lines meeting directly above the ark's center. The partition was made of a lacy white material, fairly transparent, and the stained glass windows showed pastoral scenes and biblical verses about kindness, such as, "*And the stranger, the orphan, and the widow within your gates shall come and eat and be satisfied; that God bless you in all the work of your hands.*"

Hannah had arrived in time for the end of the morning service. Very soon, she noticed shuffling movements on the other side of the partition as the men began preparing their *arba minim* for shaking: unrolling, assembling, inserting, binding, fathers helping sons, old men arranging their sets with shaky hands.

Watching the *lulavs* rise in readiness one by one into the air, Hannah considered the word *minim*. Its singular, *min*, like many Hebrew words, bore multiple meanings. *Species, type,* or *class*; also *sex*—both gender and sexuality—and finally, *heretic*. So might *arba minim* be translated *the four heretics*? Or how about *the four sexes*? The thought made her laugh ruefully. Two more sexes would be nice, since she seemed to have exhausted the supply of decent religious males for the moment. The only men available these days had the personality of a cardboard box, or had commitment issues, or were looking for some little doll to flatter their egos and keep their houses. The matchmakers urged Hannah to give it another chance, but the thought of spending another evening with any of these men made her feel physically ill.

She absently fingered the springy myrtles. Her grandmother once told her that if you boiled myrtles and put the liquid in your hair, it made it grow thick and shiny. She thought about her hair, already thinning at the top. Time for myrtle paste perhaps? She wondered, as usual, if she would get to cover her hair with the married woman's headscarf before it all fell out, along with her teeth and eyelashes. Or before she came to shun head coverings altogether as a remnant of patriarchal oppression. This seemed more and more likely as time went on. She had never planned to become a feminist—angry and selfish troublemakers they had seemed to her all her life, but with the domestic dream gradually receding, she felt increasingly conned by Judaism. Someone should be held responsible for her misery besides herself! Hannah had volunteered on many fronts to make the world a better place, from soup kitchens to combating missionary cults. But now the clearest vision of her society's ills—and also the most spine to battle them— appeared to lodge within the feminist camp. She should join them, and to hell with what the men would think. She should stop living her life according to the standards of some imaginary man who might never materialize, she thought, though not without a pang in her heart.

Her thoughts returned to her grandmother: A pious Hungarian Jewess who had covered every strand of her hair with a tight-fitting scarf, she had never shaken the *lulav* in synagogue at *Hallel* with the men as Hannah was about to do. Perhaps she never felt the loss, but Hannah felt it for her. The old lady had been extremely tactile, always fingering cloths or caressing Hannah's cheeks with her gnarled fingers. How she would have loved to hold the four species, to bury her nose in the leaves. Oh well, thought Hannah, each generation to its own service of God. Indeed, she seemed to be a pioneer for her own generation's changes, for here she was, the only one with *arba minim* on her side of the partition. Walking to synagogue she had held it self-consciously against her chest—*Woman with lulav! Unclean, unclean!*—but in the end she had encountered no one at all.

The men were finally ready, and it was time to make the blessing before shaking the species. Hannah closed her eyes and said the Hebrew words, feeling herself uplifted. Then she held the *etrog* cupped in her hand close to the *lulav* and fulfilled the commandment of taking the four species, shaking the bunch with all her strength to the East, South, West, North, up, and down. She imagined she was weaving around herself a bubble of holiness and divine aid for the coming year, and she prayed sincerely that that might be so, that her bitter lot would change.

Now her favorite moment was imminent. The *Hallel* prayer had begun, and soon all would wave their *lulavs* tall, and the energetic back-and-forth motion of branches, myrtles and willows filling the air would create an effect of a forest in the wind, or of an army on the march with its pikes and banners. Like a march of triumph after earning God's forgiveness on the Day of Atonement a few days earlier. Images of army and forest brought to Hannah's mind Birnam Forest marching to Dunsinane against poor Macbeth. Perhaps Shakespeare, while searching for the right image for his play, had wandered by mistake into some London *shul* on Sukkot and been struck by the scene—or by a *lulav*, more likely? But there were no Jews in London in Shakespeare's time. A nice thought, anyway.

Reciting the opening psalms while carefully holding her *arba minim* in readiness, Hannah glanced around the women's section. These women, she thought pityingly, praying their impoverished *Hallel* with their empty hands, like so many eunuchs standing outside the harem door. She glanced at them in their prim little hats and snoods and saw them staring back unabashedly. She did not enjoy being looked at like that. Was that envy on their faces? Greed? Were they coveting her precious species? *Well, ladies, the rest of the year I am at the disad-*

vantage, envying you your ripe Jewish lives, your delicious husbands and fragrant children. But at this festival, I win. Go die of lulav envy.

The ridiculous aspect of it all was that it was not actually forbidden for these women to shake the *arba minim* during the services. The reasons were circumstantial: one set was normally bought per household, and even in these liberal Orthodox circles it was still the husband who would be the preferred partner to use it during the *Hallel*. But a single woman had no need to share her set, no need, in fact, to share anything at all. After years of standing in line at the supermarket, looking with self-pity at the one grapefruit, one avocado and lone tub of cottage cheese in her basket, Hannah was finally beginning not only to accept her situation but to enjoy its benefits. Having her own *lulav* was a definite benefit.

Shake, shake, shake, Hannah sang to herself in triumph. *Shake, shake, shake! Shake your lulav!* She gave her *lulav* a little preparatory shove, and it quivered with readiness to do the *mitzvah* for which it was born. The congregation was now declaring, "*I love the Lord, because He has heard my supplications. The sorrows of death encompassed me, and the pains of hell got hold of me: I found trouble and sorrow; then called I upon the name of the Lord.*"

Hannah looked around once more, and suddenly wondered if, after all, the expression on the women's faces was not so much greed as disapproval. Judaism censured people who separated themselves from the community, and yet here was she, a stranger and a guest, grandly shaking her set and overturning conventions willy-nilly, like a pig doing cartwheels at a bar mitzvah. She began to have second thoughts. What kind of arrogance was this, five days after the Day of Atonement? Had she fallen into the trap of ego? But now they had reached the point in the *Hallel* where the shaking began, and Hannah forgot her reservations completely.

"*Thank the Lord for He is good, for His lovingkindness is forever!*" the cantor chanted, swinging his *lulav* around in the six directions. "*Thank the Lord for He is good, for His lovingkindness is forever!*" repeated the congregation, and the men and Hannah swung their *lulavs* likewise. The men's section became a busy courtyard of rustling greenery. Their arms pumped vigorously, the sword-like *lulavs* and bushy myrtles and willows parrying and thrusting in the air. One man's palm branch was twice the height of everyone else's: bound together with extra rings so that it would not fall apart, it was hard to miss. When its owner drove it forcefully upwards, it actually banged into one of the faux chandeliers, causing the latter to swing drunkenly and Hannah to laugh aloud.

But soon, watching the men's antics, she became strangely downcast. She realized that being the only one shaking her set on this side of the *mechitzah*, with no female companionship and support, left her feeling very alone. Rituals were meant to be done with others. Perhaps she should have left her *arba minim* at home after all.

It was at this point that it all began to go wrong. Just as Hannah finished shaking and was about to put her set down, something came flying toward her, and without any warning, a round bumpy object smashed into the side of her head.

Yelling in astonishment, Hannah dropped her *arba minim* in order to clutch at her stinging ear. She barely had time to wonder if she had been shot by a terrorist before another hard object slammed into her shoulder. This was followed closely by a third whizzing into her eye socket. Hannah screamed again and, clutching her eye, tried to decide whether to crawl under a bench or make a run for it. A round yellow object rolled past her foot as another flew overhead and, to her horror, it began to dawn upon her that she was being pelted with *etrogs*. As she crouched there in a frenzy of indecision, a man's voice howled, "Disgusting woman!" and yet another fruity projectile came flying over the partition. Although half-blinded, Hannah saw it in time and managed to duck, and it hit a prayer book instead, knocking it to the floor. "Heretic! Feminist!" shouted another man, hurling his own missile at her. Again Hannah twisted to avoid it, and it crashed into a sharp table edge and exploded open in a mess of juice and pips.

"Help! Wait!" cried Hannah, holding one hand over her dizzy eye and waving the other about in what she hoped was a conciliatory gesture. "Wait! Help!" But no one heard her, and the *etrogs* continued to fly, only by a miracle missing her. She had never been so terrified in her life, and those few moments stretched on and on as she ducked and tried to protect herself.

Just as the barrage from the men's side was finally easing up, the women joined the fray, chanting, "Feminist! Feminist! Feminist!" Hannah screamed, "Stop! Please!" but the chants got louder and louder, the women's eyes bulged out at her and their tongues worked fiercely up and down as they yelled. One or two them picked up an *etrog* and tentatively threw it her. This gave the others confidence, and suddenly, with naked hatred upon their faces, all the women yanked off their little round hats and began aiming them at her with abandon. The hats' brims and decorative sequins gouged painfully into her cheeks as they hit their target, and then around thirty head-scarves landed over her face, restricting her vision even further and clogging her mouth when she screamed. Clawing the scarves away, Hannah shouted, "For God's sake, stop! Listen to me!" It seemed as if this just made them chant even louder, so she used all her energy to make her voice heard above the din, shouting, "You've all gone crazy! I'm not doing anything wrong! It's permitted for women to shake the *arba minim*! It's a *mitzvah*!"

The women halted in mid-throw, their creased brows and pursed lips frozen. A moment of silence ensued. From behind the partition, the rabbi's voice was heard announcing sonorously, "She is correct."

The bareheaded women, panting and with hair sticking to their foreheads, looked at each other, startled. The men were uncomfortably silent for a moment. A few women moved to collect their hats. The ceasefire, however, did not last long as one of the men yelled out, "But it just isn't done! Women are exempt! For centuries only men have shaken the *arba minim* at *Hallel*!"

"Yes! Lawbreaker!" shouted another, promptly lobbing his *etrog* forcefully over the partition. It hurtled with a loud thump straight into Hannah's lower stomach, and she doubled over, gasping in a tearful voice, "But that was due to circumstance. It was just a custom."

"Jewish custom is law!" cried the man who had cast the first *etrog*. There was a flurry of agreement. Then a large, imposing woman standing near Hannah roared, "And what about the custom to get married, huh?"

"Yes! Feminist!"

"Old maid!"

"Spinster!"

"Revolting species!"

There was a synchronized motion of arms, and a deadly shower of *etrogs* hailed down upon her, like the early rains promised in the *Shema* as a reward for good behavior. There seemed to be dozens of them, far more than the number of men in the *shul*, as if they had laid in a stock of them for just such an occasion.

"Narcissist!"

"Frigid hag!"

"Lesbian!"

"Lose some weight!"

"Wear more makeup!"

"Wear less makeup!"

"Dress up!"

"Be yourself!"

"Compromise!"

"Go to therapy!"

"Date older men!"

"Date men with children!"

"Date men in America!"

"You'll never find the perfect man! *Just get married already!*"

The women had graduated to chucking baby bottles and stiff-paged children's books, and by now Hannah was being hit every second or two with something heavy, no matter how much she twisted and dodged. A ten-year-old boy clambered on top of the ark, where he had an unobstructed view of the proceedings, and, singing "la-la, la-li-li-li"—the melody sung when a bar mitzvah boy has finished his reading—he threw handfuls of fruity toffees at Hannah, their hard corners finding their mark on her body.

Head beneath her arms, Hannah cowered under the bruising shower of objects, trying to make out with her disabled vision how many women stood between her and the door and whether she could tackle them or not. She wished for the millionth time that she had been blessed with physical strength. At last, just as she felt she was about to faint, the rabbi intervened, bellowing, "Friends, friends! Enough of this spectacle, I beg you! Leave this woman alone, and let's get back to our service. It's getting late."

People nodded, and the men began pouring into the women's section to collect their *etrogs*, while the women hunted for their lost hats. Suddenly, no one was paying her any attention at all.

"But I don't want to be left alone!" Hannah cried, looking around wildly with her remaining good eye and crookedly holding out her palms in supplication. "Can't you hear me—help me—love me as I am, with all my difficulties and desires?"

Once more, men froze in mid-stride; women stood open-mouthed in silence. Then an old woman screeched from the back:

"Help you? Picky, feminist you? You refuse to be helped! We've given all our advice!"

Everyone began shouting again and throwing their newly gathered *etrogs*. Hannah felt a surge of rage, becoming absolutely livid. She picked up an *etrog* and, taking a second to aim, lobbed it straight at the rabbi's head, guessing correctly that the community would be shocked when he went down with barely a wheeze. Picking up her *lulav*, she was ready to swipe at the next volley of *etrogs*, which indeed immediately rained down with a holy vengeance. To her satisfaction, she managed to bat them away and hit some of the throwers around her as well, though in the process splintering her *lulav's* slender stalk.

A woman howled in shock, "The *lulav*! She's using the *lulav*!" All of the women threw up their hands in horror. At that moment, seeing Hannah's successful defense of herself, the men rallied and began throwing entire sets of *arba minim* at her. Leaves flew all over the place as the bundles crashed down on the benches around her, the *lulavs* cracking on impact. Her own badly frayed palm branch was of little use against such an attack, and Hannah decided it was time to go, before the sharp tip of a well-aimed *lulav* pierced her heart altogether. Gagging on her breath, her hair and mouth full of leaves, her body throbbing, one eye closed and the other streaming, she grabbed her *arba minim* and ran from the synagogue, as the entire community—men, women and children—shouted in unison, "Freak! Misfit! Leave us alone! GET OUT OF OUR SIGHT!"

Liron and Zak's door was decorated with bundles of small red flowers and sachets of herbs. Hannah pushed listlessly at the door and entered the house. She dropped her *arba minim*, suddenly unbearably heavy, on the coffee table. Liron, wearing a striped apron over an ivory blouse, flowing pink skirt and white trousers, her hair loosely tied in a brightly patterned Indian scarf, looked up from her chopping and beamed, "Hello sweetie! Services over already?"

"No, not quite," Hannah replied limply. "I left a little early."

"You look sad. Come give a hug."

Hannah obediently walked over and hugged her friend, who smelled of lemon juice, deodorant, and baby. Liron patted her on the back, just as she often did to her son. Hannah stepped away.

"I felt weird about being the only woman shaking a *lulav*. I think people were staring at me."

"Dearest, they really weren't," said Liron, tucking escaped strands of blond hair behind her ears. "We have a group of Conservative women come pray here every month, wearing *kippot* and everything. Believe me, no one cares."

Liron was now tossing her son playfully into the air, and he giggled, dribbling all over her. Seeing that they were absorbed in each other, Hannah turned away, in the grip of a crushing loneliness. Picking up her *etrog*, she rolled its knobbly scented surface gently against the side of her face and her ear, as if listening. But no sound came from within, just the faint alluring scent in her nostrils of another, better, world.

Glove

A throaty bell splits the silence. Karin scrambles to pick up.

—Shalom. This is Netta from the Society for the Protection of Foreign Workers. I was wondering . . .

Karin sighs. The tortuous passage of a month has not sufficed to eradicate her fantasy of Bo's rich voice bobbing on the other end of the line. Surely he will soon call, admit his hastiness, error, and wrongdoing, beat his breast, beg to be rehabilitated in her life?

"Hope limps eternal," she chides herself, and reluctantly agrees to donate thirty shekels.

—Would you like to make that a regular contribution of eighteen shekels per month? *Chai shekalim?*

Karin gulps down her sarcastic rejoinder (how are eighteen shekels a month equivalent to a one-time sum of thirty?)

—Look, I'm poor . . . I'm a student.

—Okay.

Netta sounds disappointed.

—Shalom.

Karin sits in the kitchen, eating a carrot and averting her eyes from the history textbooks piled on the table. Crusaders, Provençal exegetes, disputations; right now they are about as important to her, as the Hebrew idiom colorfully had it, 'as the garlic peel.'

.

Her mind seems to be elsewhere, so she sets out to look for it outside. Children in bobble hats and stripy socks streak past, laughing. Head down, hands in pockets for warmth, she kicks at the slush until her boots are soaked, realizing belatedly that she should not have worn these cheap fur boots from China, an impulse buy from one of the many shoe shops along Jaffa Street. Permeable to water, they have quickly transformed into two sodden, leaden clods slip-slapping around her ankles. The snow has fallen rather high for Jerusalem; she cannot remember the last time it chilled the flesh of her calves like this.

Something lies dark and quiet on a clean mound of snow. She picks it up. A red glove, with a flower-shaped button above the thumb and an elasticated corduroy sleeve extending almost to the wrist. Unique, and evidently of high quality. The found object dangling in her hand, Karin wanders aimlessly, solitary, for another few minutes, until the soggy boots make it impossible to advance without kicking out her feet in an awkward sloshy goose-step. She heads for home and passes a tabby cat sitting on a wall, its tart green eyes unblinking as its head swivels to follow her ungainly walk. Nowadays, whenever she passes a cat she flinches involuntarily, recalling Bo's words on their last day together, prelude to break-up:

—You know, I've noticed that you stare into the eyes of every street cat you meet.

—I do?

She had responded absently, her attention caught by a poster advertising a lecture at Pardes.

—Yes, as if you were looking for something.

The shift in his tone had caught her attention now. Something was about to happen. She turned abruptly and searched his face.

—Looking for what?

He avoided her eye.

—Answers, companionship . . . I don't know. And that's the problem.

—That I stare at cats? That's a problem?

She was trying to ignore the fact that he had not said 'a problem' but 'the problem'—two words with a steely ring, like guillotine plummeting into wooden block.

—The thing is . . . what I'm trying to say is . . .

He mumbled something out of her hearing. Her breath backlogged in her throat.

—Yes?

—It's not enough for you, being with me. There's some lonely thing in you, way beyond where I can reach. I'm not deep enough for you; I don't really get you the way you deserve.

—That's not true . . . that's a lie, you get me plenty.

Her hand, reaching out to slap him into some kind of sense, had frozen midway and wilted back to her side.

—It doesn't feel that way. You're always somewhere behind a wall and I can't break it down.

—We're back to that again, are we?

—What again?

—You want me to be mushy, just like your other girlfriends. Some kitsch Hollywood chick overflowing with compliments, hanging on your arm all lovey-dovey. I've told you, I'm British, we don't do that. Doesn't mean you and I don't have a good relationship. 'Cause we do, we definitely do.

Now she sounded like she was trying to convince herself. There was a silence. All the blood had drained out of his face.

—A *really* good relationship, she added, digging another inch of her own grave.

There was a very long pause.

—Look. I just don't think this is going to work, he had concluded sadly. And there was clearly nothing more for her to say.

Super. You're breaking up with me because I'm lonely. That'll help a lot, thanks.

Bo's real name is Boaz, but as a teenager he wanted to be cool and different so he shortened it to something spunkier, more modern and Western-sounding. Only his parents and his boss call him by his real name. Karin speaks excellent Hebrew, having studied it at university, but she has always spoken to him in English, ever since she met him at a klezmer concert at the Gerard Behar Center and compared notes on the sax player. On the short side, with a profile sharp and angled like a palm frond, Bo is modest and sweet, athletic and health-conscious, with agile blue eyes and bushy auburn eyebrows. He is covered in light freckles the color of his hair, and also sports a cluster of four moles on his face, arranged in an unusual diamond pattern that drew Karin's eyes often, especially at the beginning. This was Karin's first real relationship since the one in Cambridge six years earlier. Her boyfriend Laurence, an overweight, navel-gazing poet and pipe addict, had walked out one night and never come back, calling two months later from Australia to ask her to ship the stuff he had left behind. She was twenty-four then. Bo came along a week before her thirtieth birthday, just in time to save her from the over-the-hill-and-on-the-shelf crisis about to drop like a cartoon anvil upon her head. The crisis was merely suspended, though; in the weeks following the break-up, it showed up in a far more lethal form. No escape.

It is obvious where her mind is: Bo has sprinted off with it. She has been unable to think since he went. Urgently needs it back.

As Karin unlocks her front door and enters, she hears the phone shrieking from the back room.

—Uh . . . hello? she wheezes, breathless from her mad dive.

It is Rivka from the Association for the Blind. Rivka rattles off her interminable speech without allowing Karin any possibility of interruption. Karin gazes absently at her reflection in the mirror, short hair sticking out at all angles, framing her oval face in a laurel wreath of fire. After what feels like two or five lifetimes, Rivka concludes:

—So you understand now that this is a very important cause. Any contribution will be greatly appreciated.

—Sorry, says Karin.

—Even a small contribution?

—I don't give on the phone.

—We can send you our envelope in the mail.

—Sorry. No.

—Are you sure?

—Yes. Sorry.

—Okay, then, if you're sure, says Rivka.

—Good luck.

Feeling empowered by her resistance to Rivka's bullying, Karin hangs the red glove up to dry on a line strung across her ceiling. She clips it with a wooden clothes peg, adjacent to three other gloves dangling there: one large black, one slim brown leather, one small fluffy pink. Now that she has four it is actually turning into a collection. Ironically enough, though, she still does not possess a proper pair of her own—she keeps forgetting to go to buy one. Perhaps if she picks up enough strays she will find two that match.

She considers them for a long time, daydreaming about their owners. Sherlock Holmes would probably have been able to glean large amounts of biographical information merely from looking, but all she knows is that somewhere out there, a man, two women, and a child have one cold hand and one warm one. Perhaps, she reassures herself, they are with someone whose hand they can hold, at least until they can get to a shop and buy a new pair. Surely the child at least will be fine. Children always have people whose hands they can hold without need for endless analyses and bickering or illogical rejection because they stare at cats. How nice to be a child.

??? thinks Karin, as her bus jolts its way round the slippery curves in the Katamonim area. The route seems to have changed while she was busy having her crisis, and she hopes that it will still end up taking her where she needs to go, anxiously runs her fingers through her short red hair. Though she is only a ten-minute ride from her house, the population here is very different. In the summer, men in stained undershirts play backgammon on verandas and in yards, bags of sunflower seeds to hand, myriad dark shells littering courtyards. Now, though, everyone is bundled up in their coats, faces shielded against the wind, and they look exactly the same as her own neighbors back in the wealthier neighborhood. All people look the same in the rain, she thinks.

She is on her way to her Judaism classes. She decided to study Judaism intensively this year. She has never been very religious, describing herself as a "fundamentalist agnostic" for many years, but somehow this year it seemed the right thing to do, having landed up unexpectedly in Jerusalem, studying for her doctorate at Hebrew University.

On the bus, she finds an old green glove with a hole in the finger lying unruffled on the next seat. It looked like a workman's glove, though only Sherlock would know whether a gardener's or a builder's. With one deft movement she appropriates it for her growing collection.

The class is on Talmudic laws. This week's topic is, aptly enough, lost objects. Jewish law requires a person to try to return a lost object if it bears identifying marks, such that the owner will not have abandoned hope of finding it. You are supposed to leave a sign with your contact details, and you ask callers to give the code, the identifying marks that prove they are for real.

Karin finds herself considering her collection. Should she have tried harder to locate the owners? The black and the pink one are nondescript and generic, impossible to return. But the brown leather and the red are expensive and unquestionably missed by their owners. And what about the one she has just taken from the bus? It is old, but maybe has sentimental value after being used for so many years? Perhaps this owner is at this moment beseeching the bus driver, Are you sure? Could you just check once more for me?

She feels a start of guilt. Surely not. Rather say that it had been left on the bus deliberately because it is worn and useless. She has not even considered, when picking up these gloves, that she might do any harm. People often do not consider, do they, that they might do harm? Most just open their mouths and begin spraying out harm at all angles like some agricultural aircraft flying over a field of beets. They are not careful with their words, as she is.

Her incipient bitterness bothers Karin. She has lately been thinking that she should just call Bo. There were misunderstandings. So much was right between them that she is not willing to forgo it without a fight, waiting around for another six long years for the next man whose company is more than just sufferable. She is not the black or pink glove! She is the red one! Bo was right for her, in a way few men are. It was simply his insecurity, triggered by her lack of expressiveness, that torpedoed their togetherness. That could be remedied—couldn't it? She should call.

The teacher, an older man with liver spots, is now saying:

—Incidentally, the Talmud introduces the subject of lost objects elsewhere, in a surprising place. In discussing the active role of the man in creating the sacred bond of matrimony, the Talmud notes: *It is the custom of a man to go in search of a woman, but it is not the custom of a woman to go in search of a man. This may be compared to a man who lost an article. Who goes in search of whom? The loser goes in search of the lost object.*

He looks around at his students.

—No arguing with that, right? When was the last time one of your lost socks showed up at the door looking for you?

The class laughs, but the thoughtful expression never leaves Karin's face.

It is raining quite heavily as she walks out into the thick night air to catch her bus home. On a bench, a man is lying under some wet newspapers and she guesses that he will be very inky by the time the rain finishes. Bo told her that he had once walked by a beggar rolling half out of his mind on the streets of New York, and had felt such pity for the man that he invited him home. The man ended up staying in his apartment for two weeks, by the end of which Bo could not wait for him to leave.

He had confessed: It makes me feel ashamed to tell you that.

Karin had remarked: I could never have done that, invited a strange smelly individual into my home. She had wanted to add, but didn't: You have an incredible heart.

His arm curled, a warm, insulating belt around her waist, and he said: You have other strengths.

She had thought then how utterly amazing he was, and how happy she was to be with him, but she had not said so. She had believed her smile would let him know everything he needed to know. Stupid smile. *F for Fail.*

When Karin gets home, she shifts the gloves so that she can clip the old green glove next to the small pink one, where it seems to belong. They swing together gently, like a little girl and her grandfather. She decides to take the lecturer's words as a sign. She will not call Bo; he has to come to her.

The following day she is actually in studying mode for a welcome change, buried deep inside her books, when the phone begins its catcalls. This time Karin just knows it is Bo; she can practically feel his warm, masculine energy emanating from the instrument.

—Hello? she cries, almost pulling the phone out of its socket.

—Shalom, says a deep male voice.

Her heart leaps. The voice continues:

—Have I reached family Abramson?

It is yet another charity call. She has finally figured out that the reason they call her so frequently is because her last name begins with the first Hebrew letter, *aleph*. By the time they get to the last letter, *taf*, the callers are exhausted, hoarse, or dead. Tomorrow she will change her name to Tabramson.

—No! says Karin grumpily.

—This is not family Abramson?

—There is no family Abramson. You're speaking to Karin Abramson. No husband, no boyfriend, no children, not even a pet lizard. Understand?

An awkward laugh. They must have to deal with their fair share of nutters.

—Ah, hi Karin, this is Kobi from the Israeli Epileptic Society.

Karin makes a face at the phone.

—We work with populations all over the country—

She interrupts him:

—Kobi, are you in a happy relationship?

—Well, yes, I am.

—That's nice for you. Very, very lovely.

—Er, Karin, I'm calling to ask you—

—Sorry, I can't give now.

—Shall I try again at a better time?

—Oh, does it get better?

Another awkward laugh.

—So can I call you again next week?

—I have to go.

Karin slams the phone down. Her concentration lost, she sits there, staring at the gloves. She stands up, and unclips the black one and the red one, slipping them gently onto her hands. The black one is a little too big, the red a little too small, perched on her fingers, the elastic sleeve choking her circulation.

—Darrrling, says the black glove in a deep voice, I just wanted to tell you you're an amazing person and I've never met anyone like you.

—Why thank you, says the red glove in a high-pitched voice. I appreciate you saying that. I feel the same way.

—I know I made some mistakes.

—I did too. I should have told you more about my feelings . . .

—No, I should have been more sensitive and not tried to force you . . .

—No, it was me . . .

—Me . . .

—I miss you . . .

The two gloves nuzzle up to each other. Karin strips them off in disgust and throws them onto the floor. She jumps up and down, thudding onto the floor each time and yelling nothing in particular. Then the phone rings again.

—HELLO? she shouts.

—Uh—may I speak to Karin Abramson?

It is another unfamiliar voice, a woman's voice. Karin does not reply, so the voice repeats its request. After a moment, Karin finally says:

—I'm sorry, I'm not in at the moment.

—You're . . . you're not in?

—No. I'm out. Call back next century.

Karin hangs up.

The next glove Karin finds is purple, with a fur ruff. Another distinctive one. She briefly considers making a sign, but lacks materials to make it with. A proper Jew, a *really* good Jew, would go home, write a note, return with cellotape and thumb tacks and a hammer and bang it up on a tree. But she just takes home the glove and strings it up on the line.

—Uh, okay folks, your attention please. Everyone, meet purple glove. She's new, be nice to her. Remember what it was like for you when you first arrived . . . I just know you're all going to get along.

How do all these absent-minded people keep losing their gloves? Do they take off one glove to light a cigarette and then, in the headiness of smoking, just drop it? Does it fall out of a pocket or a violently ransacked bag? She has filled nearly the entire length of the string in the space of only three weeks.

Before Bo, Karin would probably not even have noticed the gloves at all. Three months with him have transformed her. He taught her to observe the people on the street as never before, to pay attention to the details—the "delicates," he called them. Her default mode for wandering the streets is to be lost in a philosophical daydream, but he would rouse her by plucking abruptly at her sleeve and saying, "That old woman, don't focus on her flaccid skin and bleached hair, look instead at those sorrowful eyes, imagine what they have seen. Maybe she came over on a boat as a little girl, from a country where she lived in a huge white house with a view of the *souk*, or maybe she lost her beloved son in the Yom Kippur war, the son who reminded her of the father she never knew. There is an entire world there."

Bo taught Karin to close her eyes and enter a quiet space inside her, away from the gaggle of intellectual concepts migrating in her mind. He took her to meetings of people from many countries who spoke about politics and peace: Palestinians, Germans, Swedes, African Christians, American Jews, Israelis. He opened horizons for her, yet she could not open to him. He gave her worlds, but she withheld words. That is her custom, her way.

The day after she finds the purple glove, Karin visits the little booth where Sasha, her shoe repair guy, sits, outside the post office on Keren Kayemet Street. Sasha is a Russian Jewish immigrant who inevitably greets her with a wide smile full of yellow teeth and a wave of his filthy hands: *Ma nishma, motek?* Perhaps he greets everyone this way, but she believes that he genuinely likes her, and he has twice waved her off when she tried to pay for a small job, crying, with thick Russian *lameds* clotting up his Hebrew: "*Lo, lo tzarich, metukah!*"

Today she has come to pick up her boot, one of a pair of expensive shiny pointed brown boots she brought from America, the only high-heeled shoes she owns. The heel had come loose and he had told her to return in two days. This was last week. The booth is closed and she expects to see a sign saying that he has gone to lunch. Instead, a scrawled notice on a torn piece of paper announces that he is in hospital; for all inquiries call 0545-094-6532.

Dismayed and thrown, she dials the number, but there is no answer. She treads the street, imagining him lying in the hospital all alone, and experiences a desire to visit him, though perhaps he would have no idea who she was. Hard on the heels of this noble feeling comes the selfish one. She planned to wear those boots to a wedding this week, but now she cannot even access the boot, locked away as it is in the booth. She thumb-pads the number again but in vain.

No one answers over the next few hours either. Sad as she is for Sasha, she cannot help feeling aggravated by the situation. He always inserts the client's phone number into the bag with the faulty footwear, and whoever has the key to the booth should, from an ethical and moral perspective, have troubled to call up the shoe owners and arrange for pick up. Maybe someone is at this very moment hopping around barefoot in the cold? It is a human rights matter.

Karin chides herself for entertaining ludicrous and selfish thoughts while Sasha is lying ill. She tells herself that all this is actually a punishment from heaven for taking those gloves instead of trying to return them to their owners. Just as they now have only one glove, so she now has only one boot. As the Sages say: *Mida k'neged mida*, measure for measure.

Bo, who has a bit of a Gandhi fetish, told her about the time one of Gandhi's sandals had slipped off his foot and down onto the railway tracks just as his train was pulling out of the station. He quickly threw his other sandal onto the track along-side the first, explaining to puzzled bystanders: "The man who finds the shoe lying on the track will now have a pair he can use."

That *tzaddik* strove to reunite footwear, while she, Karin, a wicked person, is making zero effort to help the lost gloves locate their other halves. What would Bo have thought? That's just it: he would not have thought. He would have gone out, bought a huge bag of snacks, and gone directly to unearth Sasha in whatever dismal hospital he had washed up in. What her ex set out to find, he found.

She doesn't want to think about Bo any more. At home, she takes the remaining shiny brown boot out of her closet and stands it up below the line of gloves.

—Here Betty Bootie, hang out with these guys till Bernie Bootie returns. If he ever does.

A week passes. Karin gives up on the useless number, and goes to visit the booth again instead. No Sasha. She feels alarmed, pained. Is he still alive? She thinks of all those shoes, stifled in bags in their dark prison, and is happy that the gloves she rescued are out hanging in the light and air with each other for company. Poor little shoes. An unexpected tear rolls out of her eye and down her chin.

—You're going crazy, she reprimands herself stingingly, and it feels like swimming in the Dead Sea after shaving.

In front of her on the street, a woman wearing a headscarf takes a plastic bag out of a stroller, and a glove falls out onto the ground. It is a red glove and from a distance Karin has the impression that it is an exact match for the one she has at home. For a moment she experiences a powerful urge to keep silent, just let the woman walk on so that she can take posses-sion of the glove and finally own a pair. But instead she shouts, "Excuse me!," not once but several times, until the woman turns around and notices her wild gesticulations. When the woman picks up the glove, Karin sees that it is not the same design at all—no fancy button, no long sleeve.

The woman thanks her, walks on. Karin advances a few steps and then a cup of coins is rattled so loudly it is practically in her face. It is the beggar woman sitting on a stool on the corner of Keren Kayemet and King George streets. Karin has walked past her a million times. This time, for some reason, the coins' rattle roots Karin to the spot. She notices for the first time the woman's disheveled hair, lopsided nose and sensitive brown eyes gazing dully out from under her ghastly torn wooly hat. The old woman—is she even old, or just beaten down to a pulp of ugliness?—puts down the cup and reaches out her hand, palm open.

—Please, please, dollar. Please, please, ten dollar.

Karin looks at her, remembers the Judaism class a few weeks ago on the laws of charity. The most fundamental charity situation is when your brother, who has fallen low, opens his hand to you. Give. Do not be stone-hearted.

—Here you go.

She takes out her wallet, and before she can change her mind, places a one hundred shekel note into the plastic cup.

The woman's face, a pastiche of features that would not have looked out of place in a Picasso painting, breaks into a shocked smile. She proceeds to caw a volley of blessings at Karin's receding back: *May you have children and wealth and all God's bounty.* Karin turns to smile awkwardly at her, and then walks on, the cracked voice following her volubly until she rounds the next corner.

—Shalom, Mrs Abramson? This is Etty from the Association for Autistic Children. Do you have a minute?

—Good morning Etty. I have no doubt you do excellent work, but in order not to waste your time, let me inform you that I give to my own charities and not on the phone.

—Not even a small contribution? Eighteen shekels?

—No, sorry. But keep up the good work, and I really wish you the best of luck. Shalom.

Karin replaces the phone, and reaches for her pen.

Dear Bo,

It's been four months, and I am more or less recovered, but there's still stuff I need to express to you. It's important sometimes to speak things aloud, to get them out of your brain and into another's ears.

I'm not trying to get anything from you or get back together. I ran into Yuval at the supermarket and he told me you're doing well and have a new girlfriend. Apparently you've even asked people to start calling you Boaz. I confess I was surprised; I thought hell would freeze over first.

Anyway, what I want to say is that I'm grateful I met you. You changed my life, in so many ways, both subtle and significant. Since our break-up I've embarked on a new trajectory which I think will take me to good places.

You complained that I never told you, while we were together, that I love you. As I mentioned then, I was brought up in a family that never said those words. I do not recall even one occasion when they were said in my hearing. It was assumed that true emotion is expressed not in speech but in action. Too many people in this world employ those words facilely toward people whom the next moment they unhesitatingly abuse in some way. My parents were, and are, very principled people, and they do not treat words lightly.

While I now see theirs as an extreme stance, and I hope to one day tell someone I love him, I still hold that phrase to be incalculably sacred, to be used only when expressing no less than a willingness to commit for a lifetime. Accordingly, I still cannot really say that I definitely loved you. But I do know, Boaz Bar-Shalev, that I definitely gloved you.

What is that? I hear you ask.

To glove someone means to send all your heart's warmth their way, so as to defend them from the winter cold—simply because you would do anything to protect them and make them happy. It means that your skin is a second skin wrapped around theirs, fitting all of their curves and crevices, following them in their highs and lows and trying to serve as a barrier from the worst of the blows. It also means knowing that you are one of a pair, and doing your best not to get lost, because that leaves the other glove on its own, which is pretty useless (believe me, I know).

Yes, I did glove you, very much so. And I really apologise for not telling you at the time. To some extent, behind the excuse of my upbringing, there was simply a lot of fear, I admit. And I know you suffered because of it.

I'm happy to have had the opportunity to say this, and I bless the time we had together.

All good things,
Karin

Gently she lays the letter and her pen aside, and curls up in her beanbag, hand upon her face, thumb inwards. Soon she is soundlessly asleep, while above her serene face the gloves swing gently in harmony on their line, as the spring current wafts through the open window the promise of fresh life and love.

Snobsk

October 2000

An extraordinarily strange incident took place in Jerusalem on the twenty-fifth of October 2000. The twins, Binyamin Zev Ben-Artzi and Adam Kossowsky, left the country, the last people that young Jerusalem society would have expected to do so. They were seen at dawn on Ussishkin Street, trundling heavy suitcases into a waiting white *Nesher* cab, the eagle that was to carry them to the airport from whence they would fly back to their ancestral home in Fair Lawn, New Jersey. From the number and size of the bags, it appeared they would not be returning for quite some time.

Four years earlier, a similar *Nesher* had transported Matt and Adam Kossowsky to their new home in Jerusalem. Of average height, with faintly olive skin, agile light brown hair flopping over their foreheads, and long eyelashes, these two with their indistinguishable faces soon presented a social discomfiture for the young English-speaking circles of Jerusalem. Bored with themselves and their Shabbat table talk of Simpsons and Seinfeld, the young adult denizens of Rechavia, Katamon, and Baka wished to make the acquaintance of these—and all—newcomers, and, of course, to date them if all applicable. But how to make small talk on street corners to Matt (*Adam?*) when he might be Adam (*Matt?*). It did not help matters that they had gone and bought themselves the identical black jacket for winter.

The trick, it was soon discovered, was to look for the small dark mole buried in the delicate skin behind Adam's ear. Upon discerning furtive peeks around the region of their head, the twins saved themselves from further molestation by immediately identifying themselves, though not always with good cheer: *"I'm Adam." "I'm Matt, for God's sake, get away from me!"* In conversation, however, it soon became apparent who was who; there was no confusing the forthright activist with the reflective student. The sensitive viewer might discern the dissimilarity simply from the look in their eyes: raging energy—Matt; Adam—introspective stillness.

But all this was before Matt became Binyamin Zev, naming himself after his idol, the Viennese prophet of the Old-New Jewish State.

"What!?" bellowed Janet Kossowsky down the phone, when Adam told her of his brother's official name change at the Ministry of (*take a number—wait for four hours—I'm sorry, you have the wrong documentation—no, it's wrong—I said no! Are you deaf? Come back tomorrow—come back the next day—crying will get you nowhere—oh, OK, stop crying, I'll see what I can do—thank you so much for visiting, and welcome to Israel*) the Interior. "What's wrong with the name Matt Kossowsky? He was named after your *Zaydie* Morris! It's a slap in *Zaydie's* face, an insult to his memory!" She descended into speechless gurgling.

Adam felt almost as upset as his mother. It was as if his twin had declaratively cut off from the family tree and created his own bloodline. If he wanted to become more Israeli, why couldn't he have taken his Hebrew name Matisyahu/Matityahu, or even the more modern-sounding Matan? And why, furthermore, did he have to change his last name? Adam foresaw the puzzled looks at parties: "What did you say your names are? (*guffaw*) Sorry, didn't mean to be rude, it's just funny, you know, twins, with (*ha ha*) entirely different surnames. You know." A serious individual with a bright future ahead of him, Adam wished no part of this circus. And, after all, what a ridiculous name to choose. It had four separate elements to it—*Binyamin,*

Zev, Ben, and *Artzi*; and Matt was insisting that all four be used at all times. Their witty friend Emma had already essayed "Binzev B'Nazi" for a while, till Matt threatened to smack her. "BZ" was tried by several but "Bee Zee" (on American lips) sounded like *"Busy,"* while "Bee Zed" (other nationals affiliated with the Queen) came across as *"Bee's Head"*; and both met with prohibitive frowns. "Binhead," Emma's other idea, elicited a sworn oath to conduct voodoo on Tom Cruise if she did not instantly desist (she did, in fear and trembling). So Binyamin Zev Ben-Artzi it was henceforth, for all but the young man's far-flung parents and for Adam, who had difficulty dropping the name that had always been a part of himself.

"Will you also be changing your name, then?" Emma asked Adam one day, in a chance encounter at the Machaneh Yehudah *souk*, while old Yemenite women elbowed them with great dexterity, first from one side and then from the other. "I have some ideas, if you want. How about Zevulun Ben Og? Or Paltiel Ibn Achashverosh?"

"Certainly not." Adam's eyes glittered. "I remain the first man, formed of moist dust and God's breath."

"Poetic, 'eh?" Emma said approvingly to the man selling them persimmons, who replied, "Five shekels ninety" and handed her a bulging bag of orange fruit, luscious as the fruits of Eden.

On the deepest level, though, Adam was actually pleased with the change. It was high time they had separation surgery, he and his impossible yet mesmerizing brother. In their childhood, he had sought Matt's protection from the bullies who otherwise would have eaten this shy kid alive. Even in college, just knowing that Matt would always drop everything and rush to help him was comforting. He had clung to Matt's strength, feeling like an eggshell under a large hovering bird that, while it protected him, also blocked out the sun, and at times stepped thoughtlessly upon the fragile thing that was Adam's heart.

Yes, 'twas time. Their paths were clearly twisting away from each other, and this might catalyze the discovery, finally, of Adam-without-Matt, whoever that might be. He resolved to move as soon as possible out of their shared apartment on Bilu Street, to dwell with strangers with unknown childhoods and hygiene habits. Matt was his only relative in Israel, and the only person who had known him forever. But there was always the phone, and Jerusalem was like a village, really. Very local.

Moreover, if Matt could change his name, then Adam could allow himself to grow a beard, as he had been contemplating for a while. It came through in a lovely silky brown, with tints of red at the edges. He did not tell his mother. The grapevine hummed with the news: "Matt has a new name; Adam, a new beard." This proved very useful for acquaintances tired of mole-hunting, and the city sighed with relief.

After some searching, Adam found a studio apartment in the Rechavia neighborhood, on Ussishkin Street—an old apartment practically buried in ivy, surrounded by pine trees and palms. Over the next three years, Adam worked at a hi-tech company in the mornings, and spent the rest of his time studying Talmud at a yeshivah near his house. This was his first time studying Talmud systematically. He had dallied with it ever since he first encountered it in college, which had left him dazed at the Jewish universe that had sprung up before his eyes. After no small measure of frustration, Adam finally began to experience mastery of the Talmud, of its difficult Aramaic and its associative mode of argument. He felt gripped by its infinitely creative mind, clearly seeing before his eyes the multicolored tapestry of the world of the Sages: brilliant, unruly men hanging out in Babylon two thousand years ago in the academies of Sura, Pumbedita, and Nehardea, or in Palestine in Tiberius, Sepphoris, and Caesarea, traveling back and forth, discussing, clashing, analyzing, ruling the law and even, on occasion, killing and resurrecting each other, as in the case of Rava and Rabbi Zeira. Thirstily he drank in their approach, desiring nothing more than to learn to think as they did. "This," he would grandly tell his study partner after deciphering a difficult section, "is to think like a Jew!"

During this time, Adam phoned his brother infrequently. Binyamin Zev, for his part, never called, preferring to drop in unexpectedly while on his way to his mysterious activities.

In time, Adam felt as if he was becoming more and more himself. Even his asthma had improved, and he breathed more easily at night. He met a nice girl—steady, wise, of South African origin, in Israel six years already—by the name of Alison, and they began to see each other regularly. Adam loved having a girlfriend. He relished the mere word, with its rich promising "r's," and wished he could hoist Robert Burns bodily from the grave simply to articulate the word as it deserved: *Girrrlfrrrriend.*

If Alison was around when Binyamin Zev visited, Adam would feel an edge of alarm rising in his gullet, and a desire to ask her to go buy some milk, preferably from somewhere far away, like Eilat. His brother's success with women was every man's bane, and particularly Adam's. In their last years of high school, Matt had smuggled numerous women into the house. Discovering a new woman almost every morning in their shared bathroom had made Adam feel disgusted and envious in equal parts. Those females always bore a look that spoke simultaneously of smug gratification and a guarded uncertainty. They were like turkeys being fattened in November, suspicious that there must be a catch somewhere and puzzled by the pervasive smell of cranberries. When the twins finally separated for college, he to Princeton and Matt to Penn, Adam forgot all this. But when their respective decisions to immigrate to Israel coincided, the twins decided for convenience to live together and see how it went. A mere three days had passed before Adam crashed blearily at 7 a.m. into a dancer named Lilach emerging from their bathroom holding Matt's toothbrush (or was it his own?!). Then all came flooding back. That day he sat down and wrote a poem:

> Brother,
> Thou art a land of tuft green,
> weeds spurting through holes in the Judean dust.
> Sweltry sun fries those presuming to dwell,
> to do anything more than to step apace.
> A land that consumes its inhabitants;
> the stranger coming near shall die.

He had left this poem tacked up on the bathroom mirror for a long while, hoping that Binyamin Zev would ask him about it. But his brother remained quite uninterested in any outpouring from Adam's pen. He would have glanced at it, thought Adam bitterly, only had it been signed "Theodor H." Eventually the writing blurred from the steam, and the note fell off into its last resting place behind the washing machine.

His protective feelings toward Alison, though, were not the only reason Adam found his twin's visits increasingly vexing. The more religious Adam became, the more Binyamin Zev delighted in needling him, and had even recently joked with Alison that if he were to grow a beard like his brother, he could have his wicked way with her and she would never know. Alison had replied quite even-temperedly that this would be quite impossible, since she and Adam had decided to be *shomer negiah*. Deliberately mistranslating the phrase, which meant "guarding from touch," Binyamin Zev retorted, "What, you *save touch*? For a rainy day, you mean? Do you think touch is something that runs out?"

"Absolutely!" rejoined Adam. "Yours was spent by the time you were eleven."

"Oh dear, whatever shall I do?" said his twin in a falsetto, batting his eyelashes. Adam suggested acerbically, "Push your hands into soil ten times, like an unkosher knife. That might do the trick." His brother had punched him on the shoulder, a little too hard, always a little too hard.

Later, when he had gone, Alison said, "Adders, read my lips: *You're my man.* I'm not interested in him."

Adam could not hear it. Pacing, he complained, "It's incredible! I resemble him so exactly that I bet even God ends up punishing me for his sins! Yet he's always been a million times more successful with women. I can't fathom it."

"Exactly how many women do you need?" Hearing her irritated tone, he hurriedly dropped the matter. The truth was that it was time to let go of his expectations from Matt. Constant immersion in the world of Torah was helping Adam cast away old resentments and enragements. And anyway, Matt seemed recently to not to be doing all that well. He looked stressed, with huge circles under his eyes. Adam felt a little guilty for not asking what was going on. The next time he heard Matt's shave-and-a-haircut knock at his door, he sat up straight and resolved this time to be a *mensch* and a perfectly loving brother.

"Enter!" he called. Binyamin Zev walked in, carrying a plastic bag and wearing old jeans and a tight T-shirt that emphasized his biceps and read *"Israel: Just do it!"*

"Howzit Binz?" said Alison.

"Good," said Matt. He unloaded a mound of *rugelach* onto a plate, oozing chocolate, and with a smell that would charm the very angels out of heaven.

"Farewell diet!" cried Alison, and lunged for a pastry, only pausing briefly to make a blessing before consuming it rapidly. The bringer of the goods sent a squishy *rugele* likewise sliding down his throat, *sans* blessing, of course. Adam closed his eyes, and, carefully imagining all of the ingredients—flour, eggs, cocoa and sugar—making their way from around the globe to form this delicious treat especially for him, he entered a state of gratitude, and from within it enunciated the blessing aloud: *Blessed art Thou, Lord our God, King of the Universe, who created all kinds of grains.* Alison said "Amen," and he bit in.

For a second, all of them sat there, teeth blackened and sugary, forgetting everything that ever was or ever would be until the end of time. Then Adam said, tongue poking into the crevices of his teeth, "Did you know, if you eat enough of these, it's as if you've eaten bread? So you have to *bensch*?"

"Fascinating," said Binyamin Zev.

Adam grittily clung to his resolution to be nice. "D'you want some tea?" he asked.

"No tea for me." With a loud yawn, Matt stretched his arms out across the table, taking up a large part of it and almost knocking over Alison's mug. Adam looked sorrowfully at his own arm. Since he had come to Israel, he had not set foot in a gym, and it now resembled a bleached bone next to his brother's thick brown log of a limb. "Have you spoken to Mom?" he said.

"Yeah," said his twin, straightening up from his yawn. "The usual, you know. Drowning in work yet still hosting a shazillion people for Rosh Hashanah."

"She always sounds so industrious," said Alison a little anxiously, as if she would be expected to measure up one day soon—an assumption that turned Adam all a-flutter.

"Where's Dad hangin' these days?" asked Binyamin Zev through the mangled cadaver of his second *rugele*.

"Japan. I think."

He yawned again. "Dandy."

"And what's with *Bubbie*?"

"About the same, maybe a little worse. Not much time left now, I reckon."

"Gosh!" said Alison, putting her hands to her cheeks. "I didn't realize. That's so sad. You'll be flying back to be with her before it's too late?"

Neither brother responded, and she raised her brows. "Adam?" she prodded.

"Well," Adam eventually responded, "I did promise myself I wouldn't leave the country unless absolutely necessary. Going to the States always throws me three steps backward in my learning. Though it does seem like the right thing to do, I guess," he said reluctantly to his brother.

"Oh no, no, no, no!" Binyamin Zev exclaimed, raising his hands. "Folks, I've made two visits Stateside since I got here, and that's more than enough. I ain't leavin' Israel's borders again unless it's for a very good reason. *Ma pitom!* Too much to do!"

"And what exactly *do* you do?" said Adam sardonically. After three years he still had little idea of Matt's movements and it irked him.

His brother licked his fingers. "Lots of important stuff, bro'. Strengthening. Planting. Weeding."

"You're a gardener now?" As soon as this left his mouth he regretted it. Not only did he sound childish, he also knew that there was no point being sarcastic about Matt's life, as the man was perfectly capable of doing almost anything. He had worked as a translator, horse trainer, business consultant, stockbroker, opera singer, waiter, salesman, teacher, and even as a construction worker in Tiberias for a few weeks. And those were just the things Adam knew about.

"Sometimes, yeah." He grinned. "But I meant it more metaphorically. Planting seeds for the future, so to speak. Weeding out bad elements. Stuff I can't really talk about to you folks."

"Hello, can we get back to your neglected grandmother?" said Alison

"Our no longer conscious grandmother," Binyamin Zev pointed out defensively.

"May she live to a hundred and twenty and all that, but, hey, what if there's, you know . . . a funeral?"

"Even less reason to go!" Binyamin Zev shrugged as he reached for another chocolate bun. "Dead people don't care."

Alison turned to Adam, who shrugged likewise. She shook her head in disgust. "How long has she been this ill?"

"About two years."

"Must be a real burden on your mother."

"Have you ever seen a giant stressball masquerading as a human? That's my mother!" Binyamin Zev said. "Wish the old lady would hurry up and get it over with. If you're gonna die in your old age, don't schlep it out, that's what I say."

"What do you mean, *if you're gonna die in your old age*?" Alison demanded. Rising to his bait again, thought Adam; she needed to learn to ignore him, as he did.

"Well it's just such a waste of good death," said Binyamin Zev, leaning back and putting his arms behind his head. Adam hastily got up to re-boil the kettle, his long *tzitzit* swinging below his shirt as he loped away. He poured the water as he tried to cool down his temper, in his irritation overfilling the kettle, which meant wasted water—a crime in a country that needed every drop. Matt thought he was so cool, with all his neologisms and creative use of language. Someone should inform him that, in doing so, he had placed himself in the illustrious company of Humpty Dumpty and Mrs. Malaprop.

While regretfully pouring out the excess water from the kettle, Adam breathed deeply and tried to think kind thoughts. It was almost Rosh Hashanah, a propitious time to abandon old patterns and adopt new behaviors. He planned to compress this year's thoughts and deeds into a tight package and offer it to God: *Here, this is the old me. Hold onto it while I redecorate.* He was looking forward to the service at his yeshivah. The rabbi's voice, normally an intimidating bass, became a startling soprano, which broke into tatters during *U'Netaneh Tokef*, causing the more sensitive yeshivah boys to cry into their prayer books.

SNOBSK 61

This was one place where a man could cry and not be ashamed. Adam wished there were more.

He could hear Binyamin Zev explaining himself: "Look, you can die in your bed, old and sick, or you can give your life up for something greater. Which would you choose?"

Despite himself, Adam let a snide comment shoot out from the kitchen: *"Tov lamut be'ad artzenu?"*

He instantly regretted it, but could not find a way to retract his words. Binyamin Zev looked over in his direction. "Yes, actually," he said. "It *is* good to die for one's country. A most noble way to go, dontcha think? Kind of a new luxury for Jews, who've been dying for everything but." Without waiting for a response, he added sharply, "And if you're gonna quote a great man, worth ten times all your Talmudic learning, have some respect there, little bro'."

Little bro'. As if the ten minutes' start he had into this world made him infinitely wiser.

"Don't mock your brother's heroes, Adam," Alison scolded. "Um, by the way, who are we talking about?"

"Joseph Trumpeldor," Binyamin Zev clarified. "The it's-good-to-die-for-one's-country guy." Though the kettle boiled loudly behind him, Adam lolled in the kitchen doorway, his feelings by now entirely out of control.

"Binz dearest," he said, over-pronouncing every syllable, "I'm afraid he's no longer anyone's hero except your own. I read in last week's paper that the majority of Israeli children think Trumpeldor is the headmaster from Harry Potter."

A crease formed between Binyamin Zev's eyes. Then he said quietly, "You know what? You're one hundred percent right. Ten points to Adam. The education in this country is up the yamahoo. And when your kids don't know about the heroes of history, you've lost your country. Might as well just hand it over right now to the Palestinians—*'We've failed. Your turn!'*— and flee back to America, tails between our legs." He shook his head and fell silent. Adam was shocked to see a tear forming in his brother's eye. He quickly turned to grab the kettle so that no one would see his eyes pricking in response. He came inside and refilled the boiling water into Alison's cup. Silence reigned. Adam sat down.

Though by this point surrounded by weeping men, Alison remained oblivious, and in that charming, light way she had, asked, "So Binge, when's your next stint of *miluim*?" Matt was always doing reserve duty—he seemed to spend a quarter of his time in Israel in some hole, guarding a hilltop caravan with three settlers and one mangy sheep.

"Next month."

"Where will you be this time?"

"Near Shechem."

Alison frowned. "Dangerous?"

"Nah, I'll probably end up spending all day stirring the platoon's tea with a broom," said Binyamin Zev, leaning his chair back on two of its legs and popping yet another *rugele* into his mouth.

"And shooting a few Palestinians in your spare time," said Adam. This time he knew he had gone too far. His brother's chair came down with a thud. Adam pulled his teabag up and down in his cup with fast, jerky motions. He could not bring himself to do the right thing and apologize. He wished Matt would just get up and leave them alone.

Looking puzzled and angry, Binyamin Zev finally exclaimed, "What's with you? You've known me your entire life. I'm not some macho, toast-brained maniac. I'd never shoot except in self-defense."

"Uh-huh, " said Adam, though he knew it was true.

His brother's voice rose. "You understand nothing. After all these years, not a word I've said has sunk in. So I'll tell you again for the millionth time: there is a firm middle ground between nutso Kahanist and brainwashed post-Zionist! It's called pragmatism! It's called being connected to your people! Oslo's architects could hand over half our land and no one cares as long as there are photo shoots and Nobel Peace Prizes. We have to act, we who still give a flying fart about the dream. We have to take charge and get it right, before it's too late."

Adam glowered. He could not argue—his brother knew a lot more on these topics than he, closeted in his yeshivah. His silence irked Matt further.

"Adam, for Chrissake, we can't risk losing our country and returning to the Diaspora merry-go-round—here a pogrom, there a pogrom, old McHitler had a farm! Right? *Ee-ay-ee-ay-oh I'm dead!?* Do you get it? Tell me you get it, or I'll shoot myself right now, I swear."

Alison and Adam looked at each other.

"But we're *here*," said Alison tentatively. "We've built roads, towns, schools, everything. We're here to stay. The Holocaust is over and it's not coming back. Why be paranoid?"

Binyamin Zev sighed. "No one's here to stay. Look at the Romans."

"They had a good run for their money."

Binyamin Zev thumped the table. "That's not enough for us! We need more than a good run! Without Israel we're dead, don't you understand? A pile of bleached bones in Slaughterville, Poland! Raped in Kishinev and disemboweled in Libya! Just a bunch of flabby Jews, *machering* and finagling and lobbying for our lives, at the mercy of *goyim* in London and Paris and Fair Lawn, New Jersey!" His eyes seemed redder than ever, the sickly circles making them bulge. Adam and Alison sat frozen into silence. Adam's tea had sloshed out at Binyamin Zev's thump, and the dark liquid flowed in small rivulets onto the floor. "Murdered by some drunk *muzhik* imbecile who blames us for his troubles. All that blood spilt into lands not ours! Simply wasted!" Adam grimaced, but his brother plowed on. "They're right, the good old Pals! You own a land through your blood and your dead!" He thumped the table again, and the other cup rocked unsteadily. "They have their dead here, buried under their olive trees. Our blood must seep into this land to make it ours! Only this land, and no other, ever again!" The last words were said in practically a whisper. Alison shuddered and glanced over at Adam. He looked away. Nothing disturbed him more than when his brother was like this.

There was a pause. Binyamin Zev rubbed his eyes as if very tired. Alison said in an artificially bright tone, "So, what's your grandmother's name? I want to *daven* for her."

No one answered.

"Nu? What's her name?" she pressed them.

Adam eventually mumbled, "It's Freydl."

"Feygl," corrected his brother.

"Freydl!"

"Feygl!"

"Freydl! Freydl!" shouted Adam, and threw a *rugele* at his twin, who chucked it straight back, bellowing, "Feygl the Bagel, with a hole in her heart!" He burped loudly and shoved his chair back with a screeching sound, standing up. Pushing the nearly empty plate away from him, he announced with a groan, "I think I ate too much. Keep the rest." Then he picked up his car keys, nodded to them—"Time to go! Cheerio!"—and in a blink, was gone.

An uncomfortable pause followed. Alison said, looking at the door he had slammed behind him, "Shame, man. I'm worried about him."

Adam sighed. "I feel so distant from him these days. He's like a stranger." He stared morosely at the table. "He's always had this obsession with death, but it's gotten much worse. That's not Jewish, the death cult! Jews want to live, to say *l'chaim* for one more day."

"Anyway, didn't Herzl die of syphilis?" Alison giggled. "Not a very noble way to die!"

Adam laughed dryly. "Don't ever mention that if you value your life. Matt once flattened me just for saying '*Herzl-Shmerzl*.'"

She began mopping up the spilt tea. Adam said in a deliberately casual voice, "You know, he used to have visions of Herzl . . . ."

"Visions?" She squinted at him.

"He said Herzl came to him in his dreams. And Jabotinsky, Ahad Ha'am, Gordon. He would, um, hang out and yabber with them at night." He blushed. "I overheard him. Full-length conversations."

She frowned. "What about?"

"How to save the Jews, I suppose. I dunno. I shouldn't really have told you. It's his inner sanctum." He cleared his throat. "I'm an apostate, I'm not allowed entry. The stranger coming near shall die."

Alison fiddled absent-mindedly with Adam's *tzitzit*. "Why? You're a Zionist too!"

"Yeah, but not as in Herzl and the gang."

"So what? You're connected, you're committed, that's good enough."

"True. I mean, I do think this country is ours, by divine right, as well as by history."

"See?"

Adam scratched his head. "No, but Alison, at bottom it's just land, and we've managed without it before. It's more important to stay Jews, and not lose our moral compass trying to dominate another people. It's Jews, not Israelis, who survived for over three thousand years, and that's our real task, to continue that. If we're not Jews, who will be?"

Alison nodded. "Matt would never agree with you. He's the most stubborn person I ever met. But he really cares, and I respect that." She sipped her tea thoughtfully. "But what on earth was all that about your grandmother? Wishing she would croak already! That's plain sick! And you're not much better. I'm surprised at you."

"Well, she's really old. She's been quite senile for years now. Also, we never had much of a connection. She lived—"

"Not even knowing her name! Pathetic!"

"Look, we all called her *Bubbie*. Even *Zaydie* did. Her name was never mentioned, not in my living memory. But it's Freydl, I'm telling you."

Alison smiled. "Freydl it is, then. What was she like, Freydl?"

"In her heyday she was quite a handful. You tended to want to get out of her way, otherwise she would grab you for intimate chats about the purpose of your existence, or to shove a piece of *kugel* into your mouth. You never knew which, either."

"So you did talk?"

"Not much. They originally lived in Phoenix near my aunt till *Zaydie* died, and by the time she moved to New Jersey to be close to my mom she was already senile. So we hardly knew her."

"That's so sad. Where was she from?"

"Somewhere in Eastern Europe. Romania I think."

"A *little* more precise?"

"I don't know, she had this thick accent. Romanian, or Hungarian, definitely one of those. Or was that dad's mom? I forget. She lost some relatives in the Holocaust—two sisters and her parents, if I'm not mistaken."

"Honestly, I don't get your family. You never call your parents, and you know nothing about your ancestors! Doesn't it bother you?"

"Well, where do your folks come from, O fount of knowledge?" he rejoined. She opened her mouth to speak, but he continued, "No, wait, wait, you told me already, hold on, don't say anything. Snobsk!" he shouted triumphantly. "Or is it Snotsk?"

"It's Snovsk! And Minsk and Vilna. All South African Jews hail from Lithuania somewhere down the line."

"Fascinating."

"Don't be so arrogant!" said Alison stiffly. "Family's important. You are where you come from."

"On the contrary! Family's oppressive. They pile expectations on you till you stagger under them and drop dead. You're supposed to live their lives for them, fulfill all their bankrupt dreams. In my opinion, you aren't where you come from, you're what you do to pull away from it!"

"The Maharal says that your soul chooses your parents, to continue their path in your own unique way."

"Uh-huh!" said Adam sarcastically, thinking of his workaholic father and his hysterical mother, whose paths he urgently hoped he had not continued.

Alison urged again: "Family is tradition."

"Tradition is the mummified corpse of religion."

"OK then, family is destiny. Like my great-grandmother Pnina Bracha, the pious woman of Snovsk. She inspired me. She's part of the reason I came back to Judaism, to Israel."

"That's nice. Really."

His girlfriend exclaimed loudly in frustration, "How can you be so casual about it? Don't you see that these ancestors of yours are the very people who continued being Jews, as you said we must do?"

"Yeah, along with the Jews of Yemen, Tunisia, Turkey, Libya! I don't see why I have to be into all things Eastern European just because I care about Judaism. God never said, 'Thou shalt eat gefilte fish and wear the fur of dead animals on thy head!' Except for Torah, their lives were very different from mine, and frankly I'm just not interested. I sometimes feel that these Polish *alter kakers* stand between me and God and block out the light."

The discussion seemed exhausted—and Adam certainly was—so he stood up and said it was time for him to be getting back to the yeshivah. Rosh Hashanah was only four days away, and he felt upset about this evening's interactions and wanted to get himself into the proper mindset. But Alison was like a dog worrying at a bone.

"And what does Matt think about it? About family?"

"Matt? Are you kidding? He says family are a thorn in your side, an outdated social structure. His real family is the Jewish people. That's all he needs."

"Ach, man. He thinks Jewish history started in 1897 in Basel."

"He's just rejecting weakness. He hates weakness, has done since childhood. When we were younger, whenever he was upset he would knock me down to feel better. It made him feel strong."

Suddenly Alison looked at him queerly, as if she had understood something. He did not like that look at all. Avoiding her eyes, he picked up the garbage and they walked out together into the Jerusalem night, fresh with the smell of jasmine blossom.

The day before Rosh Hashanah 2000, Binyamin Zev Ben-Artzi tossed in his bed. He could not sleep; he felt queasy and turbulent. He wanted to be at peace with his brother, he wanted Israeli children to know who Trumpeldor was, he wanted people to call him by his full name, he wanted to stop having one-night stands and find an intelligent girlfriend like Alison, he wanted to serve his people. He wanted so much.

If you will it, it is no dream, Herzl remarked.

"Yeah, yeah," said Binyamin Zev. "You've said that before." He had no patience this evening; he was feeling quite unhinged.

Something's seriously amiss my friend, Herzl observed sternly.

"I know that! But what to *do*, Teddy? What to do? Gatecrash the Knesset? Put up posters? Run for prime minister? Dress up as you and parade around the countryside, preaching like Zarathustra to the post-Zionism-riddled masses? What?"

Theodor turned over in his grave on Mt. Herzl, but said nothing more. He had done his bit; now let others do theirs. Bad things were coming, and nothing could be done. Binyamin Zev put a hand to his abdomen. Something inside was burning up.

At 2:37 a.m., Binyamin Zev woke with a start. He had been dreaming of his grandmother. She was floating around in some milky substance, reaching out a pleading hand to him. He called her name, but he found that he was calling, "Alison! Alison!" The red neon light of his alarm clock shone on his sweaty face. Binyamin Zev realized something was terribly wrong. He felt as if a suicide bomber had exploded in the lower right hand region of his belly.

"Aargggh!" he moaned, clutching convulsively at the spot and knocking his alarm clock off its stand. "Jee-zus! What the hell . . . ?" Intense pain seared him, radiating outward from that one point until it drenched him.

I'm being punished for my comments about my grandmother—by the God I do not believe in.

He scrambled in his mind for another explanation.

I'm going to die, here in my bed, of rugelach overconsumption. How ironic. It is good to die for your country's baked goods.

"Je—aarrrrrrgggh! Help!" With shaking fingers he dialed Adam's number.

The ambulance rushed to Shaarei Tzedek hospital with Adam following right behind in Matt's car. His cell phone rang: a breathless Alison was on the line.

"On my way! What's wrong with him? Do they know?"

"They think appendix."

"Well thank God. I thought it was something life-threatening."

"Actually I think it's quite serious," said Adam soberly. Alison sucked in a breath.

"I have to pray for him," she said. "What is your mother's Hebrew name?"

"Er . . . ." said Adam.

"Guess what?" whispered Alison. "That nurse is from Minsk!"

"Great." Adam leaned over his brother's recumbent body. He had never seen Matt look so vulnerable or puny. He suddenly had the illusion that he was seeing himself on his deathbed, from a point hovering above, as in a near death experience. The thought made him nauseous.

"He's opening his eyes!"

"Dude," said Binyamin Zev weakly. "Where am I?"

"In the hospital," said Adam, barely concealing his joy and relief. "They took out your appendix. You'll be OK."

"Hi, Beanz," said Alison tenderly, patting his blanket. "We missed you."

"So it wasn't the *rugelach*," muttered the invalid in relief.

"They said you'll have to be here over Rosh Hashanah. But we have it all organized. We'll come in and be with you."

"What about *shul*?"

"We'll find a *minyan* in the neighborhood. Don't worry, we'll make it happen." Adam smiled.

"S-sure?"

"Of course we are," said Alison. "We wouldn't dream of being anywhere else."

"*Toda*," said Binyamin Zev weakly, and closed his eyes again.

"I was thinking," said Adam, leaning on the railing of the hospital bed, "that when you get better, we should talk more. I don't know you anymore."

"Mmm."

"I think that I felt the need to pull away and then you did, too. But I'm my own person now and I'd like, you know—to go back to how it was before. Do you know what I mean?"

"Ad," said Binyamin Zev, straining to speak. "Spare me the psychobabble. I'm just too darned sick." He closed his eyes. Adam took his brother's hand in his own for a few seconds and then tiptoed away.

And it came to pass after all these things that the windows of the heavens burst open, and riots and violence spread over the land. Thus did begin the lean years, which the Arabs did name "the Second Intifada" and the Jews did name "the Situation," and many lives were lost and many ruined. And it did not find favor in the eyes of the Lord, and the Lord hid His face, and the heavens cried.

And Janet Kossowsky, she whose mother trembled upon the face of the abyss, did turn on the TV after the Rosh Hashanah meal she did cook for her sister and her brother-in-law and the Levines and the Posnanskis and the Chaits (each according to their families and the house of their fathers) and her widowed neighbor, Mrs. Grossberger. And the images of violence made her quake most dreadfully. And she did call her son Matt's home phone and cell phone, but joy came not thereof. And she knew that her other son, Adam, who had transformed into a religious freak, no longer answered the phone on Sabbaths or festivals. And she panicked, and her household became like unto hell; yea, thus it was.

And Janet Kossowsky did harass her ex-husband and the Israeli embassy, and they told her once and they told her twice that the disturbances were localized and the chance of danger to her sons was slim. Yet peace did not come to her mind, but she could do naught from afar but worry, and she did so, for she was a great worrier, known throughout the land.

And it came to pass that throughout the festival of the New Year, Janet Kossowsky did repeatedly dial her son Matt's number, sometimes thrice in a row, and she did worry muchly, for he had never ignored both phones for so long beforetimes. And she did weep and moan, and neglect her dying mother and her standoffish sister, and she did rail against her ex-husband; and her appointment with her therapist was still three days hence, and this was very evil in her eyes.

And it came to pass, after the festival of the New Year was complete, that Adam did finally answer the phone, and Janet Kossowsky did yell so loudly that it was like the big bang all over again, and the angels of the Lord were affrighted that a new universe would begin oscillating in a suburban home in Fair Lawn, New Jersey.

And Janet Kossowsky felt herself just about to break in two; yea, thus did she feel. Amen. Selah.

In the early hours of the twenty-fifth of October 2000, Alison's eyes were full of tears. "I can't believe you're leaving," she wailed in agony.

"Back soon," Adam said glumly, putting a shirt in his suitcase.

"Don't go," she begged.

"I have to. I can't have my mother's untimely death on my conscience."

"I hate her for being so controlling."

"Forgive her, she knows not what she does."

"Oh please! She's not a baby."

"Ali, she's worried sick about us, and she's just lost her mother, and she's all alone. Have a bit of sympathy. She needs to know we're safe so she can sleep at night. We'll just be there for a little while, till she recovers."

"Oof!" wept Alison. "*Till she recovers?* That's forever."

"Only for a short time, I promise. Just while she needs us there."

"I need you, too! There's an Intifada going on here, if you hadn't noticed! How will I survive?"

"You'll survive because I need you to." His voice rang harsh and curt in his ears. He struggled with himself but lost the battle, unable to bring himself to speak aloud the words he would three days later pen to her from afar, safe behind the protective barrier of email:

In chill dawn light, with neat-pressed hair
and full frank smile, you bless what's near
and pare life's mess to illuminated essence
till heart doth bare its shy confession—
that 'tis you, you, you alone
for whom I stumble on
for every fumbling step
leads back to you, my home.

Twenty minutes later, a narrow band of the black sky began to glow, and then dawn blushingly ascended above the rooftops populated with conical white solar heaters that made Jerusalem's roofs look like an elevated cemetery.

The *Nesher* van backed up to collect the suitcases with a loud beeping, fit to wake all the inhabitants of Ussishkin Street.

Binyamin Zev, who since his discharge from the hospital three weeks previously had lived with Adam and been tended to by him, climbed slowly into the taxi. Adam looked around sadly at his sweet little home in Israel. He had found a sensible Danish woman to sublet from him on short notice, but he was leaving behind his precious books, and this showed that he intended to be back very, very soon. He too alighted, sitting down heavily next to his brother.

"Where's Ali?" said Binyamin Zev.

"We were up all night, so I told her to go home and sleep. Can't believe we're leaving."

His brother shrugged. "Nu, *ma la'asot?*"

The back doors slammed. The driver got into his seat and revved off up Ussishkin, swerving left onto Betzalel. The brothers watched in glum silence as the taxi drove past Shalom Falafel and the Pargod Theater and left the quaint houses of Nachlaot behind.

"Did you sleep?" said Adam.

"About an hour. I had a dream. About my appendix."

"Your—?"

"Yeah. I dreamt it ran away, and I had to chase it all over Jerusalem. We were running through Machaneh Yehudah, and it kept turning corners and disappearing, and then I saw it disguised as an old Arab woman selling figs, but when I came to grab her, she told me to go away or she would call the police."

Adam laughed in delight. "It's Gogol in Jerusalem!"

"Google?"

"Never mind."

"Anyway, then suddenly she—it—whatever—came to me, and I saw that under the Arab headdress it had a blonde wig, and it said in a high woman's voice, something like '*Take me out, handsome.*'"

Adam shook his head in disbelief. "'*Take me out, handsome?*' Your appendix was *flirting* with you? Oh man, you've been too long without a good woman!" His laughter was very loud, and several sleepy passengers turned and glared at him.

"There's more," said Binyamin Zev in a whisper. "It ordered me to boil it into soup and eat it, and then I would feel better. It ordered me to buy carrots in the market to put in the soup.

All the sellers clapped their hands and shouted to get my attention."

"*Appendix soup?!*"

"It suggested I also get some *kneidlach* for extra flavor."

Adam thumped his brother on the back. "You're outright insane, Matt! What did they put in those painkillers?"

"*Chevreh!*" shouted the driver in Hebrew. "Keep it down please."

"*Slicha,*" said Binyamin Zev.

"*Amerikakers,*" muttered one of the passengers, and the others tutted at the loud Americans. Binyamin Zev moved his mouth close to his brother's ear, and said in a low voice, "I found out yesterday that they buried it."

"Buried what?"

"The hospital—they buried my appendix in the ground. It's traditional Jewish law; you have to bury all organs removed from a Jewish body. Shouldn't you know all this, Talmud-head?"

"I do, actually, appendix-head."

Wearily Binyamin Zev closed his eyes, and mumbled, "It's bizarre. Yet strangely comforting. My appendix, in Israel's soil."

Adam nodded sympathetically. The van full of slumbering passengers sped down the Jerusalem-Tel Aviv highway in silence.

Four months and sixteen days later, a Boeing made its way across the Atlantic on the JFK-Tel Aviv route. Passenger Adam Kossowsky spent the entire trip studying a page of Talmud and dreaming of his girlfriend. His brother had remained behind for a while to keep his mother company, and also to do the rounds of American campuses with his new lecture: *Zionism or Zionwasm? The Jews must choose!*

The plane also bore the coffin of Frayndle Shneiderman, nee Kaganov, born in the country of Moldova and subsequent citizen of Phoenix and Fair Lawn, gathered to her ancestors at age ninety-eight. Adam and BZ had finally persuaded their obstinate mother and aunt that *Bubbie* must be reinterred, and that, in accordance with her own wishes, her final resting-place must be the Har Hamenuchot cemetery in Jerusalem, close to her grandsons and to her people. To paraphrase her own words:

If her daughters wished to visit the grave, they could damn well travel to the Holy Land, whatever the political situation.

That excellent old lady. May her memory be for a blessing.

Cages

December 2001

Sometimes a long moment of joy can change the past. Two whirlygig months had swept away much of Immanuel's disappointing relationship history, replacing it with a cheerful present: Sarah, from El Paso, Texas. Aged twenty-seven and Orthodox for the past five years, she was as sweet and sharp as tea with *nana*. In Immanuel's eyes, she seemed pure and constant, like Jerusalem's very stones.

Immanuel's mouth always split into a wide grin the moment he lifted the receiver to phone her.

"Hey, you," he said, voice full of smile. "Special treat today! Where's the only normal patch of land in all of Jerusalem? Where do men, women, and children walk around, Arabs, *Haredim*, everybody together with no suicide bombings in sight?"

Sarah guessed: "The Knesset?"

He laughed loudly. "No, sillyhead, the zoo! Meet you there at two."

"Where Sarah?" demanded three-year-old Hudi, his accent heavily Israeli.

"She's meeting us at the zoo, kiddo." Immanuel swung Hudi over his shoulder, informing his ex-wife, "Back at six-thirty." For a moment he looked at her silently washing dishes, her long auburn hair in a greasy band, her back hunching into her neck. He found he could no longer remember how she had been before.

The day was overcast, a dark ivory sky, and the Biblical Zoo was quiet. The animals too seemed subdued; in fact, many were altogether absent. Hudi cried when instead of the promised leopard, they found an empty stall.

Immanuel was displeased. "Where are they all? We should ask for our money back. We didn't come to see an exhibit of cages."

"It's become the 'Biblical Cages Zoo,'" said Sarah, smiling.

"Yes!" Immanuel gestured. "On my left, the cage where Joseph was imprisoned in Egypt. And on my right, where Samson was kept before he brought the house down. A real moneymaker!"

Sarah laughed. "You are the cutest rabbi I ever met." Her possessive gaze made Immanuel tremble.

"That's not difficult," he retorted, and she laughed and began to tell him some rambling joke involving a rabbi and a leprechaun. His attention wandered, as he considered where he should buy the ring. He had bought the last one in New York, but his next visit to the States wasn't until Passover. Where money for that visit—never mind for a ring and a wedding—would come from, God alone knew. Hopefully the lecture tour would come off and solve both problems.

Sarah suddenly looked around. "Where's Hudi?"

Immanuel sighed. "That boy will be the death of me!"

They ran up the path, calling his name.

Hudi was running up and down the railings in front of the bears' enclosure, hollering, "*Dubi! Dubi!*" Sarah took his hand and ran up and down with him, giggling. Finally she collapsed, out of breath, onto the bench where Immanuel sat watching.

"So how did class go today?" she asked, still gasping for air.

"Good. The women are really getting into it now winter *zman* is under way. We covered almost a whole *blatt* this week. I told you, only the really motivated girls came this year; everyone else chickened out. At least we can be grateful to the Arabs for winnowing out the lightweights."

"Huh. I never thought of it that way." She moved closer to him. "So will you learn Talmud with me this Shabbat?"

"Sure."

"I bet they really like you. You're an amazing teacher."

He shrugged and smiled. "They're good girls."

"I'm jealous," she said, looking up at him.

"Don't be. Oh, wait, sweetie, I can't learn with you this Shabbat, I have to teach a group from Michigan at the Hilton."

Sarah stamped her foot. "*Sad face!*"

"I'm sorry, little sadface. I'd much rather be with you than with a bunch of geriatric Americans, but we need this money. This group pays top dollar."

She frowned. "Mani, this is—it's insane. The whole beauty of Shabbat is the aspect of rest. Why is the rabbi I'm dating always working on Shabbat, while my friends get to relax with their non-rabbinical men? It's all backward."

"Sarah, I do *not* work on Shabbat. Let's be careful with our language. Halachically it's acceptable. I'm being paid for the preparation time, while the actual teaching is free."

"Whatever," said Sarah with a little pout.

"No, not whatever." Immanuel waited until she looked up at him again. "I contribute to their Shabbat experience with my teaching and that's important. Also, I've told you before, these people are my best connections for my teaching tours. Can't you understand that without all this I don't make ends meet?" His hands made distinctive chopping motions in the air as he spoke.

"So change professions," she said irritably.

Immanuel raised his thick brows. "Sarah! I'm surprised at you. Aren't you proud that I teach Torah? What could be more honorable than to continue my father's and grandfather's work? To pass on God's words to the next generation?"

"Yes, yes, I'm proud." She paused. "I *am* proud and I'm sorry. I shouldn't have said that. But, seriously, don't you think that if you stopped teaching on Shabbat, God would provide?"

"He might. But there are no promises." He shook his head. "I learned that the hard way when I lost two jobs last year. God didn't step in when hundreds of kids canceled their Israel programs this fall, right? And God doesn't have to face my bank manager with a fifteen thousand shekel overdraft. God leaves me to deal with the mess. And if I want to teach Torah and live in the Holy Land, I have to compromise on something. That's reality."

"I just think . . . I just think that a little faith goes a long way."

He shrugged and said angrily, "At least I'm still here. Ask my rabbi friends who've scooted off to make a living elsewhere where their faith is!"

Sarah attempted a final stab. "Can't I at least come with you to the Hilton for lunch?"

Immanuel sighed. "They won't pay for your meal, and we can't really afford their overblown prices, right?"

"I suppose so," said Sarah, in a very small voice.

His voice softened. "I'm sorry, sweetheart, that's how it is. Listen, I'm only human; I'm doing my best. If we're to have a future together then we need to face things as they are. My next wife—and I hope my last!—will understand that marriage isn't all roses and kisses. There are sacrifices to be made." He looked at her meaningfully. "Don't you see, I'm doing all this to support Hudi and the person I'm going to marry...." He didn't finish. Sarah blushed and he was afraid he would blush too.

"God willing," she murmured. A few moments later, she said, "I guess you're right. It's important to have money." She nodded and seemed reconciled. Immanuel felt happy, as if something important had just occurred. They sat for a while, hands inert upon their laps.

"*Dubon!*" yelled Hudi, throwing a stone over the railing.

"Hudi, don't do that!" said Immanuel sharply. Three large bears lazed at the top end of the grounds, and a small white one loped between them, nosing at their flanks tenderly. Immanuel turned to Sarah and looked at her intently. "I'm sorry we argued," he said.

Sarah blushed again. "I want to hold your hand," she said softly. He pulled away from her, and she sighed. "Isn't—isn't there some rabbi who allows just holding hands? When two people are serious?"

"No," said Immanuel firmly. "No rabbi I would hold by, at any rate. Look, this is just as hard for me. At times it can drive me crazy. You know, Rina was so beautiful when I met her, and I—well, wanted to be with her, and that's why I rushed things, and ended up married to a stranger." He inhaled deeply and nodded several times. "The very first Friday night sitting with her at the

Shabbat table I knew I'd made a terrible mistake. But it was too late."

"I'm sorry."

"Well, I was a fool. But there's no *tzaddik* on this earth who doesn't sin."

Sarah said quietly, "What's to stop you from making the same mistake again?"

Immanuel frowned, pondering. "Well I'm older now and wiser. And believe me, you're not her, thank God!"

"We'll just have to wait, then."

Hudi had lowered himself to a squatting position and was chewing on a twig.

"Hudi! That's dirty, put it down!" Immanuel ordered him.

"*Abba*, look there, doggie!" shouted Hudi, waving the soggy stick.

"That's not a doggie, sweetie," said Sarah. "It's a li'l *dubi* bear. See, that's his *Ima*." She pointed at one of the larger bears.

"She's not paying him much attention, is she?" said Immanuel. "Another lousy mother."

But Hudi persisted. "Doggie! Doggie dog dog!" He stood up and ran around in circles, barking and flapping his hands. Immanuel looked on indulgently. "Kids just say whatever comes into their mind. Don't you wish adults were like that? My last relationship was full of secrets. Promise me we'll always be really honest with each other, and not hide things?"

Sarah was silent. Then she said, not looking at him, "I actually do have something to tell you."

"Anything," he insisted.

She pointed hesitantly at her wrist. "See this bracelet?" It was wide, made of flat woven brown leather, with red jewels inserted at intervals.

"It's beautiful. You always wear it."

"Well, there's a reason." She unclasped the bracelet and showed him, engraved in the band of pale untanned skin, an inky snake coiled around her wrist, its tail in its mouth.

"Ugh! Sarah, that is one ugly tattoo."

He saw her flinch and added hurriedly, "Don't worry, sweetheart, you'll just keep hiding it under that bracelet."

"So—you don't mind?"

Immanuel hesitated for the tiniest of seconds. "No, it's OK. Anyway," he added brightly, "I think there are techniques to remove tattoos now, with lasers or something." He paused, and then laughed. "You know, whenever I go to the strip-and-dip, I see these really *frum*-looking men—beard, *peyos*, the works; they look like Moshe Rabbeinu. Then they undress and it's showtime: hearts, skulls, dragons, you name it. I guess one can't completely erase the traces of a former life, huh?"

"I guess not," she whispered.

"I mean, look," he said, pointing to his son, who was now screeching *wee-oo wee-oo*, imitating the ambulances he heard constantly these days, "here's my memento from my former life. His parents aren't together and aren't in love, and that's not his fault." He sighed heavily. "*C'est la vie*. So don't worry, I know you came a long way to find God. You didn't know tattooing was wrong back then."

Sarah's lips shook. "There's something else."

Immanuel stiffened. "What else?"

Her features shifted; she looked scared. "You know how I dropped out of high school?"

"Senior year. You went backpacking across Europe."

"Yeah. And I did a number of things that year, to make money."

"Now let's see." He smiled. "I remember. You were a waitress in a bar and some dumb hick almost broke your jaw when he threw a beer mug at another drunk. And there was a car repair place where you helped the mechanic for a month."

"Yes."

"So? You're a funky girl! Not like these other women I've dated who head for home as soon as they break a fingernail." He laughed.

"Well, there's more."

"Yes?" He waited.

"So . . . this might be . . . be hard for you to hear. But I want you to know who I am, so . . . so here it comes."

"How bad can it be?" He laughed again, but he felt his neck muscles tighten into rock.

"Bad," said Sarah dolefully. Her eyes dulled and she cleared her throat. "For a short while—like a couple of weeks—I worked . . ." She struggled to get the words out.

"Nu?" he said, the word shooting out of his mouth like a bullet.

"I worked—I gave massages. To men." She paused again and sighed. "And a few even—oh, this is so hard—they paid to spend the night."

She covered her face with her hands. Immanuel blinked several times, and then turned and roared, "Yehudah Yisrael Rotter! Be quiet, for heaven's sake!" The little boy froze, then threw himself down and bawled.

"Now wait," Immanuel said to Sarah slowly, trying to make himself heard over his son's wailing. "I'm not sure I heard you right. What exactly happened?"

She did not look up, staring instead at her hands twisting in her lap. "What you heard." She made a tiny motion with her head toward the prone child, choking on his tears. Immanuel stood up abruptly and swept his son to his feet, wiping his nose and dragging him to the railings by his arm. "Look, Hudi!" he said roughly. "Look at the bears! The big bear and the little one!"

"Doggie!" sniveled Hudi, and continued sobbing, his body limp. Immanuel returned but would not sit. He said in a low voice, "But you? Of all people, you?"

The words came out in a jumble. "I didn't want to, but my wallet was stolen and—I—there were no other jobs around. I didn't plan it, it just happened."

Immanuel stood up and took a step backward, still staring at her. "My God," he said weakly. "Couldn't you have just phoned your mother?"

A moan escaped Sarah's mouth. "She was always such a loser. I couldn't be like her, sponging and scrounging—"

Immanuel shouted, "How many, Sarah? *How many?*"

She looked up at him, tears wending their way down her cheek. "I—I don't exactly—four? Seven? I'm not sure. I've blocked it out. Does it matter?" By now her voice was barely above a whisper. "As soon as I had enough money I left town."

"Sarah, I need . . . to think about this." His face gave away his feelings.

"Don't be like this," Sarah pleaded, trying to pluck at his sleeve as he pulled away. "I know it's awful—but I never did anything like it again. I'm so ashamed. I've done *teshuvah* for it every Yom Kippur—every day—for the past eight years. Surely God's forgiven me?"

He replied in a hard, distant tone. "Nobody can know what God thinks."

She reached out for him again but he shifted another few inches back. Shuddering with grief, she cried shrilly, "You always told me that a *ba'al teshuvah* stands in a higher place than a *tzaddik*—remember? We repent and then it's wiped out."

"Only if the same situation comes up again and the person resists repeating the sin."

Sarah jumped up. "But I did! I did! You don't know how many times I've been flat broke since! But I never . . . Oh! You're judging me, you're judging me so harshly—" She choked on her words.

Stonily, he faced the other direction. "Sarah, I can't! I need to think!" Without looking at her, he got up and walked to Hudi. Bending over, he wiped his son's nose and kissed him. He did not turn around, even when he heard Sarah cry from behind him, "Call me! Please! Immanuel, call me!" He ignored her until she gave up.

Her footsteps as she fled down the path were almost noiseless, but he heard every one.

"It's absurd, absurd," said Immanuel to Hudi as they wandered back to the gate.

"*Abba*, look at the birdies!" Hudi stretched his little hand toward the artificial island where the flamingos strutted.

"I thought she was so pure. I can't get my head around it." Immanuel laid a hand on his son's long curly hair. In a few months, on Lag Ba'Omer, he would take him to Mount Meron and cut the tresses in the traditional *upsherin* ceremony, alongside dozens of other long-haired three-year-old boys. He had been certain Sarah would be there with him, but now he did not know. He suddenly wondered if he had ever really known her.

Hudi shouted and jumped, and the birds flapped, startled into flight. Sarah's words jounced around in Immanuel's brain, and he began to feel ill. Swallowing, he muttered, "I mean, I'm not stupid—I knew she must have been with men before she became religious. One or two, maybe. But this?" He shuddered. "How can a woman do that? Give her most precious possession away for a few dollars?" He considered himself highly intelligent, but women, he felt, would forever leave him confounded.

"*Abba*, wanna choklic!" Hudi shrilled. Immanuel stopped and looked at his son. His desires, at least, he understood.

"I'll do my best for you, kid, I promise. I'll find you a good mother, one who respects herself." Despondently he took his son's hand.

"*Abba!*" screamed the little boy, pulling away his hand and crying. In his hysteria, he forgot the object of his desire, and could only yell brokenly through his tears, "Wanna! Wanna! Wanna!"

Back at last in his one-bedroom flat, Immanuel sat on the sofa, trying to regain his old world where things were as they seemed. He found a gauzy blue scarf of Sarah's draped over a cushion, and picking it up between thumb and forefinger as if it were diseased, stuffed it behind some books. He could live without her, he told himself; he had a rich and fulfilling life. Angrily, he turned on his laptop and checked his email.

From: Mfrohwein@ShootsOfTorah.org
To: "Rabbi Rotter" <rabbiir@hotmail.com>
Subject: Tour
Dear Rabbi Rotter,
It looks like it's happening. Whistle-stop tour of the States, starting January 9th. Eight different cities in New Jersey, Tennessee, and California. We'll arrange home hospitality at kosher homes. Everyone's very excited about you coming.
Please confirm.
Mindy Frohwein

"Finally!" Immanuel exclaimed, flinging a jubilant fist into the air. He began banging away at the keyboard with great speed.

Dear Mindy,
Yes, confirm! I had thought I might have miluim then but it's been postponed. To remind you, the fee we spoke of was $800 per gig.

Sincerely,
Rabbi Immanuel

The next email was:

From: alps@mxos.com
To: rabbiir@hotmail.com
Subject: Speaking engagement in Kansas
Dear Rabbi Rotter,
We understand you are coming to the States and we have heard
what a dynamic speaker you are. We would love for you to
lecture to us. We are a small Conservative community and will
be able to pay you $300 for your time. Please let us know.
Andrew Alpert
Educational coordinator, Temple Beth-El, Kansas City

Teaching Conservatives was iffy. Personally he did not
care—Torah was Torah—but they would have to agree to no
outside publicity, because if it got out, his reputation might
be forever ruined in Orthodox circles, and *Shoots of Torah*
would have to disown him. But this, at any rate, was plainly
not worth the effort, not at that price.

Dear Mr. Alpert,
I'm afraid that I will not be anywhere near Kansas City on this
trip. Perhaps next time.
Sincerely,
Rabbi I. Rotter

Well, he thought, at least the tour's finally come through.
He had sent dozens of emails to set it up, using up all his
connections, typing until his fingers were sore, and now he
was reaping the reward. Immanuel felt proud of himself. His
third tour and he was only thirty! Plenty of time to become
as well known as Rabbi Shraga Feivel Sirkes, a charismatic
speaker who he knew for a fact was booked solid for the next
two years. Immanuel looked forward to the time when he too
would be chased and could just sit back and take the book-
ings.
    Now, at last, he could tell Jonah he was coming. He
adopted an upbeat tone, trying to forget the day's events.

To: JonahElman@aol.com
From: rabbiir@hotmail.com
Subject: Get ready!
Yo Jonas!
I am coming to visit you in the Wild West, so make me up a bed! Have you settled into the new school yet? Do you miss us? Gevalt, man, it's so easy to earn money in the US—I don't blame you for leaving. I hear Leib's also going to Golus; he got an offer in Toronto. If it wasn't for my kid I might think of it myself. I love Israel but it's a struggle, and if some crazy Arab doesn't kill me, the taxes and miluim will. If I didn't lecture rich Americans, I'd be surviving on my own shoelaces fried in shmaltz.
Remember what zany idealists we used to be? Kollel camp—three weeks for free! Were we total tzaddikim or just really dumb??? (Both, probably!) Now I've graduated to $800 a shot, and about time.
I'm thinking I should contact some people in the UK (know anyone?) or those other English-speaking countries where people walk around on their heads. Wherever there are Jews, there's work for the likes of us ;-) So hopefully everything will be all right, God willing.
Make sure that bed is comfortable—don't you dare give me the lumpy sofa like you did last time!
Love to Malki and the kids,
The Man

Immanuel sat staring at the email he had written, and wistfully remembering times when he could just enjoy the teaching and not worry about the pay. Closing his laptop, he took out his weekly planner and a pen, and after hesitating for a few seconds, struck a line through the words *"Trip to Golan w/ Sarah."*

Money saved! he told himself fiercely. *You should be pleased.* He felt like punching something but instead took out his Talmud to prepare class. He was soon immersed in the Aramaic letters, though this time they refused to belly dance for him as they usually did.

Sarah stood in silent prayer, eyes squeezed shut, lips moving soundlessly, body rocking back and forth in wide arcs.

She raised her fist to her chest and thumped hard on her heart. It made a hollow, dead sound.

Forgive us, our Father, for we have sinned.

She beat herself again, hard.

Pardon us, our King, for we have transgressed.

Her body flung back and forth until it seemed she would take off and soar through the window. At the end of the silent prayer, when personal requests are made, she whispered, "*Please forgive me, and make him forgive me. Please forgive me and make him forgive me.*" She chanted this over and over, trying to dislodge the lump of grief sitting in her chest.

Two weeks passed. Sarah waited by the phone. It was clear to her who must make the first call. She felt herself becoming embroidered into the telephone. Wherever she was in her apartment, she was connected by an invisible fiber to that autocratic metallic jangle. In the first week, she missed her aerobics and Torah classes, ignored friends and let her food stocks run low. She just sat at her computer, doing the proof-reading and editing that paid the rent, waiting for the phone to ring. And crying.

The only class Sarah attended was her rabbi's. She had not missed one in three years. He taught a dozen or so women in the Old City, in an exquisite house through whose upper windows the Western Wall and the dark trees on the Temple Mount were visible. Sarah loved walking to the lesson, her heels ringing on grubby cobblestones, breathing in the beige-gray architecture and narrow alleys. Apart from a beggar and some yeshivah boys in velvet skullcaps, the streets and the square were empty. True, it was winter, the slackest season, but the tourists had gone from scant to nonexistent since the outbreak of the violence. Everyone now avoided the Old City, like former fans ignoring a has-been starlet, who waits forlorn and inebriated, old makeup caking her eyes. But Sarah had stayed loyal. She had a feeling that the Old City would not easily forgive these fair-weather friends. The stones remembered; they would chill those fickle hearts.

Rabbi Benchimol let out a preparatory cough and the women quieted down and took out their notebooks. All except

Sarah were married, their hair covered in a variety of wigs, hats, and scarves. One had wrapped two bold scarfs around her head, entwined and twisting like mating snakes. Another wore a black hat that resembled a wok. Sarah sat with her legs crossed, chin on her hand, staring at the rabbi's lined face, which calmed her as nothing else could. It radiated light, she thought, like the *Shechinah*.

As he drew a breath to speak, Sarah leaned forward attentively. He frequently chose topics bearing a message for her, as if direct from God. Immanuel had always scoffed when she said she believed God speaks through people. He did not believe in that level of divine intervention. But she just knew that Rabbi Benchimol was her own private prophet, and she needed guidance now more than ever.

He began. "Hillel said: *Whoever does not study the Torah deserves death; whoever makes unworthy use of the crown of Torah learning shall pass from the world.*" The rabbi looked up. "Now, ladies, what does the second part mean?"

The woman with the wok hat immediately answered: "Torah learning should be done for the right motives only."

"Yes," said the rabbi, "Torah *lishmah*, for its own sake. Correct."

Sarah, searching for her private prophetic message, immediately reflected—had she kept her Torah learning pure? No! She had wanted to use it to impress Immanuel, to make herself look knowledgeable. All those women with their advanced degrees in Jewish studies whom he had dated frightened her— when she imagined their learned feminine voices, her mind filled with a babble of Aramaic phrases. How could she possibly compete, she who had only begun reading Hebrew properly at twenty-two? So she had taken to listening in her Torah classes for quotes that she could slip into their conversations, or for memorable ideas that would impress him, instead of learning it for her own growth. Yes, that was it. She had used Torah learning to catch a man, and that was why all this suffering had come upon her. Once again Rabbi Benchimol had opened her eyes. She could hardly breathe for shame.

"Listen, now," the elderly rabbi demanded, "listen with your heart. Later on in *Avot* this idea is repeated by Rabbi Tzadok.

He says, '*Make not the words of the Torah a crown to magnify your-self, nor a spade to dig with. Anyone who derives worldly benefit from the words of the Torah removes his life from the world.* What's the meaning?"

"Well the spade to dig with is probably money. Like, you shouldn't take a fee for Torah teaching," said a young woman with a blond wig. Several students glanced instinctively at a plate on the table, full of twenty shekel donations for the lesson. The rabbi coughed delicately.

"Yes, well, Maimonides, the Rambam, *paskens* that way. Rather chop wood than desecrate the Torah by making your living from it. But then, you ask—"

"—how do Torah teachers today allow themselves to be paid?" exclaimed the wok-bearer.

"Precisely. It's a problem. So it was decided, far better that rabbis earn a wage honorably than that they be scroungers. It became acceptable to receive money for Torah, and now—" Rabbi Benchimol smiled and pointed at the plate, "—we rabbis are the wealthiest members of society, yes, no?" Everyone laughed loudly, for it was well known that he had nine chil-dren to feed and lived extremely simply, not even owning a car.

Sarah went home resolved to learn Torah only for its own sake. She would not be caught making that mistake again. Now that she had learned her lesson, God would surely be kind and return Immanuel to her. But another week passed, and nothing. Sarah wondered whether she was being too proud. Perhaps she should break the silence. But something always stopped her from phoning him. So she bore the waiting patiently, as a punishment for her sins.

At last, tired of being at home, she mustered the strength to go with her friends Emma, Shari, Hannah, and Alison to make packages for lone soldiers.

"Nu?" they said, a multi-headed monster of curiosity with drilling eyes, all speaking at once:

SHARI: Has he popped it yet?

HANNAH: When's the date?

ALISON: Can I be your bridesmaid?

EMMA: Can I come with on your honeymoon?

"Patience," was all Sarah would say, as she stuffed plastic bags with wafers, *bissli*, and *bamba*. She refused to speak about it further.

Afterward she went to the Old City for her weekly class. Perhaps this time she would approach the rabbi after class for advice as to whether she should call Immanuel, for she trusted him more than anyone else in the world.

"'*All my life I have been among wise men, and I have found nothing better for a person than silence*,'" Rabbi Benchimol read out. "Later, in chapter three, we will see a similar statement. '*Silence is a fence to wisdom*.' Now in Western society, thanks to our dear fellow Yiddel, Sigmund the Great, it has become the fashion to tell all—to your psychologist, to your spouse, or on television on the Opera show, why not?"

"Oprah!" the women chimed in, laughing.

"Lovely, fine. But this approach is wrong. Some things should never be said. We are an inward people. We are not Christians; we don't have confession. There is no confession except before God."

Sarah stared at him. Once again he was undeniably talking directly to her, this mouthpiece of heaven. She heard and understood. *I spoke things to Immanuel that should not have been said. I spoke wrongly.* Still, it was hard to imagine that keeping secrets from him was the right thing to do.

The rabbi continued, "Take Joseph, for example—he held himself back from revealing all, though he was on the verge of tears, until his brothers' repentance was complete. We can't just blurt out the truth whenever we feel like it; that's selfish. What if you're at a wedding and the bride is ugly? Shammai says if she's ugly, she's ugly, don't lie. But Hillel says no, in every case the bride is beautiful—you tell her she's gorgeous. And we hold like Hillel."

Sarah's mind wandered to her years in college when she had first encountered the overdone bride, a white macaroon in lashings of green eye shadow and pink lipstick, eyelashes mascaraed into rigor mortis, hair sprayed into solid rock. Would the sage Shammai enter such a wedding and heartily declare, "*Mazal tov*, O hideous mutant"? The thought made her giggle a little. *At my wedding, I will not be overdressed*, she resolved.

A simple linen gown, no sequins or frills—one that might even be worn afterward on Shabbat. She imagined herself sitting in a white chair covered in shiny cloth, lightheaded from fasting and excitement, as her friends fussed over her. Immanuel would be wearing an immaculate black suit, sitting in a room off the hall, respecting the custom of not seeing her before the wedding; gentle melodies sung by his friends and his rabbis would float him into matrimony. Immanuel had a beautiful voice, she reflected, and it would be a shame she could not watch him at that moment. Then with a jolt she remembered that Immanuel was no longer hers, and her breath caught in her throat. She clamped her teeth firmly, trapping a scream.

The rabbi was still talking: "Speech is powerful, and it's our Jewish power. *Hakol kol Ya'akov*. Once it's out there, it's on the rampage. It can't be recalled, like a bag of feathers shaken out into the wind. So restraint is necessary. Take Aaron the High Priest. When he heard that his two sons had died in the Temple, we are told *And Aaron was silent*. The word for silent, *vayidom*, has the same root as *dom*, a word we find by Joshua when the sun miraculously stopped in the sky. So this is not just silence, not just stillness, it is a suspension of all normal activity. Aaron, like the sun, overcame the laws of nature; he did not cry out at the most painful news of all. And that's what Jews do: we bite our tongues as we suffer."

"The Jews I know don't bite their tongues when they suffer," said the wok lady, this week festooned in a pink squashy hat that looked like a cow's udder. "They complain endlessly until you just want to throttle them." Everyone laughed except Sarah. Her mind was elsewhere. *Yes. I will be strong. I will not cry out. Like Aaron, overcoming nature.*

She did not speak to the rabbi after the lesson but went straight home. She also did not call Immanuel.

A time for speech, a time for silence.

Immanuel raised his head from his Talmud and stared yet again at the phone. Those seven digits danced through his head, a band of thieves stealing his concentration. His hand rose off the page toward the receiver; but he let it drop again. All he could think about was how foolish and gullible he felt.

He had almost proposed, yet she had been a stranger to him all along, at least in what really mattered. He felt betrayed, lied to. Or was it his fault, for not taking sufficient interest in her life? Perhaps he had talked too much about himself, never asked the right questions? His turmoil kept him awake at night. All her sweetness and loveliness now disgusted him; it was a sham. Yet somewhere inside him, he missed her terribly. But he could not phone. For no matter how far down his throat he reached, there were no words there for her, not even a half-digested sentence that could pass for human speech. Whenever he thought of phoning Sarah, all that emerged from his gullet was a wispy hoot: *Who? Who?*

In the weeks following, Sarah kept herself busy. She made no effort to contact Immanuel. At times her cheeks would suddenly burn at the pictures that must have filled Immanuel's imagination. The rest of the time she was numb, as if hundreds of little pebbles stopped up the chambers of her heart. His silence indicated that Immanuel must be extremely angry. Perhaps, she began to believe, she really had never deserved him. She should marry a man like herself, one who had done dishonorable things in his life—someone who had been a cokehead, or pulled wings off bats, or been arrested for shoplifting. That was her level as a mere *ba'alat teshuvah* from Texas—not worthy to marry a rabbi from a long line of rabbis. What had she been thinking?

Eventually, word got around that Sarah was now available again, and a matchmaker phoned. She had in her files a nice British man, twenty-eight, tall and handsome, a former drummer in a rock band who was now on the right path, studying in a yeshivah the Old City.

"A drummer?" Sarah was satisfied. To a man like this she could comfortably show her tattoo on the first date. But when he phoned and launched into that awful artificial first conversation, although he was friendly and nice, Sarah found she could not bear it. She stopped him and awkwardly apologized—it was her mistake, she was not ready to meet him. He sounded disappointed. She felt bad, but was unable.

Putting the phone down, Sarah wondered if she would ever be ready again. Does one ever fully recover from being stabbed in the heart?

I wonder, she thought, *if Aaron the High Priest, years later on some random morning, suddenly let out an endless howl that split the heavens wide open.*

Immanuel walked through downtown Memphis. The day before, his hosts had cooked him an enormous supper of lamb and sweet potato pie, and afterwards his lecture had gone down smooth as a ripe plum in that plush purple synagogue. People crowded around him, exclaiming in their Southern genteel style, "Wonderful, young man, simply wonderful, such interesting ideas, so original"—all except for one old man who told Immanuel in a slow, quavery drawl that he spoke far too fast; he had not understood a word.

Now, with some free time before the flight to Los Angeles and the perfect January weather in Memphis—a chilly sun, jacket weather—he went to see the Peabody Hotel. He intended to catch the hotel's famous duck march, but it was still early, so he hung around in the lobby nibbling peanuts. He hated this feeling of loneliness. On the plane to New York he had thought about Sarah, remembering her riotous stories of the seven months she had spent in that city before fleeing its madness; thinking about the engagement ring he had intended to buy on this trip. Embers of sorrow burned still, no matter how he tried to smother them. He had stared with red-rimmed eyes at the black Atlantic below and thought dully, *The Zombie Rebbe comes to America.*

Perchance a wonderful woman would come to one of his lectures, as Sarah had in Jerusalem. Someone who wanted to move to Israel. Perhaps, now that he thought about it, it would not be so terrible even to stay in the U.S. for a couple of years. He could put away a tidy sum in the land of steak and money before returning. He could not leave Hudi, of course; but perhaps Rina could even be persuaded, for the right sum, to move back too for a while so that Hudi could be nearby.

Finally, there seemed to be some activity. Tourists were gathering, lining up next to where the red carpet rolled. Hudi would have loved the ducks; he would have shouted *birdie*—or *doggie* or *wabbit*. A deep loneliness threatened to topple Immanuel momentarily, but just then he saw an elderly woman he had met at the synagogue the previous night waving vigorously at him. Politeness demanded that he wave back and smile.

"Ah, hello Rabbi!" she said breathlessly, a gracious, elegant woman in pearl earrings. "Seeing the sights?"

"Yes, I am."

"Going to see Graceland later?"

"No, unfortunately I don't have time."

"You should see it, you know. They say Elvis was a *Shabbos goy*."

"Really?" Despite himself Immanuel was intrigued.

"Oh yes," she said conspiratorially. "For a well-known Jewish family. Well, I'm sure he wouldn't have done it had he known what the future held. Turning on and off lights for Jews? Degrading. But you just don't think much when you're young and broke, isn't that right, Rabbi? You don't always believe in yourself."

Immanuel blinked sharply in surprise. But the woman was now crying out gladly, "Ah, the ducks!"

The carpet was quickly rolled out, the elevator opened, and five ducks waddled out majestically, accompanied by a man in a red and gold jacket. "The Duck Master," murmured the woman reverently. Immanuel nearly burst out laughing, but he contained himself. Children shouted and pointed, as slowly the ducks walked along the carpet, up the steps and into the fountain. Just as suddenly, it was over.

"Well there you are, our local wonder. Anyway, lovely to see you again, Rabbi. Safe flight." She hurried off. Soon, the crowd dispersed, and Immanuel was alone with the ducks. He looked around. He was tired of the shallow opulence, the hotels and huge suburban houses. His eyes yearned for the modest apartments of Jerusalem, with their clean white stone.

He felt his gut wobbling peculiarly and it was not due to peanuts. Without warning his knees buckled, causing him to sit down abruptly, his backside thudding painfully onto the lip of the fountain. He put his head in his hands.

What am I doing here? My son needs me. My students need me. These strangers don't need me—I'm their entertainment, their spiritual dancing bear.

Immanuel's fists clenched and his vision blurred.

No more tours! No more Shabbat work! I'm sick of it. God—do You hear me? Help me find another way to support myself and stay in Israel! Dear God, I don't know what to do anymore, I don't know what to do.

He waited for a few minutes for some sign, as the ducks splashed his back. But God did not speak to him that day in Memphis, or at least Immanuel heard nothing. Eventually, he stood up and rubbed his eyes. There was a tour to complete— the plane to the City of Angels beckoned, and so did a couple of thousand dollars. That was reality. He left and did not look back.

Postscript

August 2002

The late summer sun blazed upon the newly returned Wall-deserters, who hurried in droves, anxious for their annual wail. It was Elul, the month of repentance. On her way to the Western Wall, Sarah walked past Immanuel. She did not have time to hide her face or pretend to be someone else before he saw her.

"Sarah!"

A slight nod was all she could spare him.

"Hi! How are you?"

"OK. You?"

He shrugged. "Scraping by." The exuberant energy he had always possessed was gone. The word 'lifeless' came to mind. Not wanting conversation, she nevertheless could not help her curiosity.

"Aren't you the big star now?"

"Not exactly. There's enough for me and Hudi, I guess." Sarah recalled the little boy with a jolt, her ache to hold him after she could no longer see him.

"Rina still makes her impossible demands," continued Immanuel. Sarah hardened her heart. She didn't care.

He squared his shoulders and affected his old charming tone: "I've been thinking about you a lot lately."

She stared at him.

"Listen, how can I say this? I'm sorry I didn't call. I felt it might be less painful that way. Couldn't we . . . put it all behind us and start over?"

Can you forget my past, or I yours?

"We had so much going for us. It's worth another try, no?"

She said nothing.

"Sarah, I said I'm sorry. What more do you want—for me to get down on my knees?" He was angry now, and adopted his pedagogic voice. "You know, the Talmud instructs us to walk away from sins that we've atoned for. Otherwise it's like a dog returning to its vomit. Let's not . . . ." He trailed off, sounding suddenly unsure.

Certainly a dog should not return to its vomit.

Silence looped around them. A group of Hasidim in tall fur hats passed, skinny legs in nylon stockings below knee-length coats, like a bevy of black swans, huddling close to hear the old rebbe in their midst speak. Some South American tourists posed for the camera, and a tour guide explained the history of Herod's handiwork. A bride walked down to the Wall to pray as her friends ululated and whooped, and Sarah's eyes followed the white train trailing in the dust.

Finally, Immanuel put out his hand in a gesture reminiscent of the Kotel beggars: "Sarah, please. Let's sit down and talk."

His crestfallen face was now exactly like Hudi's when he wanted a cuddle. She badly wanted to comfort him. So tempted to make it all better. All the warmth she had felt for him was emerging again, pressing against the clamps she had put in place, ready to rise to the surface. A small word, a small gesture or smile, and all would be healed.

But instead her hand moved automatically to her chest and found the boulder still there—the one he had created. She shook her head and mumbled, "Not a good idea. As you said—a dog . . . a dog—"

Even now she found she could not bear to hurt him. Still clutching her chest, she turned and walked away from him toward the women's section of the Wall. There, squeezed between the sharp elbows of pious women, she shed her tears upon the pockmarked, stained, imperfect stones.

Biblical Zoo

So that was what tranquility felt like. Raquel remembered now. A subtle taste, like a drop of honey on the tongue.

"Thanks so much for coming," said Sarah, linking arms with her. "I've had a hard week and had to get away."

"You look a bit spooked, to be honest," said Raquel.

"Yes, this zoo is kind of haunted for me. By that teacher guy I dated before I met you."

"Ah—the ghost of a failed relationship?"

"You could say. Anyway, I really don't think I could have come alone." She squeezed Raquel's arm affectionately.

"Yeah, we'll stick together and survive it all: terrorism, bombings, and men." Raquel smiled. She felt compelled to maintain a wall against Sarah's pain, trying desperately to protect that rare feeling of joy.

The two women were leaning on the wall of the elephant compound, breathing in its grassy animal smells. A warm wind blew Raquel's spiky black hair into her eyes, and her hand brushed at it ineffectually. A young mother passed by pushing a pram. Sarah smiled sadly. "I remember we schlepped all the way out here in the middle of winter with his kid but there were almost no animals in sight."

"Seriously?"

"Oh, and get this. He told me we were going to the most normal place in Jerusalem, where Arabs and *Haredim* mix freely, and I thought he meant the Knesset! I'm such a nerd. No wonder he dumped me."

"Now, now! None of that!" Raquel tutted. "But he was right about one thing, I'll give him that." She appraised the scene before her: a ring of tall trees and weary grass yellowed by the Mediterranean sun, alongside somnolent animals, all subtly hued by the tangerine-stippled sunset. "This really is the only normal place left in Jerusalem, where you can actually walk around safely, actually breathe. What a relief." She inhaled with a smile.

As if on cue, a siren in the distance splintered the quiet moment. A second siren followed, and Sarah's face fell. "I hope everything's OK."

Raquel had, thankfully, become less aware of these sirens. Ambulances raced behind her house daily on their way to Shaarei Tzedek hospital, and at first her heart had galloped with them in Doppler waves up the street. Gradually, though, she had learned to shut the sound out, though somehow she remained aware of their number. One siren meant some unfortunate soul had suffered a heart attack, no doubt. Two might signify a car accident. But three or more spelled disaster. When the sirens fused into a viscous, pulsing sea of sound outside her window then Raquel would mutter, like a mantra, "Bad news for the Jews. Bad news." Then it would be time to turn on her TV, bracing herself for the now clichéd images of shattered glass, body bags, and stoic *Zaka* men picking up the pieces. And witnesses, always using the same words, with hardly a variation, like actors endlessly auditioning for the same gory part.

Raquel sighed. "I wish I were an animal. Life would be so much simpler."

"What, trapped behind bars all day, under people's stares? No thanks."

"I suppose you're right."

At that moment, Emma, who had gone in search of chocolate, rejoined them. Emma's and Raquel's parents were old friends from the Zionist youth movement, Bnei Akiva. In the first encounter between the next generation, when Raquel's parents came to Manchester to visit, three-year-old Emma Claire overturned a bowl of trifle pudding on five-year-old

Raquel's head and made her cry. The victim lunged back with a plastic shovel, completely missing her target and falling flat on her face, and this made her attacker laugh so hard that she tripped over a tree and cracked her head open, necessitating seven stitches. This seminal incident established the tone for their friendship thereafter.

"What're you lot nattering on about?" Emma demanded, opening her chocolate bar with much crackling.

"We were just thinking that the animals should be free to run around," Raquel explained.

Emma continued ripping at the packaging with her teeth. "Hmm. The lions'd have a blast, but I reckon it would ruin the teddy bears' picnic."

"She's right," said Sarah. "We can't have wild animals roaming around. Take your pick: it's them or us."

"Us!" decided Emma. "Anyway, I think they're comfy in this zoo. It's dead nice here."

"Yes, it is nice," said Sarah. "There's a really calming atmosphere. I was just saying that here, no one cares what tribe or race or religion you're from."

"You sound just like John Lennon," said Emma. "I liked him. Why do the good men always get assassinated?"

"It's all topsy-turvy," said Raquel. "Here, the animals are caged, while people walk around; but out there, the people all live in their little segregated ghettos, while the animals roam free."

"Especially Jerusalem's cats," added Sarah.

"I've had an idea!" Emma said through a mouthful of nougat. "Maybe each animal in the zoo corresponds to a group outside!"

Raquel smiled. "You mean like the penguins would be the *Haredim*, in their little black and white suits?"

"No, the *Haredim* are the parasites on the elephants' backs! OK, OK, keep your hair on," Emma added hastily, as she was deluged with tuts from her friends. She grinned sheepishly, bits of chocolate between her teeth.

"I think the monkeys would be the *Sephardim*," suggested Sarah.

"Oh, right," Emma sputtered. "Who's being racist now?"

Sarah reddened. "I just meant they're warm and chatty and . . . and family-oriented."

"'Course you did!"

"Don't look at me like that! I'm half Sephardi myself."

Raquel said, "Hey, and all those animals that are AWOL are the Israelis who've moved to L.A. They're planning to come back as soon as the children finish college."

Emma succumbed to a fit of giggles, choking and spraying chocolate-hazelnut fragments everywhere. Though she laughed with Sarah at the ridiculous sight, part of Raquel's mind stood to one side, registering sluggishly that this was the first time in ages she had laughed with friends. Could she string together enough of these moments to call them "fun"?

"I swear to God, I'll get all those chocolate bits back in my gob if it's the last thing I do," said Emma, pretending to feel around on the ground.

"Emma, you're revolting! Get up!" said Raquel.

Emma reluctantly stood up and flung out an arm majestically. "Onwards to the rhino!"

The rhinoceros's bulky form lay inert next to several giraffes. A woman in blue overalls was trying to persuade a young giraffe to move away from the gate, where a man holding large armfuls of leaves waited to enter.

"Amos! Amos! *Boyna!*" she shouted, waving her arms and jumping, but the giraffe ignored her. Another siren sounded in the distance and Sarah frowned again. "We must listen to the news when we get home."

"I'm not listening to the news anymore," Raquel declared. "Yes!" she said, firming her resolve. "As of now, the radio and TV are on early retirement."

Sarah looked scandalized. "You can't just cut yourself off like that."

"Can't I? What choice do I have? I can't paint, I can't think, it's unbearable, it's like my mind's been . . . invaded."

"By Orcs?" said Emma helpfully.

"And all I can think about is the next blast and the next shooting and the next massacre. My mind's been taken over— and not by Orcs, you irrelevant person!" she snapped at Emma, who had opened her mouth again to speak. "By violent destructive people, and by the media who bring it all into my house."

"But—what's the point of living here if you're not involved? Might as well be back in England!"

"Look, I had everything in London—family, friends, money, a good job. I *love* London. I do!" she said defensively. "I only left because I'm Jewish. Because London makes no sense for a Jew."

She struggled for the right words. Jewish life in Hendon had been akin to living in a country composed of separated blocs of land. There was your house, the synagogue, your friend's house, the Jewish social center. Outside of these islands lay foreign soil, with a different yearly cycle, different values, almost a different language. The Palestinians were always talking about territorial contiguity. Now Raquel realized that she had come to Israel for precisely that.

"It's like this," Raquel continued. "Here the signs in the street are in Hebrew, the products in the corner shop are kosher, the bus driver wishes me *Shabbat Shalom*. Here being a Jew makes sense. My daily life connects to the Torah. After two thousand years we can finally live the myth! Live in a land where giraffes have the names of prophets! Believe that tomorrow the wolf will lie down with the lamb and there'll be real peace! Do you follow me?"

"To be honest, I lost you at the bus driver," said Emma. She had been clutching the chocolate wrapper, and now she licked it clean. "What's all this got to do with switching off the news?"

"Don't you get it? This isn't what I left England for. I came to live out a dream, not a nightmare. It's turned into all blood and guns and bombed cafés. The wolves have run wild and are slaughtering the lambs. I want my old Israel back."

Emma said in a cynical voice, "Sorry, but that peaceful Israel never existed. You've been through too much Bnei Akiva brainwashing if you ask me—too many videos of Jaffa oranges and scuba diving in Eilat."

"It does exist. It does!"

"Come on, lovey, wake up. This is the reality!"

Raquel shrugged. "Then I'll make my own reality."

"We have to remain strong, not run away," Sarah urged her.

"Amos!" roared the frustrated zookeeper, dancing a jig around the immovable giraffe. *"Nu, be'emet!"*

As they walked back along the wooden slatted walkway, Sarah remarked, "Oh listen, guys, I've been invited to a singles weekend. Shall we go?"

"Ugh, did that last year!" groaned Emma.

"Well, how was it?"

"Pants."

"Excuse me?"

"Tedious, awkward, foul, vile, insufferable, hellacious, rubbish with a capital C. I could go on."

Sarah looked over at Raquel for confirmation. Raquel nodded. "What she said."

"Basically," said Emma, "what do you get if you throw a bunch of beautiful brainy women together with some gormless nebby males, and leave them to stew together like a bad cholent for twenty-six hours?"

"Depressed," said Raquel. "Very depressed. Very, very—"

"Plus a week's stomach ache, with lots of gas. You get my drift. Don't need to go away for that—can get the same thing at home, and save five hundred shekels."

Emma saw that Sarah seemed disappointed. "Look, I don't want to put you off. I guess it's no worse than those soddin' *shadchaniyot.*"

"Oh, come on!" said Sarah. "The matchmakers mean well. They care about us."

"Bunch of interfering yentas if you ask me."

"Your problem is that you're too picky."

"Picky! Me? Before you slap me with nasty names listen to this, right. Last month, this woman calls me up with a great bloke for me. Intelligent, she says, good-looking, generous, sense of humor—"

"Sounds wonderful—"

"And aged twenty-one! I say, 'Excuse me? *How old?*' She says, 'Twenty-one. You're twenty-four aren't you?' I say, 'No, I'm thirty-two.' 'Oh' she says, sounding all flustered, 'so you're not twenty-four?' 'Well I *was*,' I say patiently, 'when I met you eight years ago. But it like, changes, from time to time, you know.'"

"But—"

"No, listen! Just listen! They're barmy, every last one of them. There's my mother's friend Mazal who called me up last week with an offer of a really nice fifty-year-old Kurdistani accountant-slash-mountaineer who produces his own cheese by sifting it through a loincloth. She didn't take the hint after I turned down the sixty-one-year-old Hasidic chess genius with the doctorate in neurohydrolics and a squint!"

"I don't believe you," said Raquel. "These people don't exist!"

"I swear to you on the grave of my gerbil, it's all true! I don't know where she finds them. Seriously, she must advertise in the *Oddball Times*! Then there's the mad woman on my street who wants to set me up with random men she met at the dentist because they have similar teeth to mine. Not to mention the time someone tried to set me up with—wait for it—my very own brother. How much more mental can you get?"

Sarah looked a little pale. Raquel stopped and put her hands over her face, making Emma pause her rant. To her friends' astonishment, Raquel began wailing, "I can't go on! I can't! If I don't find someone soon I'm going to die."

"We're all going to die," said Emma, philosophically. Sarah put her arm around Raquel's trembling shoulders and walked a couple of steps with her.

"It just feels like there are no men left in the world," whispered Raquel, leaning on Sarah for support.

"Half the human population," Emma objected from behind them.

"I always pitied those desperate women who are obsessed with marriage, but I think I've joined them . . ."

"Oh no, puh-leez! I'd have to stop being your friend."

Sarah turned around. "Emma, please be quiet! You're not helping!"

". . . and I used to meet men at lectures and concerts and parties but no one goes out any more since the Intifada started. I'm sick of lurking at home with my four walls and my books, rotting my life away."

"I thought I noticed a strange whiff," murmured Emma very quietly.

Raquel straightened up, accepted the tissue Sarah was holding out, and blew her nose. She took a moment to gather herself and then looked over at Sarah and ventured a weak smile. "I'm sorry for being so pathetic. I'm just in such a rut. I don't even get offers anymore; it's as if I've ceased to exist. My nineteen-year-old niece just got married. What's wrong with me?"

"Nothing!" said Sarah emphatically. "Your knight will come at the right time, you'll see."

"Starry, starry knight," hummed Emma. Raquel accepted more tissues from Sarah and began to calm down.

"Hey!" Emma waved her hands to get their attention and ran to catch up with them. "I've just had a brilliant idea! Internet dating!"

They both looked at her. Raquel grimaced. "What? As in putting your picture up for strange men to look at?"

"Someone told me yesterday about a site called Frumster. Give it a whirl! Why not?" said Emma defiantly. "Isn't it better to choose your own dates instead of relying on batty match-makers?"

"Personally I'd be terrified. But go for it, if you think it will work."

"Why thanks, maybe I will! And it wouldn't hurt you, for that matter, to stop sniveling and get back in control of your life!"

"That's what I love about you, Emma—you're so sensitive."

Emma shrugged. "A friend is a person who tells you the truth when no one else will." Then, throwing the empty wrapper on the path, she began skipping toward the front gate, singing at the top of her voice.

Sometimes, Raquel thought, bending over to pick up the scrap, *I wonder what planet Emma's from.*

And when they're coming to take her back.

Very soon, I hope.

Sweet Dreamer

*Behold, O Lord; for I am in distress . . . outside the sword
bereaves, at home it is like death.* (Lamentations 1:20)

August 2002

With watercolor pencil poised in midair, Raquel
daydreamed. Behind her flat on Berlin Street, tall pines were
giddy with birdsong. She looked down at her painting, which
was nothing more than a pell-mell of brackish colors, and laid
her pencil aside. She had hoped that ignoring the news, despite
all the guilt, would enable her to paint well again, but it had
not.

School was about to start, and she still had much preparation to do. The outing to the zoo had been fun but it would be
a long while till she would be able to do something like that
again, outside. *Outside.* This word had once signified long walks
in the sun and wind, breathing in Jerusalem, feeling amazed at
simply being there ("Jerusalem! My home!"), or trips to Judean
and Samarian red-roofed settlements inhabited by proud Jews,
wild and sturdy like the local scrub; or hikes through the green
north, with its shades of England, or through desert wadis. All
the spicy, pungent smells and tastes of this country had until
recently been laid out like a spread table; but now such trips
felt far too dangerous. Now, "outside" conjured unwelcome
images of security guards in sunglasses leaning on iron barri-
cades and lethal buses stampeding in the streets.

Every time Raquel saw a bus, she imagined steel frames twisting, buckles flying through windows and landing in breakfast cereals, wedges of glass hurtling and puncturing. Raquel had ridden only two buses since October 2000, and she had hurriedly alighted from one of them after just three stops, when a strange dark man in a bandana got on. The saddest thing about not riding buses was being denied the opportunity to stand up for old ladies with whiskers and polyester headscarves, coming from the *souk* with bulging bags. Even that simple act of kindness had been taken from her. Now she prowled up and down her flat, trapped indoors.

Sarah still took buses. "I believe in God," she explained.

"Well, I also do," said Raquel defensively, "but who knows how God works? Maybe God helps those who help themselves?"

"No. Look around you. That mother who stopped her child from taking buses—then he got blown up at the local pizzeria. It was his time. We can't do anything. Only pray, and accept that ultimately God has His own plan."

Sarah still prayed every day, while Raquel had stopped months ago. Perhaps that was a mistake. Maybe only those who prayed to God were watched over by God? She did not know. In her youth, the questions raised in her Jewish philosophy classes, of free will and foreknowledge, divine providence and determinism, had seemed *so* interesting and *so* philosophical. But now that they meant the difference between her own life and death, she found these questions without answers practically worthless. A metal detector was infinitely more useful than a thousand wise books in this town where Death strolled at leisure.

"Look," Sarah told her, "if you lose your relationship with God, you lose everything. I don't understand this any better than you do. But the Talmud says that God crushes those He loves with sufferings. That gives me some comfort."

Raquel thought: *With a God like this, who needs enemies?* But, afraid to say the words aloud—afraid that Someone might be listening—she did not pursue the argument. Thus theologically irresolute, she took the safer course and steered clear of buses, or tried to, for even walking to school she had to pass buses and the crowds of people waiting at bus stops. She found herself eyeing people's midriffs for bulk where it did not belong: every potbelly an explosive belt, every pregnant stomach a ruse. Taxis were expensive, and not safe either. Once, soon after the outbreak of the violence, her taxi pulled up next to a bus at a long traffic light. Raquel kept glancing at the bus and finally burst into tears, positive she was about to die. The driver, muttering in his raspy voice, *"Kapara, neshamah,* it'll be all right," forced her to accept his personal book of Psalms for her protection. This just made her cry more.

Only on Shabbat did Raquel feel calmer walking about. Not that the terrorists stopped their bloody work on Shabbat; but with no buses, and few cafés open, there was an illusion of peace, and Raquel could take a walk without looking over her shoulder every two minutes.

The rest of the time, Raquel stayed inside her flat with its security barrier of pine trees. Painting, with the radio and TV silent, she could pretend she was in Hendon, or New Zealand, or anywhere else in the world where things were calm. How ironic—back in London as a teenager, she had longed for Jerusalem, imagining she was already there. Now, it was reversed. How had it come to this? The world had gone mad.

Her painting a lost cause, Raquel turned to her rereading of *Lord of the Rings.* After a few minutes, the phone's persistent ring invaded Middle Earth. Raquel hoped it would not be her married friend Frieda who had taken to calling every few days, urging her to go out and socialize, impatient with her fears. *We can't give in!* Frieda would preach. *Get out there! If they stop Jewish people from meeting and having families, that's another victory for them. We should have kicked them out when we got a chance. Now look what's happened. It's all our fault, you know, all predicted in the Torah, Book of Numbers: "Kick out the inhabitants of the land, lest they be pricks in your eyes and thorns in your side." Rashi got it dead right in his comment on the verse: "They'll hedge you in, enclosing and imprisoning you, so no one can enter or leave." So true!*

Raquel would listen wordlessly, unconvinced. As if single people were to be the new soldiers at the front, fighting terrorism with wine and parties! She wanted to scream back, *It's all very well for you, you silly cow! When you cry, someone's there*

*to hold you! Try lying under your blanket with ambulances screaming
outside and only a stuffed bear to cuddle instead of your beefy husband!*
She never did, though. Just laughed politely and abided, or—
when she could—avoided. Frieda meant well, she just did not
understand how hard it was immigrate alone to this country
that was simultaneously more home than home and also
bedlam, with all rules of normality abrogated. Frieda's husband
was Israeli, and he played the game with ease, while Raquel
struggled to survive with the language and social codes only
half understood, lacking the circles of support from kindergarten to college that propelled native Israelis into jobs and
marriages. Not Frieda, nor Raquel's family, nor her colleagues
at school—no one understood the experience of twin battering
rams, carnage and solitude. Only her fellow single immigrants
did. To them Raquel clung as her real kin, tested and true.

Luckily, it was not Frieda on the phone, and Raquel
answered in relief, "Hi, Sarah!"

"How are you, sweetie?"

"Thank God."

"Thank God good?"

"No, just plain 'thank God,' no cherries or whipped cream."

"Hmm. Any men on the horizon?"

"Nope. Not even a small boy."

Sarah's voice took on a persuasive tone. "You know, Emma's
idea, to do Internet dating, is not a bad one. You should do it."

"You first!" Raquel retorted.

"No, you! Why not just try it?"

Raquel felt very tired of being told what to do. "I just can't.
What if I was rejected? I couldn't bear it."

"I understand. Poor *bubbeleh*, you sound so sad. Listen—
why don't you come with me to hear Rabbi Benchimol? He's
giving a special *shiur* about *teshuvah*."

Raquel groaned inside. Not that rabbi again. She had
already refused three times. "Well . . . where's he speaking?"
she said reluctantly.

"In a gorgeous house in the Old City."

"The Old City! Oh my God, Sarah, could you think of a more
dangerous place? Why don't we just go hear Rabbi Mohammed
in the Deheishe *shtiebel*? And stay on for *Ma'ariv* while we're at

it?" Hearing the hysterical note in her own voice, Raquel hated the person she had become.

"Oh, c'mon Raquelush, the Old City's no different from anywhere else these days. And you can't just sit around going moldy at home. I'll pay for the cab. Come!"

Raquel rolled her eyes and reluctantly went to get her coat. Thirty minutes later she found herself sitting next to Sarah in a large salon full of peacockish women in headscarves. Raquel felt embarrassed to be sitting there with these earnest Americans and was already regretting coming. The rabbi had a stark yellowish face and beard, and was smaller than she had imagined him to be—almost shorter than herself. He made some inaudible joke, and then, smiling, began:

"OK, ladies! I want to teach you a very beautiful lesson for Elul, this holy month of repentance we've been given. Here we are, and it's almost the Day of Judgment, and you're getting a bit depressed thinking about all your sins, I bet, yes, no?" The women grinned uncomfortably. Glumly, Raquel prepared herself for the *mussar shmooze*, the scolding that would prod them into repentance, but instead she jumped as the rabbi shouted, "Well, this is not allowed!"

Smiling, he continued. "Aha! Everyone thinks that Yom Kippur is the saddest day of the year. But it's not, it's the *happiest* day. By all means, think about your sins, and repent; but remember, when you're depressed, you are serving the evil inclination. *Ivdu et Hashem b'simcha.* Joy is the only mode in which to serve God, yes, no, mm?" He spread his hands widely, beaming. Sarah gazed ardently at the rabbi and Raquel wished she had someone to adore too. "Listen now, ladies, listen with your heart. Here's a deep, deep message, very fine. The first verse in the Torah portion of *Emor* says '*Tell the priests: Do not become impure for a dead person.*' The plain meaning is: A priest cannot bury someone, or even be in contact with the dead, because that defiles his purity. OK, I hear you say, nu, I got it, very nice, lovely, fine—but what's this got to do with Elul?"

Now his voice became strident and sing-song. "Comes the Izhbitzer Rebbe and asks, 'Why can't priests touch the dead? Why is that so terrible?' The answer is: Because priests have to be *happy*! Their job is to channel joy into the world for us.

Aha! So what is this death, then, that they must not touch?" He glanced around meaningfully as they waited for his answer, and Raquel looked down, fidgeting with the woven tablecloth. When no one spoke, he waved his mottled hands excitedly around his head, and his thin voice rose to a crescendo. "It is sadness!" he shouted. "Our sadnesses are our death. They're literally killing us, yes, no?! So the message is this: We are all priests! Listen now, before it's too late! Abandon death! Leave your sadness behind and serve God with pure *simcha!*" The '*a*' of the last syllable echoed for a moment off the high stone ceilings. The women stared at him, pens limp between their fingers. He nodded serenely, and, making a calm blessing aloud, drank some water from a disposable cup.

Raquel wrote on her pad: *Leave your sadness behind.* She traced the outline of the words until the ink soaked through to the pages below. She was suddenly feeling a strange mix of emotions—a vague anger, a fragile hope. It was an uncomfortable feeling.

"But Rabbi," objected one of the women, who appeared to be wearing an upside-down wok on her head, "doesn't the law allow a priest to become impure in order to bury his close relatives? How does this fit in?"

"True, true." The rabbi removed his *kipa*, blew dust off it and then replaced it. "Hmmm, so what would the Izhbitzer say to that?"

Sarah raised her hand tentatively. "Maybe there are times when it's correct to be sad. You have to be willing to be sad for things that matter enough. Those things, they're—they're like the close relatives, the exception." The rabbi was silent, and Sarah quickly added, "I don't mean depression. I mean sadness and grief. We need to feel those emotions sometimes, don't we?"

Raquel found herself nodding in agreement, and stopped, self-conscious.

"Yes, thank you, maybe," said the rabbi. His voice took on a louder tone. "But anyway, ladies, remember the fundamental message—in the words of the Talmud: *Rachmanah liba ba'ei.* God wants your heart! Yes, He wants it big and juicy and full of joy, not all shriveled up like some old potato." His hands curved out an imaginary potato in the air, and the women tittered.

"So whaddya think?" Sarah said as they walked back to Jaffa Gate through the dimly lit streets. Raquel looked at her, thoughts chasing each other inside her head.

"I was surprised," she said. "It was as if he was talking directly to me." She felt relieved that she had something nice to say for a change. She suddenly realized how much she appreciated Sarah. She was glad that friendship existed, to spin from the rough materials of camaraderie and common trials the precious gold of family.

"Exactly! Incredible, isn't it?" Sarah twirled gaily around, her arms outstretched, skirt billowing out like a purple-blue mushroom. Raquel shushed her, afraid to make noise on this deserted street with the Muslim quarter just a hop and a stab away. She said in a low voice, "But what you said was the best, though. There's a time for everything. Even—though I hate to admit it—even pain, I suppose. If the situation is important enough."

Sarah nodded modestly.

It took her several weeks. Yom Kippur and the festival of Sukkot were long past, and the wrinkled leaves were venturing the long drop from the trees when Raquel finally made up her mind. *All right, Raquel, it's just not happening, face it. You're thirty-four; you need to get married. There's a time for painful risks, and this is it—so go ahead! Defile yourself!* She would do it. She would try Internet dating. So she sat down one night in late October, fortified by a glass of tea with milk—the only proper way to drink it—and Mozart on her stereo, which drowned out the over-loud tick of an antique clock on the shelf. She did her best to ignore the damp rot flaking gently from the high ceiling onto her desk, and to avoid glimpses of the ancient armchair in the other room, slumped opposite a small TV which she had covered up with a *challah* cloth bearing the legend "*Shabbat Shalom*." She kept from her mind the tiny kitchen, lizards scurrying across its floor, and the hat-rack upon which a previous tenant's grubby raincoat sagged like a condemned man. It ought to be thrown away, but what if its owner returned and became angry?

No, it was not a cheery flat. No matter how much lavender-scented oil she burned, there was a permanent smell of decay. But this was all she could afford on her teacher's salary in this neighborhood, near the concentration of English-speaking singles who were her tribe, her lifeline. In England, with a successful job in design, she was well on her way to owning her own place. Here, the first decent job she had found paid about a quarter of her former salary. Needing to live alone, with no patience at this age for another's woman's flaws and dreams, what remained was to cover the old walls of this oppressive little coop with cloths and colorful batiques, and to make believe.

After a large gulp of tea to calm herself, Raquel turned on her computer and loaded the Frumster site. The site hit her in a blast of colorful words in red and orange and blue: *Profiles, Searches, Successful Matches, Singles' Cruises.* Small boxes danced in every corner, waiting to be clicked: *Look up member, Singles events, Dating central.*

Raquel spent a few minutes getting used to the site, clicking on various buttons and trying out a few searches. There were clearly several dozen men to meet in Israel alone, and only a few dollars stood between her and contact with them. Her blood quickened in desire to gain entry to this club, and abruptly, before she could change her mind, she clicked on *Join* and paid the member's fee. She was asked to pick a username, and chose *Galadriel.* She had always thought that the elf queen's name sounded like a Hebrew word, though Emma had once tried to translate it and not come up with anything more sensible than "God is the wave of my maple tree."

Next she had to wade through long lists of categories, each with a little box next to it:

☐	*Single (never married)*	☐	*Smoker*
☐	*Divorced*	☐	*Rarely*
☐	*Widowed*	☐	*Never*

Impatiently, she filled them all out. Then she wrote and rewrote her description until she was satisfied:

*I teach English and art in a high school. It's nice to be with
children—except when it's not. ;-) I'm artistic, sensitive, refined,
thoughtful, fun, and a great listener. I'm fairly tall and slim, with hazel
eyes. Attractive.* She hesitated for a long time over this word.
Was she really attractive? With her long nose and thin lips?
Someone might get a rude shock when he met her. In the end,
she deleted the word.

*I love animals and nature, long walks, cafés, and concerts, but also
curling up with a good book, especially fantasy and romance. I do see
movies occasionally—but don't ever take me to see a horror movie if
you don't want me screaming in your ear. My prayer is to find someone
truly outstanding: spiritual, sensitive, cultured, kind, with a poet's soul.
Someone who will know me even better than I know myself.*

The clock struck midnight, and as if in echo, a tremendous
boom rang out outside, terrifying her. Each time she heard
a loud noise or bang she was convinced the war was at her
doorstep. Once a parade of children marching up the street
singing "*Am Yisrael Hai*—The Jewish People live" had sent her
hurtling under her desk; it took all her powers of reasoning
to convince herself it was not a band of marauding Arabs
intent on a pogrom. This time, however, Raquel took a deep
breath, and ignored the loud sounds from outside. If it was a
bomb, it would just have to wait. More important things were
demanding her attention right now.

Her profile finally finished to her liking, Raquel clicked *Who's
online?* The screen instantly filled with two orderly columns of
photographs, each with its username. These were the serious
men, the ones actively searching right at that moment. Raquel
blinked in awe—here were portals into the souls of strangers,
seated at this very instant at computers around the world. She
could click on any of these pictures, and a map of a person,
his complexities and his simplicities, would open up for her. It
was so miraculous that it ought to be illegal.

With a sense of voyeurism and an odd guilt, Raquel began
clicking and time stopped. The world might be full of men
after all.

The next day, Raquel walked slowly up Gaza Street, her
tired vision swaying like the palm trees. She had looked at the

profiles until 3 a.m. but had found no poets, at least not in Jerusalem. Afterward, the adrenaline and the buzz of helicopters flying over her home toward the Knesset had held sleep from her. She had been forced to down a glass of leftover kiddush wine, which always had the effect of an abrupt clout to the head. It also spared her from having another one of her dreams, featuring incomprehensible, babbling dead people who, of late, were visiting her almost every night and making her fear sleep itself.

Up ahead, at the bus stop, a young couple laughed. Raquel was always astonished at loud expressions of happiness nowadays; what she expected instead to see out on the streets was streams of wounded people shuffling along like phantoms on crutches, with eye patches and disfiguring burn marks. Where on earth were all the wounded? *Indoors, bloody indoors.*

Seeing the youth's hand raking absently through his girlfriend's hair, Raquel was amazed. Did they think they lived in some sleepy village where the only things that exploded were overripe figs? Where did they find the courage—the indifference—to be so happy? The sight of the young man's long eyelashes and dancing blond springlets threatened to rupture Raquel's self-containment; she passed by as quickly as she could, forgetting even to check out the rest of the people at the stop. But fate held no respite for her today, as she encountered several other men directly one after the other, confident Israelis, chunky and tanned, their arms swinging boisterously as they hummed to themselves or walked briskly on. Not one gave her a second glance.

"Oh God!" Raquel resolved to send a message to a Frumster guy that very night, come what may.

Looking through the Jerusalem profiles again, the best option seemed to be *SimplyShim*. Well-traveled, principled and sensitive, he was pictured with a book and had a thoughtful look to him. Most important, Raquel sensed a certain safe quality in him. Biting her lips, she wrote him a brief note:

Hi Simply Shim (or can I call you Shimply Sim?)

I love traveling too. I sketched my way through Italy, Holland, and France—I wish I could go back! What countries have you visited?

In the *Sent mail* box, next to her message, Raquel saw a little
orange *Unread* sign. She stared at it nervously for a long while
waiting for it to change but eventually went to bed as helicopters juddered across her patch of sky. In the morning, the sign
was blue and said *Read* and there was even a message:

Shalom dear lady :-)

*I took a six-month trip around South America, and I've been to
India, Nepal, and the Far East, as well as parts of Europe and America.
You catch me away from home now too, but in the wilds of Gaza, unfor-
tunately doing reserve duty. Tell me more about yourself*

Shim

Excited, Raquel wrote back immediately. She spent the next
five days corresponding with Shim. She imagined him sitting in
some huge old cement structure full of cockroaches, high above
tangled wires and corrugated iron huts that spat gunfire in his
direction, and could not imagine how he managed so frequently
to access email.

Shim wrote that he had spent almost a hundred days in
reserve duty since the start of the current Intifada. He was in
a special unit called up frequently to the front lines. He did it
willingly, but it took a terrible toll. *A large percent of the guys in
my unit are getting divorced. I'm so glad I wasn't married during this
period—it might not have lasted.*

Raquel phoned Sarah. "I'm so scared!"

"You haven't even met the guy!"

"I know! But I don't want to walk into a situation where
marriages fall apart!"

"Relax! You're not marrying him just yet."

Raquel wrote:

*The rabbis say, "Who is strong? He who conquers the evil inclina-
tion." I see that as real strength, facing terrors daily. I admire you.*

Shim replied:

Re: Strength

*They say the recipe for the army's success lies in a rule called
"hatira l'maga" i.e. don't fire on your enemy from a distance—rather,
engage him in face to face contact, then you'll overcome him. I also used
to think I need to face things in order to win, but I don't anymore. Now
I think if you can stay away, if you're not needed on the frontline, then*

do . . . you'll save yourself damage. Damage to yourself is not strength. It won't help the Jewish people if everyone gets divorced or goes nuts.

Raquel's fears remained unabated. "Sarah, how can I not be scared? He's in Gaza, bang in the middle of it all. I want to stay right here in my safe little bubble."

"Safe little bubble?" Sarah laughed. "Honey, you live in Jerusalem, remember? Your local supermarket is the battlefront! Your local café is the trenches!"

"Yes, but at least here I can close my door on it all. I'm afraid that if I'm with him, he'll drag me into it all. He'll tell me all these traumatic stories and I'll have to listen."

"There are doors in relationships too."

"Not in my relationships!"

"In every relationship," Sarah said firmly. "Just learn to use them."

"OK, but what if he's really armyish and loves guns and stuff?"

"He already told you—he's just doing his duty. You guys really need to meet. You don't know him yet."

"I'm so *confuuuuused!*" Raquel wailed. "Why is it so complicated? Back in England I didn't have to deal with all these issues!"

"No, but you had to deal with something much worse."

"What could be worse?"

"English men!"

Raquel managed a laugh.

"Listen," said Sarah in a soothing voice, "he sounds like a great guy. Just meet him. You'll take it from there."

Shim was due to return on Tuesday, and Raquel pressed him to meet her immediately. He warned her he would be tired, but eventually gave in. On Tuesday morning, she laid out a purple dress with little flowers and some stylish black boots in readiness. At school, she logged on to the site during every break, staring at Shim's profile, sounding his name out in her mind. She felt as if she already knew him, his eyes, the way he moved his arms. She was extremely disappointed when he phoned in the late afternoon and said breathlessly, "Sorry, sorry, Arafat's making trouble and I can't leave Gaza. I'll be in touch."

"Bloody Arafat! Can't he mind his own friggin' business?" said Emma. Emma was a lunatic, but she certainly gave a good rant in defense of a friend.

"Yeah!" Raquel echoed indignantly. "Some of us are trying to get married here!"

"Selfish goat. He's got Suha—can't they just go live on the French Riviera and leave us alone?"

"Do you suppose Yasser and Suha met on Frumster?"

Emma hooted down the phone. "Ha! Nine-million-year-old terrorist, close resemblance to iguana, seeks trophy blonde for seedy international purposes? I wonder, when he was filling out his form, what kind of headcovering did he put down?" She affected an outlandish Arabic accent. "*Rabak!* What is this? *Black suede kipa?! Black hat?!* Why does this website have no category called *I wear a Keffiyeh in the shape of Palestine on my head*? A curse upon your mother's moustache, Zionist fascists!"

Raquel laughed till she cried.

That night Raquel sat, feeling lonely and depressed, in her old armchair, her eyes fixed abstractedly on the soiled raincoat dangling from its hook. Suddenly she reached out a foot and kicked it. She felt a deep hatred for all of them, all these men who loved war and death. It was an exciting game that saved them from facing life's real challenges—to be a *mensch*, to deal with the banality of life, wife, children and work, the daily challenge of decent behavior, resisting grandiose emotions. No, that was too dull—so they rushed around brandishing their toys and shouting puffed-up slogans, dying by the dozen but without the courage to live. *I wish I could wake up tomorrow and discover they had all gone, leaving us to go back to the Israel we love—to a thriving economy, and to our nice hikes, buses, cafés, and parties. To our plans for a meaningful hook-up for that wolf and that lamb.*

The raincoat swung mournfully and Raquel sighed.

If wishes were buses, then I could ride.

Raquel and Shim arranged to meet the following Sunday. However, Shim got called back to Gaza yet again, and then Raquel had to go to England for her nephew's bar mitzvah, replete with hordes of family and far too much greasy food. All week long she battled relatives who asked, with a wink and a leer, "How's your *social life?*" This was a very thinly disguised way of saying, "Good Lord, girl, aren't you married yet? You're about to hit your sell-by date!"

Raquel always smiled sweetly and said, "We'll get there, God willing," and then they all said hastily, "Oh, yes of course. Jolly good."

Patronizing gits. She was too nice to thrust her nails in retaliation into their wounds, though they surely deserved it. She knew exactly what to say: *How's your anorexic teenager doing? How's your pompous lump of a husband who can't even see how stupid he is? Why does your wig always look like something the cat dragged in? Jolly good, jolly good.*

The only person who seemed to truly understand was her gay uncle, in from Berlin for yet another masochistic, painful attempt at rebuilding his connection with the family. *A fraternity of misfits*, she thought, burning with pity for him and herself.

Then there was her mother and the pathetic tremble in her voice as she begged, "Are you quite sure you don't want to come home? I'm worried sick about you." She told Raquel yet again about the awful dreams. Souls from the other side were warning her that Raquel must return to England or something terrible would happen imminently. In the past Raquel had always snapped, "Oh mum, not that rubbish again!" But now, herself plagued nightly by dreams of the talking dead, she no longer felt as convinced that her mother was merely experiencing random neurons colliding in gray matter. Perhaps there really was a psychic gift in the family. "Do you really think the dead send us messages?" she said in horror to her mother one day over lunch. "Oh, absolutely," her mother replied. "It's a known thing."

No, she insisted to herself. *I don't believe in ghosts.*

It was difficult being in England, but also in some ways very easy. Too easy. In this lovely house where she had grown up, she could finger the little dresses she had made for her dolls and remember a dreamy, glad child for whom every day was a new adventure, skipping down London's streets and crunching the mounds of red leaves beneath her boots. Now, sprawled on her soft pink bedroom carpet, lying perfectly still, she wondered if she could still retrieve that girl from underneath the years of trauma and loneliness. She no longer knew. How could she heal from the trials of life in Israel if fresh wounds kept coming every time some other horror occurred? How could people stand it? Perhaps her mother was right and she should return to England. In the face of all the violence, her love for Israel festered and became stale. Yet still she clung to her romantic notions, like an abused wife unwilling to let go.

In London, Raquel did a lot of shopping, relieved to be able to be in a crowd without fear of being blown up. The rest of the time she spent curled up in the den, watching TV shows. But her pleasure was ruined by the news, where commentators sounded off knowledgeably: "Israel has used every means of force—deportation, destruction of homes, assassination. It's about time they realized force can't create security." Raquel hurled her slippers at the screen in frustration. Who were these British who took upon themselves to decide that everything was the fault of the Israelis? Weren't the other side to be held responsible for anything, not ever? Only once, toward the end of her trip, when she heard someone say, "Do they think they can keep the Palestinians in their cages forever?" did she suddenly feel sympathy. Surely there must exist innocents on the other side who, like her, were not filled with hate, who were simply suffering from decisions made by idiots in power that destroyed their lives. Who would actually rather make peace than fling Raquel and her people bodily into the sea.

Every time something appeared on the news about Israel, as it did far too often for a country that was famously the same size as Wales, her sister, sprawled on the other couch would urge, "Darling, what's holding you there? Come back here and live with me!" But Caroline, heels dug deep in Anglo-Jewry, had never experienced the magic of Israel as Raquel had. For her, Israel was a holiday location with the advantage of lots of kosher restaurants and the Western Wall.

And anyway, said a pragmatic voice in Raquel's head, *chances of meeting a new Jewish man in London are slim—and back in Israel awaits my Shim.*

The voice lied. When Raquel returned battlescarred from England, an apologetic email from Shim informed her that he had met someone else.

"How did this happen?" Raquel wailed to Emma. "He had no time to even meet *me*! Where did this woman come from all of a sudden?"

Emma said unhelpfully: "It must be Fatima from Gaza City."

Raquel called Sarah. "Now what do I do?!"

"It wasn't meant to be. Go back to the site and try again."

So try again she did. Very soon she became hooked, surfing the site every night, reading profiles for hours and writing messages, though rarely actually meeting up with a man, for something always seemed to get in the way. When an enormous telephone bill arrived to her shock, she replaced her modem with DSL. From that point on, Frumster became her life. Current events meant checking who was online. This was so much better than the news. Far fewer fatalities.

The world shrank into the fourteen inches of her screen. She loved that she could stare at the faces in their little boxes whenever she wanted, with no visiting hours or feeding times. The pictures came online and logged off, avatars for those distant lives. She noticed that many men had submitted pictures where they faced to one side, as if ashamed to be caught there, or as if their digital camera had sneaked a picture while they weren't looking, and then furtively posted it on the site muttering, "I gotta help this loser get married." The hopeful pitches seemed endless:

I'm laid-back, nice . . . I'm a fun, cool guy . . . Hey, there, thanks for dropping by . . . I've been told I am the best uncle in the world . . . A serious learner, frum . . . Friends tell me I'm a mensch . . . Ladies, take a look at my profile! Modesty aside, I am a superior specimen!

Eventually all the words and voices blurred together into one huge babble of self-promoting loneliness banging around inside her head. But still she could not drag herself away from the site. She marked papers in front of the screen, watching as men logged in or signed off. They came and went in batches, depending on the time zone. When she went to school in the morning, a few early risers in Israel and Europe were online, together with the West coast men and the East Coast night owls. But when she returned in the evening, everyone was awake and active, and the site would proudly announce 169 *online now!*. She imagined the men across the continent and over the ocean, bored at their desks in law and accounting offices or in university libraries.

She soon became familiar with the habits of particular individuals. *Seaview* obviously had no access to email during the day, as he only logged on at night. *Blatt* had set aside Sunday as his day to find a wife. And *Nush-nush* seemed to be online twenty-four hours a day. "Don't you ever sleep, *Nush-nush?*" Raquel would murmur at his skinny bespectacled photograph. She puzzled over how a religious man could be online during Shabbat, when using the computer was forbidden. The riddle was solved by Emma, who laughed roundly at her friend: it was his computer that was on all the time, not him. Of course. Raquel was reminded that these profiles were not people—the profile could be online when the person was not. She kept forgetting this, for it was with the profiles that she had a relationship.

The website also let her know when someone had looked at her. *UJ335* from South Africa looked at her profile every day or two. "What d'you want from me, sonny?" she said, clicking on his profile every time as if it would reveal the mystery; but he never made contact.

"It's amazing!" Raquel declared to her friends. "You know when someone across the world has seen your profile. You know what they're doing, what they're looking at. I feel omnipotent! I know how God feels!"

"You really don't," said Emma. "God's not busy turning into a cabbage while glued to some dating site."

"Au contraire, my love, that's exactly what He's doing," said Raquel. "And this is why the world's gone to the dogs." She stuck out her tongue at Emma, who made a horrible face back, crossing her eyes and slapping her forehead while making various ghastly sounds.

Raquel found the correspondences with men in America to be the richest, with long emails back and forth and ever-deepening confidences. They became Raquel's new friends and she was no longer lonely. Now, when something new happened in her life, instead of phoning Sarah or Emma or Frieda, Raquel wrote of it to Victor from Seattle, Rafi from Austin, Buzzy from Cleveland. She fell in love with one's sense of humor, another's depth and a third's modesty; and as she gave and received compliments, she felt more and more vigor returning to her heart. She began planning a visit to the US, a dating tour. *Please, God, if You do listen to prayers after all, one thing only I ask: help me with the money for this. Much love, your servant, insignificant mortal, Raquel.*

School became a game, the computer the only reality. Only on Shabbat, with the computer once more a graceless metal box on the desk, was Raquel forced to remember her other, "real" life. For the first time ever, she disliked Shabbat. She dutifully went to meals with other singles, but during the insipid conversations that never led to a date, her thoughts were on the Frumster men, wondering what they were doing at that moment. These Jewish men were her new hobbits and dwarves, and she was their elven princess.

Over time, however, Raquel realized that while this Frumstermarket appeared full of delicious-looking products, at the check-out counter her cart was always empty. Victor suspended his membership without warning. Rafi got into a relationship with someone else. Buzzy lost interest and wrote only sporadically. She was alone again, and all the men who contacted her seemed so lackluster, their profiles so unimaginative, that she could not bear even to write to them.

"Couldn't you think of anything else to say?" she sighed to *Chatanooga Jew Jew's* photo. He seemed very eager to meet her but his description began and ended with *My friends tell me I'm a good guy. I love sports and children, and want to have a large family with many Shabbat guests. Looking for my better half, my best friend—a woman of valor, a true "Eishet Chayil."*

And when Raquel found a man with some imagination and dared to contact him, he was never interested in her. She modified her profile but it made no difference. They often simply ignored her letters, which hurt terribly. Feeling her lifeblood draining away, she finally ceased searching and surrendered herself to the misery of her former life, schlepping herself through the incessant round of work and sleep. Her students made merry in her classes and she no longer bothered to discipline them. Her flat was dirty but she did not clean it. At night, the dead people returned, howling at her with vague, formless mouths. She caught herself wondering how her mother managed to understand their messages but even the thought *Oh God! Now I'm as mental as my mother!* barely moved her. And the bombings and shootings and stabbings continued, whether she listened to the news or not. Politicians changed their minds every week. Men with blood on their hands were released from jail for political reasons, only to murder again. Soldiers shot children and inquiries were set up. Endless traffic jams piled up behind roadblocks. Israelis left for Canada and L.A. and England. There was no light at the end of the tunnel— and by now no one even remembered life before the tunnel.

One afternoon in late December, Raquel saw a dead rat in the street, caught in a rusty trap. She stopped and stared at its glassy eyes and small stiff paw, flung out as if petitioning the heavens for clemency. Without warning, her legs buckled, and she staggered against the wall, liquid rolling from her eyes as if a sluice had opened in her head. Her legs barely carried her home; hours later she was still shaky. Emma phoned and began blabbing away about her fabulous boyfriend, while Raquel listened miserably. To distract herself she turned on the computer and checked for mail as Emma talked. Suddenly a piece of classical music, Handel's *Messiah*, blasted from the speakers, and Raquel dropped the phone.

"Crikey!" yelled Emma's voice from the floor. "What was that?"

Picking up the receiver, Raquel explained, "Sorry, sorry, a long time ago I set the computer to play that when a message comes in from a Frumster guy. Hold on a sec." She checked her inbox:

Frumster member Sweetdreamer has sent you a message.

"Emma, I'll call you back." Raquel hung up and logged on to the site to read his message:

Greetings, dear searcher—search no more!
For when a lock meets its key,
then the soul greets its Maker,
and thanks Him for making
a half-soul
whole.
You're amazing! I want to know you. I want to take a stroll with you in the beautiful streets of Jerusalem. Write to me soon
Jay (Sweetdreamer)
P.S. Did I mention that I like you?

Gongs and clappers sounded in Raquel's heart, as if a troupe of folk dancers had run amok inside her. She clicked on Jay's profile. He was thirty-two, and lived in Pardes Hannah (where was that?). Slim and tall. The picture revealed a handsome man, with soft chestnut curls, a wide smile, frank brown eyes. Raquel stared at his picture for several long moments. She experienced a peculiar sensation that this man was connected to her in some profound way. She had to drag her eyes away from his face to read his description:

I recently returned from several years in the States, with an advanced degree from an Ivy League school. I enjoy learning Torah and Kabbalah. I also like movies, hiking, and waterskiing; love reading (classics, moderns, sci-fi) and music, especially baroque. I'm also a published writer. I thank God for my successes, and for my failures too.

I'm a romantic, so don't expect anything less than sunsets, flowers and fiddles, candles, the whole shebang. I take my life seriously but need to laugh often or I feel something dying inside (extra points if you like Python/Far Side/The Onion) My ambition is to learn something new every day, support my family, and never stop cherishing my beautiful wife. When I go, I aim to leave behind a better world.

Raquel had stopped breathing. She wrote back at once.

Jay, I love your profile. I feel sure that we have loads in common and can't wait to talk more. I can tell you haven't been here for the past couple of years. Jerusalem's streets aren't so beautiful now, they're empty of people, like that verse from Eichah: "How lonely sits the city, that was full of people; she has become like a widow." I don't dare to go to restaurants or the cinema anymore. This city was once so vibrant, but now the image that comes to mind is that of an old woman schlepping a massive burden on her back, so bent over she can't see anything but her own scabby feet. It's been truly awful witnessing this, like watching it happen to your own mother.

Raquel felt pleased with what she had written—she hoped her letter would impress him, though she wondered if it was a tad too heavy for a first email. She kept watch at the computer. Half an hour later, the little orange *Unread* changed to a blue *Read*. But it was only hours later, after Raquel, exhausted from surfing aimlessly, had practically fallen asleep at her keyboard, that his message finally came in:

Dear Raquel,

Thank you for sharing your feelings about Jerusalem with me. After several relatively worry-free years in the US (except for the failure of a serious relationship) I am slowly soaking up the awfulness here. Not that I was oblivious of it there, but it's different close-up (I don't need to tell you).

Not to discuss politics too much, but I must admit that with every new wave of violence I've moved further right. I used to think the right-wing were blocking peace with their unattainable dream of greater Israel, but now I think it's Peres with his pie-in-the-sky New Middle East who didn't get what we're up against. Enough with the Utopias; someone has to get real. People are dying and we have no partner.

Anyway, on to more pleasant things. Such as your name Raquel, ringing in my ears like a sweet bell.

Let me tell you that I really want to move from Pardes Hannah (my parents' home) to the most amazing city in the world. I'll come visit Jerusalem soon, and then we can meet up.

Jay

Despite the late hour, Raquel immediately wrote back.

Dear Jay,

Your comments are spot on. The worst thing is about it all that it's affected my religion too. What am I supposed to think about God when His chosen people are shot, mutilated, and slaughtered? It's like we're His punching bag. Aren't we fools, for believing each time, for praying despite it all? Did we learn nothing from the Holocaust? My faith is in tatters.

Raquel read and reread her words, feeling an awe of sorts. He was drawing out of her a voice she did not know she had. The message sent, she tried to sleep, but colored lights pranced in front of her eyes for many minutes. Eventually they faded, leaving her to the sound of her breathing. This time she heard nothing of the helicopters overhead or the sirens yowling in the night.

Three days later, Raquel lay on her bed, one arm across her stomach, the other flung over her eyes. How surreal. In a brief time, this stranger, this random man, emailing her from some pothole up North, had become more important to her than life itself. With a flick of his wrist, Jay had opened up some rusty portcullis inside her and ambled breezily into her holy of holies. It moved her and terrified her in equal parts.

At school she checked the computer every break and wrote as much as she had time for. She taught on autopilot, not entirely aware of what words were coming out of her mouth (had she really taught them that the capital of Australia was Melbourne?) And she fantasized constantly about her wedding. Mid-April would be good—it was almost four months away, long enough to arrange things, and her relatives could stay on for Pesach if they wished. Maybe a trip to Eilat could be thrown in—they would feel safer there, far away from the bombs. She hoped no one would stay away, as had happened to a friend of hers whose sister had pleaded that she was not afraid for herself but could not bear to risk leaving her children without a mother.

She would design the invitation herself, she decided, doodling on a pad. It would bear their initials, a J and an R, with lots of curls and flourishes. Then their names, intertwined, with leaves growing from the letters: *Jay and Raquel* . . . . Damn! She must remember to ask Jay his surname. She always forgot, there was so much else to write about.

She read the old emails again and again. She already knew many of his phrases off by heart.

You are one terrific lady.
I should snatch you up while I still can.
Your opinion means so much to me.
When I write to you it feels like home.

They made her feel limp, like one of Dali's floppy watches. Jay planned to come to Jerusalem in a week to flat-hunt, and they would meet for the first time. The week stretched ahead like seven years instead of seven days. She occupied her mind trying to decide where to go, to make the first date a special one they would remember for the rest of their lives together. The promenade in Talpiot? The Old City? Yemin Moshe?

A message alert came in from Frumster and Raquel sat up quickly. They were still communicating through the site. They should have moved to regular email already but Raquel loved the thrill of the alert in her inbox: *Frumster member Sweetdreamer has sent you a message.*

She read it greedily. Jay was finally opening up about his previous relationship back in the U.S. Raquel felt repugnance for this woman who had caused her sweet dreamer so much angst. She must have been crazy to let him go. Jay expressed his confidence that it would be different this time. He also wrote in a postscript, *Can you send a photo so I can have a face to talk to? I'd love to see your hazel eyes—first in a picture, and then, reflecting the sunset . . . .*

Reading this she panicked. She owned no digital photo of herself, or even a scanner. Then she remembered her photograph on the school website. Looking at it, she blanched. She was not smiling, and the colors were way off. She bore a close resemblance to a corpse—skin milk-white, and eyes dark holes in her skull. She stared at it for a long time, and then decided that she was being silly. Every sensible person knows that the camera always lies. So she wrote back, directing him to the school website to see her image.

Then, since he had been so open and she now felt safe enough to match his confidences with her own, she told him about her relationship history and its discontents, decanting vinegary feelings last shared with a therapist some three years previously. For years now, she told Jay, she had suffered from a maddening pattern, whereby new relationships seemed magical at first but somehow always became increasingly dull until they fell apart. The therapist had tried to help her break out of this; but since then it had worsened to the point where now even the initial magic was gone, and all she felt on the first date was a bland emptiness. It was no surprise, therefore, that the men often rejected her. It hurt so much; they failed to understand that she only needed someone to bring her back to life with his love. She wrote:

But now all that will change. With your help in fighting off my demons, I can feel again.

Jay. To say your name is to pray all my lost prayers.

The next day, no messages came in. All day Raquel checked repeatedly in increasing panic and disbelief but her inbox remained empty. By evening, anxiety had spread in a lump across her midriff and up to her head, where it lodged, throbbing. What was Jay doing for so long away from email? She already knew intimately the delicate motions of his mind, but of the prosaic details of his day-to-day she knew next to nothing. Ignoring her mother's anxious messages on her machine—who had patience for her absurd ravings?—she phoned Sarah.

"Oh sweetie, I hate to say this but I think you got in too deep too quickly. Email's dangerous—believe me, I'm speaking from experience. I once emailed someone for a month, and I really thought he was my soulmate, but the moment I met him I knew it'd never work. Email distorts things, especially for people with a lot of imagination like you. It hides what's real and implies what's not."

"I see." But Raquel was not listening—she was checking her account again. By midnight, her head was buzzing so ferociously she could hardly sit up.

"What is it? What's happened?" said Sarah sleepily.

"Oh God, I'm so sorry to wake you up, but he's not responded yet! I can't take it!"

Sarah yawned loudly. "Raquel, listen, you've known this man for four days! You know nothing about him—"

"I looked so horrid in that photo!" Raquel whimpered. "He found me ugly—that's why he's not writing!"

"You're beautiful! I'm sure it's not the photo." Her friend's voice softened in sympathy. "Hey, you know nothing about his schedule. He may have taken a trip somewhere. Stop being silly and go to sleep."

"You don't understand," mumbled Raquel, clutching the phone, "he's not like that." As she hung up, she whispered dully, "*We're* not like that."

Raquel spent the night squirming in her bed, and got up the next morning fusty and glowering, her hair all spikes. She had dreamt again of corpses shouting gibberish at her but once again had not caught their message. She felt as if something had detonated in her, turning her organs to mud.

Still no email. She hated him. Did he not at least have the decency to write and admit her photo had put him off? Should she write and explain that she did not really look like that? It felt so humiliating. Raquel stomped into school, plunked her bag down on a chair in the staff room and went to slam shut a window that was letting in chilly air.

"*Boker tov*," said Marly, a fellow English teacher in her fifties. Raquel could not force her usual smile. She managed a nod, and rifled noisily through her bag for her papers.

"Yes, I'm upset, too," said Marly and sighed. "Another *piguah*. It's just unbearable, unbearable. I just want to tear out my hair, to lie down and die."

Oh, another attack? What a surprise. Raquel continued to rummage. *Well I don't care anymore. Letting those murdering animals out of jail—what did they expect? This stupid bloody country, everyone killing each other instead of communicating like human beings. Insane, they're all insane.*

"I have a sister up there, in Hadera," Marly continued. "I was so worried till she called. They've been hit a few times. It's not just us Jerusalemites; we forget that sometimes."

Raquel slapped her papers down on the table with a grumpy thump. Then she froze, and said, "Hadera? Is that near Pardes Hannah?"

"Oh yes, right next door."

Raquel lunged for the newspaper from the next table. She struggled frenziedly through the Hebrew, wishing she had studied the language more diligently at Ulpan. The details were all there: Seven people killed, twenty-four wounded. A car packed with more than 100 kilograms of explosives had pulled up next to a bus near the Karkur junction. On route 65, near Pardes Hannah, the previous day at 11 a.m.

"Oh my God, oh my God," muttered Raquel. "The names of the dead—where are the names?" Her eye ran over the profiles and then halted abruptly. There! Yaakov Wolfson, aged thirty-two, from Pardes Hannah! There was a blurry picture of a young man with a grave expression, short hair and soft eyes. It did not look much like his Frumster picture, but it had to be him; she felt it deep in her abdomen. There could be no doubt. *Yaakov equals Jacob equals Jay.*

"Raquel, what's going on?" said Marly, putting her arm around Raquel's shoulders. Her eyes filled with concern. "Not someone you know?"

"Yes—no—I . . ." stammered Raquel, and picked up the paper again. Where were the funeral details? "Marly, I have to go. Tell them I had to go."

"Are you crazy?" yelled Sarah. Raquel, in the back of a cab traveling northwards, held her mobile phone away from her ear. "He doesn't reply for a day so you assume he's *dead*?"

Raquel collected her emotions carefully, as if they were crumbling leaves on a lawn. "Yes, it's him, Sarah."

"Did he ever tell you his last name?"

"No. But I know it's him."

"Gosh, Raquel, this—this—I'm speechless." But she wasn't, and she continued, "You're gambling that your sweetheart Jay is this Yaakov guy with his fuzzy photo! And the stakes are a five hundred shekel taxi to Hadera and your sanity!"

Raquel said quietly, "I can see you can't listen to me right now. Talk to you later." She switched off her cell phone and leaned back, watching the flow of the passing landscape. Even under these circumstances it felt good to be finally out of the city, to see an uninterrupted arch of sky, fields and orchards. Raquel remembered how beautiful Israel could be. She had missed it.

Soon she closed her eyes, trying to prepare herself for what was to come. There was an odd peace underneath all the turmoil. A clear breath she had never felt before gathered deep in her lungs.

The road to the cemetery at Pardes Hannah was a mass of cars, so the taxi had to drop her off far from the entrance. It was much warmer here than in Jerusalem, and she stripped off her coat. Feeling drugged and yet strangely focused, Raquel followed the sluggish crowd. From a distance, it seemed, quite far off, came a moaning sound; Raquel was not even sure it was human. Impatiently she began pushing through the throng, elbowing aside the damp bodies, squeezing herself between heads and backs, collecting other people's sweat on her face and arms. She had no idea if it was over already, but she pressed on, sliding, stumbling once or twice, pushing blindly onward. *Jay. Jay.*

As she got closer she could hear the sounds of speeches—eulogies. She passed people crying, and still she pushed forward, dry-eyed.

I'm coming. I'd planned our first meeting a little differently. I'm sorry, Jay.

Finally she stumbled into the innermost circle, and there was the body, stiffly wrapped and covered with a white prayer shawl. There was no coffin and she was glad. She could not bear to think of him inside a dark box.

Raquel stood for a few minutes, allowing the words of the eulogies to wash over her, registering only a mass of blotched, grieving faces ringing the body, and from the Hebrew speeches, the single word Yaakov, over and over.

Oblivious of the dull pain in her limbs, Raquel began inching forward toward the body, stretching forth her hand. She would touch him—at least that, in lieu of a life together; at least that. *Jay.*

She was almost there when a dark woman with peroxide-blond hair and expensive sunglasses caught her arm, pulling her back into the crowd. Raquel tottered and would have fallen, but the woman held her firmly and dabbed at her face with a tissue. She whispered sibilantly in Hebrew, "You were close to Yaakov?"

Raquel swayed. Her throat burned and the sun beating down made her head swim, though her heart remained a hunk of ice. The woman's eyes behind the dark sunglasses blinked like a scuttling lizard. She repeated her question. Raquel nodded weakly and replied in English, "I'm his widow."

The woman pulled her hand away as if she had touched something rotten. Raquel wanted to explain: *A priest may come into contact with the dead—for close relatives.* But instead, she turned away. Gasping, hand over her mouth, she began shoving her way back out through the mourning throng.

Raquel took a bus home, her first in two years. Her head jolted against the window and she did not care. In fact, she spent the entire journey praying for a Palestinian rock to come ripping through the window and split open her head. Then at least she could see Jay, in heaven, if there was a heaven. She wondered if Jay could see her from wherever he was now.

When she arrived home hours later, with blistered feet and smudged eyes, Sarah was waiting for her at the front door. She put her arms around Raquel's lanky frame and Raquel slumped against her like a long-limbed doll.

For the next couple of hours, despite Raquel's repeated insistence that she just wanted to be alone, Sarah sat with her and made sure she ate. Finally she left and Raquel went immediately to turn on her computer. Of course there was no email from Jay. How could there be? God had finished playing His sick joke and was laughing now at His handiwork.

I hate you God. And there I was thinking You might want to help me raise a Jewish family in Israel. Silly, silly me!

She wept, bashing her fist upon the desk and wishing it were her head. When she had calmed down a little, she turned back to the screen and dizzily opened Jay's profile. There he was, smiling, brown-eyed and earnest, looking so very alive. What would happen now? Frumster had instructions about how to remove your profile—*I'm married and I no longer need your services. How do I remove myself?* But there was nothing saying, *I've been blown into smithereens and no longer need your services. Please remove me, for I cannot remove myself.*

Should she write to them?

Dear Frumster,

I'm sorry to tell you that Member 1743 was recently murdered. Please remove him from your lists as he is no longer a very good catch. Or at least modify your categories: Single (never married), Divorced, Widowed, Dead (never married).

Dead, never married. Never lay next to his cherished wife, watching her smooth face golden in the slatted light of dawn, haloed by her hair on the pillow. Gone, leaving behind only a bloodstained bus seat and a ruined heart.

Dear Frumster.

Please remove Sweetdreamer from your lists as he belongs to me now. To me alone.

The next day Raquel did not go to school. She unplugged the phone and ignored the knocks at the door. Tearing a long rip in one of her T-shirts, she put it on and sat on the floor with the blinds down, unaware of the ceiling flaking on her head. She felt the sweet love that had been circulating in her bloodstream curdling in her, the black dirge in her heart, the void gaping at her center. So much had been left unsaid. With all her greedy joy at his compliments, she had forgotten to ask him so many important questions, or even simply to say, *I like you too.* Too late now.

All day Raquel felt she was about to throw up, but she forced down water, and lay on the floor and it passed. In the afternoon, she got up and went to her computer, and once again opened Jay's profile. She read his words again through puffy eyes. Suddenly she noticed the link at the bottom of the screen:

Send a message to Sweetdreamer! You have already sent sixteen messages and received twelve messages from this member.

Impulsively Raquel clicked on it, and typed, her fingers moving of their own accord:

Jay, my love, what a brief time we were given together on this earth. I know you are my zivug, ordained by God forty days before I was born. What shall I do now?

Then anger swelled. Palming away the tears, she pounded at the keys:

Jay you owe me an email! How you could you leave me without more of your sweet words to remember you by? You stupid, stupid man! Didn't I tell you buses are dangerous? Your body was mine, your soul was mine—how could you be so careless with my possessions??

She sent it, then got into her bed and lay under the covers, fully clothed. In her mind, dead people with shadowy mouths and elongated arms danced and beckoned on a hill of bones.

The following day passed somehow. The phone was still unplugged. She heard Sarah calling her name outside her window and tapping persistently, but did not get out of bed. In the evening, she picked up her paintbrush and painted circles within circles in oranges, reds and yellows on white sheets of paper, dozens of them. Then she slept for seventeen hours straight.

On the morning of the third day since the funeral, Raquel got up. She felt different, as if awakening from a strange dream. She was starving, and grabbed handfuls of crackers and hummus and whatever else she could find in her fridge. There was still a deep aching sadness in her, but she was surprised to find herself also looking forward to school, to her pupils' impish expressions, as if she had not seen them for weeks. She showered and put on clean clothes, then stumbled around her pigsty of a flat, running a wet rag over sticky surfaces and putting away loose papers. As she passed the moldy raincoat on the hatrack, she reached for it and crossly threw it down by the door. Today would be its final day cluttering her house.

Raquel unlocked the front door. Clouds were gathering; it would rain.

She returned to get an umbrella from her room, but on impulse, turned on her computer instead. Before stepping out again into her life, she wanted to read what she had written. She was a fool, she knew, sending a dead person a message; but it was a goodbye of sorts, and goodbyes are important.

When the message box opened, she was poised to click on the message she had sent, to reread it—but her hand froze on the mouse. The message marker had changed from the orange *Unread* to the blue *Read*.

Raquel blinked at the little marker. An icy sensation spread up her spine. What was going on? Had she made some mistake? *What was this?* She could not even articulate the idea rising in her mind. It was unthinkable, horrendous.

She stood there, paralyzed. Perhaps a minute passed, though it felt like forever. Then she had another thought:

What if a new message comes in?

She gasped in horror and was finally galvanized into action. Shuddering uncontrollably, she moved her limp fingers on the mouse, quickly positioning the cursor on *Delete Your Membership Permanently*.

She clicked it.

She pulled the plug. The screen flickered once, then became black. She sat for several minutes, motionless, just looking at the lifeless screen. Then, with leaden limbs, as if in a dream, she slowly returned to the front door and re-locked it.

Bending over stiffly like an old woman, Raquel picked up the crumpled raincoat by the door. She slipped her arms through its sleeves, and sat down in the sagging armchair, buried in the coat's rank folds, its greasy collar upturned against her face. Her nose wrinkled but she did not move. Her mind empty, she watched the sky darken and the walls close in upon her like a tomb.

Katamonsta

BLOGNAME: KATAMONSTA
WARNING: THIS BLOG MAY BE HARMFUL TO YOUR HEALTH. PLEASE CONSULT YOUR DOCTOR UPON FIRST SIGNS OF NAUSEA OR DEATH.
ABOUT ME: My name's Emma. Grew up in Manky and now reside in Katamon, J-town, Israel (I'll change that to "live in Katamon" when I actually get a life). My friends think I'm crazy. My enemies think my friends are crazy.

August 19th 2002

Hello again, blogfellows! Today I learned that I am the queen of shortcuts. It only took me forty minutes to walk from the zoo in Malcha back to Katamon. There are a lot of back passages and cut-throughs (what we used to call "ginnels" in the old country) in Katamon—you need to know them to get around, otherwise you can spend three hours getting from your house to the *makolet* down the road.

My friends R and S taxied it back but to be honest, I couldn't be bothered with their company anymore. Sorry to bitch but R has become the biggest Bridget Jonesy *kvetchbag* ever. All she can think about is tying the proverbial knot. She once had personality, I remember, back in kindergarten (love ya, R).

Funny, but I realized that what I do at work is also all about finding shortcuts—how to get things done when the budget doesn't quite stretch. So it's like an *organising principle in my life*. Wow! So that's what an epiphany feels like. I've always wondered. Kinda fuzzy and nice and swinging in your face. Like furry dice.

POSTED BY EMMA   2 COMMENTS

September 1st 2002

My boss Itzik is very intellectually challenged. We just hired a bunch of foreign workers hailing from somewhere in Asia for some repair work we've been asked to do at Yad Vashem, the Holocaust museum. Of course, they all have these odd Asian names like Hi Lo and Fu Manchu, but Itzik isn't even attempting to learn them. First he called them all Ting (his pronunciation of "Thing"?) but that wasn't effective, so I, the wonder-woman of shortcuts and efficiency, suggested we number them from one to sixteen. This worked excellently. Now you can hear him shouting, "Seven! Where's Twelve today? Two, get that mud off your shoes before you walk all over the tiles!" And they just take it from him, the daft buggers. Well, I guess they need to eat; and there are worse things in the world than someone not knowing your name.

POSTED BY EMMA   2 COMMENTS

September 10th 2002

Zounds! I spend my life surrounded by whingeing singles. Yes, friends, the Jews can no longer claim to have a monopoly on suffering. There is a new demographic for self-pity. Jesus wept! (He was a thirty-something single too, our Yoshke. But he was lucky. He was crucified before the matchmakers could get to him.)

So here's my tuppence 'orth: Whoever invented marriage was one sick bazook. Married people are so dull, it's so obviously all a trap to get babies into the world and prevent revolution. Marriage is the opium of the masses. Hello! Has no one read such excellent works of feminism as *The Cinderella Complexion* or *My Mother Mein Kampf*??? We don't need to hide behind a man anymore, we're liberated. The prison door is swinging open but no one's walking out. There are loads of things they don't tell you till it's too late. After I begged and threatened, one of my married friends told me some of the secrets. Like after you get married you're always tired, even if you've just slept the entire weekend. And like if you see a couple sitting in a restaurant with nothing to say to each other, they're married. Anyone yapping away vigorously is either still single or is with someone who is *not* their spouse. I really thanked her for being honest with me (poor duck, she was then abducted by men in suits). The whole marriage thing is just as much of a conspiracy as who shot JFK or JR and I wish someone would make a documentary and blow it wide open.

And it's even worse if you're Jewish. The number of your offspring doubles or triples, and, as if you weren't tired enough, you spend all your free time going to the bar mitzvahs of all your friends' brats. And look at all these married Orthodox women with their hair covered in those repulsive shapeless snoody things! Who was responsible for that bright idea? "Hey, *frum* babes, let's all put our heads in cloth bags! Hooray!" It probably works to stop them from thinking too much, especially if the elastic is tight. I can imagine the super-religious man proposing to his girlfriend (who he's known for about ten seconds). He gets down on one knee and holds out a little velvet box. The woman takes the box and opens it demurely, and inside there is a sequin-studded tea-cosy for her head.

"My little *ziskeit*," says the gent, "I want you to spend the rest of your life with your head in this lovely sack."

"Oh yes, yes!" gushes she. "Amen to that!"

He smiles dreamily and adds, "And when it gets a bit threadbare we'll cut holes in it and use it as a nappy!" (That's *diaper*, you pignorant Yankee doodles—do I have to translate *everything* for you?) She blushes, and accepts upon herself sixty years of bad hair.

Look, I'm religious too (well, more religious than Stalin or Ozzy Osbourne, anyway) but I think that's going a bit far, to have to cover your hair for the rest of your life. How come your hair is suddenly so provocative the day after you get married when it wasn't the day before? And why do ultra-Orthodox women shave their heads completely bald and then *cover it anyway*?

By the way, I noticed that the Hebrew for "will you marry me" is "*hatinasi li*" which sounds suspiciously like "*hat in a silly*."

Say it ten times fast and you get *"in a silly hat."* You heard it here first, folks.

P.S. For those of you who asked—and also those who couldn't give a Horton's hoot—things are finally getting better at the office. I am training my boss Itzik, using classic Pavlovian techniques, to understand that if he shouts at me I will work slower. (He has also learned to salivate when I ring a little bell.)

POSTED BY EMMA   5 COMMENTS

September 18th 2002

You know, women are really fine being single; it's men who can't manage on their own. When God said "It is not good for man to be alone" he was talking about Adam, not Eve.

And yes, *Shy Shadow*, your comments are well-taken. Not only was Yoshke single but in fact God Almighty is single too. There are no other singles likened unto Him; He is, was and always will be Single. And I learned once in the name of Rabbi Soloveitchik that we are supposed to imitate God—it's called *imitatio dei*. So there we have it: us singles are in da God zone! Stick that in your *gemora* and smoke it, rabbis. Pah!

Actually, the only reason I would want to get married is to stop all the nosey parkers asking me when I'm getting married. It's the only solution with one hundred percent guaranteed results. My friend P suggested a less painful way might be a hard blow to the bonce with a sawn-off log—to the nosey parkers or to myself, either one is fine. She's going through a divorce, poor doll—yet another reason not to get married.

R said I might be able to get one of the foreign workers to marry me for a permanent visa, but only if he has an IQ of sixty or less and likes women who bear a close resemblance to a meerkat. I told her she wasn't at all funny but she said I had to publish it in my blog because of the nasty things I said about her. The truth is that Eight is quite good-looking, if you squint at him through a dirty window on a moonless night.

I have taught Itzik to understand that I am not Manchurian, I am Mancunian. He is really coming along nicely.

POSTED BY EMMA   1 COMMENT

September 26th 2002

OK, OK!!

I may be against marriage, but it would be nice to have a man to do stuff with. And I am so bored of the male flotsam that's washed up on these Katamon shores! So I'm gonna do the Internet thing! I'm not desperate or nuffink, it's just that all the losers seem to wash up around the Palmach street supermarket and wrap themselves clammily around the yoghurts. I just want a normal boyfriend; is that too much to ask?

So I'm going on to this website called Frumster. Stay with me, I'll do it now and report back in real time. I'll need a Username. I think I'll call myself *Monsta*.

Oh my word! Didn't expect a multiple choice test. If I fail will I be forbidden to Internet date? I mean look at all possible answers to *What is your religious observance?*

Modern Orthodox (liberal)
Modern Orthodox (machmir)
Yeshivish Modern
Yeshivish Black Hat
Hasidish
Sephardic traditional
Shomer Mitzvot
Carlebachian
Traditional and growing

Hell's bells! You've got to package yourself into a little box, so you can find someone who lives in exactly the same little box. To pair off with a beast of your own species, like in Noah's ark. And what in God's cabbage patch is *Carlebachian* when it's at home? I know that Shlomo Carlebach was a hippy rabbi and his followers are happy-clappy flakey types. But would someone really define themselves as that? Wait, I must do a search of Carlebachian men forthwith.

Wow, check this one out—I swear to God, I've just splattered cheese sandwich all over my screen:

Name
RebDude
This is how I describe myself:

I like the outdoors and sometimes live in a tent.
This is what I am looking for in a mate:
Someone who likes goats and knows how to make tasty
jams.

One down, five thousand nine hundred and ninety-nine
to go.
OK, I've cleaned my screen, but I still don't know what
to tick. Help! I wear black hats sometime, but I don't think
that's what they meant. *Modern Orthodox (machmir)* seems too
religious. I could land up being approached by a real caveman.
I remember once I dated a newly observant man who'd gone
off the deep end. His views were so unripe—brings to mind
those little grapes that taste so sour you wonder why they
are being marketed as a foodstuff. I remember he had these
stumpy fingers and didn't stop twisting them in his beard, and
he announced in his deep Californian drawl:
"I'm not interested in seeing movies. And I expect my wife
not to either."
I said, "But what if she wants to?"
He said, "I'll put my foot down."
I said, "On her head?"
We did not part as friends.
OK, I know you're in horrible suspense, so here's my decision. I'm going to categorize myself as *Shomer Mitzvot*. For
all you millions of gentile folk reading this blog that means
(at least to me) just plain old Jewishly observant, the basic
package. It'll do. Anyone who has a problem with that can
shove off, before I start my lecture on Judaism as a religion of
praxis, in modular dialectic opposition to the Christian faith-
based creed (I surprised you, didn't I? Hah! Shot down and sat
upon!).
Onwards.
Do you wear skirts or pants? You can tell this is not a British
site—"pants" in Queen's English means underwear, though
the word has probably never passed the Queen's lips ("My
husband's pants and I . . .")
I really don't think the question "Do you wear skirts or
underwear?" should appear on a dating site—except possibly

for Scotsmen. Certainly not for nice Jewish gals. Bleddy Americans.

Will you cover your hair when you get married, and how?
With a flowerpot, every Tuesday.

How often do you pray? How often do you learn Torah? What is your Jewish background? What is your college background? Do you smoke? Are you willing to relocate?

Arggh! Nobody expects the Spanish Inquisition! When are these questions going to end? I still have to write my personal essay and I'm already completely knackered. This is worse than A-level Biology with Mrs. Boyner.

OK, here's the personal essay. I only had the energy to spew out the following:

I'm stunningly beautiful—I've been told I look like a model (airplane). I'm energetic, witty and driven (by a chauffeur.) Also a pathological liar (I'm lying about that too). (I'm hoping that this last sentence will cause any of you who are robots to malfunction, as I do not wish to date a robot.)

I'm looking for someone with a great sense of humour, who loves people, and is RELAXED! No chain-smokers, religious freaks, or repressed homosexuals please. If you have commitment problems, go commit them elsewhere.

Please be a somewhat intelligent conversationalist—if I want to talk to a wall I'll go to the Kotel. And TALL; I don't want to get romantic with your bald spot. Basically looking for someone solid— liquids and gases need not apply.

Yeah, I know, crap effort, but I just want to get to the search.

Finally, the search! Hooray! I'm going to tick off all of my ideal characteristics—the exact age, weight, background, college education, religious philosophy, and attitude toward capital punishment I want in my ideal man. I am now awaiting with trembling earlobes and bated kidneys for it to produce the Ultimate Man . . . Uh-oh! The screen barks at me:

No members match your search criteria. Having problems? Widen your criteria!

Go widen your own criteria, you daft gits.

Right. I've lowered my standards and presto, I found some men! But they're all either too short, or too religious, or too educated, or not educated enough; and if they are tall, normal, and educated then they inevitably look like a bullfrog. ☹ One man seemed nice till I realised he's French. Ugh! Puke!!! I'd rather be dragged backwards through a bush by inebriated yaks.

Some of these men must have filled out these forms while they were asleep. Who are these nebs who put themselves down as *Single (never married)* and also *With children*? Now that's what I call alarmingly honest. Save something to tell on the second date, sugar. And who are these clowns who write they're *Modern Orthodox machmir (= strictly religious)* and then go on to say they never learn Torah? What are they, Modern friggin' Greek Orthodox priest *machmir*, for Blog's sake, that they don't learn Torah? Ignoramuses, more like; probably don't know their *machmir* from their Vermeer.

Oh and here's one who has given me an apoplexy (whatever that is). He has literally written *"No fatties please."* I swear to you on the life of Elijah! Ooh, I could just thrash him. I hope he dies totally *alone*! . . . in a rat-infested garret with no *heating*! . . . in friggin' *PARIS*!

POSTED BY EMMA   8 COMMENTS

October 1st 2002

OK, more on the enthralling Internet search for Mister Emma. This site is proving disappointing. I sent in a photo of a monkey as my main picture but they wouldn't accept it. I just thought it might make my profile stand out from that of the other six thousand women. And anyway, how can they know that's not really me? I might have a serious skin condition. Some of these men are definitely less attractive than a nice good-looking baboon.

Anyway, I've contacted men with names like *Golem* and *Spittoon* and *Mensch* and *Menschlich* and *Truemensch* and *BigFatMensch* and *IAmTheWalrus*. Some of them wrote back that I'm not religious enough (and who are you to judge? The Lord Almighty Himself?) or too tall or too witty or too English. Some of them did not even have the courtesy to reply. Well, all

I can say, in true Israeli style is: *"I don't put on you in the slightest! You interest my bottom! Jump to me, you rubbish!"*
POSTED BY EMMA   6 COMMENTS

October 17th 2002
Well. I went out with *Spittoon*; he was actually kinda short and shiny, so the name fit. Lawdy-lawd, he was so dull—every sentence began with "back in the old days" as if he was 152 years old. And I met *YetAnotherMensch* for coffee at Masaryk, but he talked non-stop for two hours about himself, and when I finally said, "Perhaps you want to ask *me* a question?" he said, "Uh, sure—where's the bathroom?" I additionally walked around the industrial zone in Talpiot on a fruitless search for a *milchik* restaurant with a totally obstropolous vegetarian slaphead whose name I've wiped from the hard disk. None of them were worth the effort of moving my bum off my chair and missing a rerun of *Friends* (or even of *I Love Lucy*).

I have discovered some natives who have infiltrated the Frumster site, though entirely unburdened by a knowledge of the English language. How courageous are these Dibs (Dear Israeli Brethren); they let no obstacle stand in their chosen path. "If you will it, it is no dream," as good old Hurts-all used to say (understandably this did not particularly satisfy many sleep-disturbed Viennese people, who preferred instead to go across the road to Ziggy's couch for dream analysis).

So I received a message from *Yar8n*, who is a
Good Israelien guy with kind hearth.
Stabl, religus ect. ect.
Intrest, help, good relations, wan4t to meat kind Jewi6sh woman with simlar.

Odds Bodkins! I can't go out with someone who has numbers in the middle of his words! Need a bloody calculator just to understand him!

I wrote back: *"Than9k you but I don't thi7nk we have the right chemis3."*

Ugh! I feel like reporting these wallies to Frumster, they just clog up the site. Call the plumber ASAP.

Anyroad up, I don't like Israeli men for the most part. They're so macho and knowitall and all they talk about is politics and religion and the army. Whereas English men can talk about football and the weather and—er—tons of other fascinating things.

It's quite amazing—when you read all these profiles everyone sounds like a saint. All they want to do is learn and grow and do *mitzvot*. They're all so spiritual. Where are all the selfish prats I know in real life? Here's one feller who's built like Schwartzenegger and whose photo makes him look so gormless that you feel sure he couldn't read his own name if it was tattooed on your forehead. In any other life he'd be a truck driver looking for a good time, but here he is, a Looby Hasid who says his lifelong ambition is to learn Torah and to host guests at his Shabbat table. Oh, the beauty of Judiasm.

I see on the site that *"The JSingles cruise is almost sold out of inside cabins."* I am going to write to them and ask if perchance there are any outside cabins still available? Frankly, I'd settle for a bench in a lifeboat, or even a spot floating in the sea alongside the ship, tied around my waist by a thick rope. All the better to make a quick escape, I reckon. I have no interest in single cruises, except for Tom, and he ain't single right now. (Tom my love, I will wait forever.)

I think R is about to join the site. Very exciting, I will be able to go spy on her profile and maybe send her fake messages from a cross-eyed seven-foot airline steward called Garp. Other friends are "not exactly inspired by my experiences," or so they say, and have declined my repeated urges to leap on the bandwagon. Wimps.

POSTED BY EMMA   12 COMMENTS

October 18th 2002

Oh, and another thing that infuriates me is that every second man writes in his profile that he's looking for an *"Eishet Chayil"**

*[literally a "Woman of Valour," referring to the superwoman from Chapter 31 of Proverbs, who is traditionally praised every Friday night in a song before the meal.**]

**[you get footnotes too in this blog. All part of the service.]

Now what does that mean, they want an *Eishet Chayil*? She doesn't exist; the whole thing is a myth, a metaphor. Look, even the first line proclaims "*A woman of valour who can find?*" Answer: "No one! *She's a fantasy. Duhhh.*"

So I decided to create a new profile of myself based on the "Woman of Valour," to show these men what their ideal woman really looks like. Stay with me, peeps, and open your Bibles at Proverbs 31 if you don't know what the 'ecky thump I'm on about.

Here's what I wrote:

My day is busy—I get up at 4am and make breakfast for everyone. By 6 or 7 I've already bought a field or planted a vineyard or two.

Then I might go to the gym in order to gird up my loins and make my arms strong. I also do arm-stretching exercises with the poor people who show up at the gym. I really like to exercise in their company as thus I feel both fit and rich.

Then I travel to Eilat or the Lebanese border to buy my groceries; it's important to me to buy my food from as far away as possible.

Now, boys, I'm a woman of means and thus a good catch, mind. I have my own clothing business, so my afternoons are spent looking for wool and flax, or spinning, or making scarlet clothing for my family (I find it protects them from the snow).

But don't worry, I'm an old-fashioned gal and I don't expect you to take any part in the running of the household. In our marriage, all you'll do all day is sit at the gates of the cities or go visit old-age homes, and though everyone will know that that is all you do, you will not be embarrassed at all. Seriously. Because you will have such an amazing wife.

And by the way, I should add that I am not at all pretty or attractive; in fact I'm just one level above hideous. But I fear God, and that's the most important thing—right?

Yah right!!! These religious boys, they're all *Tosfos* this and *Shulchan Aruch* that, but when it comes to the crunch they all want a gorgeous babe if they can get her, just like any red-blooded male under the sun. So much for *Eishet Chayil.* Pah!

POSTED BY EMMA   17 COMMENTS

October 20th 2002

I sent my new profile to S and she told me that this time I'd gone too far, making fun of a beautiful piece of Torah. She said that learning this chapter was one of the things that made her want to be a religious Jew, that this description of a woman full of industry and dignity was so different from the self-absorbed female role models she had grown up with, yadda yadda yiddle (ect. ect. as *Yar8n* would say).

"All right," I said, "don't get your knickers in a twist. It's just a little joke."

R told me I'm wasting my life. I said, "What's happened to your sense of humour? Was it outlawed by the Knesset when I wasn't looking?"

R said sorry, she's having a hard time right now. I forgive you, ducky. (But I will ask—is there a site for acquiring friends with a sense of humour? And if so, will I have to tick a hundred little boxes to get in?)

Anyway, no one has responded so far to my profile. Can I just say that if anyone is stupid enough to want to correspond with an ugly hyperactive clothing saleswoman, he deserves to be single for the rest of his life. And for the next three reincarnations too.

(BTW, do carnations have reincarnations? And if so are they called reinhumans? I think I was definitely a carnation in a former life; or perhaps a piece of kelp.)

POSTED BY EMMA   5 COMMENTS

November 18th 2002

Greetings, ladies and gentile men! Sorry haven't written for a while. Lots been happenin'. Finally, someone of my way of thinking wrote to me on Frumster. He said he thought my profile was hilarious and that he laughed for an entire hour after reading it. Anyway we met. He's a tall redhead from Canada and my mother is over the moon coz he's a DOCTOR. We've been seeing each other for a few weeks now. He's dead bright and we have a right smashin' time together. I knew that somebody somewhere would get my mindset if I just waited long enough. On this blog I'll call him W (no particular reason—his real name is Ilan).

POSTED BY EMMA   24 COMMENTS

December 27th 2002

Wotcher, fans, I'm back! I've been dating W for two months now. Things between us are really cushty and it's utterly fab, though I'm not thinking of the M word so don't even get me started. But I am going to do the hosting thing and make Shabbat lunch. Show him I can be just as domesticated as all the other fillies. He sounded pleased and is even cooking a cholent (an inedible Jewish food that looks as if it's already been eaten once).

But it won't be a conventional meal, don't worry fans—I have a little plan. I'm going to invite Karin, Ariel, Joanna, Kfir, Lucy, and Irena. I've spent all day in the kitchen giggling.

POSTED BY EMMA   9 COMMENTS

December 31st 2002

Narf! Things did not go quite as I imagined. I laid out a beautiful table, including the white tablecloth I nicked from the rabbi's house when I was nineteen. I put the carrot salad, roasted sweet potatoes, pumpkin pie, orange juice, and mango juice on the table. Everyone came in all smiley, and W looked really chuffed. I was waiting gleefully, with my tenters all hooked. But it was only when all seven were present that they looked at each other, and there was this moment of dawning realisation. You could see them blushing the same colour as their hair. What a sight! Totally priceless, bloggies! And so interesting, the different shades. Ariel's hair is dark russet, Karin's pixie cut is a flaming sunset colour; Irena's mane is a light pop blondy orange-from-a-bottle. I swear, dear readers, it was truly beautiful, like an art installation in my own home! I literally had to restrain myself from running out into the street to invite people in to look.

I clapped my hands and said in my best Scottish accent, "Welcome all ye redheads! Praise be to the Lord who hath made the colour orange! *Nu*, let's wash!" I winked at W, and only then did it hit me that summat was amiss. His face looked like desiccated coconut and my heart sank exactly like when I was six and was caught red-handed filling the dinner ladies' handbags with chocolate sauce.

There was this awkward silence. I smiled at everyone and herded them out and the meal got going, but the atmosphere stayed uncomfortable and the meal was short. Afterwards, I said to W, "What on earth is the matter with all of you?" and he told me that I had been insensitive. He said, "These people all thought they were invited because you liked them, not because of their hair colour."

I said, "Of course I like them! I just wanted to be a bit original! Why are you being so uptight about this?"

He put on his most poncy patronisng voice and said, "Emma, have you ever read Martin Buber?"

I said, "'Course I have." (Never heard of him.)

W said, "Well, you just turned your guests from a Thou to an It."

Considering I thought he said I turned my guests from a Thou to a Nit, which made no sense at all, I couldn't think what to say, so I just stood there gawping for a minute and then said, "Sod it, I thought you of all people could understand my sense of humour. I mean what's the bloody point?"

"You can't make a joke of everything, Emma," he told me. Now, I *hate hate hate* it when people say that to me and I never thought my beloved Ilan would, and it made me feel like yesterday's cheddar wrapped in last year's socks, so I put on my coldest voice and we had a li'l ol' spat and then I said, "Well I see you're not really into it anymore."

"Not so much, no," he said.

"You're really overreacting," I said.

"When you begin to understand what happened today, you can call me," he said patronizingly. That made me so angry I just said, "Goodbye then," in a very deadpan voice, and showed him the door in silence.

I am writing this three days later and my heart is still squelching around in my feet. I'm asking myself, "What in the name of all that's frog went wrong here? Did we really just break up over a mild prank?" And thus, here I am, my friends, with no one to take me to the New Year's Eve party on Nadia's roof.

Alone again, naturally . . . .

POSTED BY EMMA   31 COMMENTS

January 5th 2003

Thank you all for your condolences. Good riddance to bad rubbish, indeed. *Anonymous*, if you're going to tell me I have less emotional intelligence than a tin of dogfood, be brave enough to give out your name. OK, my love? Don't be a pillock.

Well, with no love life to speak of, let me tell you, dear blogreader, about the supermarket on Palmach street.

See, this is no ordinary supermarket. This is the place where all the Katamon singletons come to stock up. This is where you'll meet the ones you'll never run into at singles events or on Internet sites, coz they gotta eat, right?

The best time to meet people at this location is on a Friday morning. It's also at that time that you realise why the street is named for the Palmach, the pre-State army corps—coz when you're in there on a Friday morning, if you don't know how to fight your way with sharpened elbows into the queues that sprawl endlessly up each aisle, you're going to find yourself still there after everyone's gone home, spending Shabbat with the frozen peas. It's a wild place.

So on a Friday morning, we Katamon singlettes put on our lipstick and our second-best T-shirt (our best one is reserved for strolling casually down Emek Refaim) and pose next to the veggies, looking seductive and gorgeous while at the very same time like someone who would make a superior mother and worth choosing from all the rest (to paraphrase one of our own, "If you pick me, will I not breed?").

Did you know there are twenty ways to pick out tomatoes, of which only five are attractive to men? You did? That's odd, as I just made it up. But someone should really do that experiment! It's extremely important to us Katamon singlushkas to become familiar with the best man-catching way of choosing vegetables. Which vegetables, for example, would be considered by an eligible Jewish XY as most redolent of a nice Jewish home? Beetroots (for the borscht)? Or potatoes and onions (for the cholent)? These are questions of supreme existential import, and no one is guiding us in this matter. Help! Crisis! Where are all the rabbis, social workers and crazy old women when you really need them?

Speaking of experiments, let me digress for a moment to proudly say that I have thought up several very important psychological experiments. Most of them revolve around toilets. An underappreciated cultural resource, toilets. So in my first year of university I was feeling kind of depressed, lonely, bored, etc. etc.

and I thought of a great way to test how depressed I really was. We all shared these four loos which stood in a row, and being psychologically minded, I invented the "Toilet Method of Introspection." This is great because use of the facilities constitutes a good random sampling of times every day. The four toilets in my dorm represented Happy, OK, Mildly Depressed, and Super Depressed (aka "My Life is in the Toilet"). Whenever I needed to use the facilities, I would enter the one best reflecting my state of mind. Well, to my surprise, I noticed that I quite frequently used the "OK" one, so I learned that I was happier than I thought. It was very enlightening. I am now working on my Second Theory of Toilet Dynamics, which suggests that certain psychological types will be more likely to use particular toilets. Type A's for example would probably barge to the nearest loo, whereas shy types would go for the furthest one so no one will hear them expressing their bodily functions, heaven forfend. This could be of ginormous interest to advertising companies, who could put up different kinds of ads on the backs of different toilet doors based on the new "toilet profiling."

Woohoo, I'm going to be rich! Befriend me while you still can!

POSTED BY EMMA   29 COMMENTS

January 16th 2003

Shock! Horror! The supermarket is under new management—it's now called "Mr Cheapo"—and everything's been switched around. I saw all these people walking round and round, unable to find anything, and I bet a lot of people had to eat pineapple gnocchi with chicken-deodorant dressing for supper last night. I've been three times and each time I walk in I say, "Hey! Fruit! What you doin' over there, buddy? Get back here, now!" I mean life is hard enough for us singles as it is without shifting our eggs all over the place. Cruel, cruel world.

One good thing about no longer dating W-whose-real-name-is-Ilan is that while he really wasn't all that religious—believe me, that prat was quite a heretic in some ways that shocked even sinful me—for some reason he only ate food with certain strict kosher certificates. So whenever I went to the supermarket to buy us something, I spent hours squinting at all the labels looking for the right set of symbols that meant that the coffee had been slaughtered in the most kosher way and had no little adhesions in its lungs. It's such a relief now to just grab whatever's on the shelf—that is, after all, what I came to Israel for. If I want to squint at food, I can do it in the UK, where fewer people will shout rudely at me for blocking the aisle.

I must say, by the way, that the weirdest people show up at the supermarket. Yesterday I was standing at the counter behind two people. The first looked from the back exactly like your typical middle-aged national-religious Settler-type codger— he had a big bowl-shaped *kipa*, dangling *tzitzit*, sticker on his backpack saying "Hebron now and forever" etc. etc. In front of him stood—I was convinced—his skinny wife wearing typical woman-Settler clothes: striped long-sleeved shirt, with awful unkempt frazzly hair sticking out of baggy-snood-item on head (see my entry on <u>snoods</u>). Anyway, after a few moments I realised to my shock that Settler-Guy was actually there with stunning-young-blonde-in-short-skirt who was waiting behind the check-out counter and told him to hurry up. And what about dowdy-skinny-snoody woman, you ask? Gulp! She actually turned out to be a *man*! With dreadlocks! The snood was actually a rasta hat!!!

          POSTED BY EMMA   22 COMMENTS

January 20th 2003

What does Katamon even mean anyway? Anyone of you blogmeisters know?

Personally I call it *Katamoan*. This place can get extremely tiresome. OK, it's good to be with other singles, as you feel more normal and people don't ask you insulting questions all the time. And yet it's not really normal when you think about it, to be doing the same thing in your thirties/forties/fifties as you were doing in your twenties—swanning pointlessly around Ohel Nechama and bringing endless Riesling to endless meals full of pointless chit-chat, and meeting endless pointless guys (have you ever seen an endless pointless guy? not a pretty sight) and it's all so bloody POINTLESS and ENDLESS! Doesn't anyone have just one tiny point or end for a cute little Katamonsta who is soooooo tired of it all? SOS!

The natives—the Israelites, da Hebrew man—they call the singles community "The Swamp." Anyone who wants to know why is invited to simply tag along to one of our local singles events and witness the swamp creatures who've emerged from the deep for the occasion. Ugh does not even begin to describe it! Big Fat Ugh with Thousand Ugh dressing!

Come to think of it: weren't all those early Zionist pioneers famous for draining swamps? Yes in fact, that's what they did all day—drained swamps! Calling all Zionist pioneers—your services needed here chop-chop! Get that witch of En-Dor here pronto to revive them from the dead!

Harrumph. Anyhoo.

I, in fact, believe that Katamon stands for "Cat or Man," which is essentially the choice I'm trying to make right now. It's either one or the other, and at this point I don't really care which (is there a website for finding cats, too? *Catster? J-Cat? Stroked You at Sinai?*).

Or alternatively, somebody once told me that Katamon is the Cat in the Moon. Yeah! I don't see why the Man in the Moon shouldn't have a pet. He probably gets really lonely up there. (Know how you feel, my duckie!) Hold on a mo'—*he's* single ... oh no, not Jewish. Damn.

The Cat in the Moon—a new book by Dr Seuss:
The sun did not shine
It was too wet to play
So we sat in the house
All that cold wet day.

I sat there with Sally
She sat there with Harry
And I said, "How I wish
I had someone to marry!"
POSTED BY EMMA   4 COMMENTS

January 22nd 2003

More on the supermarket (don't tell me—I *know* I currently have the most exciting blog on the web). I found a packet of forty toilet rolls labeled as costing 3 shekels. I was so happy coz I once heard there's a law that says you pay whatever the label says; but when I took it to the counter the girl there said I had to pay the normal price, 35 shmeks. That was annoying! And then I found a can of mushrooms costing 119 shekels. I got really irritated and asked the Arab worker, Samer, how we're supposed to shop if all the price labels are wonky. He looked at me funny and told me that that's what the mushrooms really cost. Who would pay 119 shekels for mushrooms?

I went to a wedding last night. They had this enormous *challah* (that's special Jewish plaited bread). It was about five foot long, the *exact height* of the bride. Incidentally the word for bride in Hebrew is *kallah*, which is very similar to *challah*! Coincidence or freaky mystical random thing? (Cue Elton John's "I want to Eat the Bride" (Ugh, a bit too much Christian symbolism, methinks).) Anyway, they passed around pieces from it, and we singles were expected to eat them as it's a *segulah*, a special charm meant to help you get married. At every wedding we poor singles have to eat the magic *challah* and drink the magic wine and we're even given pieces of the magic plate that's broken at the betrothal, and some singles are so desperate that they eat that too, no doubt. Heck, why don't they also give us fragments from the glass the groom breaks to remember the Temple? We could use them to gouge out small areas of our faces, to show that we remember that we're not building a good Jewish home which is like a miniature Temple. Bad, bad singles.

At *my* wedding no one will have to eat anything they don't want to. In fact, just to make sure that doesn't happen, I am planning to serve no food at all. Or drink. In fact, I think I will hold it on Yom Kippur. Don't snort! It'll keep costs down and I'll be in a white dress anyway which is convenient.

Well it doesn't bleedin' matter what I plan for my wedding, does it, seeing as the prospect is currently somewhat about as likely as a penguin winning the Nobel Prize, or peace in the Middle East.

OK, it's 3:52 a.m. and I'm tired of entertaining you. Go back to your own loser life.

POSTED BY EMMA   0 COMMENTS

January 25th 2003

Peeeeeeple! Why should I bother to spill my guts out here if you aren't going to comment? Sniff! *Lioness of Israel* always has thirty or forty comments on her blog. People often burst a systole arguing over *her* stuff. Then again, she does believe that part of Israel should be split off and become a theocracy governed by descendants of Rashi and Hillel the Elder, with her cousin Shaltiel as king. I guess that's a tad more controversial than my local supermarket. Hmm.

Hey, the Arab who shouts in Yiddish is back! ☺ He walks through the streets shouting *"Alte zachen!"* (actually, *"Alteee zacheeeeeeeeeeyen"*). It means "Old things" and he wants us to come out and give him second-hand stuff. It's like a tradition, from the early years of the State or something. He used to come around all the time before the Intifada started and I would give him old stuff all the time, including things of my roommate's that I thought were ugly. Though he refused to take the Kaja-googoo albums, for some reason—he actually backed away, holding up a *hamsa* and muttering some kind of curse.

I'm SO happy he's back! I wish I could give him my old boyfriends to sell to tourists in the Bethlehem square. No, actually what I *really* wish is that I could give him my friend R who doesn't stop moaning about being old and single. That'd teach her a thing or two.

POSTED BY EMMA   6 COMMENTS

February 5th 2003

A mysterious thing happened on a bus today.

But first, a small digression regarding Israeli buses. Many of my friends no longer take buses coz they're scared of sudden death, but they're missing out. Israeli buses are amazing. They are microcosms of Israeli society. You'd think a bus is a simple thing but it isn't. When you get on an Israeli bus, your mind learns to automatically scan the seats and the people, and eliminate all the non-options so you can speedily work out where to park your bum.

First of all, no one wants to sit down next to an Arab, in case he's in an explosive temper. Personally I think that in a bus that size it doesn't make much difference where you sit—if it's seventy-two virgin day and Allah's in his Akbar, you're pretty much canned soup anyway. But you never know, I guess, and the truth is that I avoid them too, just to be safe. I feel a little sorry for them, though. I know how they feel. People wouldn't sit next to me on the school bus for years, though for different reasons probably.

Next, as a woman, I can't sit next to any ultra-Orthodox men. They don't like it, it's too intimate, the whole sitting next to each other thing, coz our *sleeves* might touch and have lots of little baby sleeves before the next stop. The ultra-Orthodox have their own buses, which are segregated, and I wish they'd stick to them, but unfortunately they also use the ordinary Egged buses alongside us plebs. Things are normally fine, but sometimes there's a spot of trouble when the selfish gits want the world to revolve around them and their extreme beliefs and they ask people to move. Highly annoying. I have to say, though, that personally I was once on a bus when an ultra-Orthodox ultra-old very frail chappie got on and was standing at the front because all the empty seats were next to women. He was swaying dangerously and so I got up so he could sit down, but the bus driver yelled at me to sit back down and ordered him to sit down already and not be so stupid. That old man literally went the colour of a beetroot stain and sank into the seat next to me looking like a dog that's been kicked by its master. Well, that's respect for the elderly, I say; that's tolerance. Marvelous.

Speaking of the front, you can't sit in the front row as that is reserved for the elderly and the disabled. And you never want to sit anywhere near two or more Israeli teenagers because they are incredibly loud and stupid. And you can't sit next to someone coming back from the Machaneh Yehudah *shuk* because the seat next to them is taken up by their shopping trolley containing a billion plastic bags full of vegetables and burekas.*

*[an incredibly greasy and yummy pastry, though not nearly as fattening as it sounds because luckily the vast majority of it flakes onto your shirt or is blown away by the wind]

And of course you *have* to let the woman with the baby sit in the accordion middle part of the bus so that she can hold the pram (that's *stroller*, you damn Yanks!). And you can't sit on the side of the bus where the sun comes in coz you'll fry. That leaves not too many seats for your tired tushy. And when you actually do find a seat, an old lady gets on at the next stop, or a pregnant woman, and you have to stand up for them. Well, that's Jerusalem.

In fact, I once had an idea for a board game, called "Ottobus" (that's Hebrew for bus, though I know it sounds like the name of a German pervert). The game board would be bus-shaped, with walls and windows and rows of seats. There would be painted cards with little feet representing people who get on the bus and want to sit down, who would be as follows:

Ahmed the Arab

Zalman the Dos

Takelu the Ethiopian immigrant

Yevgeny the Russian immigrant

Candy the American tourist

Julie the Baka leftist hypocrite who lives in an Arab house

Emma the unbearable English snob

Tzachi the Arss*

*[= uncivilised hair-gelled individual with tight jeans and a huge Star of David necklace]

And so on. By rolls of the dice, the seats get filled up, but people can only sit down according to a complicated set of rules. For example, no religious woman can sit next to a religious man and vice versa; no Jew except for Julie can sit next to an Arab; no one can sit next to Candy except for Takelu, because Candy takes up one and a half seats and Takelu has the waistline of a pencil; and no one at all can sit next to Zalman coz he wears a heavy black coat in the summer with no deodorant and the smell of his BO is instant death. Etc. etc. etc. Oh, and if Tzachi, or indeed any Israeli under seventy, sits next to Emma the English snob, she has to get up and move. (She moves a lot.)

In addition, there would be special "argument cards," which might be something like, "If when you turn over this card there is a secular person sitting next to a national-religious person, they must now have an argument about the Oslo peace process. Roll the dice to see who clobbers who. The loser has to get off the bus and go limping home, muttering, 'They're destroying this country.'"

And then there are the "naff Egged driver" cards, which mean that the bus swerves, and any player who is standing because he or she did not find a seat has to fall on the people seated nearby, which gives you ten embarrassment points— and fifty embarrassment points if they are ultra-Orthodox and opposite genders; and if Candy falls on someone, then that player goes to hospital and is out of the game.

And when you turn over either the "KABOOM!" card or the "DID YOU KNOW THAT MORE ISRAELIS ARE KILLED IN ACCIDENTS THAN IN TERROR ATTACKS?" card, the board is picked up and shaken violently so that all players fall out of the bus, and the game ends.

Anyway, I digress. I was going to tell you what happened on the bus. So I'm coming back from a party in Tel Aviv one night, feeling pleasantly buzzed from drinking an entire bottle of Golan Heights Merlot. I catch the last number 13 at the Jerusalem Central Bus Station, and it's completely empty because it's late and people aren't taking buses so much at the moment because they want to go home and not to the Abu Kabir Forensic Institute.

So there's not a soul on the bus except myself and good ol' Mr. Nahag, the bus driver. The very next stop, this dude gets on. "FWORR!" I think. "Haven't seen such a fit bloke for years!" He's nicely tanned, great torso, good cheekbones, all the important things. He walks the length of the bus and then plonks himself down next to me! *Davka* next to me, with all these empty seats available! Well, these are tense times, and I couldn't tell if he had come to chat me up or blow me up, right? True, the guy has these incredible blue eyes, but that doesn't prove anything because there are lots of Arabs with blue eyes from the time when the British Mandate was having lots of man dates with the local Fatimas.

So here's the two of us, sitting next to each other on this totally empty bus, and it all feels really dodgy and I'm trying to work out if I can lose enough weight in five minutes to be able to escape through the window, just in case he looks like he's pulling the cord, know wot I mean? I venture a look at him, and he's staring straight ahead as if everything's perfectly normal. I kind of cough and he still ignores me, so I say to him:

"*Slicha*—this seat's taken." (In English. I can actually say that sentence in Hebrew, but I always speak in English when I think I'm about to die—it seems a more polite way to go.)

Well that gets him, and he turns and looks at me for a long moment and then says, "By who?"

"My great-aunt Ethel," I say. "She's getting on at Dover."

He totally surprises me by going with it.

"Well, when she gets on I'll be happy to hand over my seat." He says "hand over" so it sounds like "hand Dover" and I laugh because I love puns and I don't think terrorists know how to make them so I'm feeling relieved.

Dangerous extremist 0, Harmless nutter 1.

His English sounds good, though his accent is weird and I can't place it.

"OK," I say, "so what's the deal? Why this particular seat?"

"I always sit in this seat," he says.

"And if someone's already sitting there already . . . ?"

"I shoot 'em," he says. I raise my eyebrows.

Dangerous extremist 1, Harmless nutter 1.

Then he smiles.

There is no doubt, ladies and yentlmen, that the man has a stunning smile. I am temporarily paralyzed and stop reaching for my housekeys, with which I had planned to gouge out his eyes.

Then he dazzles me further by turning to face me and saying, "I want to get to know you."

Even with his weird accent, I can't fool myself into thinking he said "I want to get to Noyu" (city in Liberia—not kidding!) or "I want a ghetto, no ewe" or anything else that might make more sense. No, I heard it, plain as the Pope's nose! He wants to get to know li'l me!

I don't know whether to feel flattered or scared, and I can't decide which script in my brain to open: "Hot Hunk" or "Terrorist" (they are in fact different from each other, though if you saw me malfunctioning at a singles event you might never know that.)

"So—er—what do you want to know?" I say cautiously.

"Everything," he says.

I point out that would take some time.

"I have plenty of time," he says. That makes me feel even better. It seems he's not planning to end his life—or, more importantly, mine and Mr. Nahag's—in the next sixty seconds. The score is now *Dangerous extremist 1, Harmless nutter 2*.

Then he says in a completely random fashion:

"Look, I can see you're hesitating, so I'll start off our conversation, OK?"

"OK," I say, warily.

"So I was thinking today, Armenians can't be great scientists."

"They can't?" I say.

"Well, the problem is that if they ever discover something important it's going to be very difficult to refer to it."

"I haven't the froggiest what you're on about!" I say.

"Look," he says patiently, like he's talking to a retard, "we call it Newtonian physics, right? After Newton, yes? Just add the ending 'ian.' But all Armenian surnames end in 'ian' because it means 'son of'! So say this guy named, for example, John Azarian stumbles onto something, what will we call it? Azarianian physics?"

"You're a loony," I say.

"No, I'm serious. I once met a guy who was called Yanian. I mean, if he discovered a new theory of, say, covalent stochastic equivalences they would have to be called Yanianian equivalences. See what I mean?"

"Not really," I say.

"It would be even worse if his first name was Ian," he adds, nodding.

"So—are you Armenian then?" I say, scrambling for rational ground while simultaneously fishing for some info that might help me choose a script. He ignores my question and carries on.

"You've got exactly the same problem in trying to define that indescribable quality that makes a real Loch Ness monster—it would have to be called 'Nessness.' It just doesn't fly." Terrorist or no, the man is clearly one banana short of the bunch. I abandon my two old categories in favour of one new one: *Dangerous nutter. Code Red!* Indeed, dear readers, there are other risks in Jerusalem besides human bombs. The place is swarming with people who are off their trolley, thinking they're Jesus, King David, and suchlike, when most of them really *aren't*.

That's it, I decide, I have to get off this bus right now. I have every intention of pushing the bell, but for some reason my hand doesn't move. Instead I hear myself say, "You're really weird, you know that?"

Without even pausing he says something like (I will try to reproduce it here accurately): "What's weird? What's normal? What are all these norms we have to listen to? Why do entire groups of people have to believe the same things? Like why am I not allowed to sit next to you until all the other seats in the bus are full? Why can't I just start talking to a pretty girl if I want to? Who made all these things up? Are there little molecules called 'norms,' like little Norman invaders, floating around in the air, which shoot up your nostrils and *wham*, you're normed? Or are we actually free to invent our own reality and dismiss these norms as a repressive socialization mechanism?"

I'm gobsmacked. I shake my head and tell him I have to go. The truth is, his speech was so long that now we've reached my actual stop. He gets up to let me out, but then the cheeky monkey follows me right off the bus! *Chutzpah!*

I don't want him to see where I live, so I sit down on a wall and he talks to me (well, more like "at me"—so much for wanting to hear all about me! Typical male!) for another thirty minutes, about yet more barmy stuff that I can't even remember now, and then suddenly he says goodnight and walks away. I sit there, feeling simultaneously shaken up and let down, asking myself, "Emma Claire, what just happened?"

A minute later he returns. "I forgot something," he says.

"What did you forget?" I say, looking around on the empty wall.

"Your phone number," he says.

By now I'm totally and utterly confused by this whole chain of events and have no idea what to do. He's definitely kooler than the Katamon kats but I don't know really know him from an octopus, and there still seems to be a whiff of something strange about him. I can't place him at all.

Well, turns out he has telepathy as well coz he says charmingly, "I'm sorry if I seem a little odd. It's been a while since I had a girlfriend and I've forgotten how to talk to women."

"Oh," sez I.

"Look, let's just meet. No pressure, just for fun to hang out."

Well, I do fancy him rotten, and I really want a man in my life so I sigh and say, "OK."

"Good," he says.

"But *I'll* call *you*," I say. "Give me your phone number."

And he does. And after dithering for about a day I call him. So now I have a "meeting" with this alien life form on Sat night. His name's Modi. I know nothing else about him except that he has an intriguing mind and a fab smile. I think I've flipped my lid.

Life. Just when you think you know it, it buys bell-bottoms and dyes its hair purple.

POSTED BY EMMA   52 COMMENTS

February 8th 2003

I was so nervous the whole of Shabbat I spilt kiddush wine all over my white skirt. Got some very odd looks.

Thank you for all your comments, blogpals, but I'm going to ignore them and go meet with Modi. S says I'm crazy and he might be a stalker and I should meet him only in well-lit places. She's not happy because I told her he doesn't wear a *kipa*. I haven't dared tell her that, never mind not religious, I'm not even sure if he's Jewish, and indeed he might be best friends with Sheikh Ya Booty and Fat Yassir. (And to my reader *Whirling Dervish from Derby*, thanks for trying to explain to me the difference between holders of blue or orange ID cards who are Israeli and non-Israeli Arabs. I hear your point that there is a third option between "nice Jewish boy" and "I want to blow you up and throw you into the sea." But I agree with *Qwerty Gerty*: Arabs are loyal to the Arab cause, being Arabs, and so you can't trust any of 'em. Definitely not alone on a dark night, anyway.)

Well, my brother told me Modi is probably short for Morde-chai, but I think it could just as easily be short for Mohammed or Mahmoud. Bah! (Arabic for "Pah!")

POSTED BY EMMA   75 COMMENTS

February 9th 2003 5 AM

Back.

It was really nice; he's such an interesting person and he also smells nice. Those two almost never go together. Though I wish he wouldn't talk quite so much; my brain has the bends.

I made subtle inquiries about his background but didn't get far. He told me he grew up in Jerusalem, spent several years studying in Germany and the States, came back and studied at the Hebrew University. His father's a businessman and his mother's a nurse and he has five siblings. None of the above narrows things down in the slightest, and so I still don't know if he's a bro' or a cuz, as say in these parts. Well, what kind of question was I supposed to ask that wouldn't seem downright rude?

"So—will ours be just another story of *girl meets goy?*"

or

"Tell me, Modi, do you fondly remember your circumci-sion?" (Not a bad one, in fact, except that talking about circum-cision is pretty impolite on a first meeting).

Anyway, right near the beginning I asked him, "So what's your ambition in life?" I like to ask that; it opens them up and then I can make fun of them later.

He replies, "Emma, my ambition is to sit on every bench in Jerusalem with you."

I thought that was quite a sweet and romantic answer, though the proposed activity itself seemed fairly dull. But for the next six hours we went around sitting on every bench in Rechavia and I actually had a good laff. I never knew that every bench is different! Some are wood and some are metal, and some of the wooden ones are warped or have chunks missing as if someone's nibbled them, and the metal ones have the Jerusalem municipality lion engraved on them. And some had plaques on them from people wanting to honour their departed ones by providing repose for the esteemed bottoms of Jerusalem. One had been overgrown by a bush and we sat with our heads in said bush for a few minutes till I felt something crawling into my ear and screamed. One amazing bench I've never noticed before, on Rashba street, is made of white stone, with two black stone pigeons perched on it, facing each other. We stayed on that bench for a good while, having lotsa fun. I ain't forgettin' that bench in a hurry. Yar!

And then there was this bench that some guy called Itai wrote all over, "Why don't you love me anymore?" I was saddened that he had his heart broken by a piece of furniture, which no doubt had initially seemed a safer bet than a human. Well, as I always say, "Life's a bench and then you die" (groan now or forever remain silent).

Modi is a bit shorter than me but that doesn't bother me like it usually does coz he has a real presence; most of the time I don't even notice. Anyway, don't worry, all my screaming fans, I'm not allowing myself to get emotionally involved with him till I find out who he is. And after all it was just a hanging-out, nothing serious.

I have to go now, I'm so tired I've fallen off my chair and am typing this with my toes.

POSTED BY EMMA   144 COMMENTS

February 14th 2003

OK, so we've met twice more and the man is still a mystery to me. I still can't muster up the courage to ask straight out, and the circumcision question just doesn't seem to come up naturally, know wot I mean, 'Arry? So we talk about very general things. Well, actually it's mostly him talking. I don't mind coz he amuses me, though at some point I will probably want to say something—such as "Hi, my name's Emma." No, just kidding. Actually we have already talked about some really personal stuff. Though somehow it never quite tells me what I need to know.

On our last meeting he brought along a banjo, and every time we moved to a new bench he would diddle away at some tune he made up. He's too cute! We've covered the benches in the Sacher park and all around the Rechavia and Nachlaot neighbourhoods. I'm really getting into this now. Wouldn't it be great to be able to say I have sat on every bench in J-lem?

Oh, and the lad took my cellphone when I wasn't looking and changed all the instructions to Swedish. I don't know how to change it back now because I can't read the menu. I can't tell you how inconvenient that is, so the fact that I still thought it was a hoot is a bad sign. Uh-oh, I think I'm falling for him.

Don't worry, blogmates, I swear to you I'll find out next time who he is.

P.S. Oh, how sweet—he just called and we spontaneously met up, and he gave me a Valentine's Day heart. It's a bit unusual—it's made of banana bread wrapped in surgical bandages—but it's the thought that counts.

POSTED BY EMMA   165 COMMENTS

February 18th 2003

I tried, I really tried!! I took the subtle approach and very very casually said, "So, Modi, tell me more about your background. Where is your family from?"

But he answered "To tell you the truth—I'm half Irish, half Humpty-Dumpty."

I replied, "Begorrah, why that's a rare chance as we're also descended from the original Sir Humpty of Dumpty, and the proof of it is that we have his eggy face on our family coat of arms, bejaysus."

Well, what else was I supposed to say?

POSTED BY EMMA   103 COMMENTS

February 23rd 2003

OK, you can all stop your naggings and thrashings about. It's over. ☹

Here's what happened.

He picked me up in a car it turns out he had all along (so why was he on that bus?? Yet another mystery.) We were driving along and I took his CDs out of the glove compartment. As I flicked through them I said, "You know that every single one of your CDs is in the wrong cover?"

"I like to be surprised," he says.

I put on a CD of "Hits of the 70's" (vile!) and we drive along in silence while I churn over how to ask my date politely which branch of the Abrahamic family he's descended from, and whether he's a member of the Islamic Jihad and is planning to kidnap me in exchange for 1000 prisoners (in which case he needs to realise that there's no way I would fetch that price. Maybe two prisoners and a goat.)

I'm feeling really tense by now, because it's way time I got this clear, and to be honest I'm afraid of the answer. At this point his cell phone rings—normally he turns it off—and he answers it in rapid Arabic. I break into a light sweat. When he hangs up I say real casual-like,

"So who was that?"

"My grandmother," he says.

"Why do you speak to her in Arabic?" I say.

"Because that's the language she knows," he says.

"And do your parents speak Arabic?" I say.

"Yes," he says. "We all speak Arabic."

"Oh," I whisper. "I see."

"Is there a problem?" he says.

I say, "I think this was a big mistake. Can I get out?" thinking, if he's going to kidnap me, then now is the time to run for it.

"What, right now?" he says. We're driving past the Cinemateque down toward the Old City.

"Yeah. Stop here," I say, kind of choking. I realise that I've been in denial, but it explains everything. Why he never mentions doing army service, for example, which is something every bog-standard Israeli bloke will mention within the first half hour of meeting you. Why he didn't want to tell me what school he went to or where he lives.

"I just can't continue seeing you, Modi," I say, trying to be nice about it. "I'm sorry."

He just stares at me with those intense blue eyes, and I see hostility in them. Thousands of years of hostility between his people and my people. It pains me so much I just want to hug him and cry. But now there's too much empty space between us for that.

"I want you to know," I say, "that I don't hate you personally. I actually really like you. But this is just wrong. It can't lead anywhere; we come from two different cultures. I should never have agreed to meet you." (Pure Hollywood!!)

Still he says nothing.

"Take care of yourself," I say and without looking at him I get out of the car. He drives away, leaving me there, standing in the freezing cold above the Gei Ben Hinnom valley for which hell is named.

And it is. Absolute hell.

I'm too upset to write more now, I'll continue tomorrow.

POSTED BY EMMA   84 COMMENTS

February 24th 2003

So here's the next part of my sorry tale.

I stumble around for a bit, then walk up the road toward the Old City and find myself, without meaning to, at the Kotel.

I haven't been to the Kotel for years. I never liked it. Bunch of people praying to a wall. Why would God the Omnipotent be present at this wall any more than anywhere else? Also it gives me the willies when a lot of Jews get together and wail. I think after two thousand years of wailing, we're done—this is the dawning of the Age of the Smile.

Anyway, it's really windy and cold, but there are quite a few people down at the Kotel, mostly religious types. I don't really feel like going down to the Wall, and I feel self-conscious in my jeans, so I just sit at the back, watching the people come and go. Next to me this middle-aged potbellied Israeli is talking on his cell phone, saying:

"Yeah, the guy's gone to pray—some multi-millionaire, even he doesn't know how much money he has. I drove him around Jerusalem of heaven and Jerusalem of earth. He left his

Christian wife behind, thank God—what do I need with Christians? She stayed in the hotel, blow-drying her hair."

I take this as a clear sign—that I shouldn't listen to him anymore. I get up and go to the Wall. I walk right up to it and find a free spot between all the polyester-bloused bewigged matrons. I touch the cold stone and I say in my mind, "I've just met my soulmate and he's an Arab. God, if You exist, can You explain this?"

I pick up a prayer book but I feel so rubbish and I don't know what to do with myself. Then it hits me that this must be God's punishment to me for being so crap at religion all these years and so cynical about it all. I don't know what to do with that thought, so I just go sit down on a chair and cry a bit and don't move for about an hour.

As I'm leaving the Wall, the guard at the exit stops me. "Why are you so sad?" he says. This really pisses me off. In Israel you can't be left alone for a second.

"It's the bleedin' Kotel," I snap. "People come here to be sad!"

"No, but you're going through something," he says. "Need to talk?" He motions me aside and lowers his voice. "Talk," he commands. He must be really bored. He's a young, dark chap with a pockmarked face. I shrug. What the hell, things can't get worse.

So I tell him, "I don't know what to do. I'm in love with a non-Jew." I don't tell him he's an Arab. He probably hates Arabs, all the Sephardim do coz they actually had to live with them all the years. He looks at me as if he doesn't understand my point.

"Well, we all do sins," he says. "Take me. I'm traditional—" he takes a *kipa* out of his pocket to prove it to me—"but these girls come to the Kotel half-dressed and I look at them. I'm only human."

"But I feel like I'm being punished by God," I add, feeling stupid.

"Could be," he said. He's really being helpful and I am *so* glad that I struck up this conversation.

"Well then all I can say is that God's being really childish," I say.

"Well who says it's a punishment? Maybe it's a gift!" he says.

"A gift? To fall in love with a non-Jew?"

"Why not?"

"Are you thick or just plain stupid?"

"You just have to take what God throws at you," he preaches at me. "Take me. My dad doesn't work and we're twelve children. I'm the oldest; I support the whole family. I said to my mother, 'We have no money, why do you keep having children?' She said, 'I like children!'"

"Intriguing," I say.

"You could get married in Cyprus," he says.

"This isn't helpful!" I snap at him. "I won't marry a non-Jew!"

"Shhh," he says. "Sorry. You're wearing jeans and *tzitzit* . . ." (he fingers my beige pashmini from Marks and Spencer) ". . . so I thought you were Reform." What a flaming moron! Me, wear *tzitzit*?! I'm plotzing to slap him good and red, but I just shake my head and say through gritted teeth, "*I'm—not—Reform!*"

"He could convert," he points out.

I reply, "It's not that simple."

Then he says, "All right tell me the truth. Was he no good in bed? Is that it?"

"Piss off!" I retort, and start to walk away. Bloody froggin' sleazy Israeli.

"Sorry!" he shouts after me. "Just remember, you're lucky. You have your arms, your legs, your health; you're a pretty girl. You should see some of the handicapped people who come to the Kotel. Think of how hard it is for them."

"RIGHT!" I yell. "CAN I GO NOW?"

"There's a reason for everything," he says. "It's all from God. Find out the reason."

"OK!" I shout. "I'LL DO THAT THEN. GOODBYE NOW."

"Smile!" he says. "I'm not letting you leave without a smile."

I walk away. And you know what? I'm actually laughing.

POSTED BY EMMA   191 COMMENTS

February 26th 2003

So we have a difference of opinions amongst my friends and family:

H says he was definitely not a terrorist as he would have killed me already by now.

R says I've gone completely spare and should go straight to the police.

S says I should never have hooked up with someone not religious anyway, as it just creates messes. That's rich coming from her—she dated a rabbi who destroyed her life.

My brother says it's still not entirely clear who Modi is. He thinks it's perfectly feasible that he's a Sephardic Jew whose grandparents and parents speak Arabic.

P agrees but says I should still keep away, coz it's a known thing that Sephardim hit their wives, so safest to quit it now before he starts with the beatings. I think she's become just a tad bitter since her marriage went all a-squiff.

All I know is that I'm out of control and every time I see one of those little puffy chocolate crembos I feel a need to bring my fist smashing down on it. I've already made two kiddies cry. Bad bad Emma.

POSTED BY EMMA   143 COMMENTS

March 2nd 2003

I can't stand it, I have to call him.

No, I mustn't.

But I have to.

Can't.

Have to.

No no no.

Argggggggggggggggh . . .

POSTED BY EMMA   30 COMMENTS

March 3rd 2003

All right all you cleverblogs, you've all been discussing my personal life and its ramifications for the continued viability of the Jewish people for weeks now, so put your money where your mouth is and let's take a vote.

Who says I should call him up, and who says I shouldn't? Come on, let's 'ave 'em.

POSTED BY EMMA   412 COMMENTS

March 5th 2003

OK, I counted the votes and it's 203 saying I shouldn't call, 176 saying I should call, and one person wanting to interview me for the *Jewish Chronicle.*

But guess what, me old bloggies? I'm going to ignore the vote and call anyway. You can just shut it, all right?

POSTED BY EMMA   19 COMMENTS

March 6th 2003

Um . . .

I don't know what to say. Maybe I should have listened to you after all.

He reluctantly agreed to meet me and we met up and he sat there glowering at me for a bit, and so I said, "Look I just want to know. Who are you? Are you Jewish? Just tell me straight, once and for all."

So he tells me that I've got *chutzpah* but he'll tell me because he likes my dimples, that he *is* Jewish, he's from Bukhara, in Uzbekistan, where they speak Arabic. I know Uzbekistan is part of the former Soviet Union and then I begin to freak out because second to the French, I *hate* Russians. But before I can even finish that thought he tells me that he's sorry, he just lied to me and actually he grew up in Ramallah and his uncle is Faisel something or other, the head of the Palestinian Front for something or other. He said that he had to lie to me for my own protection, coz if anyone found out they would kill us both, in a kind of reprisal of the Romeo and Juliet thing. So we must never meet again and I must never mention to anyone about meeting him. Well, I'm picking my jaw up off the ground and wondering if now is a good time to say "er—is it a problem that thousands of people have been reading about you on my blog?" when he says he's sorry, he's just lied to me again and he's actually the product of the union between a deaf Nazi who fled to Brazil in 1945 and a Swiss woman adopted as a baby by Saharan Bedouins. No, woops, actually he's a particularly tall pygmy who converted to Zoroastrianism after he had a vision of a giant jellyfish. No, in fact, he's a former spy for Israel who had plastic surgery to disguise his real face, which is triangular and purple. Actually, he's really a woman who—

I start hitting him and yelling, "Tell me the truth! I just want the truth!"

"Why do you want the truth?" he yells back. "We were getting to know each other, having a good time! What difference does it make where I come from!"

I keep hitting him. "It makes a massive difference! I can't marry a non-Jew!"

"Marry?" he shouts at me. "Who was talking about marriage? We were just hanging out!"

"You bloody twit, I've gone and developed feelings for you!" I shout, and then I burst into tears and stop hitting him.

He looks at me for a bit with those true-blue eyes and sees that I mean it. Then he says, "OK, then here's the truth. The real truth. My father is Muslim Arab. He grew up in Umm el-Fahm. My mother is an American Jew. They met in Jerusalem and got married in the U.S. So what am I—Arab? Muslim? Jew? You tell me! My parents are anarchists. They see people as human beings, period. And so do I. So technically, I'm both Jewish and Muslim, OK? Does that help? I've been to the synagogue and to the mosque, but I don't practice any religion. So?"

I let this sink in. Then I say, "Why couldn't you just have told me that from the start?"

He says, "I didn't think it was that important to you. I didn't think I needed to sign in before hanging out with you!"

I say, "You're lying. You deliberately avoided telling me."

He thinks for a bit and then says, "I guess I was scared of your reaction. That you would reject me before knowing me. I wanted you to like me."

I say, "I'm sorry. I'm really sorry." And I get up and leave.

And no, before you ask, I'm not going to call him. He may have told me the truth finally but I'm never going to trust anything he ever says ever again. And I know he's technically Jewish but I still think of him as an Arab; or rather, my brain thinks of him as both Jewish and Arab and then it short-circuits, and I can't handle that.

But worst of all—and what I'll never forgive him for—is forcing me to blurt out my feelings like that. That's just not the British way.

So this is the end of the saga. You can all go home!!

Fin! The End!!
Come on, I mean it. On yer bike! Sod off, the lot of you!
POSTED BY EMMA   209 COMMENTS

June 9th 2003

Hi-de-hi punters. It's me, your old pal, Emma Claire, back from the dead. Sorry for the above comments and for my long absence. I was just a weeny bit upset.

You probably want to know what happened, right? Well, I never called him again. No, I have no idea where he is now or what he is doing. If anyone meets him she's welcome to him as far as I'm concerned, and good luck to them.

No, there've been no men in my life since then—one or two stupid dates, nowt to write home about. But I just want to share that today I saw the most *stunning* ultra-Orthodox man. He had on a long stylish coat and a gorgeous grey wool scarf flapping out behind him, and these thick brown-blond *peyos* and light green eyes, and his face was so gentle and beautiful I just wanted to go up to him and touch his cheek.

Course I didn't, are you off your nelly? Do you think I want to start a political incident?! I just stood and watched till he was out of sight.

The Fellowship of the Ring

May 2005

Scene: Night. An apartment in Jerusalem. The furniture (sofa, armchair, three folding chairs and a coffee table) is old and cheap but comfortable. There is a large painting on the wall and a phone on a small desk. On the coffee table are glasses and a jug of lemonade, as well as platters of cut vegetables and cake. Next to the legs of the coffee table are some nicely wrapped presents.

As the lights go up, we see five women on stage. Three are sitting on the sofa. The first has long shiny brown hair and is immaculately dressed. The second is wearing a headscarf and denim skirt. The third is tall and gangly, with a pale face and dark hair. The fourth woman is sitting in the armchair; she has short spiky red hair. The fifth woman has medium brown thinning hair and delicate wrists and is standing.

(The first woman on the sofa is in the middle of introductions)
SHARI: . . . and you know Alison, and this is Karin.
KARIN: Pleased to meet you, Raquel. By the way, is it OK with everyone that I grabbed the armchair?
SHARI: No problem at all. It might be a bit of a wait. (*Looks at her watch*) I think Sarah had a lot of things to do today—relatives flying in, et cetera.—so she might be a while. Which means we have time to catch up on everyone's news! So tell us Raquel, if you're not too exhausted from your plane ride, how's life in England?

RAQUEL: Not bad, not bad . . . It's not Israel (*Sighs*) but it's home, and after all, my whole family are there and they are *so* happy to have me close by. I do miss it here, and I hope we can come back at some point, but Julian doesn't like Israel much. He's very English. (*Laughs awkwardly*) You know, cricket, the Queen, tea with milk, *Antiques Roadshow*. He just laps it up.

KARIN: (*Laughs*) The Queen! What better reason for staying in England?!

SHARI: I still can't believe you married Emma's brother! Let's see the ring.

ALISON: What? You married Emma's brother? How did that happen?

RAQUEL: (*Giggles, and shows off her ring to everyone.*) Here it is, the monstrosity, it belonged to his grandmother. What can you do? (*Shrugs, but is clearly proud.*)

ALISON: So nu, how did it happen? Do tell.

RAQUEL: Well, we've known each other since we were tiny tots. Our parents are best friends. I never saw him as a man; he was always just Emma's spotty annoying brother.

KARIN: More annoying than Emma?

RAQUEL: Yes. And spottier.

ALISON: (*Impatiently*) Go on with the story.

RAQUEL: Well, things weren't going so well for me in Israel. In fact they were bloody awful, definitely the worst time of my life—

SHARI: Oh, I'm sorry.

RAQUEL: Wasn't *your* fault. Anyway, so I decided to move back to England just for a bit. I just had to be somewhere where things didn't explode all the time, just for a little while. Recover my sanity.

(*All nod sympathetically.*)

KARIN: I get that. Things haven't gotten any saner since you left, believe me.

ALISON: Tough times. Anyway, go on.

RAQUEL: Well I hadn't seen him—Julian—for about seven years, basically since I moved to Israel. Soon after my return, I ran into him at a friend's Sunday brunch. He'd changed so much I hardly recognized him. Seriously, I walked right past him! He was totally offended. The truth is that he'd lost half his body weight, his skin was clear, and he actually looked good! And as soon as he got over his deep insult and started talking to me, I discovered that he was so much more mature than when I had last seen him, and with a good solid job to boot. Not at all the silly boy I'd known before.

ALISON: Solid job, always important.

SHARI: Speaking of which, did Adam start yet at Netpoll?

ALISON: Sunday. But we're talking about Raquel right now. Go on.

RAQUEL: (*Raquel pours herself a drink and then offers the others. All except for Hannah accept.*) I was impressed, I admit. But I still didn't think anything of it because he's so far from my usual type.

KARIN: Which is . . . ?

RAQUEL: (*Dismissively*) Oh, you know, those romantic sensitive types with puppy-dog eyes, you know what I mean. Julian's not that kind of man at all. His eyes look more like a squashed hedgehog's. (*General laughter, slightly embarrassed—the women are not sure how to take this.*) Well, at least that's what Emma says. I think they're beautiful. Anyway, with most of my London friends married and boring as mud, he and I ended up spending time together, going to concerts and things. But just as platonic friends. I wasn't even ready for a relationship. Couldn't even bear the thought. Well, at least I thought it was platonic, but . . . .

ALISON: Aha! No such thing as platonic friendship.

RAQUEL: Yes, well, he started sending flowers and other romantic doo-dahs and I couldn't resist the onslaught. Hey presto, a few months later I found myself engaged. Astonished but engaged! And then married! Mrs. Julian Kahn! Me!

SHARI: (*Exhales*) A miracle. Mazal tov.

KARIN: Nice story. It's always best when it sneaks up on you and bites you in the backside, the natural way.

ALISON: Well, you look great.

RAQUEL: Thanks.

ALISON: You've put on a bit of weight and it suits you. Rounds you out.

RAQUEL: (*Bashful*) Well actually, I'm pregnant. Due in October.

(*More fuss is made, but Raquel waves it away.*)

RAQUEL: We can talk about it later; enough about me. How about you all? What's been happening? I've been so out of things. I'm rubbish at emailing, I know.

(*There is a pause. No one knows who should go first. Finally Alison speaks.*)

ALISON: Well, as you know Adam and I got married in 2001, and we now have three kids. For a few years now, Adam's been learning Torah half day, but he's about to start a full-time job—frankly, we need the money. He still plans to become a rabbi, but it just might take a bit longer.

KARIN: And how's Adam's twin with the weird name? I met him once, uh . . . .

ALISON: Binyamin Zev?

RAQUEL: BZ?

KARIN: Yes. Interesting character.

RAQUEL: He's going out with Emma.

KARIN: (*Jaw drops*) No! Emma didn't tell me.

SHARI: Yes, they're pretty serious. I think it's scaring her how serious.

KARIN: (*Pause*) Wow. I can't imagine the two of them together. It must be quite—you know . . . .

SHARI: Intense. Yes.

RAQUEL: Intense is an understatement! They picked me up from the airport yesterday, which was really sweet of them but then they spent most of the journey arguing at the top of their lungs about whether Israel should attack Iran or not. At one point they almost ran the car into oncoming traffic.

ALISON: That's about par for the course.

RAQUEL: In the end I told them that *they* should attack Iran. Guaranteed to wipe out all life forms in a matter of minutes.

ALISON: Adam and I always argue about which one of them is crazier. (*Hastily adds*) Though we adore them both, of course.

KARIN: Who is your candidate?

ALISON: Not telling.

KARIN: Ha! I can't wait to see their children.

RAQUEL: I plan to keep any offspring of that particular union a million miles away from my precious kids. *Just kidding,* Shari. Don't forget I'm her sister-in-law now. No escape.

SHARI: Emma's lovely! I loved living with her. It was the most fun I've ever had in my life. I was devastated when she moved to Tel Aviv.

RAQUEL: (*Soothingly*) We all love Emma. 'Twas all in jest.

KARIN: We adore Emma.

(*Shari looks over at Hannah and asks if she is OK, pointing at a chair to indicate that she can sit down. Hannah shakes her head and remains standing.*)

KARIN: (*Looking at her watch*) I hope we can get started soon. I'm meeting someone afterwards.

SHARI: She'll be here soon.

(*Pause*)

RAQUEL: So Shari, your turn, what's with you?

SHARI: The usual. You know—teaching eighteen-year-old girls medieval Jewish philosophy. Always a challenge. That's it, nothing new.

ALISON: She's hiding something, I can tell.

RAQUEL: What are you hiding? Tell us.

SHARI: Nothing!

ALISON: Come on, Shari. Tell us.

SHARI: (*Hesitates*) Well . . . but it's a secret. You know what the rabbis say: 'Blessings only adhere to what's kept out of sight.'

ALISON: Oh, come on! You can tell us!

KARIN: (*Interjecting*) I know.

RAQUEL: (*Surprised*) You? You only met Shari last week. You know her the least of all of us.

KARIN: Yes, but I am good friends with *him*. The person Shari is currently in a serious relationship with.

ALISON: What? Who is it?

RAQUEL: Wait, I bet it's Washy, that redheaded doctor that Emma dated three years ago? Tell me I'm right!

ALISON: Washy?

KARIN: His real name is Ilan. Emma called him Washy because he reminded her of George Washington. Something about his teeth.

RAQUEL: Ilan? Ilan! I remember him well. I really liked him. I hoped he would actually stick around but Emma managed to repel him, too. That stupid meal. (*Turns to Shari and notices that she looks upset.*) Hey, sorry we let your secret out. But we won't tell anyone, will we ladies? (*Everyone shakes their head vigorously.*)

ALISON: So where did you meet him?

SHARI: On Frumster.

RAQUEL: (*Snorts*) So that site is good for something after all.

ALISON: And it's going well?

SHARI: (*Small pause*) Yes. But I don't want to talk about it, I don't want to put an evil eye on the relationship. I've had bad experiences with that.

RAQUEL: (*Hastily*) No, no evil eyes. Only good eyes, very good eyes.

ALISON: Yes, best of eyes and best of luck to you, seriously.

(*Suddenly Shari bursts out crying. The others fuss around her, and hand her tissues. She dries her eyes awkwardly, apologizing.*)

SHARI: I'm sorry, this is so embarrassing.

KARIN: What's up?

RAQUEL: What's wrong, Shari?

SHARI: Nothing's wrong, that's the problem. (*Starts bawling again*)

KARIN: Huh?

SHARI: It's all going so well, I'm not used to it. I keep waiting for it to end, thinking it's not possible but—(*crying and laughing at the same time*) I think he's about to pop the question. He's taking me to the Kotel next Monday and he's acting all strange and secretive.

RAQUEL: Well, that's wonderful.

KARIN: Fantastic. So can someone explain to me why she is crying?

SHARI: (*Noisy nose-blowing*) Sorry. I've come to believe that this would never happen to me. After 176 men, who would have believed number 177 would be different? It's a miracle.

RAQUEL: Wow, Shari, I'm so happy.

SHARI: No don't, please don't, it hasn't happened yet. I shouldn't have said anything. The evil eye . . . (*Starts weeping again*)

(*The phone rings. Hannah hurries to answer it, looking relieved. She says, "Uh-huh . . . no problem, we haven't started yet . . . yes, see you soon" and returns to her place.*)

RAQUEL: And Hannah, what about you?

HANNAH: (*Shrugs*) Me? I've been working for the past year training businesswomen in assertiveness techniques and teaching business English. I volunteer for Kolech, the Orthodox Jewish Feminist organization, and I also do yoga and pottery. That keeps me busy.

RAQUEL: Cool.

HANNAH: (*Sarcastically*) Oh, did you mean am I in a relationship? No, I'm not.

RAQUEL: No, I didn't mean . . .

HANNAH: I haven't been in a serious relationship in over six years.

RAQUEL: That's OK—

HANNAH: I'm so glad that it's OK.

SHARI: Hannah, she was just asking how you are.

HANNAH: These days it seems as if that question means only one thing: "Tell me about your love life." Excuse me, I have a date with my bladder. (*Exits stage left*)

ALISON: Is she OK?

RAQUEL: What's with her?

SHARI: She's just going though a hard time right now.

RAQUEL: I don't remember her being this sarcastic.

SHARI: I don't think we should talk about her behind her back.

(*Awkward pause*)

KARIN: Well, why do people make all this fuss anyway? I'm in no rush to enter the gilded cage. People should just chill out, you know?

SHARI: Um, how old are you, if you don't mind my asking?

KARIN: I'm thirty-five and I don't have a problem with it. I've got time. My life doesn't feel empty just because there's no man in it. Why should it? I work, I go out with friends, I have

relationships, I live my life. That's normal, in my eyes. Whatever needs to come along will, all in good time.

SHARI: (*Flustered*) Uh, ok...

(*Stage goes dark, with spotlight on far left. Hannah appears in the
spotlight.*)

HANNAH: And what is a full life, after all? Where are we
going, as women, as human beings? What does God require
of us? To act justly, love mercy, walk humbly with God. We,
clay and dust animated by a soul, are subject to so many laws
and ideas and aspects, moral, ethical, societal. So how does it
all boil down to that one verse: *It is not good for man to be alone?*
And was that not said of Adam, rather than Eve? Then why
this terrible need that has me crying into my pillow at nights?
Why this awful vacuum at my core, darkness upon the face
of my abyss? All I want is to be a rounded human being, to be
dignified. Why this torture? How can I navigate this obsessive
babble of weddings and rings and couplings? How can I leave
when it is my own apartment? Why did I offer to host this
gathering? Stupid, I'm just stupid.

(*Spot dims and lights go back up on the stage.*)

RAQUEL: (*Looks at her watch*) So where is she?

SHARI: In the bathroom.

RAQUEL: No, I mean our guest of honor.

ALISON: Our blushing bride.

RAQUEL: Or she will be, this coming Tuesday, God willing.
And I hope she shows up before then. Where is she? I'm dying
to see her!

ALISON: We can't start the evening without her.

KARIN: She'll be here any minute.

RAQUEL: We're not going to do that whole pathetic
bride's hat thing are we?

KARIN: What bride's hat thing?

ALISON: You take a piece of wrapping paper from each
present and stick it on a paper plate. At the end of the evening
she has to wear the plate on her head.

KARIN: What on earth for?

ALISON: For fun.

RAQUEL: It's the stupidest thing, believe me.

KARIN: Sounds bizarre to me.

ALISON: It's fun. I've done it at a lot of bridal showers. It's symbolic, preparing her to cover her hair as a married woman.

KARIN: With gift wrap and disposable plates?

RAQUEL: (*Shakes her head*) Stupid.

SHARI: I have to agree. It makes a mockery of the religious act of head covering, which has so much more meaning that some silly plate on your head.

(*There is a knock at the door.*)

ALISON: Aha! (*Exits stage right. Hannah returns from stage left*).

RAQUEL: (*Brightly*) Hannah, I really love your apartment. Great painting!

HANNAH: (*Subdued*) Thanks.

RAQUEL: Who's the artist?

HANNAH: Gershuni. (*She sits down on one of the folding chairs, the one farthest from everyone. Enter Emma, Alison and a tanned, good-looking well-built man in his thirties, wearing a T-shirt on which is written* DID I SAY YOU COULD READ THIS, SUCKER?)

SHARI: (*Rising*) Emma! Hi! (*They hug.*) Hi, Binyamin Zev. How are you?

(*BZ sticks out his hand. Shari hesitates, then shakes it very quickly and lets it go.*)

EMMA: Sorry so late, traffic on Highway 1. I swear to heaven, snails were overtaking us on the hard shoulder. I exaggerate only slightly.

BZ: (*Echoes*) Only slightly. The slugs, however, were actually speeding by and to that I will swear upon the grave of my dentist.

EMMA: Dr. Samuel Jacobs. Stubbornly alive and well in Fair Lawn, New Jersey, no matter how many oaths Beez takes on his grave.

BZ: So, while Israel prepares for disengagement, we celebrate an engagement. Poetic justice, hey? Balance of the world and all that. Shame about the thousands of people who are about to lose their homes for baked beans. But don't let that spoil the mood. (*Looks around*) Which one of you is the lucky ducky? And where's the beer?

(*Pause. All except Emma are staring at BZ in bemusement.*)

ALISON: (*Shrugs*) I tried to tell him. He doesn't really do the listening thing.

BZ: (*Small pause, looks around again*) So Ali wasn't joking? Tonight *is* a women-only thing?

RAQUEL: Yes it is. That's why it's called a hen night. If we wanted you to come, we would have called it a poultry night.

BZ: What on earth is a hen night?

SHARI: A bachelorette party.

BZ: Not fair! You women are always having these funky events and excluding us. It's illegal, you know.

RAQUEL: No it's not. Go away.

BZ: (*Falsetto*) I can be a woman for an evening.

EMMA: You couldn't be a woman for a second. You haven't the first clue how women think.

BZ: (*Blows her a kiss*) That's what you're here for, to do that kind of thinking for me, sugarplum.

EMMA: That makes about as much sense as a walrus in a wheelchair. And don't call me that, sugarbum.

(*Hannah gets up and exits stage left.*)

BZ: (*Shrugs*) Oh well, I guess I'll go sit in a café. I still have 200 pages left of *Countdown to Crisis*. I'll see you all at the wedding! Bye, babe! *Au revoir*, all!

(*BZ blows several kisses and exits stage right. Emma sits down on a folding chair.*)

EMMA: So—hello! How is everyone doing?

(*Everyone murmurs great, fine, and thank God simultaneously.*)

EMMA: (*Not even listening*) OK, now we've got that out of the way, where is the *kallah*?

KARIN: Should be here any minute. It's already nine o'clock.

RAQUEL: (*Anxiously looking at her watch*) I hope nothing's gone wrong. Till she's actually got that ring on her finger I won't be able to sleep.

EMMA: I can't believe she's marrying that guy! That guy! The blokey who messed her around and broke her heart!

SHARI: People change.

EMMA: I wouldn't date any of my exes again, even if they said they'd become Mother Teresa herself. What a stonky bunch of losers.

(Shari looks offended and Karin giggles. Emma does not notice.)

EMMA: There were some right old wallies, remember Quels? Shari, I chewed your ears off about them, too. I can't even remember them all. Only a few choice ones come to mind. *(Ticking off on her fingers)* The one obsessed with all things cactus; the one who told me I had Marilyn's mind and Einstein's looks; Mr. Giant-Squid-Face; and of course, the terrorist who wanted to cart me off to Hezbollistan. Oh my bloody Gawd, I've wasted years of my life. Thank God for BZ, though he's no bed of roses either, I can tell you.

RAQUEL: And once again, even on Sarah's big night, Emma makes it all about herself.

EMMA: Sorry, was I being insensitive as usual? No, seriously, I'm really happy for her, as long as she's happy. Look, I'm always talking utter twaddle, you know that. I mean. Take what I said a minute ago. Who would want to be romantic with a very short and significantly dead Indian woman, however saintly? Just ignore me.

(Enter Hannah)

EMMA: Hannah darling, it's been absolute yonks! How are you?

RAQUEL: Don't ask her that.

EMMA: Oh, OK. How aren't you? How weren't you? How will you be? Who would you have been? Oh wait, is this your seat? *(Starts to rise)*

HANNAH: *(Hurriedly)* No, no, sit, it's fine. Have a drink.

EMMA: Thanks. *(Pours herself a drink)* So they're really going to get hitched, after all they've been through?

SHARI: I'm sure it'll all work out fine. You should see them together. They're adorable.

EMMA: I *would* have seen them together, if they hadn't gotten engaged about ten milliseconds after they started wrestling round two. Ding!

SHARI: Well, she didn't feel the need to go schlepping it out. She says she knew immediately.

EMMA: She refuses to go out with him for three years, and then when she says yes—bam! *(Snaps her fingers)* Wedding bells, just like that.

RAQUEL: After what happened last time they should really make sure. This all seems so rushed.

HANNAH: Yes. What's to guarantee he won't hurt her again? Once bitten . . .

EMMA: (*Enthusiastically*) Oh yes, how does that proverb go?

(*Raquel snorts at her.*)

EMMA: Seriously, I've forgotten. Once bitten, twice smitten?

RAQUEL: Exactly.

EMMA: (*Nods*) Great proverb! Twice smitten, I like that.

SHARI: No, she says he's changed, and it's not just lip service. She can see it in the little things and the way he treats her and his kid. And she's changed, too. She says it wasn't only his fault, everything that happened. It's important that both people learn to take responsibility. Blaming men is childish.

EMMA: (*Shakes head vigorously*) No, no, no! It's always the man's fault.

ALISON: Uh, remember the Garden of Eden?

EMMA: In my Bible, all Adam's fault.

ALISON: You don't say.

HANNAH: How old is the child?

RAQUEL: Almost six.

KARIN: Amazing. To be willing to take that on.

SHARI: Sarah *is* amazing. If anyone can do that, she can.

(*A knock. Shari goes to answer, exits stage right.*)

ALISON: So what does your Bible say about Potiphar's wife?

EMMA: Innocent till proven guilty.

ALISON: Jezebel?

EMMA: Lovely lady, definitely didn't deserve to be ripped to death by dogs. Aardvarks perhaps.

HANNAH: Emma, I'm the first one to read the texts in a way that is sympathetic to women, but I think you've gone completely off the edge.

EMMA: One person's edge is another person's ledge.

HANNAH: Uh . . . I really don't know how to respond to that.

(*Shari returns with Sarah, who is wearing a long, patterned dress, beaded necklaces and bracelets. The women clap their hands and break out into* Od Yishama, *a traditional wedding song. Emma ululates—a piercing sound somewhat like a car alarm, traditionally emitted by old Yemenite women at celebrations and suchlike.*)

SARAH: (*Blushing*) No, no need really. Shhh, everybody.

(*The song dies down, there are hugs all around, congratulations, and mazal tovs.*)

SARAH: It's so wonderful to see you all here. Raqueli! I am so glad you came out. (*Hugs her again*)

RAQUEL: Wouldn't have missed it for the world.

EMMA: What does that actually mean? Why would the world want you to miss it? What could it possibly benefit the entire world if you—

ALISON/RAQUEL: Emma, shut up.

EMMA: (*Irritated*) It's your turn to shut up. I shut up yesterday.

RAQUEL: Sarah, my love, I know I'm not going to get much time with you before the wedding, so do you mind if I ask you something in front of everyone?

SARAH: No, go ahead.

RAQUEL: Are you sure you're doing the right thing? I'm really sorry to ask, but you did this whole thing so fast that my brain can't keep up. Immanuel is still registered in my mind as the man who was so disgusting to you that burning alive was too good for him. You're not upset that I'm saying this?

SARAH: No, I really understand. I guess it's hard for people looking at it from the outside.

RAQUEL: I'm just concerned.

SARAH: I appreciate it, sweetie. I guess my short answer is . . . well, most of you know the story of why we failed, I mean, the first time around. I was furious with him for not accepting my imperfections. But I finally realized that if I don't forgive him after he begged me five times, and allow him another chance, then I am doing the same thing to him that he did to me. I mean even a prospective convert to Judaism is supposed to be refused only three times, and here I was refusing him five.

EMMA: Six if you count the time he came over on Purim dressed as a monk and collapsed on your doorstep.

KARIN: (*Giggles*) Oh my God. Who could resist that romantic gesture?

SARAH: I, for one. I poured a bucket of water on him and told him to go away. But anyway, back to the point. So one morning about two months ago I woke up and thought, Sarah Mosry, just who do you think you are? Get off your throne of judgment and give the man a break! See him as more than he is, instead of as less; see his future, not his past. That's what you wanted from him, so you do it now. And, yup, it wasn't easy but here we are, and with God's help it'll work.

RAQUEL: But Sarah, don't you want to take time and see whether he lives up to his words? I mean how long did you go out for the second time—three weeks? And now you're getting married already? I'm literally dizzy.

SARAH: Look, we were practically engaged last time, so we'd already done all that. And the important thing is that I saw he had changed. He treats Hudi differently—doesn't take his temper out on him. He seems gentler.

ALISON: (*Approvingly*) Very important.

SARAH: I don't want to talk about him or his mistakes anymore. It doesn't feel right. Let's just say I'm focusing on his good points, and trusting that he won't hurt me in that way again. It's always a risk anyway—even if you've known each other for twenty years, at some point you have to leap into commitment and that's a different ball game. Zero risk factor is only when you're both dead.

EMMA: And even then you never know.

HANNAH: (*Emphatically*) I would rather be alone my entire life than have to be married for even one hour to a man who does not respect me.

(*Pause. Everyone looks at her.*)

SARAH: I hear you, Hannah. But (*hesitantly*) see, respect comes from knowing who each other is and maintaining open communication, even in tough times. In fact, the respect actually comes from the way in which you weather the hard times, and Lord knows we've worked on that plenty. But sorry, I really don't mean to sound patronizing. I remember how women who get married start to preach to their single friends.

EMMA: Exactly! They start blabbing away as if they're the friggin' Elders of Zion! Smug marrieds! I won't be doing that, just watch me.

SARAH: (*Grins*) Hmm, so you're planning to tie the knot too? In the near future, perhaps, to a Mr. Beez?

EMMA: I never said that! Don't even dream of starting that rumor! (*Changes subject quickly*) So let's see your ring. Gi' us a look!

(*The hand with the ring is shown around; everyone oohs and ahs.*)

SHARI: Oh! You have to tell them how he proposed.

EMMA: You won't believe this, Raquel.

SARAH: (*Smiles*) He hired a guy dressed up as a nine-foot high bear to come to my building and shout my name into a megaphone until I came out.

RAQUEL: What? Where did he find a guy dressed as a nine-foot bear?

SARAH: Apparently that's his profession. He does shtick for weddings.

EMMA: A shtickmeister.

RAQUEL: I see.

SARAH: Anyway, I emerged wearing a skirt over sweatpants—very romantic—and stood there with my mouth open as the bear handed me a bunch of roses and a note.

EMMA: The note said, "If you can *bear* to be with me for the rest of your life, please say yes very loudly." Groan!

SARAH: Mani was hiding in the bushes. I had to say yes three times before he heard me and came out.

EMMA: All the neighbors clapped and cheered.

SARAH: So I'm now standing there bawling, wearing all these old yukky clothes, and Mani's blushing and speechless with his shoes caked in mud. In short, we looked a complete sight.

EMMA: There are pictures.

RAQUEL: So you just stood there?

KARIN: Well, he couldn't exactly sweep her up in his arms and run off into the sunset.

ALISON: Religious people do get short-changed when it comes to romantic gestures.

EMMA: All it needs is a bit of ingenuity. He could have hired a crane to sweep her up and carry her off.

KARIN: Or gotten the bear to do it.

EMMA: No, inside the bear was another religious man.

KARIN: Oh.

EMMA: He could have paid a woman to—

SARAH: (*Interrupting*) Anyway, it's been amazing ever since. Stressful but amazing.

RAQUEL: (*Laughs*) OK, you've convinced me. You both have my very best wishes and I am sure you're going to be deliriously happy. Mazal tov! (*They hug again.*)

SHARI: (*Claps hands*) Oh, this is going to be the best wedding, the highest of the high! I can't wait!

SARAH: Neither can I, believe me! Tuesday is too far away.

(*Od Yishama is sung again. The women begin dancing, and suddenly the stage is flooded with purple and pink and green headscarves, and wedding dresses and cakes and huge rings fly through the air as confetti and streamers rain down. Colored spotlights dance and the music swells. The women link arms and stand swaying together, faces upturned toward the audience as the song gets louder and louder, a chorus of angelic voices taking up the refrain. The music hits a final note, the last words "ve-kol kallah!" echo for a moment, and then the curtain drops to wild applause.*)

THE END

(*Silence descends. BZ emerges from stage right in front of the curtain, carrying a book on which is written "Crisis in Conflict." He tiptoes forward to the tune of "Pink Panther" and tries to peek in through the curtain. The curtain wobbles wildly and he is rebuffed at every turn. Giving up, he exits stage right again.*)

THE END

(*Hannah emerges from behind the curtain at stage left, and stands for a moment looking both angry and forlorn, which is not easy, even for an experienced actress.*)

HANNAH: Ugh! I *hate* modern literature! Even if the hero and heroine despised each other's guts for most of the story and had nothing in common, they always end up kissing in the sunset! A woman on her own is never the happy ending! And this is how people end up making terrible mistakes, desperately looking for the romantic dream, wanting to be swept off their feet and carried off on a white horse. Women need to be taught to love and respect themselves and not compromise! Marriage is *not* the final destination! Many couples are trapped and miserable! Hollywood poisons our lives. What, you think flying headscarves and confetti is the pinnacle and that curtains equals happily ever after? Well, I don't plan to be fooled by it. I can face the loneliness. I'm strong. I'll hold out till it's absolutely right, and won't compromise everything I've built until I meet someone who really respects me. Do you hear? (*Shakes her fist*)

THE ... END?

(*Sarah emerges from stage left and puts a hand on Hannah's arm.*)
SARAH: You're right, Hannah, happily ever after *is* a fantasy. But when we find a good relationship then it *is* real. It's a step up in our evolution. It's a level of love and commitment, humility and suspending judgment, and we can't achieve it on our own. You have to risk and allow someone into the vulnerable space, not stay walled up in fear and anger. You have to enter the unfathomable mystery that keeps men and women together, for this is how God created us, to yearn for that beloved other so much that it hurts. It's normal. And I'm telling you, it was only when I could soften and pray, open my eyes and really see where Mani was headed that I could get past my wounded ego. I had to bring God into it, look for His guidance. I'm so grateful for everything I've been through, even the pain ... Hannah, listen! What I'm doing is not romantic fiddlesticks! On the contrary, it's real. It's the realest thing possible! Don't you see? By holding out for the perfect man you are making the very same mistake as the romantics! I truly believe it.
(*Emma emerges from stage left; says in evil stepmother voice:*)
EMMA: I smell psychobabble. Fee-fi-fo-fum.
(*BZ joins her, nodding*)

BZ: Spiritual psychobabble, sugarplum.

EMMA: Beez, we have to save her before it's too late. (*Quickly approaches and lays a hand on Hannah's other arm.*) Now don't listen to her, dearie. You can be single for your whole life if you want to! Yes, that's probably the wisest choice. Stay single! Be firm! What do you need a man for anyway? Men are just silly pillocks!

BZ: Hey!

EMMA: Well, not you Beezibub, you're a sensible pillock.

(*Hannah shakes herself free, and with a terrible shriek of frustration, runs offstage.*)

SARAH: Good grief, Emma! Now look what you've done.

HELLO?! WHAT THE . . . ???

(*Alison peers around the curtain, no longer wearing a headscarf, with half-eaten sandwich in hand.*)

ALISON: Whoa! I thought the play was over so I started my supper but then I heard weird noises. What's going on?

SARAH: (*Wringing her hands*) Disaster upon disaster.

EMMA: We're just being postmodern out here.

ALISON: Ugh, there's far too much of that about these days. Why can't they just keep fiction where it belongs? (*Takes another bite and says through a mouthful*) We don't even get paid properly for these bits.

EMMA: You're so right! And I can't take much more of this rubbish! Look at me! Right from the start I'm given the most clownish dialogue about cheese sandwiches and drunken yaks while everyone around me gets to play high drama and tragedy. Then I have to blog *on and on* for ten thousand words without a break like an utter cretin! And now this play, well—what can I say, I come off even *less* intelligent if that's humanly possible, and the bloody thing is just neverending, look it's *still* ongoing at this very moment! And I'm *soooooo*

tired and I wanna go home! In fact, I demand to be paid over-
time for this speech I'm making right now. I tell you, I can't
take much more of this. We must force that stupid author to
stop or we'll never get to leave.

(*Shari and Raquel have entered during this speech, and chime in:*)

SHARI: Yes, that author! Look what she did to poor
Hannah. Why couldn't she have a happy ending too, like the
rest of us? Plenty of feminists get married.

RAQUEL: Yes, plenty! This must stop now.

EMMA: *Yalla*, let's do it!

ALISON/SHARI: Go, Emma, go!

SARAH: EMMA, NO!

(*It is too late. Emma has jumped off the stage, with BZ following
her. They move purposefully with aggressive looks on their faces toward
the back of the theater, where the author sits with her laptop. Hurriedly
the author clicks to shut down her comp—*)

The Hidden of Things

March 2009

"An interesting story." The Scot always began his critiques with the same three words. Indeed, the deep creases in his freckled nose spoke of interest in everything. "But I didn't like the main character. Selfish bitch, I'm glad she died."

The breathless girl said, "Oh, did she die, then? I wasn't s—"

"Nonsense!" interrupted the boy with the neon green shoelaces. "She doesn't die. Read it again."

The breathless girl rummaged in her handbag for a tissue. As she leaned forward, her tight jeans garrotted the cellulited flesh at her hips into rounded mounds, and a thin line of red material was revealed above the denim rim. Her bag, painted with light pink hearts but otherwise entirely transparent, contained sunglasses, assorted lipsticks, pens, a magazine, feminine hygiene products and numerous used tissues.

"All right, all right, don't quibble," said the professor. The weather was unusually fair for March in London, and the sunbeams sidling in through the large windows made the students squint. The professor continued:

"It is, in fact, unclear if the mystery at the story's end is intentional. That needs more work, Astor. But the protagonist comes through well. We get a good sense of her misery and self-destruction; she rebuffs the help offered by the best friend and parents and the mysterious homeless person. Most important, when she ends up being hit by a jeep, seemingly a random event, we sense that it really is her own choice, to end her own life. Your metaphors bring that out nicely. Well done, Astor. Your best writing yet."

"She definitely died," muttered the Scot.

"Definitely not!"

"I said all right!"

When the story's author returned home, she locked her bedroom door. She had dreamt the previous night that her bedroom was an enormous football field open to the sky. When she tried to undress and go to sleep, strangers had approached the fence and stared, their noses pressed to the wire.

Her real bedroom was curtained and carpeted, its cupboards overflowing with expensive clothes, many unworn. She had tacked cloths over the five large full-length mirrors. Two electric guitars leaned in a corner, an unmarred layer of dust on their surfaces. TV sounds came from the next room. First a man's voice, and then her mother's voice, practicedly neutral:

". . . the police, but as of yet there are no leads. The shocked community has rallied 'round the family. Back to you, John."

She thought back to the writing class and felt bruised. Why was the Scottish boy so glad to see her character die? The character was not selfish, just confused. She couldn't help it. Curling up tenderly around her middle, she pulled her blanket over her head, and reassured her arms and legs and thighs and stomach and hair, "You're safe. Just stay out of sight."

Much later she slipped out to the Torah class. Her father was still up when she returned.

"Went to a party," she lied.

He looked at his watch and laughed. "Midnight? I remember when you used to crawl in, smashed out of your senses, at 7 a.m. Welcome to the old fogies' club."

"Dad—I've decided to move out again. I feel recovered."

"Eh? That's fine, Astor. Whatever makes you happy."

She moved to a studio in Hackney, and began to attend three Torah classes a week. They were taught by a young man with a black beard and pallid skin, and his brown-wigged wife, in their tiny flat. A baby cried frequently, unseen, from a back room.

Without telling her mother, she gave away almost all of her clothes to charity shops. Now, when she walked the university corridors, bustling with students in pre-faded jeans, people still recognized her—but always with a measure of uncertainty, for she looked different now, different enough that she could insist they were mistaken and duck away. It was this more than anything that convinced them, for such a constrained person could not possibly be the spotlight-hugging Astor Megablaster.

But her ruse was not always successful. Once, she ran into an old acquaintance, an energetic young man who knew her instantly, calling and waving from several meters away. She nodded coldly. What was his name? Hadn't she had a fling with him? That did not mean that she knew his name. His face did not seem too familiar either but you didn't always see them in the darkness, your drunken eyes and nose buried in sweating flesh. Indeed, she remembered one boy who had insisted on covering her face with his hand the entire time they were being intimate. It was so warped. This was why the Bible used the term "to know." It had intended something else, something with a face.

In the meantime, here was this man, acting like her best friend, whooping and slapping her shoulders and shooting questions at her in a staccato discharge. She shrank from him, flinging answers as she retreated:

"Contemporary music studies and creative writing . . . Hackney . . . No, not anymore . . ."

He shook his head. "Honestly, I don't get it. You had it *made*, babe, you were *there*. So what the hell are you doing here?" He surveyed the dreary corridor. She put her hands up defensively.

"I wasn't *there*. I wasn't anywhere! I was in paparazzi hell, I—"

"Well, it's the world's loss." He grabbed her by the wrists and examined her thoroughly before she squirmed free. "Hot as ever, Astor. You were always the life and soul, dancing on

the tables and getting it all on, 'ey? Good times! Want to come
tonight to the Temple of Beat? Top DJ in from Amsterdam!
Let's pump it up!"

The Temple of Beat. Images flooded her mind. Strobe-
flashed caverns, bodies writhing madly to crashing rhythms
and unsubtle prose, vigorous activity in dark corners, four-
teen-year-olds in bikini tops vomiting on the floor.

"No thanks." She took a step backward and turned to go.

He said, "Astor, you've changed. Is everything OK?"

"Couldn't be better. Good to see you,"—she had finally
remembered, "Darren."

Over time, university became increasingly loathsome to
her. The college displayed, at his own request, its founder's
stuffed dead body in a glass case at the entrance. Each time
she passed, she wanted to spit at him for denying his body
its natural end, the dignity of disintegration in dark dirt. An
idol at the entrance to the temple, he symbolized all that was
wrong with the place.

She met with her professor to discuss her writing. "I'm
pleased," he said. "When you first came, your sentences sank
under heaping helpings of clichés and adjectives, but—and
can I credit myself here?—your writing is now delicate and
concise, a joy to read. You've learned about revealing only
what's necessary. You've learned the secret of less is more.
Have you given any thought to publishing?"

She looked at him, surprised. "No. I'm planning to give
up writing."

"You're not serious?" He seemed affronted. She wished
people would not become so invested in her life.

"Look," she said, "I owe you a lot. You told us to write our
worst fears, our deepest shames—"

"Which you did. Wonderfully."

She nodded, suddenly shy. "I've been to a million therapists, but . . . when I started to write my stories, I saw what
lay under all the anger. You showed that to me."

"Hey, don't underestimate your anger. It was the engine
for your songs. Excellent songs, by the way, I've been meaning
to tell you. Your album—"

"Was nauseating," she said flatly. "But I've written new songs this year. Much better, I think."

He pursed his lips. "So you *are* writing?"

"Not fiction."

"But why not, for heaven's sake?"

"Overexposure. Too much of me comes through in my stories. No music to hide behind."

"Oh. I see. You shouldn't be ashamed of what you are."

She stared at the desk. The professor reflected briefly, tapped absently on the edge of his desk with a pencil.

"Astor, you know my beliefs. The true poet feels compelled to undress for the masses. We conspire with him to pretend he is cloaked, but all know that his writing is a mere fig leaf, that the emperor has no clothes. That is writing: a pact between voyeurs and exhibitionists."

He leaned forward. She scraped her chair backward a few inches, avoiding his eyes. "As I've told you all many times, we write what we cannot say. I wrote my first novel to carry my rage at my father. I couldn't speak of it to anyone, so I spoke of it to everyone." He nodded and spread his hands toward her in a gesture midway between resignation and challenge. "If you aren't willing to do that, then I would say no, don't write."

She glanced up at him briefly from the lowered angle of her head, sensing his disappointment. "I can't. Eyes are too brutal."

Oh wise professor, do not individuals need their privacy, or society its secrets? Listen to what the Kotzker Rebbe said: "Not all that is thought should be said; not all that is said should be written; not all that is written should be published; not all that is published should be read."

He leaned back with a rueful shrug. "Well, don't bare more than you can bear. But Astor, if you change your mind, let me know."

She nodded in relief.

One day soon afterward, a few minutes before class, the breathless girl said, "Astor, can I ask you a personal question?"

"Yes."

"Well, what's with all these baggy skirts? Jeans looked so stunning on you."

"I like skirts."

"If I had a great figure like yours I wouldn't hide it under—"

"I like skirts."

"Yes, but—"

"Tell me something," she interrupted her. "Why do we have to see everything inside your handbag? Can't you spare us your Tampax and used tissues?"

The breathless girl froze. The Scot's childish snigger erupted loudly nearby. Everyone turned to stare in the sudden silence.

Feeling ashamed of her sharp tongue, she hastily gathered her things to leave. It was at that moment that she decided she would not return.

Her mother stopped talking about the Tory minister's latest philanderings and put down her fork with a loud clatter.

"Astor, I'm not blind. I always watch what you eat. You haven't touched your shrimp. Tell me what's going on."

"Nothing. Leave me alone."

"Tell me!"

There was a silence. She shrugged. "It's not kosher."

Her father said straight away, as if he had prepared for this moment for months, "Don't worry, it's just a phase. A phase, that's all." With efficient motions, he reached over and shoveled her food onto his plate. The TV was muted but a subtitle flashed onscreen: "*Next up: Rob dumps fiancée for masseuse!*"

"Is her clothing a phase too?" her mother asked acidly. "Where did you buy that blouse? It's positively Victorian, Astor."

Her face was expressionless. "My name is Esther."

This time even her father, mouth full of shrimp, winced as if she had spat out a curse.

"Dad, that was Grandma's name," she said angrily, "so it's my real name, not that *goyish* version you gave me."

"*Goyish!* Where did you learn that disgusting word?" her mother demanded. "I will not have racism in my house!"

She did not respond. Her father swallowed his food, and reached for his glass. He said in a carefully measured tone, "We didn't want to expose you to anti-Semitism. We wanted a normal childhood for you."

"Call that normal? Walking around ashamed of my identity?"

He drank some more wine, delaying his reply, then said quietly, "My mother went to the camps for being a Jew." His daughter was startled. He hardly ever spoke of that time. "When we came here she instructed us to keep a low profile, to blend in. I have honored her wishes, and if you care for her memory, so should you." He gave her a hard look, and a hint of mockery entered his tone. "The Biblical Esther also kept her faith a secret. Her uncle Mordecai commanded her to. Did you know that?"

Red patches appeared in Esther's cheeks. Her mother burst out: "Look at you, sleeves to your knuckles! Soon you'll be wearing a burqa from head to toe, with a slit for eyes. Then it'll be farewell daughter, hello bloody postbox!"

It is God's glory to conceal, Esther thought.

Her father sighed. "Lynnette, she's just acting out." He did not look at his wife. They almost never looked at each other anymore, it seemed; only at the TV, computer, and food. Oh, and at her, of course, for particular purposes only.

"Come on now. Remember her gothic phase? Her piercings phase? Her . . ." He trailed off but they all knew what he meant to say, as he flicked a glance at her face, thin but no longer skeletal. "She tries on identities like fancy dress costumes. She's done it all, including superstardom and making a bundle before she even left school. She's not run-of-the-mill, our girl, and she has to try things out, but she'll finish university too, and turn out fine. So she's trying religion now, so what?"

His wife made a stifled noise.

"Darling," he soothed, "don't react to her every whim. From now on she'll give herself the attention she needs. We've done enough." The prongs of his fork stabbed through the crust of his pie, raking through the soft cooked vegetables inside. His daughter pushed away her plate and stood up.

"Oh spare me your analyses, for God's sake. I'm not your one of your precious patients." She stood there for a moment, as the two of them stared at her. They seemed to be waiting for some other reaction, some kind of understanding. A subtitle ran across the screen: "*Next up: Olette's stripping for charity!*"

Esther went in one last time to the university to bid goodbye to her professor and thank him, trying to ignore the wrinkle of disgruntlement in his forehead. Afterward, she encountered the breathless girl, carrying a new green leather handbag.

"Um," said Esther, forgetting the girl's name. "Wait, please. I wanted to say I'm sorry. The Jewish Sages say shaming someone in public is like murder. I must ask you to forgive me."

The girl giggled nervously. "Oh—well, thanks. I mean let's not exaggerate, I'm still alive, aren't I?" She pinched the exposed fold of her stomach as proof, a mawkish smile on her face. "I'm sure you didn't mean it, Astor. No harm done." She tried to put her hand on Esther's arm, but the latter just nodded awkwardly and moved away.

"No harm done." Esther sat on the old sofa in the tiny flat, wearing a floor-length skirt. The young woman in the wig quietly nursed her baby under a cloth. "You can embarrass someone, you can murder someone, you can do what you like—because you don't really mean it, and so you're not responsible. A sick society, Bayla. The Torah has saved my life. I'm so happy I met you and Aryeh Leib. But I wish my parents understood."

"Oh, Esther," Bayla said. When she spoke, her eyes glanced upward as if turning to other spheres. Esther was always trying to catch her eye and keep it, as if competing with God for her attention. "Don't cut off contact with them. They were God's partners in creating you."

"I'll try. They're difficult people." She listened to the small sucking sounds coming from underneath the white cloth. "Bayla, I noticed at your *Shabbos* table that the women sit in silence while the men sing the songs. Why?"

"It's forbidden for men to hear a woman's voice. It's considered a form of nakedness."

Esther considered this information, which in one fell swoop negated her entire career to date. She found that she approved. "I've never before just sat back and enjoyed other people's singing. It was liberating."

"I told you, you have an innate Jewish modesty." Bayla shifted the baby to her other breast under the cloth in a swift, practiced movement. Esther marveled at the young woman's poise. She could turn into a dignified act even this awkward conjoining of greedy little mouth with milky balloons of flesh. "Your very name means hidden," Bayla continued. "I wonder if you were born under the sign of the moon. That's a good sign for keeping secrets, the Talmud says. When's your birthday?"

"I'm a Scorpio," said Esther. The other woman nodded sagely as if that was what she expected to hear. This topic held little interest for Esther, and she continued to press her. "But is it only singing or a woman's voice in general that can't be heard?"

She laughed. "Only singing, of course! Otherwise how could I talk to my husband, or the grocer?"

"Oh."

"You sound disappointed!" she chided. "Esther, Judaism is a religion to live by, to be normal by."

"I know that."

"No, really. Be careful. I've seen newly religious people go *meshuggeh* taking on all kinds of things God didn't command."

Esther frowned. After a pause, she said, "So can a man listen to a woman singing on the radio, or on a CD?"

"Well, my husband wouldn't. But, well, if the man doesn't know who the singer is or what she looks like, it might be allowed. I'll ask my husband if you want."

"It'll never work."

Her agent pushed pens around his desk then stuck one in his mouth, making his thick northern accent even more incomprehensible. "Using an alias is a really daft move. You're blowing all your hard-earned name recognition. And how can

I promote a disc if you won't put your picture on the cover? You're killin' me, love. You're cutting our sales to the bone."

To her dismay, she could not stop her voice from shaking. "But the new disc is about my music, not my body. It's a whole different sound, and a different me."

He screwed up his face and tried to put his arm around her, but she moved away. "Lovey, you've gorra gorgeous voice and great lyrics, and I'm a big fan of your new sound, right? But selling these days is about a lot more. Don't forget it was your . . ." he hesitated, uncharacteristically delicate, "er—very out-there pics that finally got us to number one. That's the world we live in."

There was a stony silence. Cautiously he ventured, "And what about touring?"

"For women only."

He spat out the pen. "Sod that for a lark. You might as well tear up your contract right now."

She set her teeth. "I'll get the damn thing out myself."

And with a lot of trouble, she did. She chose the name *ElleUsive* for herself, and for the album, *Seen/Unseen*. The cover picture showed a blurry, genderless figure lurking in the shadows. She conscripted all her old contacts to help her get the disc out, all sworn to silence about her true identity. She spent a lot of her own money advertising in all the right papers and magazines, and drove around London plastering posters until her fingers ached. The first single released was *Holding Back*, a quiet, dreamy song with few words and much silence. She forced herself to wait patiently.

She struck lucky. A DJ at Radio One heard the CD and was hooked. He said the songs were "fiery yet tender, like an English Sinead O'Connor." Soon the single was climbing the charts, and myriad media lips flapped earnestly with the question, "Who is *ElleUsive?*" Every time she heard them, she held her breath in fear of discovery. The talking heads loved the mystery, and drained it to its dregs. One morning, a besotted young fan from Leicester was interviewed on Breakfast TV.

"I dream of her at night," he said. "Her voice fills my head. I'll find out who she is if it's the last thing I do."

The presenter smiled patronizingly. "Any ideas yet?"

"I've studied the album cover," he replied, "and I have some leads. Also, I plan to use a computer voice recognition program—I'll match her voice against albums from recent years. Maybe she did backing vocals to some band. Or at the very least I can pinpoint her accent and find out where she's from."

"A latter-day Henry Higgins!" chortled the presenter. "Well, best of British luck."

Esther shivered uncomfortably. She suddenly knew the hedged-in feeling of the fox at the hunt. A few days later, her name was suggested by someone, though whether as a result of the young fan's research or a leak was unclear. Some scoffed at this suggestion. The glittering, crowd-loving Astor, queen of publicity, would never put out an album anonymously. But many others were convinced, and it rapidly became a given. Most of the mavens chirped their approval of her musical transition "from hostility to yearning," but a few were disappointed and claimed she had "copped out" and "lost her gumption and pizazz." Tauntingly, they challenged her to show herself.

As for the public, the idea of forcing her out of early retirement appeared to please them tremendously. Throngs of reporters and pimply teenage boys showed up at her parents' house; she heard them screaming in the background of her mother's messages on her machine. Infuriatingly, her mother actually sounded pleased. With a shock she understood that her mother preferred her as she had been before. This knowledge made her snappish for weeks.

Astor is back! It made the last item on the evening news, the so-called "dead donkey slot" generally reserved for newborn pandas and talking dogs. They showed the old pictures of her, her spiny mauve-and-blonde hair, black lipstick and shiny black blouses, the scanty swatches of red leather that passed for a skirt, her face, covered in piercings, scowling into the microphone. Subtitle: *Where is Astor and why is she hiding?*

So frightening was her picture, was the mere idea of becoming that unhappy person again, that the very next

day Esther called a travel agent and fled to Israel, till the fuss
should die down.

In Israel, at the seminary for newly religious women,
everyone wore long skirts and tights. Though many girls
sufficed with calf- or ankle-length skirts, Esther's hems swept
holy soil every time she moved. Wet circles spread under her
arms in the heat, so she bought larger blouses that billowed
away from her armpits. Their sleeves covered her hands and
only her fingertips stuck out. She liked it that way: *The glory of
the king's daughter is within.*

She had never been to Israel before but it seemed the
right step to take. She had left her parents a message that
she was going away but without saying where, unable to face
objections that Israel was too dangerous when they failed to
grasp how threatening her existence was back home. After
her arrival, she did not call them once.

Thus isolated from the world for seven weeks, amongst
people who had no idea of her past and did not care, she
finally found a calm of sorts. She wrote down everything she
was taught, read books on the soul, on prayer and on being
a Jewish woman. She even learned to read Hebrew. But she
found prayer very difficult. She lurched through the collection of syllables in a foreign tongue, feeling stupid and frustrated and not as if she was talking to anyone. She asked her
teachers repeatedly, *How can I pray?* They replied, *Call out to
God, speak to Him, make it a habit. Ask Him to help you pray.* She
asked, *But who is God?* They told her *King, Father, Beloved.* But
when she said the word God softly to herself, there seemed
to be no Being behind it, just an absence, a flapping curtain.
No Face.

Her teachers told her to wait; these things came slowly.
She told herself to be patient, and to trust. But she was not
used to waiting, or trusting, or inhabiting the bottom of the
ladder alongside the unskilled and inept. A rabbi suggested
that she imagine a person she really loved and then multiply
that by ten, but Esther got stuck at the first part. She watched
the other women daily as they prayed with a devotion that
made her loathe herself.

Finding the Mediterranean sun unbearably bright—
England's hottest sun was still yellower than this white
heat that bleached the insides of her eyes—Esther wore
sunglasses, even indoors. She went out only at night, and
then mostly to the Western Wall. She would try to pray, and
end up instead watching the guard handing female tourists
shawls to drape over their bare shoulders or midriffs. Or she
would peer through the partition at men in black who unin-
hibitedly cried, "*Tatteh, Father,*" their bodies swaying like trees
in a storm. No one ever stopped her; no one paid any mind
to yet another bundled-up religious woman in the streets of
Jerusalem. She spent many days in silent meditation behind
her sunglasses, gladly secreted in her capacious clothes.

Jerusalem! She was astonished by the place. As with
everything in her life, she had come with low expectations,
and indeed found crowded buses full of irritable sweaty
people, cracked and dirty pavements, police and soldiers
visible everywhere. Yet the city had a transcendent pulse to it
that London lacked; the ordinary person's mind, even when
buying vegetables, was halfway in the sacred, just by virtue of
breathing Jerusalem air. Somehow, people who vehemently
disagreed with each other's fundamental beliefs managed for
the most part to jostle together without incident, in a delicately regulated co-existence resting on unspoken covenants.

And when Esther did make the effort to connect, to
converse with the Jerusalemites she met, she found herself
amazed at their sincerity and their uncomplaining sacrifice.
They were so kind, constantly inviting her to their homes,
even those who were clearly not well-off or barely spoke
English. She felt embraced, as if she had finally reunited
with family. One of her fellow students invited Esther for the
weekend to her American cousins in Bnei Brak. The husband,
a soft-spoken man with a tall round fur hat, would not look
directly at Esther when he addressed her, a fact that made her
absurdly happy. The wife was fat and garrulous, and seemed
able to produce huge amounts of delicious greasy food from
her small kitchen without breaking a sweat. She was proudly
informed by sixteen-year-old Chaya Udel that the nine children she saw constituted only a *part* of the family, who

numbered fourteen children all told. "No, of course this isn't the biggest family in the neighborhood," scoffed the teenager, adding a Hebrew phrase for protection from the evil eye. Ticking off on her fingers, she explained that the oldest, a girl of twenty-five, was married with three children of her own; the second, a boy, was somewhere in America; then two more boys and a girl, all married, to Esther's astonishment.

The remaining nine children (from Chaya Udel all the way down to baby Rucheleh) slept squished three to a room. There was no spare bedroom, and Esther and her friend had to sleep on mattresses on the closed balcony. And yet, seated in a corner and watching the littler children tumbling over each other, shouting boisterously in Yiddish, or pulling at her sleeve to ask her endless questions ("Do you have a car? How big is your garden? Are you Jewish? Why don't you live in Israel? Is England in America? Can you go to America and bring back our brother Gedalyoh, he's gotten lost?"), she realized that she infinitely preferred this cramped four-bedroom home to her parents' house in London, four times the size.

A part of her, however, wondered what lay beyond Jerusalem and Bnei Brak—was there another Israel? So on her last day, she skipped class and went to the beach. Not the separate beach where only women swam, but the mixed beach in Tel Aviv. She sat at the back, watching. Where once she would have seen people enjoying themselves on a hot day, now all she registered was hundreds of bodies. Bodies bouncing around everywhere: flabby and compact, hairy and smooth, brown, white, and piebald, with rounded bellies, extruding vertebrae, covered in scars, warts, moles and patches of pinkish dry skin. Hard to believe, she reflected, that she had once lain there amongst them, sunning her limbs, before they became bony and grotesque; seeking admiration, yet always ready with a nasty gibe against male predators. More than once she had looked up to find a strange man staring, and once she had even woken to a hand laid upon her thigh.

Later, of course, came all the greedy cameras, guzzling her figure with their clicking lenses, her body a valuable commodity. Often she only found out precisely what they had captured of her when she opened the paper the next day. At the time she claimed that she did not mind, that she welcomed anything good for her career. Now she could not imagine how she could have sat there dressed in only a few inches of fabric, the private and the public hopelessly mixed up.

She suddenly remembered how impressed she had been upon meeting a nudist. "*And they were both naked, the man and his wife, and were not ashamed,*" he had declaimed proudly, "and thus we return humanity to Eden and reverse the curse." Back then it had sounded spiritual, even utopian. Now it just seemed perverted. A society without shame was not paradise, but hell. "*Doesn't Anyone Blush Anymore?*" That was the title of the talk that had led her to Bayla and her husband. Her own answer had been "No, should they?" It seemed obvious, but she was intrigued enough to drive for an hour in the rain to unfamiliar territory in Northwest London. There she had met some people dressed in neat dark clothing—"medieval relics" her father would call them—who claimed otherwise. A rabbi spoke of how the brazen Moabites defecated publicly before their gods, while in contrast, the windows of the Israelites' tents faced modestly away from those of their neighbors. Apparently, it was the spiritual descendants of these Israelites who still blushed, while the rest of humanity had lost all shame. Driving back, she had committed to memory the verse the rabbi had quoted: *How goodly are thy tents, O Jacob.*

"*Ahalan,* sweetie." A hairy man in a wet swimsuit grinned at her, interrupting her reverie. She looked around at the hundreds of firm, tanned limbs in bikinis, then down at her over-large blouse, long skirt and laced shoes—and laughed in disbelief. He laughed too, misunderstanding. "Pretty! From America?"

She shook her head at him. "What's wrong with you? Are you insane?" She pointed around herself in a semi-circle and raised her eyebrows at him meaningfully. His face was a blank. She waved him off and sat there for a long while, feeling perplexed and disjointed.

Back in England, she discovered a large pile of fan mail and wilted bouquets waiting at her parents' home. Her song, though now dropping rapidly, had made the top ten. She did feel gratified; but somehow, seven weeks of mumbling Hebrew had made ambition and success seem transient, cobwebs obscuring the mirror of truth. She told her parents to throw the entire pile of letters away unopened, carefully avoiding her mother's disappointed eye.

Esther hoped that the album would continue to quietly sell on its own for a while longer. This would pay for trips to Israel, since almost all of her savings were gone, spent on drink and drugs and hospitals, given away to long-gone friends or stolen by spurious paramours. She felt now that she could not tour anymore, even for a female audience. The idea that she might never perform again, once so terrifying, now gave her great peace. She hoped the newfound quiet would allow in more joy. More God.

In her absence, she was pleased to note, the media had moved on to buzz around fresh carrion. Their short attention span, precisely what had once provoked her to ever more extreme antics to keep the public eye, was now a reason to be grateful. Her parents, though, would not easily forget their horror at her sudden disappearance, and to Israel of all places. For weeks afterward her mother called her at odd hours to make sure that she was still in the country. Ignoring the phone was futile; her mother simply left the same message time after time:

"Your mother again. Call me please."

But this harassment too ceased eventually and Esther was finally left in peace until the day she received a hand-delivered card at her Hackney flat. It contained two words only, in careful handwriting with long capitals: "*Beautiful Astor.*" Her hand trembled, holding it, and she felt immensely perturbed to think that someone knew her private address. From then on she looked around whenever she went out, and triple bolted her door at night.

Esther spent the rest of the summer in Torah classes, and began to attend synagogue every Sabbath. The place was small and overflowing with old wooden benches and lecterns. The prayer books, yellowed from much fingering, were stained at the pages for the Sabbath services with the lipstick smears of the women who buried their faces in the books, screening out the world. The women had their own floor, high above the men, behind a criss-crossing brown lattice partition that her mother would call a chicken coop. You could see through the lattice only if you held your face sideways against it, which she did, feeling its wooden slats pressing into her cheek. Through the holes she could piece together visual fragments of the men below—an ear, a *kipa*, a hand resting on a prayer book. She wondered if the lattice left red diamond-shaped marks on her face, like the marks left by the *tefillin* on the men's arms in the morning when she came to the synagogue on weekdays, the only woman present. On those days she would slip through the back so as to avoid the men coming in at the front, her long skirt tangling in the brush, collecting burrs. Later, while plowing through the morning blessings, she would pick the burrs out absentmindedly, making a neat pile of them on the ledge.

Esther's Hebrew fluency had improved, but prayer was still a challenge. She had heard a rabbi speak of the mystical idea that the word for "world," *olam*, came from the same Hebrew root as "to hide." The beginning of enlightenment, he explained, is in understanding that until now one has been living in darkness. Esther understood this well: she was experiencing a growing light in her life. But still she was not happy. She did not feel she knew in any kind of meaningful way this God that everyone was so busy worshipping. Light was not something she could love or know or pray to. She yearned for a connection to something that could be named and seen. In the meantime, the light she felt around her began to bother her. She even found herself squinting.

One Monday morning, Esther found an American woman standing in the women's section of the synagogue. She felt an immediate visceral hatred toward this bronzed stranger, waltzing into the sanctuary in her tiny pink shorts. To her chagrin, she soon discovered that this woman knew the service well, closing her eyes and praying by heart, covering her face with the *siddur* and swaying like the most devout of rebbetzins. When the men began to sing the Psalm before taking out the Torah, the stranger joined in loudly, her pronounced accent making her voice even more prominent. Esther squinted through the lattice and saw several men look up and frown. A few seconds later the service halted completely, and there were loud *Shhhh*'es. She burned at the idea that they might suspect her of this travesty. The American woman, however, simply leaned forward and hollered through the partition: "What's up with you guys? If you don't like my voice, sing louder. Get your thoughts out of the gutter, people, and back on God!"

Esther blushed—for the shrill vulgarity of the woman, for the men, for herself. After a second, the men continued, more loudly, and from then on ignored the stranger's singing. But Esther was scandalized. Mercifully, the American never returned.

A month after the first, another card arrived in the same handwriting. This time it said, "*I know you, lovely Astor. Your music speaks your soul.*" Esther ripped it up into small pieces, flinging them through the window. In her morning prayers, she put a special emphasis on the sentence "*and keep us far from evil men.*" She hoped someone was listening. To her, it often seemed that all her prayers blew away in the wind, just like the fragments of paper.

Esther had never told her mother what she had done in Israel. She had let her think it was just a holiday and a refuge from the newspapers. Bayla encouraged Esther to reveal that she had attended a seminary there, and that her life now revolved around Torah and synagogue. Finally, Esther sent her mother an email telling her of the changes in her life. She lived to regret it, for her mother began calling her continuously, her voice high with anxiety: "Astor, these people have modesty patrols. They'll beat you up if they see your ankles."

Don't disconnect. Partners in creation. "Mum, this isn't Afghanistan. These are civilized people."

"You're turning into that handmaid in that novel by Margaret Whatsername! You'll wear a red cloak and become a baby machine!"

"Mum, with all due respect, could you separate between my life and fiction? First of all, red's not a modest color; we don't wear it. And sec—"

Her mother would not let her finish. "And back goes the clock two thousand years!" she moaned. "Why did we even bother with the feminist revolution?"

"To be honest, I really don't know."

This made her mother's voice rise to shrill. "Then I'll tell you! Trips on your own to Paris and New York, that's why! Singing, modeling, writing, that's why! Parties, boyfriends, your own car, your own money, owning your body—everything you've ever enjoyed, your freedom, your very life!" She sighed heavily. "Listen to me, listen how I'm yelling at you. How did we come to this? My darling, the world was your oyster; and now you're throwing it all away."

But oysters aren't kosher. "Mum, you don't understand."

"You're right, I don't understand. Do you mean to tell me you'd freely choose a life of sewing and cooking and babies and—" she stuttered with frustration, "—and endless laundry over all the exciting things you could do with your life?"

"I freely choose happiness."

"We gave you everything you need to be happy! Everything!"

"Everything except protection."

"Protection?" spat out her mother. There was a pause. Then her voice changed, and Esther recognized her mother's flat, professional voice—the one she used for reporting murders on TV. She could practically see her counting off on her fingers. "Now let me see, Astor. We live in the best neighborhood, we sent you to the best school, we drove you everywhere, and bought you your own very expensive and safe car. How could we have protected you more? Explain this to me. Really, I'd like to understand."

Esther sighed. "You just don't get it. Just look at your daily reporting. Murderers, rapists, adulterers, they're everywhere, all products of your so-called enlightened society that uses pornographic images to sell yogurt. But religious men control their animal urges. They're gentlemen. Religious people can be quiet and shy, and they're appreciated for those qualities. Religious women don't have to build superstar careers to be admired, or sleep with a man just to get him to love her. She's respected as a woman!"

"What—" her mother said in her thinnest voice, "what a gross caricature of our values. It's downright insulting."

"Yes, it took me a long time before I saw it myself. I had to be shown."

Her mother exhaled and appeared, finally, to have run out of steam. Esther suddenly felt a mild compassion for this woman who had brought her into the world. She said, "Mum, I'm happy. Can't you be happy for me? Please?"

She waited. Eventually her mother said hoarsely, "I'll never get it. It sounds like a cult. But it's your life, so live it."

Her father was less accommodating. "Astor, I strongly advise therapy."

"No, Dad. That's not where I'm going now."

"That's precisely what's worrying me—are you going or being taken? Why not choose more moderate forms of Judaism? These fanatics will squash who you really are. You're still vulnerable, and you're being drawn deep into a society that doesn't allow you to think."

"You're so patronizing! You know nothing about them!"

"I know enough," he persisted. "Go to analysis. Become familiar with your true motives. The philosopher said, 'Know thyself,' and I'm sure that the Torah, as a book of ancient wisdom, does too. If, after you reach a real understanding of yourself you still want to do this, I'll respect your decision and leave you in peace."

No, Dad, you're mistaken. Not everything must be revealed. For there is the hidden of things:
pulsing of wombs . . .
weeping at night . . .
reptiles under stone . . .
whispering passions . . .
Redemption is not found in talk shows, frying our innards under studio lights.

God is not found in the shrink's office, plucked like a growth from our murky minds.

One evening, returning home from Bayla's after midnight, Esther found a man lurking on the street near her place.

"Astor!" he beamed, approaching her with outstretched hands. Her body was instantly covered in goosebumps.

"No," she said, backing away up the steps toward her door. Her hand fumbled for her key. He stopped, his palms held upward toward her.

"Astor, please." A deep bass voice. "Don't see me as a stranger. That hurts. See me as a lover you don't yet know." He moved toward her and her heart shot into her throat. Seeing this, he urged, "Your music called me here. This was meant to be."

She dug her hands urgently into her bag, but the key eluded her grasp. He came up the steps, and before she knew it had taken hold of her arm in an iron grip. His touch sent a jolt through her. No man had touched her for a long time. She cast around frantically for the best course of action. In the past she had had no problem hitting, biting, and scratching stalkers. But she did not want to behave like a wild animal now; she did not even know if she had it in her anymore.

"Please," she said weakly, trying to pry herself free. But he held on, and looking intently at her, brought his other hand up to her hair to stroke it. "You're even more beautiful now, without all that make-up," he murmured. "I understand this change you went through. From girl to woman."

The street was deserted. With reluctance Esther decided to resurrect her old, violent self—she had no choice. Mustering all her energies, she let out a piercing yell and started flailing her head violently from side to side and thrashing her arms about. She succeeded in knocking away the hand that was at her face. Then she turned from defense to attack, kicking out at his legs. Grunting, eyes wide in pain and astonishment, he finally let go of her arm in order to slap away the oncoming blows with both hands. She took the opportunity to shove him hard in the chest with a strength she had forgotten she owned, and he toppled down the stairs and fell hard onto his hip on the asphalt, where he remained, moaning. She was not going to wait for him to get up. Locating her key at last, she stumbled in through the front door, tripping over her long skirt and ripping its hem. Before slamming the door, she screamed over her shoulder, "If you ever come near me again, I'll kill you!"

Safe inside, she ran to the front window. Through a crack between closed curtains she watched him slowly get up and, with a reproachful and appalled look at the building, hobble away.

Esther did not call the police. She could not face their sniggers, or risk finding herself in the morning papers. But buried memories surged up uncontrollably, and the feel of his hands remained on her for hours, long after she had showered.

First thing in the morning she would look for an apartment in the most religious Jewish area she could find. This must never ever happen again.

"It was disgusting! Why is a man allowed to molest a woman at her own doorstep?" she complained, feeding the baby. "It's a free country for everyone except women."

"You really shouldn't be on your own," said Bayla. "We'll find you a *shidduch* and get you married."

Ignoring Bayla's words, Esther extracted banana mush from the baby's fine hair. She was not ready for anything like that. Her shameful past would surely repel any nice man. She needed to build a new life first, prove that she had changed. Moreover, there was a possibility that due to her choices, her reproductive system might be permanently damaged—something she hardly dared to think about.

Bayla continued, "But—and don't be offended—you should really change your style. You know, being modest doesn't mean being dowdy, wearing clothes three sizes too big. Dress neatly and in quiet colors, cover yourself nicely, that's enough. If you draw attention to yourself you defeat the purpose."

"I know that." But she continued to wear the same clothes, and a few days later, took out a long cotton scarf and wound it around her head. It instantly made her feel so safe that she began wearing it all the time, even in bed, taking it off only to shower.

Bayla blanched when she saw her next. "Esther, it's not appropriate for single women to wear headscarves. People will think you are married. The scarf is the boundary mark of a woman who is off limits."

Esther said in a hurt voice, "*It is God's glory to conceal.*" Bayla just shrugged. "But why?" Esther pleaded, feeling tears at the back of her eyes. "Why can't I cover my head? The men wear *yarmulkes* and black hats on top of them. Why can't I wear just one layer?"

"Because you're not a man." Bayla sighed. "This isn't good."

Yet with the head covering on, Esther felt protected—not just from intruders but even, somehow, from the light that constantly grew, surrounding her. If she could only block out the light, she felt, perhaps she would finally be able to see the Face.

Within ten days of the incident, Esther had moved to a very religious neighborhood. She loved the way, even late at night, people walked the streets with their children, or left their doors open, chatting to neighbors. Fear did not dwell in these streets. She did not mind living in a room the size of her parents' walk-in closet—all she needed was a bed and a door that locked. Moreover, the walk to *shul* now took ten minutes instead of an hour and a half.

One Friday night she arrived in the women's section to find the wooden lattice gone, replaced by a transparent glass partition. She turned in shock to the rebbetzin: had modesty been thrown to the winds? The old lady laughed at her.

"No, dear, it's a window on our side, but for them it's a mirror. So we can see them, but they only see themselves. Isn't that clever?"

But that's unfair. Do they know?

She sat in her usual seat in the front row, right next to the partition. During the service, she looked down at the men, dazzled by the absence of the slats, unused to being able to see them in their entirety. She saw many new things: an old man with a cane; three little blond boys with their dark-haired father; a young teenager sporting an over-large black hat, like a child dressed up for Purim. She could not believe the richness of detail she had previously missed.

Esther remembered one of the teachers in Israel speaking of the experience of watching Hasidic men in their swaying hundreds on bleachers at a *tish*. The teacher described how she crowded alongside the Hasidic wives and daughters in their special white aprons at small windows high above the men, jostling for a glimpse.

"It was a sight I will never forget," the teacher reminisced. "And in some ways, I felt, it was even better than being down there with them. You see, girls, we learn from the Izhbitzer Rebbe on *parshat Toldot* that there are two modes in life: *being* and *seeing*. Isaac represents being. He lived in Israel for his entire life, and his feet trod only holy soil—but he was blind and never actually saw the land. Moses, who represents seeing, in contrast saw the entire land spread before him, but never set foot in it. Girls, in *shul*, men are Isaac and women are Moses. We can't be down there, close to the Torah, but we can see what the men can't—we can see them!" All the women in the room had nodded, recognizing the truth of the words.

Indeed, at this moment, looking down, Esther felt a strange power, a superior knowledge. It reminded her of days gone by, on the occasions when she would spot a man she wanted. She knew that all she had to do was approach him boldly, stand in a certain way, laugh in a certain way, and touch him lightly on the arm. They could never resist her—or rather, their own desire. Only later, when they had grown bored of her, would she feel powerless, and then she would do all the humiliating things in the world to try and get them back.

Esther cringed and moved her arm as if to brush away the memories contaminating the pure air of the synagogue. Taking a deep breath, she directed her eyes back to the praying men below. The congregation reached the end of the *Lecha Dodi* hymn, welcoming the Sabbath Queen as a bride. For the last verse, as usual, everyone turned around toward the door, to bow to the incoming Bride before turning back to face the front and the Holy Ark.

But now Esther saw something she had never noticed before. While the women turned again to the front relatively quickly, the men remained facing the back for a minute, until the tune was over. This meant that for a few long moments, the men and the women actually faced each other, like the cherubs, one male and one female, adorning the Israelite ark. At this revelation, Esther felt some thought agitating inside her, pushing to surface.

The word for face is the same as the word for inside: panim, pnim. When you meet someone face to face, your inner worlds meet.

Around her, on the second floor of the synagogue, the women were silent. A few closed their eyes; a few hummed the tune. But down below, the men, their faces upturned, sang rowdily, almost breaking the disintegrating floorboards with their stamping feet. Esther felt that she ought to avert her eyes from this sight, that there was something immodest about staring at the men. Nonetheless she pressed her nose to the glass with a greedy hunger that alarmed and shocked her.

Do they know?

To her surprise, Esther found her own body moving back and forth in time with the men, her feet pounding wildly to the song, her lips mutely shaping the tune. She suddenly felt as if she was back in those sublime concerts in which she, fueled by hundreds of pairs of intoxicated eyes, would force hoarse brute screams from her gullet in strange octaves, higher and higher, until she finally felt herself blasting off in a jet of sound to some starry place beyond self.

Those moments had made everything else worthwhile. But then she had never paid attention to anyone but herself. The faces, out there beyond the blinding spotlights, were to her an undifferentiated mass, a many-headed beast named Audience, existing solely to be sated by her. Now, here in this old crumbling synagogue, held together by prayers, these strangers' faces with their starkly revealed ecstasy caught at her throat and moved her in an unfamiliar way.

The tune intensified. The men's rapture engulfed them. Faster and faster they swayed, higher and higher they jumped. They clapped and sang until finally, at the height of the chant, with their eyes closed and their arms flung joyously upward, it seemed to Esther as if these men were embracing the Shabbat Bride, embracing God Himself. Clutching her scarved head tightly with both hands, Esther suddenly cried out into the euphoric tumult, her shout swept away by the roar. Her eyes were wet, and she had never felt happier than at this moment. In another second she would surely burst with gratitude for this blessed sight, this secret knowledge, this wondrous intimacy with these anonymous bearded men, and—more incredibly still—with the God she saw reflected in their upturned faces. At long last: *King, Father, Beloved.*

Yet in some discerning place inside her, with the one sentient cell remaining in her giddy brain, she asked herself:

But do they know?

Do they know?

Do they know how naked they really are?

The Ged of El Al

"But the land which you are going over to possess . . . the eyes of the
Lord your God are always upon it, from year's start to year's end."
Deuteronomy, 11:11-12

"Many waters cannot quench the love, neither can floods drown it."
Song of Songs, 8:7

January 2014

In the growing twilight, the window reflected Ged's pale
face, blurred somewhat by a layer of condensation. He looked
down past the rainclouds to the city's mass of dirty buildings
in beiges and browns, reaching up, always reaching. In his
ten years there, Ged had never quite understood what they
reached for.

He was not sorry when Manhattan receded, the plane
hauling upward into the smooth, violet sky. He only regretted
the memories of places. Somewhere down there amongst all
that clutter and tinsel was the Starbucks where he had sat,
a lifetime ago, soon after his arrival, drinking in the sounds
and the faces and the freedom to read what he wanted. Even
the air had seemed suddenly clearer, sharp in his nostrils and
lungs. He had just bought a second-hand copy of a book called
A River Runs Through It. He loved the title, the unexplained "it."
It took courage to put such a vague, unidentified pronoun in a
title. Just then he had felt like an "it" himself.

Legs folded beneath him in the Starbucks armchair, Ged had read for hours of outdoorsmen, so different from the bearded thick-spectacled men with multi-voltage brains whom he had known all his life. He had felt a painful yearning to know these other men, so attached to earthly things. In the poetry of Montana fishing country, his coffee lay forgotten on the table, its lukewarm surface congealing.

"I am haunted by waters."

It had been a soft voice, with a friendly teasing tone, but Ged had jumped, the coffee splashing up and drenching his knees. He automatically cursed in the other language, the one from a world with no Starbucks or girls in short red skirts and an O of a mouth that made him blush.

"I'm sorry!" She pulled out a wad of tissues, dabbed futilely at the drenched cloth. He pulled away from her touch. Her hands were small and brown.

"Why did you say that?" he said, his usually gentle voice harsh and loud.

"It was just a line. From your book." She sounded mortified. "I just wanted to tell you I'd read it, but instead I wrecked your pants." She almost reached toward him again, but pulled back. "I was just showing off. Sorry."

"It's fine," Ged muttered. He stood up and—feeling like the village *schlemiel*—ran out, stained and wet.

Later he wondered how long she had been watching him read his book. Perhaps she had seen him through the café window and come in expressly to talk to him. Though he searched repeatedly for her silhouette, he never saw her again. In the city of eight million stories, hers was not to be his.

His neighbor whistled. Jolted from his memories, Ged turned to discover in the adjacent aisle seat a young man in his late thirties. The man sported wavy gelled hair, a black turtleneck and black jeans in the latest style. Ged wore ordinary blue jeans, and today his thick brown-blond hair was a bit lank. He pushed it awkwardly behind his ears.

"Look at that!" The man pointed at a small button next to the TV screen embedded in the seatback in front of him. "It's the new Personal Profilers. All the competition has forced El Al to become cutting edge."

"They definitely didn't have that when I last flew," Ged concurred.

"I'm such a sucker for a new gadget. See, it builds a personal profile of your movements during the flight—how many times you get up, what you order, how long you sleep, even in what position. Then it can recommend the best seat for you next time." He laughed. "It's the same principle as the Driving Profiler, except that we're not in danger of losing our license to be airline passengers!"

"I don't want a little spy gadget watching my movements," Ged objected.

"Yeah, very Big Brother."

Ged just nodded. A decade or so ago this statement would have been lost on him; but now he prided himself on being able to catch most Western cultural references.

"That's the way the world is going now," his neighbor added. "We're always being watched and tracked—in stores, on the street, maybe even in our homes, who knows?"

Ged shivered slightly. Neither of them pressed the start button for their profiler. A female flight attendant was closing all the overhead bins. Ged noticed her because she looked to be in her early fifties, with a lined face testifying to some life experience and smile far more genuine than those of the pretty young things who patrolled the aisles with her.

The man proffered a hand. "I'm Leon, by the way."

He shook it. "Ged."

"Pleased to meet you, Ged."

The El Al video began. Ged stared at it abstractedly, not bothering with headphones. On his outbound trip there had been one screen for fifty people; now the plane boasted individual seatback screens—touch-activated, with Internet and sockets for downloading content from mobile phones. He had, it seemed, been away for a long time.

Onscreen, sunlit coral reefs in Eilat and hotels with brushed white exteriors were rapidly replaced by camels on the desert horizon and beautiful tanned people singing, their mouths flapping in a comical muteness. Leon laughed. "This video is so kitschy. I know the tune by heart." He sang a few bars: "El Al, El Al, your home in the sky; *El Al, El Al, beitchem ba-sha-mayim*. I liked the old one better—*latoos El Al*—remember?"

Ged did not remember which one had played on his outward journey. Just remembering that trip, that flight from everything, made his muscles ache. When were the drinks coming around? He could do with something strong right now.

The day after it occurred, Ged reported the Starbucks encounter to his psychologist. He had followed the *She'elah* people's recommendation, to find a therapist as soon as he landed in New York. "You'll have a lot to deal with," they said. "You'll need help." He had contacted her the first week, picking her because Fein sounded Jewish and he wanted to be understood. Now it was their third session. Dr. Fein opened by saying:

"Ged, last time you told me you came to America to be normal. Tell me more about that."

Ged licked his lips, chapped from the New York cold. "I just want—you understand—to be a regular person. To disappear in the crowd. I'm truly exhausted of meeting people's eyes glaring at the stranger, the outsider."

At that time he still spoke a hesitant English, trying to avoid embarrassing errors. He had grown up with Yiddish. His American parents, speaking their secret language, did not reckon on their bright, osmotic child taking in every word. But his was still a pitted, peppered English, and while he possessed a rich vocabulary from his reading, his pronunciations were often laughable. In his mouth, crescent was *cress-kent*, gesture was *gestooer*. On the advice of the man from *She'elah*, he had bought a second-hand TV. The man assured him that he would soon learn to speak English exactly as the *goyim* did, and Ged thought it an excellent plan. He was a fast learner.

"But," he continued, "it is no simple undertaking to be normal. Yesterday I saw a girl, in Starbucks. When she tried to talk to me I spilled coffee on myself." Ged blushed. "I lack even the basic capacity to talk to women."

"You're talking to me."

Ged ran his hand over his scalp, feeling his short hair sprouting like grass after the first autumn rains. He still could not get used to the blunt corners of his head, where his long silky *peyos* had always dangled. Occasionally he fingered the bone below his eye socket, seeking to twirl the fine skein now gone. It was like an amputated limb that still itched.

"Yes," he said, "but I am nervous."

"It's OK to be nervous."

Ged raised an eyebrow but did not disagree.

"So what did the girl in Starbucks say that made you spill your coffee?"

Pink swept across Ged's high cheekbones as he met her eyes. "She said, '*I am haunted by the waters.*'" He did not explain further.

Dr. Fein nodded patiently as if they had forever.

The El Al video was glossy and appealing. For a moment Ged forgot he was not a tourist arriving in this exotic country. He imagined himself ready to eat spicy foods, to soak in the sun and allow the desert wind, bearing particles of sand from bones of Arabs and Jews, to scrape the pores of his face clean. Then, remembering that he was in fact a native son returning home, he experienced an even deeper joy, deeper even than his apprehension. He had missed this place, this belonging.

Ged ventured to ask Leon, who seemed to know a lot about everything, "Are tourists coming to Israel these days?"

"Oh yes, hordes."

"Really? I thought Israel had become a pariah."

"That's what the media would lead you to believe but that's because they're invested in that spin. Ordinary people are still drawn to come see for themselves."

"But what about the danger to life?"

Leon laughed cynically. "Oh come now. After 9/11 and bombings everywhere from Spain to Kenya, not to mention tsunamis, earthquakes, hurricanes, and volcanoes, people got the message—the only truly safe place is in your armchair, in front of the TV. So people say 'what the heck' and head out for Israel's beaches, which suddenly don't seem so dangerous after all, since at least Israel knows its security."

Ged smiled. "Even an armchair's not safe—there's a risk of spontaneous combustion."

This time Leon's laugh was genuine, full-throated. "I always say, if the Angel of Death wants you, he'll get you wherever you are. So just chill out and have another beer."

The sentence echoed off walls in Ged's mind. It reminded him of something from the Talmud. Yes, that was it: *Moloch homoves, mah li hocho umah li hosom.* The Angel of Death says, "What do I care if it I get you here or I get you there?" He had forgotten so much of his Talmud, it had been so long, yet the language, the way of thinking, was still inside him. He fervently hoped that if—when—he started learning again, it would all return. Distractedly he took out the in-flight magazine and began leafing through it.

As time passed, Ged got used to being alone with Dr. Fein. She was definitely Jewish but she seemed somehow so *not*, with her cropped hair and beaded necklaces, her elegant clothing in light velvets and delicate flowery fragrance, so different from his mother's moist smell of fried fish and little children. He had been afraid that he would fall in love with her, indeed, that he would fall in love with every woman he met, after being so long deprived—but there was something a little cool, a little distant about her that dampened any such emotion.

The first time she asked how he was feeling, he had flung out his arms in a wide gesture and exclaimed: "Feel? I feel like dancing! With your books! I want to do a waltz with every single one!"

She smiled slightly at his exuberance, without showing her teeth. "Why?"

He pointed to the books on her shelf. "Did you ever imagine a world where you would not be permitted to read any of these? Not a single one?"

She gave his question serious consideration. "No, I never did."

"It is as if someone would dictate to you what you can eat, all the time." Ged rambled happily for an hour about books and what he was learning from them. It took several sessions before he was willing to talk about something else, to admit more difficult feelings—such as his steady guilt at wasting time on non-Torah subjects. He confessed, "We're wired to think at every spare moment, 'Why am I not learning Torah?'" Even there, in her office, his hand fumbled at the small tractate of Mishnah he kept in his pocket. Sometimes he took it out, touching its smooth cover. But when she asked what he was thinking, he replaced it and changed the subject.

Over the course of their next meetings, he spun the story of his past. The migraines he began to suffer, the sense of suffocation, the unbearable pressure to get married though barely nineteen. All the rumors about his absences from yeshivah, his sense of being followed when he went to the Israel Museum to look at old artifacts, or to the rusty shed near the yeshivah where he kept his secular books locked up. His paranoia when the neighborhood kids squinted small curious eyes at him and giggled when he came home to Bnei Brak for Shabbat.

"How could they know?" he said bitterly. "Did the news reach them all the way from Jerusalem? So many eyes, so many gossiping mouths. Don't they have anything better to do?"

He saw again his father's silent anger, and his mother's red-rimmed eyes as she pleaded with him. How could he have become such a wicked boy, have broken the rules? He was ruining his good name and the family's, destroying his sisters' *shidduch* prospects—and for what? Some stupid books full of *goyishe narishkeit*?

"They had a lot of children and were very busy. I'd always been quiet, so they left me alone to sit reading in my room. 'This one, he's my Torah boy,' my mother would tell guests. My father would say, 'He's a quiet one, but don't be deceived—he's a cistern that retains every drop. He'll end up a great rabbi, we're sure.' Then all of a sudden I became more trouble than any of them. My mother became unable to leave the house without a nosy neighbor expressing some kind of sympathy over her troubles. I was so angry. The sympathy was killing her."

"Uh-huh," said Dr. Fein.

"I didn't mean to hurt her, doctor. I just wanted to know what was outside the yeshivah's walls."

The talks with his *Rosh Yeshivah* were particularly hard for him, for he had always revered him. "Do not be seduced by this world," the elderly man would say in his Polish-accented Yiddish, his hand resting lightly on some old volume. "It says in Ethics of the Fathers, '*He who stops his Torah learning to praise the beauty of a tree is liable to death.*' A Jew's eyes are not his own, Gedalyoh. It is written in the Shema, '*Do not be enticed after your heart and your eyes.*' You know all this, I shouldn't need to remind you."

Or: "My child, once a man starts looking at women, at the world, he will never stop until he has descended to the pit of hell. Not for nothing do we keep our eyes downcast when we walk. Keep your nose inside the Torah. Its sweet scent will guard you. The Torah's rules are our only true security."

After these talks Ged's guilt had burned in his gut, but he did not stop reading, or walking, or looking. His desires were so strong that eventually they had brought him here, to this new strange life, and now he could finally satisfy his thirst to look at many new things. Yet he still missed his parents and the neighborhood with its cramped buildings. The old rituals, the old books. Even now, free in New York with no one peering over his shoulder, he went every Friday at sunset into a kind of funk, creeping under his blanket till nightfall, ashamed that the Sabbath Queen should see him fallen so low.

Dr. Fein wrote on a yellow pad. Her handwriting was large and she was constantly starting a fresh sheet. She asked numerous questions about his parents and his childhood. Since he loved books, she suggested some she thought might be helpful to him, for example, *Siddhartha*, by Herman Hesse. Ged read it, intrigued by the transitions it contained and by the unusual religious personality at its center. Something in it spoke of his own life. "But Siddhartha was never normal," he said, returning the book to Dr. Fein's bookshelf. "Even in the end. He became a strange old man who understood the river but not his own son."

"OK. So what about Zionism? Zionism is how the Jews became normal," Dr. Fein proposed. "Today's Israeli is a citizen of the world."

"No!" he said. "No labels or ideologies for me! Just normal! Just human!"

Week after week, Ged had found himself sitting on the white leather sofa and lamenting his failure.

"Yes, OK, I've cut off my *peyos*, I wear jeans, I look entirely modern. Yet still when I see the people walking next to me on the street, I know I'm different. Superior." He pointed at himself. "Look at me, I don't learn, I read *goyish* books, I haven't prayed since I left Israel. I'm actually the worst kind of sinner, for I know the law! Yet because my mind still contains all the Torah I learned, I feel holier-than-them. It's disgusting, yet I can't help myself." A knot of saliva clumped in his throat. "For example . . ." He stopped.

"Go on," she prodded.

"Well, when I look at you, a loud voice in my head says you are not a real Jew. Your beliefs about God are—" He blushed, and turned his face to the wall.

"Speak your mind. Please."

"OK. I think they're ridiculous. You've sullied them with modern ideas, convenient ideas. You have no clue what the Torah is. You've never spent entire nights poring over every word as if it's a love letter from God."

He was both relieved and perturbed to see that she appeared unmoved. Her voice steady, she asked, "And how do you feel about God?"

He hesitated. "Oh—Him? Just before I left I informed Him that I don't believe in Him any more, so He should leave me alone."

She kept a straight face. "And what was the reply?"

"The usual. Silence." He laughed a cynical laugh. "But we have a concept in the Talmud—*shtiko kehoydo'o*. Silence is agreement. So He agrees."

Now she smiled. His hands twisted in his pockets.

"Do you honestly no longer believe in God?" she probed.

"No. I know He exists. But I've lost Him; I can't read Him the way I used to. It feels like He's stepped out of my life." Ged felt dizzy, as if an abyss had opened up beneath him. "You stop learning Torah, you cut the line."

Her sympathetic smile was small comfort.

A month after his arrival, Ged found work in a deli on the Lower East Side. He liked the people he worked with—Lyle, Maria, Denzel. He listened carefully to their conversations and tried to imitate their slang. He liked that they did not pry into his background or his peculiar English or ask why he never ate the deli food. He learned that normal people weren't as curious as he was. They weren't always poking into every nook to see what it contained.

Normality. Ged circled the subject, attacking it with the gusto he had once saved for the ancient books. What was it? Where was it to be found?

"Man, you in the wrong city!" chuckled Denzel. "Normal? Ain't no one in this place in their right mind! You gotta go someplace else! Go to Illinois!"

But Ged still searched, in restaurants, theaters, clubs, and parks, book in hand, always trying to blend in. He walked through Central Park, the Upper West Side, Wall Street. Christopher Street, Harlem, Chinatown, the Village. He went further afield, to Long Island, New Jersey, Connecticut. Looking, always looking. He did not go to Crown Heights or Washington Heights, Williamsburg or Monsey.

It made him happy just to walk by people, to observe them while not being noticed himself. Though he wore a watch, sometimes he even asked them the time, just to hear their commonplace replies—no startle in their faces, no black reflecting in their eyes. He forced himself to overcome his shyness and strike up conversations with strangers on park benches. He would ask them, "What is the meaning of your life?" Many refused to take him seriously, labeling him another New York weirdo. But he was amazed at the answers of the few who did, which often seemed to go round and round like a *dreidel* and then flop, without leading anywhere. He tried to fathom their passions but rarely did he discover someone whose way of seeing the world intrigued him deeply.

Only when he met artists, writers, philosophy students did he finally feel some kindred spirit. He had coffees with them, talking for many hours at a stretch. But when they invited him to a party, he would stand at the side, reading a book, feeling gauche and different, avoiding the women who tried to strike up conversation and refusing to return their flirting glances. The music seemed very loud and the people silly. Parties did not seem to be as much fun as when described in books, and he stopped going and stayed at home.

For a while he did not mind his isolation. He was delighted with the rent-controlled studio apartment he had been lucky enough to sublet on East 7th Street. Though it was tiny and had only one sink, he was used to small houses, and at least he finally had his own space after a lifetime of congested sharing. He was content to sit at home on the old sofa, reveling in the silence, listening to the dripping faucet, the roaring traffic, for long minutes on end, or turning on the TV and witnessing the lives there, learning the slang, spending time on this activity that seemed of such importance to Americans.

But eventually loneliness set in. The two tractates of Talmud he had brought with him as souvenirs of the old life glared at him from their shelf, their crumbling covers covered in dust. He found himself desperate to escape them, and stumbled out into the streets, searching for a girl in a short red skirt or following religious Jews with his eyes as they walked quickly down the street, hunching into their black coats to escape his fierce gaze. "They don't recognize me!" he thought in amazement. "They're afraid of *me!*" But the thought did not make him glad.

"It's so different from home!" Ged observed to Dr. Fein. "Here you can look at anything you want—jewels, clothes, women's bodies. But most of it is not yours, and never will be, so you're left thirsting after it. By us, we only look at what is ours. We look at a woman only when our parents have decided she is suitable to marry. We look into the Torah and it is ours. We look at what we love, and we love it by looking."

Dr. Fein scribbled something down on a pad. "Have you noticed," she asked, "that you still say 'we'?"

Ged reached up and opened the little nozzle above his seat, allowing cooling air to blow over his moist brow. He tended to sweat a lot, especially when anxious, and was always wiping his forehead self-consciously with a handkerchief that had once belonged to his father and was the only memento he carried of him. Though no one on the plane gave him a second glance—not even Leon, whose nose was now buried in a huge volume on American history that must have run to a thousand pages—Ged felt embarrassed, and fanned his face vigorously with a magazine. It was beginning to sink in that he was only a few hours away from landing. All that weighted past awaited him. He pressed the call button for the flight attendant. He did not particularly like alcohol, but there were times when it was the only thing that could help. This was one of those times, it appeared.

The El Al video shifted to Jerusalem. On Ged's screen, the domed mosque shone like the golden baubles on Manhattan's Christmas trees. It was followed by a shot taken from a helicopter flying over the Temple Mount. Ged marveled, for he had never seen the Temple Mount from above. After a few seconds, the helicopter flew above the Western Wall. It looked packed, and Ged idly wondered if it had been filmed on Shabbos. All those pious Jews would not be pleased to know that this camera had desecrated their holy day, and that their sacred devotions were now being shown on every El Al flight from Budapest to Beijing.

Now the intrusive camera zoomed in to the men's section. It was a storm of heads in motion, a writhing knot of black hats and white skullcaps. Ged's heart began pounding, and he stabbed again at the call button. He really needed that drink.

The New York seasons flowed into each other and months turned to years. Ged was still seeing Dr. Fein. She had helped him understand a lot more about his childhood and emotional patterns, but now the sessions just felt depressing and unproductive. Weary of threshing through his past and complaining about his present, Ged sat shrugging in frustrated silence. He refused to answer any of Dr. Fein's questions. Finally, she steepled her hands together and said:

"Ged, I think it's time to take a new tack. I'd like to go back to the waters you mentioned when we first started therapy. Tell me about the haunting waters."

Ged blinked. He looked down for a long time, and finally said, "What do you think of when I say the word 'sea'?" He looked up quickly and found her watching him with cool eyes. They had a clear sheen to them. However frustrated he was, he always found his reflection in them.

"I think calm, still, blue," she suggested.

"No!" he said. "No!"

Dr. Fein waited.

Ged needed to breathe. Fumbling furiously, he undid his seatbelt. He pushed the straps away from his body, inhaling deeply.

Now the camera zoomed even closer to the Wall, capturing its bulky stones, brushy overhang, overactive pigeons. Men squeezed close together, their eyes shut, the Wall or prayer books wedged against their noses, murmuring, chanting, unaware of the camera brazenly stealing their faces and moving mouths.

Suddenly a sharp gasp escaped Ged's lips, as if he had been punched. His trendy neighbor's head snapped around. "You OK? What happened? Shall I call someone?"

Ged stared at him. He felt the blood leave his face, his eyes like a wounded child's.

Ged looked up at his psychologist. She could wait forever, it seemed, never moving her eyes from his.

"Tell me Ged," she said gently.

"Dr. Fein," he whispered. "I dream of the sea."

"What do you dream, Ged?"

The mighty sea, the killing sea, rushing into pores and open doors. Filthy and brown, roaring and snorting into buildings, closets, nostrils, lungs.

Hands reach out and are rammed backward; heads tumble over legs.

Waterlogged screams, below the surface.

Hands float.

Ged's eyes brimmed with salt water. "The sea fills every corner."

"Sir, I'm sorry if you're feeling unwell, but I really need you to do up your seatbelt." It was one of the flight attendants, a young brunette, and her smile did not touch her kohl-lined eyes. His hand moved feebly toward the strap but stopped. His head rolled forward. The attendant tutted in annoyance, and her hand moved a few inches in his direction as if she would belt him up by force. In a cold voice she said, "The sign is on, sir. Please fasten the belt now."

Leon said testily, "Honey, give him a break! Make yourself useful and go get him a drink, OK doll?"

At that moment, the older flight attendant passed by. She said something to her colleague, who shrugged and moved away.

"Are you all right, sir?" Ged saw the flight attendant's kindly face leaning over him, waiting for his answer.

You use the word "you." Who am I? Please tell me.

He was returning to someone else's life, someone else's parents, neighbors, friends. It was hopeless, like a snake trying to don its shed skin. But the Ged of New York was gone too, slipped away through the rain-splattered window.

At this moment he was *nisht ahin un nisht aher*—neither here nor there; in limbo. Right now, he was simply the Ged of El Al.

More time passed. Manhattan transformed again from freezer to sauna, and Ged sheltered in the New York Public Library or in the shadiest parts of Central Park. Every so often he opened his tractate of Mishnah and tried to read it aloud in the yeshiva's singsong melody. But each time, the words evaporated from his tongue; only the tune remained. He talked to Dr. Fein about Freud's theories of religion, and how they compared with those of Jung. He spoke of America and Israel. He spoke of West and East. When she pushed him to be more personal, he reflected on his new job at the bookstore, and talked to her about his ongoing awkwardness with the women who floated in and out of his life.

From time to time, Dr. Fein made another attempt: "Ged, what is the sea?"

Her question dropped like a smooth round stone into a black lake inside him, and sank.

"The sea is the sea!" He shook his head. "*Der yam iz der yam*, doctor. Nothing more."

The older flight attendant leaned across in her fitted blue jacket and handed Ged a cup of water. His fingers were too unsteady to hold it, so she held his hand and helped him sip, her eyes never leaving his face. When she said something, Ged's mind did not register it. He was suddenly remembering his mother's soft green apron with the burnt hole in the corner. He had not thought of it in a decade. He thought he smelled her heavenly potato *kugel* and the wax she used to shine his brothers' shoes. His mother could not be on this plane, baking and waxing shoes. She had not flown since she was young, as far as he knew. Not even—he felt quite certain—to come out and look for him. He realized that he could no longer remember the color of her eyes.

Dr. Fein continued to nudge Ged, like a tide pushing at a sandbank. "You're holding back. Tell me more about the dreams. The dreams of the sea."

Eventually something snapped inside him.

"You're the shrink!" he cried. "You tell me, Dr. Fein! Where is the sea in me?" He raised his fist as if to strike the table, but seeing his arm reflected in the mirror behind her, lowered it slowly. She was only a woman. She had learned no Torah. What could he expect?

When Ged finally regained a sense of his surroundings, he had a faint recollection of the flight attendant repeatedly saying "Sir? Sir?" Now she was saying to Leon, "Excuse me, he clearly needs someone with him. Would you mind if I sat here for a bit? The seat over there is free."

"No problem," Leon said cheerfully, hoisting his bag from underneath the seat. The woman sat down next to Ged, who was taking small gulps of the water.

"Do you have anything stronger?" he said.

"In a minute. I want you to just to breathe slowly now. Breathe. Relax. Good."

Ged inhaled and exhaled for a couple of minutes until he felt calmer. She smiled, and took his limp hand in both of hers.

"My name's Carmela."

He exhaled his name in a gush of breath. "Ged."

"Ged?"

"Short for Gedalyoh." He tasted the long name, once so familiar.

"Yes? How nice. I've never met a Gedalyoh before."

"It's a popular name in religious circles." Closing his eyes, he said, "I wasn't always as you see me today. I grew up a Gerer Hasid in Bnei Brak, the second of fourteen children."

"Really?" said Carmela. "That's very special." Her smile was clearly an invitation to speak further. Ged thumbed through his memories like an old tome. *Children everywhere, noise, wildness. The yeshivah, its walls covered in burgundy books with gold lettering. The words of the Talmud burning black fire into his brain at midnight, making his mind swim like porridge. His yeshivah friends, serious young men who debated passionately, and when overtired, pushed each other playfully, their peyos swinging like jungle vines. They teased Ged for sitting in a corner with his back to them, a secular book concealed inside his gemora, but he was grateful to them for not telling the rabbi.*

Lonely walks in Jerusalem's spittling rain. Flowers whose delicate petals made him clap with joy. His shed—his secret stockpile of books. The Internet café he secretly frequented, glaring at the one or two other Hasidim who he suspected had come to look at porn. Saying in his mind, "Go away, I am not like you!"

He began to hate the inside of her office, and skipped weeks sometimes, but still he kept coming. He knew there was something else to unravel, but could not allow himself to go near that place. That could only come when he was ready. No shortcuts.

One day, as Ged sat in silence, his forehead knotted and sweaty, and Dr. Fein looking worn out from trying to drag words from him by force, he looked up and observed, "I've just noticed—your eyes change color from time to time."

"Oh?"

"Yes. Sometimes they're green, like mine, and sometimes more of a blue. I don't know why I didn't pick up on this till now," he said, aggravated. "After all, they never leave my face. Even when you reach for your pen. That at least I noticed at the start."

"Does it make you uncomfortable?"

Ged shrugged his shoulders, like a child.

"What does that mean?"

"It means yes—no—I like it and don't like it all at the same time. It's confusing."

Dr. Fein smiled her widest smile. He knew by now that this signaled that they had hit upon some subterranean layer of his psyche. Ged suddenly felt a wall of emotion dissolving in him and closed his eyes in a bid to keep from falling apart. He still felt her eyes upon him, and the walls continued to crumble and fall inside him. He felt great fear and great hope simultaneously. It was time to tell her, at last. The words came gushing out, as if some small boy inside him had removed his finger from a dyke.

"It all started when I went to an Internet café. December 2004, in Jerusalem. It was a Wednesday. I had discovered Google that year—my way of learning about the world. As the Google website loaded, I saw under the search bar: *Ways to help with tsunami relief.* I didn't know what a tsunami was. I clicked on it and discovered that four days before, thousands of people had died. I had not known, sitting in my cocoon of a yeshivah while the world flowed by outside. I was not sure where Thailand was, had never even heard of Sri Lanka. I felt so ashamed."

Ged recalled the pictures of the splintwoods and arms sticking up from the rubble, and the people running, some still smiling as if it was a joke. Blurred faces frozen in their final flight.

"When I finally got up to pay, I said to the boy behind the counter, 'Did you hear about the disaster in Asia?' 'Of course, what do you think?' the boy said scornfully. 'Everyone knows about it. My mom's friend from work is missing. She was in Ko phi phi.' 'I'm sorry,' I said. 'Do you have anyone missing?' he said. 'No,' I said. 'My family doesn't go to places like Thailand.' I saw his face darken, and he turned away, back to his magazine. I said 'It's terrible, isn't it?' trying to get him to look at me again, but he just nodded and read on."

"And then?"

"Then I had the strangest urge to hit him, so he would look up."

"Did you?"

"No, of course not! I've never hit anyone in my life." Ged tossed his head. "But I knew he hated me. I was not of his world."

"People inhabit lots of different worlds," said Dr. Fein. "I am not of that boy's world either."

"You're missing the point!"

"OK." Her eyebrows rose marginally, but otherwise she did not react. "So tell me the point."

"The point is that I began to understand that I was different from everyone. I fit in nowhere."

He told her the rest of the story. He remembered everything clearly, even small details.

Walking in through the yeshivah door, he had said urgently to his friends: "Did you hear about the tsunami?"

"The what?" Layzer had said.

"The Asian tidal wave that just killed thousands of people!"

"Oh, yes," said Osher, Layzer's study partner. "Entire countries smashed up and washed away, mamish." He brought his fist down emphatically on his shtender.

"I can't believe I didn't hear about it till now." Ged sat down heavily.

"Nu, G'dalyoh, what's the big deal?" Layzer smiled his boyish smile. "Millions of people die all the time. Earthquakes, disease, drought. Yemei hayenu hevel, our lives are like a breath."

Another young man, Akiva, leaned forward on his shtender toward them. "It's min hashamayim, all those people lying on their beaches, wasting their lives, bittul zman, their bodies uncovered for everyone to see, total pritzus! What could be more obvious than that? Just like Sodom! Wiped out in one big bang." He made a sweeping motion with his hand.

"Just like the flood in Noah's time," said Osher. "Washing away the corruption, for a clean start."

The pictures of wreckage, shells of houses and mounds of debris burned in Ged's mind. He could not imagine anything less like a clean start. He said softly: "Many innocent people have just lost their lives. Good, simple people."

Layzer shrugged his slim shoulders. Osher suggested, "So maybe it was because of our sins, not theirs. We're the ones who have to be good, we Yidden."

Ged was not sure he liked that idea any better than the previous one.

"You're right, it's a terrible, terrible thing. And did you hear," Akiva rushed on eagerly, "it was all predicted in Yirmiyahu?" He pulled out a Bible and opened it at Jeremiah. "Here, chapter 51. If you look at verse 39, the letters at the end spell out tsunami. Then only three verses later it says 'The sea has come up upon Babylon; she is covered with the multitude of waves.' Isn't that amazing?"

Ged felt sick. "Babylon isn't Thailand," he muttered. "Babylon is Iraq. Don't you know anything?"

They paused. Osher looked at him, head cocked. "OK G'dalyoh, OK," he said. He turned to Layzer. "Nu, let's get back to the daf, we're wasting time." He picked up the book and his voice rose in the yeshivah melody as he read the Aramaic:

"So we learned that looking over into a neighbor's plot is not considered a substantial damage. Comes along Rabbi Nachman, and says . . . ."

Ged stood up, yanked on his black hat and walked out, overhearing Layzer's puzzled comment as he left: "What's with him lately? He's acting meshuggeh."

"I spent the next day in bed," Ged told Dr. Fein. "I didn't pray or lay tefillin. I saw myself tossing, tumbling, dying—for it was myself in that sea, my brothers, my own human flesh. That was when I first dreamed of the waters. Foul and green, rushing through rooms and houses and gardens. There were no people in my dreams, only waters, engulfing all. I don't know why. When anyone came in, I pretended to be asleep. I left my room only once in forty-eight hours, to buy newspapers, for the updates." Ged told her that he had not gone to the *mikveh* before sundown on Friday. He had not even showered. But when the Sabbath siren sounded, as if by some automated reflex, he threw back his blanket and, smelling of sweat, his *peyos* greasy, put on his long black robe—*bekishe*—and tied it with his *gartel*. He went down to the yeshivah for evening prayers. His mind blurry, he walked into the old, large book-filled room, with the verse inscribed above the door: *How I love Your Torah; the whole day long it is my conversation.* He picked up a dilapidated prayer book, as the first words of the afternoon service reverberated on the men's lips:

"*Ashrei yoshvei beysecho*—happy are those who dwell in Thy house." But the words caught in his throat; he could not continue. He swayed dumbly as everyone else prayed, clapping in devotion in the Hasidic fashion. He had felt this feeling before, after visiting the Holocaust Museum, or on hearing of soldiers killed or buses blown up. But he had never yet been so paralyzed. When he finally awoke from his stupor, the afternoon prayer was long over, and the hundred or so men in the room were chanting together from the Friday night service. Ged felt as if he had never really heard the words before:

The voice of the Lord is upon the waters, the God of glory thunders.

The Lord is upon many waters.

The voice of the Lord is powerful. The voice of the Lord is full of majesty.

The Lord sits enthroned at the flood, and the Lord sits enthroned as King forever.

"Master of the Universe!" cried Ged soundlessly. "You created our weaknesses, so please hide Your eyes! For if You persist in judging us this harshly, not one amongst us shall live!"

Ged paused in his story, feeling confused and dizzy. To whom was he talking? Was it Dr. Fein? But it was dark, and there was a humming in the background.

Carmela, her name was Carmela, he reminded himself. He was on an airplane. He was telling his story to a flight attendant. Yes. He continued. "So that's why I fled to Manhattan. I guess it was the last straw."

She listened intently, the dim glow of the cabin lights reflecting off her face. The encouraging touch of her hand on his own calmed him.

"So that's why I fled to Manhattan," said Ged, squirming slightly on the white sofa. "I didn't want to sit in God's house any longer. I wanted to be out in the world. Next time death visited, I would know before a teenager at the Internet store did."

The psychologist leaned her face on her hand. "Ged, there's enough death where you come from. A Jew just has to toss a coin to hit death, and especially in Israel. Why come searching for it here?"

He tutted in that uniquely Israeli way that says *You really don't understand.* "I didn't come searching for death! I came searching for life."

She looked at him intently. She reminded him of the Jerusalem cats, staring at him with their scrutinizing eyes from the tops of walls and garbage cans.

"So, do you think God watched as those people drowned?"

He shrugged in annoyance. "What do I know of God's ways?"

"Well, do you feel God is watching you now?"

"I don't know. I hope not."

"Do you think of your rabbis and friends at yeshivah?"

"Sometimes."

"Do you wonder if they think of you?"

"Who cares?" he said brusquely.

She paused. "And your mother?"

He bristled. "Of course my mother thinks about me! If you had any children you wouldn't ask such a stupid question."

Dr. Fein said quietly, "I have two children."

He felt shocked. All this time he had never known. "I'm sorry. I shouldn't have assumed. But seriously, it was a stupid question."

She replied patiently, "That's what we therapists do. We ask stupid questions."

After this, Ged began feeling more and more oppressed by the therapy. He earned barely enough for rent and food, and the cost of therapy meant that he could not afford to study or travel as he wished. He told Dr. Fein he needed a break. She appeared flustered.

"Ged, don't run away. You're finally making real progress."

"Just a break."

"If you're planning to end therapy, we need to create closure."

"No, just a break."

She reluctantly agreed.

But the break stretched itself out and he made no contact for a long while. Dr. Fein called a couple of times and left messages requesting him to come in just once more so that they could work through what had happened, say a proper goodbye. But he always returned the calls in the middle of the night so as to get the answering machine. "I got your message. I'll be back soon."

A year passed, then another. He moved from the bookstore he was working in to a much larger store with four floors worth of books—heaven on earth. He took night courses in art, comparative religion, history, and psychology, and received excellent grades. Slowly he worked toward a B.A. He gave up his apartment and moved into a Brooklyn house with three students, two of them female. He finally became comfortable at parties and discovered that he was an excellent dancer and could draw attention easily. He became aware that he was considered handsome, and that when he smiled at women and asked them questions with his shy charm, they fell in love with him. He dated many of them and had many new and astonishing experiences. He had a couple of long-term relationships but ultimately found himself unable to respect the women, bemused by their flighty emotionality and their teasing. Most of all, he disliked their lack of interest in what he still thought of as a woman's chief goals—creating a family, self-sacrifice, and spiritual growth.

Loneliness ate away at his insides. His job became stale and he applied to work at a publishing company. That was exciting for a while, but then he got bored and went to work in an investment firm, where he made lots of money, using his quick mind to compensate for his lack of formal education. He made trips into upstate New York. He met Conservative, Reform, and Reconstructionist Jews, Jewish Renewalists, Secular Humanists, and JuBus. Yet none of these forms of Judaism felt to him like the real thing. He took up martial arts, yoga, and meditation, and found himself skilled at those too. Somehow, however, no matter what he did, his life felt meaningless. Nonetheless, he stuck with it, for he had no choice. The very thought of going back to Israel made his muscles cramp.

One day, while cleaning his room and blowing the dust off the volumes of Talmud, Ged decided to quit his job and go traveling. He flew to Atlanta and traveled by train and bus through much of southern USA. He enjoyed the changing scenery, although McDonalds was the same everywhere. He stopped for several days at various cities, sampling the food, museums, and nightlife, but found nothing to keep him in any one place, moving onward inexorably. He made it to Texas, then on an impulse, boarded a northbound plane to Illinois. He found he liked Chicago best of all the places he had been. He was delighted and amused to discover the existence of a town in Illinois called Normal. Denzel was right, after all! He was even tempted to visit but knew he would not find anything special there.

The people he met on his travels did seem different from the New Yorkers. They spoke more slowly and often seemed to have more time for him. Yet their conversations were frequently less than riveting, and he sensed that he stood out even more here than in the Big Apple, where every second person was a misfit of some sort.

Here, far away from everything, he crossed all his few remaining red lines. He ate cheeseburgers and shrimp, spent Passover in a bakery and Yom Kippur at a rodeo. But the little book remained always in his pocket. He invited random women back to his motel room, but did not allow them to spend the night, afraid of waking up in a sweat from the intense dreams that had suddenly returned after several years of peace.

He felt little committing these sins, just an emptiness that grew daily. In the long hours of traveling he had much time to think. He thought about his family, especially his mother. He had not phoned them for several years. He could still hear his father's reproaches in the final conversation, having discovered that his son was not in a yeshivah at all and had been lying to him. Most hurtfully, his mother had not even come to the phone last time. Were they worried? Had they ever tried to call the police? He wished he knew more.

As he watched the scenery pass for hours, fragments of Talmud rose from the depths of his mind, settling on its surface like pieces of a ship smashed apart in a hurricane:

The dream follows the interpretation.

Rabbi Hisda said: A bad dream is better than a good dream.

Jonah thought: I will flee abroad! For God's presence does not dwell outside of Israel. But God said, "By your life! I have emissaries whom I can send to bring you back!"

Napping on the train to Boston, he dreamt of a hazy figure, breath bubbling in its throat, floating at the bottom of the sea. In the dream he knew that this man was Jonah. But no fish came to swallow and save him; he hovered there, choking but never quite drowning, until Ged awoke at the final stop. Alighting, he caught sight of a religious Jew, and it was all he could do not to fall to his knees and beg for something, though he knew not what.

Back in New York, Ged found himself dialing Dr. Fein's number with a shaking hand. "I need to talk to you," he said. "My dreams are killing me."

The seatbelt sign finally went off, just as he finished the tale he had not planned to tell. Suddenly self-conscious, he removed his hand from Carmela's and gripped the loose metal buckle, which dug coldly into his palm.

"So I found an organization that helps people like me go out into the wide world, called *She'elah.* They said they would help me make a new start away from home. I lied to my parents and rabbi, and boarded a plane to New York. The yeshivah I was supposed to be attending in Borough Park became a job in a deli. I dropped out of sight in the big city, phoning them every few months from a payphone and lying for as long as I could, till they became suspicious." Ged sighed, then added in a monotone, "There is a chance that I ruined my sisters' *shidduch* prospects, that they had to marry beneath them. I might have destroyed my family with my choices."

There was a long pause. Carmela finally spoke. "Do you regret it?"

"No. I had to do it. I was dying back there."

"Yes, you were."

Hearing the certainty in her voice, Ged gave her a quizzical look. She explained, "I have a daughter. She ran away too."

She had hung up a new painting and her hair was now cropped very short. Otherwise everything was the same.

"So," said Dr. Fein. "How can I help you?"

"My God!" Ged cried, without preamble. "They just won't leave me alone! I grieved the tsunami, I mourned it, I changed my life. So why am I still dreaming about the sea? It's driving me insane!"

Calmly she said, "Close your eyes. Think of the sea. Think of waves, think of water. What's your association?"

"Water? Water is . . ." Ged closed his eyes and breathed deeply.

Liquid

Swimming

Cleanliness

Rain

His eyes snapped open.

"Torah."

She said carefully, "What about Torah?"

Ged recited from the recesses of his memory: "*Just as water has no taste except to the thirsty, so too Torah is best appreciated through great toil and yearning.*

Just as water restores the soul, so does the Torah.

Just as water is cleansing, the words of Torah are purifying.

Water is a great equalizer. No matter your station or class, all can drink water; thus too a scholar should not be ashamed to say to a simpleton, 'Teach me a chapter, a verse, or a letter.'"

Dr. Fein looked expectantly at Ged. He was stunned. What had the Torah to do with dreadful brutal waves crashing onto innocent fishermen and holidaymakers? The Torah was beautiful, it was ancient, it was a love letter, a guide.

"The Torah," he said slowly. "It fills every corner."

His heart constricted, and his voice broke.

"And there's no space . . . for me."

She nodded, as if she had been waiting for a long time for him to say this. Tears surged in Ged's eyes. He pulled out the little tractate and riffled through its pages. He desperately wanted to send it sailing violently across the shiny desk, to have it crash satisfyingly against the wall, its pages crumpling in all directions. In his imagination he saw himself doing it. He could almost feel the exact neuron pathways that would send the signals to his hands. But his hands remained in his lap, his fingers inserted between the pages, his thumb stroking the cover.

Dr. Fein sat very still.

After a minute, he closed the book, raised it to his lips, and kissed it gently. His breath clouded its green cover. *"Please,"* he whispered, though it was unclear whom he was addressing, *"please, please, please."*

Under the gaze of Dr. Fein's blue-green eyes, Ged wept.

At long last, Ged's whiskey arrived. He felt better but took a swig anyway.

"So, can I ask what happened?" he asked shyly. "With your daughter?"

Carmela sighed, her face looking tired under its careful make-up. "It wasn't a good time in my life. I cried a lot."

"What was it all about?"

"I really don't want to go into it."

Ged was consumed with curiosity as to the details. Perhaps her daughter was a lesbian, he thought, or had chosen a career of which her mother disapproved. Maybe she had gone to live in India in an ashram, or had become ultra-Orthodox. But it was not for him to pry.

She said, "Let's just say that I forgot that my child is not an extension of me. What she needed most from me was acceptance."

"But she came back in the end?"

"Yes, after six long years she came back. And everything's OK now, thank God." The woman seemed quite emotional. Again, Ged smelled the impossible *kugel* smell wafting through the airplane's sterile air. The woman smiled at him. "And you, you're a good son, you're going back now too. It'll make your mother so happy."

Ged brushed his hair back awkwardly and shrugged.

"To tell the truth," he admitted, "I don't know what to do. If I walk in like this, the neighbors will talk about it for the next thirty years. It'll kill my mother, as surely as if I walk in with a gun and shoot her myself."

"Maybe go in under cover of dark?"

"Yes, but what about the next day, and the next? Carmela," he pleaded, "—what shall I wear? Who shall I be? Shall I shave my head again and put on the clothes? Just for her? Or maybe even for myself?" His face colored.

"It depends on you. On who you are now."

"That's just it, I'm not sure who I am." He blinked a few times.

"It'll come." Carmela patted him on the shoulder. "Maybe check into a hotel for the first couple of days, take it slowly, make a plan. Perhaps she can come visit you at the hotel to begin with."

Ged nodded. "I think I might know more when I see her face."

She smiled at him.

"Thank you." He reached out spontaneously and gave her a hug, hoping she would not find it inappropriate.

"You're a good person, Ged," she said, and stood up.

He looked after her for a long moment, then took out of his jacket pocket a small, well-thumbed card and opened it.

Dear Ged,

It was a privilege to meet you, and to witness your search for the truth.

Remember: "Water can support a boat, or overturn it" (Shakespeare, Richard III).

Stay in touch

With warm wishes

Dr. Dawn R. Fein

Leon returned to his seat. "Feeling better, friend?"

"Yes. Thanks."

"So now tell me—what happened to you back there? You looked like you had seen a ghost."

"I did see a ghost. On the El Al video."

"Excuse me?"

Ged flushed. "Myself."

The other man laughed uproariously. "Were you one of the camels?"

"No!" He frowned. "At the Wall. They must have used old footage. There I was, praying, with my eyes closed. Myself—as I was then."

Leon's laughter died on his lips. "My God!"

"I felt like an object. *Image of Hasid praying at the Wall.* No one asked my permission. The camera just trapped me there, in my sacred moment, and pasted me next to camels and hummus and hotels in Eilat. Just another sight you can see in Israel."

"Small world!" exclaimed Leon.

Ged laughed dryly. "No privacy anywhere, right?"

Leon nodded. "You said it, man."

The lights in the plane dimmed, and the plane began to shudder under turbulence. The seatbelt sign lit up again. Drowsy forms shifted around them, fumbling sleepily for their belts. Ged belted himself up firmly. Carmela passed by holding a tray and stopped to give Ged a smile. Raising his head slightly so that she could hear too, Ged reflected:

"No, it's not a coincidence, it's a sign. The closer I get to the Holy Land, the more I feel God reclaiming me. I guess I always knew He would." He paused briefly for a deep breath, like that of a diver before jumping. "Thank you both so much for putting up with me and my troubles. I don't know what will be, but I'm sure I will be all right."

They nodded at him kindly and then departed, Carmela to her duties and Leon to stretch his legs. Ged arranged a blanket around his knees and, covering his eyes with his right hand as if saying the *Shema* prayer, sank into a deep, dreamless sleep.

Dateline Manhattan 2029

Hudi yawned and dropped heavily into his chair. It was late and his legs ached. He had managed to create enough wattage on the bike to power his apartment for the next three days, which was good, because last week he had forgotten and ended up using an entire day's worth of expensive grid electricity. But the cycling had wiped him out, and he had not yet learned his *daf yomi*, his daily page of Talmud. This feeling, that the *daf* was a chore, was a new one. For most of his life he had sped through the Aramaic as if it were a double burger with relish. But in recent months—since his thirtieth birthday last September, to be precise—his mind had turned pulpy and sluggish. As always when tempted to shirk, he reminded himself that since the *daf yomi*'s launch in Lublin in 1923, Jewish men (and now women too) had studied a page of Talmud daily, in seven-year cycles. Who was he to break the chain of tradition?

Hudi sighed deeply, and tried to decide, as often happened lately, whether he should study from a real book, or the programmed wallscreen so that the difficult words would automatically be translated. Maybe tonight he would put on the HoloRebbe and let him belt out the lecture while he put his feet up? This option required the least work but the programmers, knowing their slothful audience, had set it up such that if you closed your eyes for more than ten seconds, the HoloRebbe would shout in his Brooklyn accent, "Hey, *Schlemiel!*

Wake up! We're learning Torah! You'll sleep in your *kever* after 120 years!" Those evil *mamzers*. Hudi hated the HoloRebbe, an identical twin to his fifth grade Talmud teacher. He couldn't imagine why anyone would want to replicate him when one was already way too many.

In the end he went for the book. It was less user-friendly, but he loved the feel of it and the knowledge that his great-great-grandfather had brought it over from Vilna wrapped inside his *tallis* in the bottom of his trunk. Carefully turning its brittle brown pages to the right place, Hudi felt his self-respect returning. He had promised himself he would attend the next *Siyum haShas*, in 2034. The previous one, celebrating over one hundred years of *daf yomi*, had taken place in the George O. Bush stadium in upstate New York. What an event that was! Three hundred thousand seated, and another hundred thousand lying in glass overhead cubicles watching through the floor as the speeches were piped in, with simultaneous translation from the Yiddish. The crowd danced in their seats till dawn. Yes, people had sold their grandmothers for a ticket to that event but as luck would have it, Hudi's annual evaluation meeting with his dating coach had fallen on that day and no amount of string-pulling could get him out of it. The next *Siyum haShas* would take place—if rumors were to be believed—on a space station near the moon. Hudi was determined to be there this time, having mastered every last page of the Talmud. This time, he swore fiercely to himself, no stupid dating obligations would stand in his way, for he would be married!

Snapping out of his reverie, Hudi suddenly remembered that the following night he had Lirit's party after work. He would come home late again and have to repeat this battle with himself over his learning. *Who is wise? He who has foresight!* Better to try to squeeze tomorrow's *daf* in before it came to that. Perhaps in the morning.

Sunlight streamed in through Hudi's window and woke him up. Not real sunlight—few in Manhattan could afford such a luxury—but rather, a glorious light reminiscent of Tuscany emanating from the SunnyDay Refractor™ affixed outside the window. All the new gadgets were so expensive but this one was definitely worth the splurge.

He attended morning prayers in the basement of his building on West 79th between Amsterdam and Columbus. With over two hundred religious men living in his building there was always a *minyan*. Women from the building next door also attended, but Hudi's circles were not yet counting women for *minyan*, though many thought it would happen any day now.

Reddish *tefillin*-strap marks still visible on his arms, Hudi returned to his seventeenth-floor apartment and studied the next page of Talmud on his wallscreen while crunching through his cornflakes. After bagging the recycling and pushing it down the chute, he walked to work on the teeming First-Level sidewalk. The weather was mild, as it had been for many years now in March. Hudi divided his time looking down at Ground Level, where all the old people shuffled along, and up at the panting joggers on Second Level and even higher up, cricking his neck, at the noisy Toyota Feathers and Honda Airbeams whizzing overhead, their rich owners enjoying the view of Manhattan's tall buildings. He grimaced at these metal birds with their clattering racket. He would never be able to afford one, not in this lifetime.

Hudi worked as a spiritual coach in an Orthodox Jewish high school not far from his apartment, on West 67th. His mornings were spent in meetings with the school psychologist and with teachers. The rest of the time, students came in individually to his specially decorated office, full of warm colors and subtle scented oils. Hudi would invite the student to draw, play music, do drama or write poetry. Sometimes he would try to start conversations about their secret desires and ambitions, their feelings about God or about being Jewish. Depending on what came up, he would choose whether to learn a Jewish text together, to speak of some of his own struggles growing up, to do guided imagery or exercises, or just to listen. Most days he loved it, but sometimes he wished he could just drop everything and go play hover-baseball, his favorite game, at the 92nd Street Y.

"You have the best job in the world," his father always chided him, when he complained of exhaustion. "You shape kids' souls." Hudi did not disagree. Thank God that the World Board of Jewish Education, largely due to pressure from his father, a past president, had woken up just in time to the mass Jewish defection to the New Age "One World" schools. Their solution was to allocate major funds for the new position of spiritual coach. But this was a pilot project, with only twenty coaches in the country, and Hudi frequently felt the future of the Jewish people perched heavily on his shoulder, like a bois-terous, demanding parrot.

"Sweetie, you can only do your best," his stepmother Sarah would say to him, always sensitive to that crease of stress appearing in his brow. He was so grateful for her support. He had a close relationship with his father too, though the latter was not an emotionally expressive person, preferring to show his feelings by cornering his son for a discussion of his latest Torah insights. Going to his father and Sarah in Brooklyn every second Shabbat recharged his batteries. At times, two weeks seemed far too long.

He felt less eager about the alternative Shabbats on which he visited his mother and step-father in Trenton. Leon was a fascinating man, but he liked the sound of his own voice, and, more liberal than Hudi, would spar mercilessly with him at the Shabbat table while his mother looked on. Hudi didn't enjoy seeing the negative effect of these polemics on his teenage half-siblings, who were growing up with confused identities.

But these visits were Hudi's foolproof excuse to get away from all those crabby singles on the Upper West Side. When-ever he was forced to attend the mandatory singles' weekends, he invariably needed to take a day off work to recover his sanity.

Today was one of those days when hover-baseball beckoned. For some reason, the kids were being particularly obstreperous. One whined, "Rabbi, I donwanna write poetry," and just sat there like a lump of unpoetic clay. Another came in chewing Splattygum™ and exploded purplish shreds all over his papers before he could stop her. Hudi was gradually realizing that however excellent the project, some kids were just too immature to take advantage of it. In his end-of-year report, he would recommend that in the future an SQ—spiritual intelligence—test be devised so that the weaker kids could be dealt with by someone else (anyone but him).

The day finally ended. He walked in through his door completely shattered, and lay down in his clothes. He was sorely tempted to stay in. His brain reasoned wearily that he had almost filled his party quotient for this quarter. But then with a guilty start, he realized that he was two months overdue in calling his dating coach. The controllers calibrated annually, in some complicated way they never explained, one's party attendances together with a bunch of other statistics, including number of calls with matchmakers, meetings with dating coach, visits to dating simulator, hours surfing dating sites, and actual dates, of course. After mixing and dividing, the resulting dating score of the bizarrely random 117.5 or less brought nasty pad-calls from your regional coordinator. If the score dropped below 90, you were slapped with a large fine, on top of the annual fixed singles penalty of five thousand dollars. All this with the noble aim of stamping out that nasty species—the permanent bachelor and bachelorette—from the heart of the Jewish people.

So the choice was either going to the party, or calling up that asinine woman Bertina. Some dating coaches were good, but this one drove him mad with her infuriatingly obvious tips and pointers that she always prefaced with, "Now, Hudi, you have to understand a woman's world. Women are not like men. Learn to *listen*, Hudi." No, parties were definitely preferable as a way to drive up the score. He could always bring his Talmud and sit in a corner preparing lessons or learning the *daf*. He had done it before. Sometimes supervisors patrolled to prevent things like this—people were supposed to be socializing at parties, that was the point—but since they were all enormously fat men with greasy big beards, who sometimes even forgot to remove their wedding rings, they stuck out like Splattygum at a funeral and could hence easily be dodged. For Hudi, who urgently needed to avoid supervisors as he was always late paying his singles penalty, this fact was extremely fortunate.

As always when he caught himself resenting the laws, Hudi felt embarrassed and ungrateful. Though a mere teenager when they were implemented, Hudi knew the dating laws and their history better than most. Some of his father's friends had been involved in setting it all up, and he had studied the laws extensively for his rabbinical examinations. The initial impetus had come from the mass demonstrations of 2015, when thousands of singles stood outside the Rabbinical Council building on 7th Avenue chanting:

"Stop the hurt! Where's our Bashert?"

and waving banners such as

—*Pray for us—we're desperate!*

—*Either single or intermarried? Give us another choice!*

—*We need more babies, say the six million!*

—*Warning to rabbis: Prolonged singlehood may lead to mixed dancing!*

After being ignored for three hours, the singles stormed the Rabbinical Council building and clouted helpless bureaucrats with their signs until stopped by the police. (A policeman who happened to be Jewish ended up marrying one of the protesters, and the rabbis took credit for the match.)

There were several more riots, which spread also to other Jewish singles capitals. All this unrest led to the Emergency Rabbinical Convocation of 2016 in which the fourteen *gedolim*, the greatest Orthodox rabbis in the world, met to create a new set of rulings to deal with the singles epidemic and assure the future of Jewish demography. They published these in a six-hundred-page volume named *Ozer Dalim*. The non-Orthodox movements objected to this work's authoritarianism and restrictive attitude toward sexuality and suggested their own solutions. Weakened, however, by intermarriage, these movements lacked the power and sheer numbers of the Orthodox, and most of their singles ended up drifting into the Orthodox schemes.

The Federations raised millions of dollars under the banner "Our Precious Future!" JDate, JWed and forty other dating websites merged to create *MegaShidduchMart*. Singles' zones were marked out in cities, controllers were hired, and the system cranked into place. Thus it had remained, more or less, for all of Hudi's adult life.

Many or most Jewish singles now lived, as he did, in the special enclaves marked out for them, the *shetachs*, which had instantly—and predictably—been nicknamed the "ghettos" (recently renamed *"Begetos"* by popular blogger Jewmouth). These enclaves had been delineated within strict boundaries in Jerusalem, New York, and London, set in areas that already boasted high singles concentrations—the Katamon-Rechavia-Baka district, the Upper West Side, and Hendon respectively. The rabbis did not make dwelling in the *shetachs* compulsory, as there might be a compelling reason to live outside of those areas, but it was strongly recommended, and *"all who are strict in this will merit to be blessed."* Bottom line, all of Hudi's friends lived in the ghettos and it was almost unheard of not to.

Additionally, those above the age of eighteen—though deferments could be granted in special cases—must set up a profile on *MegaShidduchMart*, set regular meetings with a dating coach, appoint five personal matchmakers, and attend parties and social weekends. When a person turned thirty there were even more requirements—regular attendance at either computer-simulated dating or live dating workshops, more parties, sessions with therapists, sessions with image consultants. This was why nobody in Hudi's circles celebrated their thirtieth birthday anymore, opting instead to lie miserably in bed and feel their youth drain away.

All singles, young and old, also had to carry small square plastic cards bearing two items of information: Username and Dating Number. These were to be carried at all times, for you never knew when you might meet someone and want to give him or her your profile ID details. Shabbat initially presented a problem, since on the Sabbath it was forbidden to carry in the public domain. Then special belt tags were manufactured, with the necessary details printed on them. Upon meeting someone attractive, one would unhook a tag, and the other person would take it and hook it into the loop of his or her own belt specially designed for the purpose. This, the rabbis ruled, was not considered carrying and therefore breaking Shabbat, as the tag became an integral part of the belt. Initially many complained that the belts were ugly, but a more fashionable line of belts had recently come out in tangerine, and now even the trendiest singles sported them, sometimes even on week-days.

At last, feeling that he had no choice due to his very low dating score (he figured it at currently around 80), Hudi schlepped himself out of bed, put on a clean white shirt, and went. At least Lirit only lived one block down. He would prob-ably know most of her guests. They would all be from the West 70s and 80s, many of them members of the three thousand strong singles' synagogue on West 78th, *Dodi Chamak*. But there would be some randoms, selected by the computer to facili-tate more mixing. These randoms sometimes came in from as far as Omaha or Tallahassee, and constituted live evidence of the weird make-up of the database. He could deal with the run-of-the-mill *nebbishes*, geeks, or bad dressers. But sometimes people who weren't even remotely Jewish showed up, calling him Hoody and asking "so whut's that flat thang on yowr head *symbolahz?*" Hudi always asked the host to expel these guests immediately. "No, it's not rude!" he would expostulate (in a dignified way). "The entire *raison d'être* of the system is to help us find our Jewish soulmates, yet at this very moment you're undermining it! You are aiding intermarriage as we speak!"

And these non-Jewish infiltrators were on the rise, as they got more desperate. The world in general was suffering from a plague of singles—930 million out of an eight billion global population. The Gaia Sect claimed it was the earth's new way to curb the human population, just like homosexuality before it. This offended many singles, though the Chinese asked if they could perhaps go back to having two children now. Most governments recognized the situation as a dire threat and began to institute coping strategies, but these lagged far behind the sophisticated Jewish system. Hence, increasing numbers of lonely gentiles, weary of sordid meetings in bars and of ten-year-old pranksters masquerading as adults on dating sites, infiltrated the *MegaShidduchMart* system, thwarting even the rabbis' best efforts at screening.

There were also various Jewish gatecrashers, who had hacked into the site and discovered where the parties were. When the parties were organized by height, for the very tall and very short, gatecrashers generally took one look and ran out the door. But in other cases, people showed up who were entirely the wrong age group—senior citizens, or nineteen-year-olds. Sometimes married people sneaked in, and when discovered, claimed their divorces were coming through "any time now." These people made Hudi so angry he longed to whack them with some extremely heavy stone tablets.

Yet despite all the glitches and the unpleasantness, ultimately Hudi believed in the system. First, it was decreed thus by the rabbis and was therefore binding. And second, it worked. It had produced many fine marriages, and not nearly as many nervous breakdowns as was believed.

Lirit's apartment was welcoming. She had put up decorative panels with paint that changed color every half hour. She had also lit candles, now as passé in the non-Jewish world as smart phones and personal computers. While everyone else these days was using Evercandles™, Jews continued to go for the messily dripping wax ones, associated in their minds with Sabbath warmth and chicken soup. Hudi felt pleased that he had come.

"Well, hello, *mein* dear *yingele*," trilled Lirit. "Let me take that." Shoving his jacket into the Jackmatic, she made no delay in doing her duties as a hostess and motioned him over to two seated women. "Hudi, meet Michaela and Nessi."

He sat down, and gratefully activated the discreet massage pad in the chair. "Hi," he said, leaning into the comforting whirr that did wonders for his stiff neck. Now it was time for the all-too-familiar courting ritual, the pleasantries, the digging for information, the search for that elusive chemistry, and all that jazz. Neither woman looked nerdy or married. That was a start. Hudi struggled to remember what his coach had told him about making initial contact. Something about not doing all the talking himself. He could hear her saying in her nasal voice: "*Ask a question, Hudi. Appear interested, even if you aren't.*"

He smiled and made eye contact with both of the women. "So are you folks from this area? I've never seen you before."

"No, I'm from the 110s." This was Michaela. She sported long, brown hair with blonde highlights, a lot of gold jewelry and fashionably pointy clothes. "I met Lirit just last week and she invited me. They say there are some great men in the 80s so I came to check them out." She smiled at him boldly and he quickly looked away, gulping his tiramisu-flavored soda water. Lirit passed by with a platter of fried eggplant and antipasti. While Michaela helped herself, Hudi turned to the quieter Nessi. "And where are you from?"

"Jerusalem," she replied. Darker than Michaela, her face was round and soft, without the jutting cheekbones prevalent on the fat-obsessed Upper West Side. Her rapid, enigmatic smile came and went like summer lightning. Her clothes were different from anything Hudi had ever seen; they looked about a hundred years old: an embroidered peasant blouse, a long layered skirt with fraying hems, and sandals on her sunburned feet.

"So you're from the Katamon *shetach*?" Hudi said. It was more a statement than a question, as few singles these days lived outside the delineated areas if they wanted to meet people. But Nessi surprised him by firmly shaking her head.

"Oh?" said Hudi. He paused briefly then said, "Well, I was born in Jerusalem, actually." He smiled fondly. "I remember the zoo before it became a mall. I actually remember the bears —"

"But you're not Israeli?" she interrupted. She had a strong accent.

"We left when I was eleven."

She fixed her dark eyes upon him. "Why?"

Hudi met her gaze. "One word: mortgage. With a wife and three children to support, my father couldn't refuse a good job offer here. He promised us it would be temporary—but it wasn't, and we're still here. My stepmother still moans about the raw deal she got. She misses Israel a lot."

Michaela chimed in again with the typical question: "What does your father do?"

Hudi replied, feeling the familiar mix of defensiveness and pride: "He's a rabbi and educator."

"Still paying off the mortgage then, I guess," Michaela snorted, as if she had made a hilarious joke.

"Jewish educators do fine!" Hudi retorted, his brow blustery. Modern women all claimed they wanted a spiritual, sensitive man, yet still expected him to earn the seven-figure salary. It was so unfair.

Fortunately, Michaela excused herself at that point to go talk to another man she had spotted, and Hudi finally had the opportunity to try to draw the other woman into conversation. He was curious about how things had progressed ever since the Palestinian State, finally bankrupt after years of corruption and wasting billions of dollars of international aid, had declared itself a canton of Israel, notwithstanding that the latter was almost as impecunious as itself. He said in a friendly tone, "So what's going on in Israel now?"

"Can't call it Israel any more!" said Nessi flatly. "Illegal!"

"Oh right, sorry. It's the—what is it now?"

"The Joachim and Bella Slasnick State of Israel," she spat.

"Oh right, sorry, the Joachim and—"

"*Ya-alla!* You ever hear anything so ridiculous?" There was a fury in her voice, previously so quiet and measured. "After Israel spending all its cash on security barriers, the post-Zionists all left for America, and the *Kachniks* and all the other crazies are driving away the tourists and disgusting the funders. And then—no big fat surprise—suddenly there's no money left. *Nu, tembelim.* OK, let's dedicate the entire State, then! Brilliant! Goodbye Israel, hello all-new State of Slasnick—and God help us all!" She picked up her glass and downed her vodka-and-orange in two gulps. Hudi was mesmerized by the movement of her strong neck muscles as the liquid descended. He did not normally stare at women's necks as it was not modest, and he felt somewhat embarrassed. However, something in him was captivated by this woman.

She put the empty cup down and, catching him staring, frowned. Hastily looking away, he said ingratiatingly, "Well, I bet they spent the money already! Next thing you know they'll be looking for another donor! Ridiculous, hey?"

But Nessi simply tossed her head in a horsey gesture and retorted, "You think you can criticize Israel? What gives you the right, Diaspora Jew? You gave fifty dollars five years ago or something like this?"

Hudi was very taken aback. He had never been spoken to like this by anyone outside his family. But then she smiled, softening her attack and showing a set of shapely white teeth. "But actually," she said, "you are right, *davka*. Lots of fun for the atlas-makers, yes? When it becomes the Slasnick-Katzenellen-bogen-Dorfenberger State of Palestine-Israel-Judea, this name will be covering seventeen Arab countries on the map and everyone take it as the proof that the Jews want to conquer the world. *Oof! Hablaz maz maz!* So silly!" Nessi accepted another vodka from Lirit, who gave Hudi an inquiring glance. He nodded at her, and turning back to the fierce Israeli, observed:

"Actually, the name might end up a lot shorter. I heard Bill Gates might be in the running—his granddaughter married a Jew, and he wants to try to appease the hostile parents-in-law by sponsoring the State in his name. He could sponsor all the countries in the area collectively as the Gates States of the Middle East!" Hudi chuckled at the thought.

"*Yeuch!* And there is worse besides!" Nessi lowered her voice. "I hear last week that people are being now tattooed."

"Tattooed?"

"Yes, like for example to write on my neck, *This Israeli dedicated by Mr. Max Rosen of Toronto. Alek!*" she cried emphatically, as Hudi choked on his soda water. "Not if Mr. Max Rosen wants to keep alive, I tell you! Oh, yes, these funders from the Diaspora, they are bored of forests and halls and libraries, so a new fashion—let's sponsor people. And the Ofers and Yossis in Ramat Gan and Kiryat Motzkin is happily selling themselves, for fifty or one hundred thousand dollars each. What do they care, if stupid Diaspora Jew want to pay up. A little tattoo, so what?"

Hudi gawped. "I can't believe it! Tattooing—that's against Jewish law!"

Nessi's eyes flashed with contempt. "*This?* This what bothering you of all this story?"

"No, no, of course not—wait, don't go!" He almost grabbed her arm but caught himself in time. Putting on his most sincere voice—his spiritual coach voice—he begged, "Listen,

I'm deeply troubled by everything that you've told me, really. Please believe me, Nessi. I've always cared about the State of Israel—er—Bella and thingamajig Spastic—dammit . . . !" He trailed off limply, cursing donors everywhere.

"OK, OK." She smiled at him, though it may have been out of politeness. "Sorry. I still have the jet lag. But really, I must to sleep now. So see you soon, *yalla bye*." She stood up to leave. One more moment and she would be gone from his life, perhaps never to return. Galvanized into action, Hudi quickly got up and physically blocked her exit with his broad shoulders.

"Wait, please—I'd like to continue talking. Here. Here's my profile ID." He handed her his laminated card. "Can I have yours?"

Nessi stared at him and he blushed. Obviously she was about to refuse, and he was already cross with himself for screwing things up with her. Then she surprised him by saying, "*Eyn li.* I don't have one."

He laughed, relieved she had not rejected him. "Silly girl," he scolded, "coming to a party without your profile ID! Well, I can just write it down." He slid his digital pen from its place in his front pocket, and reached for his Pad.

"No," she said defiantly. "I have no profile existing at all, anywhere."

Hudi froze in mid-motion. "Uhh . . . what . . . ?"

Nessi repeated slowly, as if to an idiot, "No . . . profile . . . existing . . . anywhere."

Hudi felt a little dizzy, and, replacing his pen carefully, snatched up some storm-roasted peanuts to stuff into his slack mouth. "You don't have a profile at all?"

Nessi rolled her eyes. "No profile! Hello!? No damn profile!" She flung her arms about like an Airbeam's rotor. "What's wrong with current generation? Why we can't meet in a nature way, like our parents? Or, maximum in blind dates arranged by careful friends or elderly aunts? This is our tradition! *Tradition! Tradition!*" She began walloping out some old tune that Hudi vaguely recognized. It was from an ancient movie called Fiddle something, if he was not mistaken—*Fiddle While the Roof Burns*, he thought it was called, made by that *alter kaker*, Woodly Allen, who last year, at the age of ninety-two, had made a movie about Jews, sex, and death.

"But Nessi," Hudi said in perplexion, "aren't you religious?"

"Yes. So?"

"Then you have to carry an ID. The *gedolim* said so—"

Nessi leaned close to him, her eyes blazing holes in his retina, and said in a brash whisper. "I am member of FSM."

Hudi stepped back. "FSM?" he said weakly. The Free Singles Movement! He had read about this subversive group in the *Jewish Forward-Backward*, whose lead columnist termed them "a bunch of *behemas*"—beasts—who ignored the rabbis' rulings and cared for no one but themselves. But until now he had not really believed they existed.

"*Ken!*" she hissed. "What is this, the new *Judenrein*?! Singles must be allowed to live anywhere! Date when they want! Why they have to pay ridiculous fines and suffer from stupid matchmakers and coaches and peepers looking at profiles? This all so unhealthy!"

"But what about the epidemic?" he said petulantly. "Who's going to stop it? These measures are working; they have statistics."

"I'm not statistic!" Nessi said stubbornly. "I living by my own mind! My love life not need to be packaged or halachically solutioned. I rather be single all my life than this awful humility!"

Hudi was aghast. Single her whole life, this glorious woman? "Don't say that, Nessi! *Chas v'shalom*, heaven forbid!"

Nessi glared at him, and, without another word, brushed past him and walked out of the door. Hudi tutted. "But it *is* selfish," he muttered. "What about *Am Yisrael*?" Nonetheless, his eyes did not leave the door for several minutes, in case she decided to come back.

An hour later almost everyone had left, and she had not returned. Wholly miserable, Hudi was about to put his plate into the recycling and leave too, when a short unshaven man in dark glasses sat down next to him. This was unusual—you came to parties to meet the opposite sex, not to make new friends.

262   YAEL UNTERMAN

The man looked around circumspectly, and then said,
"*Sholom Aleichem*," extending a hand.

"*Aleichem Sholom*." Hudi never refused to shake the hand of
a fellow Yid. The man's hand sat flaccidly in Hudi's grasp like a
piece of pickled herring for several seconds before he withdrew
it. He leaned closer to Hudi, to the point where Hudi could
smell his breath.

"Listen," the stranger said in a low voice. "I have something
good." He stopped and wrinkled his nose, sniffing the air, his
eyes darting around.

"Er—that's nice," said Hudi encouragingly.

"Eck! For *you*! Good for *you*."

"For me? What is it?"

The man leaned sideways and put his finger on the side of
his nose. "An offer. Only three hundred dollars—cheap for you,
tonight only."

"Three hundred dollars? For what?" Hudi could not imagine
what the man was selling.

"To doctor . . ." He stopped again, and swallowed.

Hudi shook his head, bemused. "I'm quite well, thank God."

". . . your photos!" he finished in a sibilant whisper, making
it sound like "*photossss*." "For your profile!" he added. His eyes
shone and suddenly he launched into his patter. "Headshots
airbrushed, lightened, darkened, slimmed down, cheekbones
highlighted, chins firmed up, moles removed, noses replaced
using noses of movie stars, unsightly hairs disappeared, no
more wrinkles. Sigh no more, ladies, sigh no more! All your
photos doctored, lawyered, and accountanted!" Laughing like
some Jewish Rasputin, he reached forward and inserted his
business card into Hudi's shirt pocket. Then he pulled out
some photographs, samples of his work, and laid them out.

Hudi did not spare them a glance, glaring instead at the
little crook. He had heard that these things went on, but to
meet such a shyster at a respectable party was astounding.
And anyway, anyone with half a brain could airbrush their
headshots themselves, if it came to that, as indeed everyone
would, were it not for the Rabbis' express ban on tampering
with photos.

In the face of Hudi's scowl, the man reluctantly returned the photos to his briefcase. "Eck!" he sniffed. "I see you're not interested in my wares at this time. I'll be getting along then."

"You *gonif!*" Hudi said loudly. "You've got *chutzpah* coming to a party and pestering innocent singles!" The few people who were still present glanced over to their corner.

"*Shhh,*" said the man, placing his slippery hand briefly on Hudi's and winking at him. He picked up his case and scuttled toward the door, waving goodbye as if he were an old friend. Hudi felt the man's touch spreading on his hand like an oil slick. He rubbed some soda water on it but the sensation remained.

Home at last, Hudi logged onto *MegaShidduchMart* as he did every day. No messages. In fact, no hits at all on his profile this evening. Zero. "Doing well, Hoods!" he said to himself morosely. Slumping back into his chair, he activated all the massage pads at once. That Nessi thing had been degrading. Why had he been attracted to such an oddball anyway? Not his usual type.

"Ach, sweet *Abishter*, till when?" he said, rolling his eyes upward and putting his palms out beseechingly. "*Ad mosay?* I need some help here Lord!" He closed his eyes for a minute and breathed, emptying his mind, centering himself. Then he plugged his smart watch into the wallscreen and logged into his Callmail. To his disgust, Spampic after Spampic flicked across the screen, dozens of pictures of attractive strangers, every last one a trick, a crude ploy to market something. Hudi sighed as he realized that he had no choice but to renew his blocker software against this plague of automated messages. Would expenditure on technology never end? Would no one have pity on a poor teacher who could not even afford his singles' fee?

Finally a message from a real person came on screen. Hudi clicked his remote at the wall and the frozen picture in the inbox began talking.

"Hey, man," said his friend Avi's image, "how ya doin'? I thought of dropping by this evening but I guess you're out, you little rizzle-razzle! Actually, you told me you were going to a party, yeah, I remember now. Aaaaanyway, I think I better warn you about something. How can I put this?" Avi squinted in discomfort. "Look, here's the thing . . . um . . . someone has written something not so great about you. Uh—you're like . . . well, you're on the List, man. It's real, and you're on it. Look, just don't ask me how I know, I can't tell you. Sorry. So, see you in *shul* then, *mein kind. Ciao* for now."

It was after midnight, but Hudi immediately hit the "Call Back" button. Avi's icon—a laughing Hasid dancing on a gefilte fish—appeared on the screen, as Avi's disembodied voice said tiredly, "*Vi geyt es*, man?"

"Hey, what's with the icon?" Hudi demanded. "Get it off before I push that gefilte fish through your head!"

"I can't, Hudish." Avi sounded distressed. "This has to be a voice call only, coz if I see your face I'll have to spill the beans, and that would just, like, stench, you know. That's the pure *emes*, man."

"All right, all right, just tell me everything you know."

Avi exhaled. "Well, OK. So first of all, seems the List does exist after all."

"*Heilige Moses!* I can't believe it! The Protocols of the Zeldas of Zion?! The List-Shmist?! It's not just some kind of a joke?" Hudi made distinctive circular motions with his hands as he spoke.

"Yeah, funny nicknames aside, it's real, all right. The black-ball list exists. Apparently men's profiles get added all the time, and thousands of women look at it weekly and take it dead seriously."

"Well, shoot me down with a nanogun! Avs, I would give my family jewels to see that list. Oh, but of course, the web address is—"

"—a secret."

"Naturally."

"It's a non-Googleable site and you need a fingerprint ID to get in."

"Of course, of course." Hudi paused. "And my profile . . . ?"

"Yup, it's there, man. And someone's nuked you. I mean, your name's been *mamish* splatted, tarnished to a T. She wrote major bad about you."

"Like what? What kind of things do these wicked *veibers* write?"

Avi sounded apologetic. "Well, they write if a guy never shows up, or cancels half an hour before a date, or never calls back, or talks non-stop, or if they think he's not emotionally available. If he has revolting table manners. If he's a sleaze-bomb or has a violent temper or is a miser. They write everything. It's really not fair. If I wasn't with Tonya I'm sure I'd have lots of horrible *losh* about me up there too."

Hudi slammed his hand on the chair's massage button, and the pads ground into high speed against his back. "What did they write about me? Tell me! Details, I want details!"

"I don't know exactly," said Avi miserably. "But my source said it's pretty bad. Oh, man, you're never going to date a Yiddishe girl again!"

"Damn! This really *farshtinks*! Who was it? Which girl wrote about me?"

"I don't know." A silence. "I'm really sorry, I wish there was something I could do."

"Can't you get your source to—"

"No, no! If anyone finds out, my source's friends will never ever speak to her again. They are all totally sworn to secrecy; it's part of the deal."

Hudi let out an anguished groan. "OK. Thanks, bud."

"Nightie-night, *yingelbells*. Sorry."

The wallscreen went blank.

Hudi kicked his briefcase and yelled, "Damn!"

The next day Hudi's mind buzzed with speculations about the List, and when he was not thinking about that, he was ruefully going over his conversation with Nessi. At last he could stand it no longer. He canceled his last session with some spoiled brat, and went to play water-chess since the hover-baseball court was full.

In the evening he called his father and told him the entire story. His father might be a little old-fashioned and ignorant of the ins and outs of Internet dating, but surely he would understand that his son's being blacklisted would put his marriage

prospects in danger of extinction—and that would get his
blood boiling.

"*Abba*, it can't be right," Hudi grumbled, when he finished
the tale. "How can they be allowed to write lies and ruin someone's life?" He swallowed furiously, sensing that in another
moment he might cry.

"It's unheard of!" his father shouted. "Thousands of repu-
tations are at stake. This must stop immediately."

"What can we do?" Hudi suddenly felt like a little boy again,
looking to his confident, brilliant father to save him. Onscreen,
Immanuel's thick eyebrows shadowed his eyes as he thought.

"I'll contact Frohwein. Maybe he can do something."

Hudi smiled in relief. "Thanks, *Abba*. Love to Sarah."

"Yehudaleh, stay in touch with your sisters. They miss
you."

Rabbi Frohwein did his job thoroughly. A few days later, it
was on CNN, no less. The anchorman announced:

"Today, posters appeared everywhere regarding an infa-
mous Internet List dedicated to slandering single Jewish men."
The wallscreen image cut to Rabbi Blatspeter, Rabbi Frohwein's
charismatic right hand man. "An outrage has been committed
against our finest young men!" the rabbi said forcefully. "The
women have banded together to create this disgraceful list.
In these posters you see here—" he pointed at the large black
Hebrew and English letters, "—the *gedolim*, that is to say the
great rabbis, make it clear that this is false gossip, and that any
woman who participates in such a list is not a real daughter of
Israel and should be excommunicated. Let the public beware!"

"Thank you, Rabbi Bloodspatter," said the anchorman.
"Now back to pictures of the last polar bear, who scientists
predict will die today. We go live to the former Arctic, where
Apple Martin has the story."

Hudi clutched at his chest, relief flooding him. Thank God
for his father and his connections. The List would be taken
down, and the slanderous report about him would break up
into a million cyberspace fragments, and life would return to
normal (though not for the polar bear, sadly).

However, over the course of the following week Hudi could not help but notice that barely anyone looked at his profile. Normally, as an eligible, good-looking man, he got traffic of four or five hits a day, not to mention the computer-generated matches. Something was still very wrong. Soon, Avi confirmed Hudi's suspicions. The List was still up, and growing daily.

"What?" Hudi exploded. "They're ignoring the *gedolim*? Who do these femmes think they are?"

"Well, apparently some women did delete their reports. But unfortunately, all the posters and publicity brought even more women in. I reckon they think they're safe because rabbis can't get in, only females. The Maharats ain't cooperating either."

"Well, some female told *you*."

"Yeah, I know. And look where it got us."

Hudi put his head in his hands. "*Ribono shel Olam!* What's happening to our women? They no longer respect rabbinical authority. Who will educate our children?"

Avi sympathized. "*Eishet Chayils* are few and far between these days, man."

"Yeah, and you caught one, you lucky *mamzer*. OK, I have to go save the shreds of my good name. Scratch ya later."

Clearly, the first thing was to change his Username. With any luck, the evil report had mentioned only his Username, which could be changed whenever he felt like it, and not his Dating Number, which was permanent. He changed his Username from *Ipcha* to *Mistabra*, but he still felt very anxious. He burned to read the report. Who on earth could have posted so many bad things about him? Henya? Sharona? Surely not Maayan Tiferet? Yes, they had all been painful relationships but he was sure that he had behaved decently throughout. Mistakes he had made, for he was only human, but they were clearly through lack of wisdom, not malice. He always called his dates back, he was certain. Well, almost. Perhaps once or twice he had let silence speak for itself.

Hudi tutted. He would have to take out his dating records and ascertain which of the nearly three hundred women he had dated it could possibly be. Clearly he had hurt someone very badly and needed to ask forgiveness. But how could he, if he could not know what was written or who wrote it? It didn't take a *gadol* to guess that Avi's source was his girlfriend, Tonya. She would never let him see the site, or even make a copy of the report for him. She was too honest.

Hudi strained to think. It would not be fair to ask his woman friends or his sisters to break this female pact, apparently a covenant with the force of Sinai. He cracked his knuckles, brainstorming desperately. Suddenly he remembered the small-statured criminal he had met at Lirit's. Perhaps this man had connections in the underworld who could help. He had been so tired that night that instead of chucking the guy's business card in the recycler as he had intended to, he had left it in the pocket of his shirt, which was now in the laundry basket. Hudi retrieved it and dialed the number. The man's icon, a tall, tanned blond man of Nordic physique, appeared on the wallscreen.

"Hello?" said a hoarse voice.

"Hello, is that Mr—er—Listim?"

"Eck. Who is this?"

"My name's Hudi. I met you at a party recently and you showed me your . . . work." Hudi prayed that the man attended many parties and would not remember him.

The man gave a gurgling sniff. "*Ahhh.* Are you the young man who called me a *gonif?*"

Hudi made a face at the ridiculous icon. "Well, yes. Look, I'm sorry, I didn't mean to embarrass you."

Listim whined in his guttural voice: "The rabbis say it's like murder, embarrassing someone in public."

"Yes, I know. I'm sorry." *And what about lying and deceiving— what's that like?* Hudi hated hypocrites. But he kept his thoughts to himself. "Look, I need your services."

"Ahhh!" The man sounded delighted. "Headshots airbrushed, lightened—"

"No!" interrupted Hudi forcefully. "I actually want to know if you know anyone who can hack into a site."

"*Ah-hahhhhh.*" He hummed a little *niggun* to himself. "*Eine kleine* hacker, that's what you want?"

"Yes."

"That can be arranged, mm-hmmm. For breaking into what system is the hacking intended, might I ask?"

"It's the List."

Suddenly the man's greasy face replaced the Nordic picture onscreen, eyes bulging and nose a-twitch. "*Vos?*" he yelled. "To hack into the List? *Meshuggeneh!* It's impossible!"

"Impossible?"

"No one can hack into the List. People have tried before, believe me. Eck!" His eyes spasmed nervously, each in a different direction. "It's been protected, firewalled and hackerproofed. The only way to get in is to have someone who's already inside finger-print in. Even then, she would have to do all the keystroking. If you so much as touched it, it would shut down."

Hudi licked his dry lips. He believed that the man was playing hard to get, which irritated him so much that he wanted to punch the screen. "OK, OK, I'll give you five thousand dollars," he said. Not that he had the money, but this was an emergency. He would get it from his father.

Listim picked at a scab on his chin. "Young man," he said gravely, "this thing even a price above rubies, even a thousand gold and silver coins, cannot buy."

Oh, now he was quoting verses from Proverbs. A *Talmid chochem, noch.* Hudi hated him more with every passing moment. Bitterly he said: "You're not much good, are you? You're basi-cally saying I'd have to become a woman to get in!"

"Precisely." The man leered. "Let me know if you want a nice photo of yourself in a dress."

Hudi slammed his hand down on the off button.

What is happening? Hudi thought furiously. *Two weeks ago I was a respectable rabbi and a good catch. Now my name is mud and I'm considering cross-dressing—which is forbidden by the Torah.*

Hudi felt himself descending into a black misery. He had never felt so forlorn. After a while he became so desperate that he put on the HoloRebbe just to hear a familiar voice. The Brooklyn growl spitting out *hava aminas* and *nafka minas* calmed him. He concentrated on the *daf* and forgot his troubles for a while. Then he went downstairs for the evening prayer. During the silent prayer, instead of saying the words, Hudi looked around at the faces of the dozens of young men around him, eyes closed, fore-heads smooth in devotion. As if seeing them for the first time,

Hudi felt a rush of bittersweet compassion for them, his compan-
ions in the arduous search for domestic felicity and happily ever
after. For the first time, he was glad he lived in this building. At
least this way he was spared the daily sight of men and women
all paired up like Noah's Ark, playing with their children and
being nauseatingly coupley. How wise the rabbis were, in their
decrees. Sometimes you only realized this belatedly.

The basement emptied out, but Hudi lingered, not quite
knowing why. At last his heart opened to the prayer. He stood
very still, his lips barely moving, only occasionally dabbing his
moist eyes on his shirt cuff. When he eventually returned to
his apartment he felt better. He had had an idea—it would be
humiliating, and perhaps unsuccessful, but it was his only hope.

"Hello, Lirit? Do you have Nessi's number?"

"Who?"

"Nessi!" said Hudi impatiently. "The Israeli woman who was
at your party."

"Oh, her! No, she was a random. And anyway, you know I
can't give out her information if she didn't give you her profile
ID herself. I'm surprised at you!"

"Believe me, she wasn't a random, and anyway . . ." He
almost blurted out, "*she has no profile ID*," but stopped himself in
time. That would open up too many questions.

"And anyway . . . ?" Sharp-witted Lirit never missed anything.

"Nothing. That was the end of the sentence. It's the new
fashion, and anyway."

Lirit snorted. "Well, I can't help you, I don't know her, and
anyway."

"Well give me Michaela's number, she might know, and
anyway."

Lirit laughed. "No problem, and moreover nonetheless but."

Hudi called Michaela, but she could not help him—she
was indeed the one who had brought Nessi, but she had only
met her at Israeli dancing two hours before the party and had
spontaneously invited her against the rules. Michaela tried
to keep Hudi talking, asking his opinion of the latest *Tradition* magazine, but he politely cut her short, for time was of

the essence. He checked Spacebook but, unsurprisingly, Nessi was not listed. He ran a complete search of all engines and social networking sites for the name "Nessi," but could find no connection to one archaic yet attractive Israeli woman amongst the results. Her digital footprint appeared to be an astounding zero, which figured, as her entire being seemed to be a throwback to the last century. He tried to find the FSM movement but they too did not have a website. All his life Hudi had easily located people by Internet. How on earth did one find someone without it? How primitive things used to be, before the cavernous info-umbrella of cyberspace united everyone. You could totally lose a person, like those sisters separated in the Holocaust and reunited sixty years later. It was positively barbaric.

In increasing frenzy, Hudi paid to update his Spacebook status in 3D pop-up and his Twitter in earblasting Stellar-Sound, broadcasting the following message which he also sent hurtling directly to several thousand friends' smart watches:

URGENT DO U KNOW ISRAELI CALLED NESSI, VISITING UPPER WS NOW? ##!!

All he got back were a bunch of "no"s, and Sharona's nasty comment on Spacebook: *Trying it with Scottish sea monsters now? Getting desperate, Huds?*

Grinding his teeth, Hudi left his building and began to prowl the sidewalks, searching for a round brown face, peasant blouse, and sandals amongst all the high heels and expensive hairstyles. Three hours later he had trod his sneakers threadbare. He had scouted out all three sidewalk levels in an area covering the lower 70s through West 115th, and gone into every kosher café and eatery and restaurant, into every synagogue and Jewish cultural center. He was exhausted. This was futile—for all he knew, Nessi might have returned to Israel already. He was heading dejectedly home when he ran into an acquaintance, David, who introduced him to an attractive redhead with glasses.

"This is my friend Anishara. She's visiting from Israel."

Hudi's eyes lit up. *"Brucha haba'a!* Tell me, do you know Nessi from Jerusalem?"

"Nessya?" said Anishara.

"Um ... she said her name was Nessi. Dark girl, peasant blouse."

"Yes, Nessya. I know her."

Hope surged in Hudi's chest. "Do you by chance have her number?"

Anishara padded a friend who called another friend who had Nessi's number. Hudi bid a hasty farewell and then called Nessi. He was extremely relieved to hear her answer on the first ring. He started off by apologizing for insulting her and her homeland at their last meeting. She said nothing. He swallowed, and plowed on, humbly asking her if she could meet him immediately at his house. To his surprise she agreed, and even sounded fairly unruffled.

He arrived before she did, and punched an order into his Instashop for hummus-flavored ice cream. When she appeared, wearing a faded khaki shirt, long corduroy skirt, and beige desert boots, Hudi ushered her in, leaving the door open as he always did when alone with a woman. She reached for the ice cream and, ignoring the spoon, scooped it into her mouth with two fingers, listening with eyes half shut while he explained his predicament to her.

"But what," she asked, opening her eyes again when he had finished, "are all this to do with me?"

Hudi sighed heavily. "Look, I'm in dire straits. I need a woman to get into the system. I need to see if the report uses only my Username or also my Dating Number. If the latter, then I somehow need to erase the report. Otherwise," he sighed again, "I might as well tell my parents to spend my wedding money on a new eight-jet turbo Feather."

Nessi studied him measuredly. "I'm a woman. Why you think I betray these other women?"

"Because—" he stuttered. "Because you think the whole system is rotten! You have no allegiance to it! You don't feel bound by the whole profiles thing in the first place. And lady, after this experience, I'm beginning to understand you. We've become so dependent on profiles that anyone can be demolished with a moment's malicious typing. It's lethal."

"Uh-huh." She leaned her face on her hand and looked at him thoughtfully. There was a dribble of ice cream at the side of her mouth, and he experienced a desire to reach out and wipe it off. "So you promising to remove yourself from the dating system if I help you?"

Hudi flinched at the spots of zealous light in her eyes. What she asked was impossible—she might as well ask him to dye his feet pink and do cartwheels on the uptown train. He felt trapped, like the Israelites between the Egyptians and the Red Sea.

"Nessi," he said at last, in a soft voice, "don't you see? I can't possibly leave the system. You're asking me to abandon everything I believe in. This is the procedure our *gedolim* set up, and for me their word is God's word. This is the only hope we have to save our communities. We can't turn back the clock to the old-fashioned ways. Thousands will end up never married, and that would be a tragedy." His voice took on an urgent tone. "But what I can promise you is that I'll work to reform it from the inside. I'm a rabbi, and my father has influence. I think I can really make a difference."

Nessi considered his words, while picking her teeth with the edge of his remote. He confiscated it gently from her, and cleaned it off with a tissue as he awaited her reply. Finally she said, "I don't know. I must think."

Hudi had reached the threshold of his endurance. "Look," he said wearily, "call me as soon as you decide." He saw her out. She left a scent of flowers and fertilizer drifting in her wake.

Nessi called the next day. "Shalom, Hudi," she said solemnly from the wallscreen.

"Well?" he said anxiously.

"Well, so I entered the List—"

"You did?!" he shouted.

"Yes, yes." Nessi laughed delightedly. "No problem, the first woman I ask get me fingerprinted in, with not suspecting me for one minute. I learn to be sneaky in the FSM! And I read your report." She laughed again. "*Habibski*, this is very bad rap for you!"

A red flush crept up Hudi's face at the thought of Nessi reading all those negative things about him. "But how did you know it was me?"

"It under the name *Ipcha*—your name. You give me your card at the party, remember?"

"Wait, Nessi, just tell me: did my Dating Number appear in the report, or just my Username?"

"Just the name."

"Fantastic! I changed that, so now I'm a different person! Yippee!" yelled Hudi, cavorting around the room and singing a verse of praise from the *Hallel* prayer. Nessi grinned at him from the screen. Then she said seriously, "I also went to the dating site and manage to locate your profile even with new name. I want to see what this all about."

Hudi fell giddily into his chair and activated the massage function. "You did?"

"Yes. This very interesting, make me think deeply since yesterday about whole dating meeting thing. It change what I think of you."

"What do you mean?" As the chair began to hum at his shoulders, he found himself waiting in suspense for her answer.

"Well," she began slowly. "I learn new things about you I would not know after just meeting. You are not as much idiot as I have thought at the start. You are sensitive, bright, good guy, and idealistic."

Hudi blushed at both the damning and the praise. "Thank you."

"And I think your bad report is exaggeration and unfair."

Hudi said in a pleading voice: "Nessi! I have to know what it said! I—I want to apologize to whoever I hurt."

"I tell you a different time, when you not so upset." Hudi opened his mouth to say something, but then Nessi smiled, her even white teeth large on the screen, and asked, "So, you want to go get a cup of chicory-brew together sometime?"

Hudi blinked. "Are you asking me out?"

"Yes, *shmotek*," said Nessi, laughing at his shock. "We in FSM not so old-fashioned that we think the man is always asking out. But on our first date we talk about changing this entire rotten system and giving people back their life."

"Yes. Assuming the rabbis' approval, of course."

Nessi raised an eyebrow and shrugged but then broke out in a smile. "Whatever. We talk about it."

Hudi stretched out his hands toward her image, like a groom about to uncover his veiled bride, and beamed. "*Maideleh*, I'd love to."

They grinned at each other, the silence broken only by the massage pads doing their job discreetly as always.

On they whirred, these pads, indispensable so long as human foibles cause aches and pain; so long as humans schlep on, braving frustration and sorrow, ineluctably striving and yearning for authentic connection with God and other, for wisdom and sagacity, and perhaps, perhaps, a small taste of paradise.

And thus it shall always be, until the Messiah.

About the Author

Yael Unterman grew up in the UK and now resides in Jerusalem. After attending an Ultra-Orthodox Jewish high school, she came to Israel to pursue Torah studies, and stayed on, earning a BA in Psychology and advanced degrees in Jewish History and Creative Writing. She lectures worldwide and has published in a variety of forums. Her first book, *Nehama Leibowitz: Teacher and Bible Scholar* (Urim) was a finalist in the 2009 National Jewish Book Awards. Visit her website at www.yaelunterman.com.

Glossary

The following words are familiar to, and appear in the vocabularies of, traditional Jews and modern Israelis. Almost all stem from Hebrew, Yiddish, or Arabic. Some appear in the Ashkenazic pronunciation, and others in the Sephardic pronunciation used in modern Hebrew.

Abba: Father
Abishter: God
Ad mosay: Until when?
Ahalan: Israeli slang for hello
Alek: Israeli slang for "yeah, right!" or "as if!" (sarcastic)
Alter kakers: Old people (impolite—equivalent to "old farts")
Am Yisrael: The Jewish people
Arba minim: The four species shaken on Sukkot: palm branch, citron, myrtle and willow
Avot: Short for *Pirkei Avot*. See Ethics of the Fathers
Ba'al/at teshuvah: Newly religious person
Bamba: Peanut-flavored Israeli snack
Bar mitzvah: Coming of age ceremony for thirteen-year-old boy
Bashert: Soulmate
Bensch: To say Grace After Meals
Bissli: Israeli snack
Blatt: Yiddish—a page of Talmud; in Hebrew, *daf*
Boker tov: Good morning
Borscht: Cold beetroot soup
Boyna: Israeli slang, short for *Bo Hena*—come here

Brucha haba'a: Welcome! (to a female)
Bubbeleh: Term of endearment (literally "little grandma")
Bubbie: Grandmother
Challah: Braided bread, used especially for Shabbat
Chevreh: Guys
Cholent: Traditional food for Shabbat—a mix of potatoes, meat, beans or other ingredients, stewed for many hours
Crembo: Popular Israeli snack: chocolate-covered marshmallow on a biscuit base
Daf: A page of Talmud.; in Yiddish, *blatt*
Daven: Pray
Davka: Specifically, actually
Dos: Religious person (often derogatory)
Dreidel: Spinning top
Dubi: Teddy bear, diminutive for bear (dov in Hebrew)
Eishet Chayil: "A woman of valor," referring to a woman of good character (from Proverbs 31:10)
Emes, Emet: Truth
Ethics of the Fathers (Pirkei Avot): A collection of rabbinical wisdom from the Mishnaic period
Etrog: Citron; a lemon-like fruit, one of the *arba minim*
Eyzeh keta: Israeli slang for "how weird/amazing" or "what a surprise"
Frum: Religiously observant
Gadol, Gedolim: Leading rabbi/s of the generation
Gartel: Belt worn while praying, primarily by Hasidim
Gemora: The longer, and chronologically later, Aramaic part of the Talmud
Gevalt!: Good grief!
Golus: Exile, or the Diaspora—outside the land of Israel
Gonif: Thief
Goyish: Non-Jewish
Hablaz maz maz: Short for *Haval al hazman, mizman mizman*. Israeli slang for "Fuhgeddaboudit!" Waste of time
Halachically: According to Jewish law
Hallel: Song of praise. Collection of Psalms sung to celebrate specific festivals
Hakol kol Ya'akov: "The voice is the voice of Jacob" (Genesis 27:22)
Hamsa: Hand-shaped amulet

Haredim: Ultra-Orthodox Jews

Hasidism: A stream in Judaism, known at the outset for its revolutionary thought, today associated with strictly Orthodox observant Jews wearing distinctive clothing; its adherents are called Hasidim

Hava aminas/nafka minas: Talmudic terminology

Heilige: Holy

Ima: Mother

Kachniks: Followers of Rabbi Meir Kahane, an extreme right-wing activist and politician

Kallah: Bride

Kapara neshamah: Literally "atonement, sweetheart;" term of endearment originating with Israelis of Sephardic descent

Ken: Yes

Kever: Grave

Kiddush: Ceremonial blessing made over wine to sanctify the Sabbath and other holy occasions

Kipa: A skullcap—traditional Jewish headcovering for men

Kneidlach: Dumplings made of matzah meal and egg, traditionally put in soup

Kollel: A place for studying Torah at advanced level

Kotel: The Western Wall

Kugel: A baked casserole

Kvetch: To complain and whine

Lashon hara/losh: Evil speech, gossip

Lulav: Palm branch stripped of its fronds; one of the *arba minim*

Ma la'asot: "What can you do?"

Ma pitom: Israeli slang for "No way!" (literally "What suddenly!")

Maariv: Evening prayer

Machmir: Strictly observant

Maideleh: Girl

Makolet: Small, local store

Mamish: Yeshivish pronunciation of *mamash*, meaning truly

Mamzer: Bastard

Mazal tov: Congratulations

Mechitzah: Partition separating men and women in Orthodox synagogues

Mein kind: My child

Mensch: Decent human being

Meshuggeh/Meshuggeneh: Crazy/crazy person
Milchik: Dairy
Miluim: Reserve duty in the Israeli Defense Forces
Mikveh: Ritual bath
Min hashamayim: Ordained from heaven
Minyan: A quorum of ten men over the age of thirteen required for traditional Jewish public worship
Mishnah: The shorter, and chronologically earlier, Hebrew parts of the Talmud
Mitzvah/Mitzvot: Commandment(s) from the Torah, also used to refer to good deed(s)
Muzhik: Russian peasant
Narishkeit: Foolishness
Nesher: Shuttle company to the airport (literally "eagle")
Niggun: Wordless tune
Nu: Come on! (Also has many other meanings depending on context and intonation)
Parshat Toldot: Weekly Torah portion of *Toldot* (Genesis 25:19—28:9)
Pasken: To decide the law
Pesach: Passover
Peyos: Sidelocks, hair grown by religious men in front of the ears
Piguah: Terror attack
Pritzus: Immodesty, promiscuity
Rabak: Israeli slang: "By your God!"
Rebbe: A Hasidic rabbi, serving as spiritual leader for his community
Ribono shel Olam: Master of the Universe
Rosh yeshivah: Head of a yeshivah
Rugele/Rugelach: Pastry/pastries wrapped or rolled around a filling (in Israel, generally chocolate or cinnamon)
Schlemiel: Simpleton, fool, loser
Schlep: Drag
Sephardim: Jews of Spanish, North African, or Middle Eastern descent
Shabbat/Shabbos: Saturday, the Sabbath
Shabbat Shalom: "A peaceful Sabbath"—traditional greeting on Shabbat

Shadchaniyot: Matchmakers

Shechinah: God's indwelling presence

Shema: "Hear O Israel"—particular biblical verses said daily, as well as just before death

Sh'koyach: Well done!

Shidduch: Match

Shiur: Torah lesson

Shmaltz: Chicken fat

Shmeks: Nickname for Israeli shekels

Shofar: A ram's horn

Sholom aleichem: "Peace be upon you" (greeting)

Shomer mitzvot: Keeps the commandments, another term for religious/observant

Shtender: Book stand. Can be small, for desk use, or reach chest height for use while standing

Shtick: Entertaining activities done at weddings to make the couple happy (also has other meanings)

Shtiebel: Small, simple synagogue

Shul: Synagogue

Shulchan Aruch: 16th-century codex of law, of major importance in Jewish observance

Siddur: Prayerbook

Siyum haShas: Event to mark completion of the study of the entire Babylonian Talmud, occurring approximately every seven and a half years

Slicha: Sorry

Sukkot: An autumn festival, in which booths are built and plants (*arba minim*) are shaken

Tallis: Prayer shawl

Talmid chochem: Torah-learned scholar

Talmud: The fundamental Jewish text alongside the *Tanach* [Bible]. A compendium of rabbinic interpretations; made up of *Mishnah* (Hebrew) and *Gemora* (Aramaic)

Tefillin: Phylacteries—leather cases with straps worn during morning prayer

Teshuvah: Repentance

Tish: A gathering of Hasidim around their Rebbe, involving singing and eating

Toda: Thank you

Tosfos: A commentary on the Talmud

Tzaddik: Righteous person

Tzitzit: A garment with long fringes hanging down from each corner; may also refer only to the fringes

U'Netaneh Tokef: Powerful prayer said only during the High Holy Days

Upsherin: Customary ceremony to mark the first cutting of a boy's hair at age three

Veibers: Women

Vi geyt es: How are you?

Yalla: Israeli slang: "Come on!"

Yingele: Little boy

Yeshivah: School or academy for study of Torah

Yeshivish: Bearing a religious and social affiliation with the yeshivah world

Yid/Yidden: Jew/Jews

Yom Kippur: Day of Atonement, holiest day of the year

Yoshke: Jewish name for Jesus

Zaydie: Grandfather

Zaka: Israeli religious rescue and recovery organization

Ziskeit: Sweetness

Zivug: Mate, partner, spouse

Zman: Semester, term (literally "time")

Lightning Source UK Ltd.
Milton Keynes UK
UKOW06f1105281115

263703UK00001B/41/P